MECHANICS
OF
THE PAST

K.A. Ashcomb

Glorious Mishaps Series

Liquid Hare Publishing

MECHANICS OF THE PAST

Copyright © 2021 K.A. Ashcomb

All rights reserved.

Published by Liquid Hare Publishing 2021

Riihimäki, Kanta-Häme, Finland

This book is sold subject to the condition that it shall not, by way of trade or otherwise, be lent, resold, hired out, or otherwise circulated without the publisher's prior consent in any form of binding or cover other than that in which it is published and without a similar condition including this condition being imposed on the subsequent purchaser. Under no circumstances may any part of this book be photocopied for resale.

This is a work of fiction. Any similarity between the characters and situations within its pages and places or persons, living or dead, is unintentional and co-incidental.

ISBN 978-952-69026-5-4 (nid.)

ISBN 978-952-69026-6-1 (EPUB))

Contact K.A. Ashcomb: k.a.ashcomb@gmail.com

Follow K.A. Ashcomb's blog: https://ashcombka.com

Cover Design by K.A. Ashcomb

Edited by Emily Nemchick

To all the dreamers and listeners
Without you, the world would be a dull place to be
Thank you!

Also by K. A. Ashcomb

Worth of Luck
Penny for Your Soul
Mechanics of the Past

ACKNOWLEDGMENTS

A special thanking are needed for those who helped me to complete this book. Writing Mechanics of the Past and publishing it wouldn't have been possible without their support. Foremost, to my husband, Henri, who endured my endless questions and reading and rereading the book in various stages. He never let me give up. He always pushes me to be the best version of myself. Special thanks to my beta readers, who pointed out its weaknesses and strengths. To Emily Nemchick, for editing. She scrutinized my text and made it better. And to my older sister, Katja, who believes in me and encourages me to write. And to you, my readers. Without you, I wouldn't be writing.

"I perceive, says the Countess, Philosophy is now become very
Mechanical. Yes, Madam, says I, to Mechanical, that I fear we
shall quickly be asham'd of it; they will have the World to be
in Large, what a Watch is in Small; which is very regular, and
depends only upon the just disposing of the several Parts of
the Movement. But pray tell me, Madam, had you not
formerly a more sublime Idea of the Universe?"

- Bernard le Bovier de Fontenelle (1686)

MECHANICS OF THE PAST

PROLOGUE

an you surprise someone who knows the future? Do you try to act randomly? Can you truly move without forethought if you have a purpose? Margaret Illes was sure the universe knew what she was planning behind her eyepatch—a patch she'd earned a long time ago. But for the universe to see and to comprehend her plans or anyone else's meant it had to care. Margaret was sure there had been no extra consideration towards her in all her life. The opposite, she might say, if she had any desire to dwell on the past. She didn't.

The past was gone. The future was unknown. There was only the task at hand, and that was to hunt down Humphrey Chadwick. A man who'd proven publicly that he could predict the future and command the great beyond. One could call him a clairvoyant. She wouldn't. She had only one name for the man, and that was number five.

She'd tracked him through the city of Threebeanvalley from his hotel to the open field outside the compounds. "Tracking" might be too sumptuous a word to use for what she had done, as there had been no need to resort to any cat-

and-mouse games. She only had to read the announcements of the Great Clairvoyant Humphrey's travels in the newspapers, making her work easier than she cared for, as there was something about the hunt that made a person's heart beat the right way. A way that announced, "I'm alive and king of the jungle, deal with it!"

Margaret observed the man's subordinates as they busied themselves setting up a tent and building a stage for tonight's show. It was going to be grand, from the look of it and from the rumors she'd gathered. The great man himself would read the future, talk to the dead, and make all the ladies in the audience faint as their world views shattered. It had taken Margaret longer than she wanted to discern whether the man was a charlatan or the real McCoy, fielding the rightful crown for the clan or, in this case, for his talents. He was the real deal, forcing her back to the initial question: How to fool someone who supposedly knew the future before it happened? Would he predict her every move, or was he as blind as the rest of us, knowing only what to ask? She would find out soon enough when the others left him alone.

Margaret settled more comfortably against the tree she was leaning on, feeling the thick bark on her back. She took a cake tin out of her dark brown backpack. She used her teeth to open the green bottle she always carried with her and laced the spongy fruit cake Mr. Chadwick loved so much. He should know better than to eat all this stuff. But that just went to show, he either knew a sugary death wasn't in the cards or he recognized that the future was ever-changing, and even a man who was the master of it needed something to ease the burden of living.

Margaret carefully sealed the cake tin again and put it back in her backpack to let it marinate. She took another tin out, this time her lunch.

She ate with a healthy appetite as she listened to the workmen curse and occasionally scream as they injured themselves with loose nails and wayward hammers. What a fantastic tool the hammer was. Aerodynamic, well balanced. One swing and lives would be canceled like a lousy showpiece that wasted more money than it made. But unlike the actors, they would be goners.

The tent rose. The men swarmed around it. And the crowds lined up. Women and men and children. But there was an extra blush in the female faces, and the children were crying more from the mere fright of whether an apparition from the great beyond would appear. The men, on the other hand, looked like they had been dragged around for hours upon hours in a purgatory called the Mall.[1] Their faces were gray, and they were in that subliminal stage between unruly rage and apathy, like the darkness at the bottom of the most bottomless sea. What would win would be all down to the ladies' shade of blush later tonight.

Margaret got up, dressed in a skirt she'd stashed behind the tree, took the cake tin, and made her way to the tent, past the audience. What an excellent cover they were as they moved like ants towards the tent, squirming, bellowing in anticipation of the weird.

It was disappointingly easy to get to the backroom, where they'd arranged a setting area for tonight's star. No one was there yet. They were too busy taking people's hard-earned pennies, guiding them to their seats, and warming them up for the main attraction like a virgin for her king. All pampered. All docile. All believing.

Margaret opened the cake tin and left it there on the dressing table with a mirror where color could be added where there was none. Then she hid behind a trunk.

It would be fun to say Mr. Chadwick walked in at the same moment or he came rushing in late, not even glancing at the cake tin, but that was not the case. The middle-aged man with a receding hairline came in the midpoint, when there was enough time to fret over the performance, the mood of the audience, the cooperation from the great beyond. There was no mention of a possible threat except fear of rotten tomatoes. There had been no tomatoes, no special fruits mentioned in the newspapers, but Margaret guessed even the possibility of losing face was more than some could handle.

As Humphrey muttered to himself while covering his face with stage makeup, his hand dipped into the open cake tin. In the fruit cake went, one bite at a time.

"Mr. Chadwick, they are ready for you," the stage manager said from the door, which was nothing but a sheet.

"Give me a moment, Larry," Humphrey said.

---

1   Whatever that was. Only the future generations would know.

"Five minutes and they'll eat the poor boy alive," Larry insisted.

Humphrey stood up and walked to the trunk. Larry drew the curtain closed.

There was a frown on the clairvoyant's face. A deep one. One Margaret had seen many times before. He began to stagger, and he looked like he was going to throw up.

That was her cue.

"Mr. Chadwick, are you alright?" Margaret asked, standing up behind the trunk. "Let me help you, sir. You don't look so good."

Humphrey looked confused. They always did. "Who? Where?" he managed to ask.

"Let me help you sit down. You must have hit your head," Margaret said, calculating the weight of the man against his height and the amount he had eaten. Any minute now. He was a tall man, but despite his fondness for cake, he was slim, albeit with a bit of a soft belly.

"I'm sure I would remember if I hit my head," he said, his speech slurred.

Margaret wrapped her arm around his waist. "There, there. All will be fine soon," she said.

Humphrey squinted his eyes. "Have I seen you before? That... that... the thing on your face. I think—" he said.

Margaret guided him to the dressing table. The man slumped on the stool and soon folded over the counter.

"There you go to dreamland. Was it there where you and I met? Not connecting the dots, eh?" Margaret said. She took a dagger out of her skirt hem's hidden pocket.

"Mr. Chadwick, they are eating him alive. You'd better come before they bring out the eggs and the tomatoes," Larry's voice came from behind the curtain.

Margaret took a better hold of the dagger and moved to wait for the man at the makeshift door. When he came in, and before he could rush or alarm anyone, Margaret hit the man on the back of his head, and into a different kind of la-la land he went. She left him lying there and went to the end of the dressing room, tearing a hole in the tent. Then she put the dagger back in her skirt, went back to number five, wrapped her arms around him, and dragged him out into the night.

"We have a long journey ahead, and you won't like it,

but don't worry, I won't kill you. Not yet, at least," she said.

There was no reply. There was only dead weight with a heartbeat.

※

A screech, a thump, then silence. The machine the size of a shoebox came to a halt. A man with dark brown curls stood up from behind the golden apparatus lying on the work desk. He took a smooth gold coin in his hands from where the machine had spewed the perfectly round chip out. Levi Perri let the coin dance from one finger to another.

Here it finally was, yet he felt empty. Deep down, he knew he should be singing and dancing, as the legend of Lord Bufonite's box was true. He hadn't spent all these years running after his version of the philosopher's stone like the alchemist before him for nothing. Not forgetting the bitter reality that he had been driven out of academia for believing and daring to dream. But there was no glee in his voice as he said,

"Look at this, Otis."

Levi tossed the coin to the man sitting on a wooden chair near the workstation. The man had had his head buried in his hands a moment ago, muttering about the pointlessness of it all. They had been up the whole night and many nights before, and now morning had to be dawning already. Not that they could see the light of day here in the basement, but Levi's inner clock said the scullery maids had risen to serve their masters along with the street sweepers and milkmen a long time ago.

Despite his fatigue, the necromancer, Otis, caught the coin with ease. He flipped it in his hand and shook his head.

"This shouldn't be. It shouldn't have worked this way. You can't make something out of nothing. All the spirit does is tap into the etheric world and transport knowledge. This, this is heresy." Otis collapsed deeper into his chair.

"Yet we have done just that. Also, you forget that we come out of nothingness, and we exist. Here we are, standing on the floor made of stones, feeling the coldness and dampness underneath, and it exists as well. If we are lucky enough, we can see the stars and the moon shining at the crack of dawn, and they exist there in the emptiness. So does the coin, and if you bite into it, it's the real thing. What you and others think of as nothingness is actually something, the quintessence. Something that is the building blocks of the universe and, it seems, of the souls as well. Nonetheless, we shouldn't leave it to what we see and think. To be sure, I need you to run to an appraiser. Let's see what they make of it. It's the opinion of the collective that matters when it comes to judging worth. They might think along your lines that if something comes out of nothingness, it's illusory. If the appraiser agrees that the coin is gold, as they should, then it's gold. Change it into gems—no, actually don't. We need to see if it continues to exist."

Levi reached for the notebook from the table and began to write down all that had happened tonight, noting the time and date as well. Nothing should be forgotten. He was feeling a lot better.

He took no notice of Otis getting up and saying in a scornful tone, "Yes, master."

All he thought was, that's more like it. But it was accompanied by a sneaking intuition that the words were the only way for Otis to get out of the basement and away from the machine as fast as he could. Lately, the necromancer had only wanted to be out and about, pursuing his other desires: women, poetry, and testing the limits of his dark arts. The man had come to hate the machine during all these years, complaining about being tied down or deeming Levi's pursuit impossible. Otis wasn't a bad assistant despite his disbelief, pessimism, and other traits that made his mind too closed to be the one to dream up the Bufonite—no, he couldn't call it that. Maybe Levinite—no, not that either. The right name would come when he least expected it. But Otis had never let him down. He'd made the machine possible, risking his life and freedom for it.

"Use the one on Cobble Street. He'll swindle you if you let him, but he's the best," Levi said, raising his head up from the notebook before Otis left.

Otis didn't look happy, but he didn't protest either. There was bad blood between the necromancer and the appraiser. Levi wasn't sure why, and he was too disinterested to find out. But although he didn't care, he could still guess. Something to do with ladies. Otis and his insatiable taste for women. Maybe it was because the necromancer was curious-looking;

he was never the same when you glanced towards him. Always fluctuating between your preferences and his original features. The alchemist wasn't sure what Otis honestly looked like, but it didn't matter. It was the same as with the machine he'd made: What was, was all that mattered. Yet sometimes he feared it would be Otis' downfall, this need for outside validation, and more so, the need to be considered alluring and handsome, and how it might affect getting the machine to work. Levi considered pursuing adoration and the approval of others a waste of a life, especially the female kind.

"He has sharp eyes, and if he says it's gold, no one in the city will go against his word," Levi added.

"Did you say anything, sir?" Otis replied.

"Not as such."

Otis put the coin between his teeth. A moment later, he turned into a chestnut brown otter with a dash of white under its belly.

That was another odd feature that he hadn't known about when he'd hired the necromancer. The man was not confined to the shape and size of a human, and still he wondered about how you could turn nothing into something. Unlike with Otis, the machine of legends wasn't about magic. What he had done was pure science and mechanics—and necromancy, he regrettably had to admit. For several years, Levi had tried to get the machine to work in vain. In principle, it should have worked without necromancy, and it had worked, or so the stories went. Yet, nothing. Then he'd read about the technology of the glowing skulls they used in Necropolis. For banking. The mere thought made him want to scream, "fools!" There was so much they could have done with such a system, and they had gone and tapped the etheric world to help with their accounting. It didn't matter. He would show what machines could do with a ghost in their system.

Levi watched Otis run up the stairs and out through the crack in the basement door. He turned back to face the machine, which deserved a name. Something worthy of its function. And this wasn't about gold. He couldn't care less about gold. Devoting one's life on such matters was limiting and blinding. This was about discovery. About doing the impossible. About the machine. About changing the world. He cranked a lever on the metallic box with golden plates and flipped up two other switches. The engine coughed, and then the wheel whirred as it turned the tiny cogs. It sounded like a wheezing mouse.

Levi waited for a moment—a moment longer than he cared to—and then the machine spewed a wheat grain onto the table. In the past, producing a single grain had taken weeks. Now it got the task done in minutes. Progress, but not enough, and not fast enough. The gold coin they'd just witnessed had taken months to produce. He needed to make the machine bigger. He needed to make more of them. He needed more souls to make the work faster. Not just any souls. He required those who tapped into the universe the unusual way. Someone like his sister. Like Otis with his shapeshifting. But he needed money for all that.

When there was a handful of grains, he once again shut the process down. Levi took what had been made into his hands and sniffed them. They smelled and tasted like the real thing, earthy and nutty. Levi spat out the grain shell and made a note in his book.

He would make his maid grind them and bake him something. It would be the ultimate proof of whether the machine created more than illusions.

He let go of the pen and put the notebook inside the breast pocket of his jacket, which was draped over the chair's back. Levi took a rag from the table next to the apparatus and covered it up. He took the jacket with him and moved to the basement door, glancing over his shoulder at the other doors and then at his work desk, where his future lay among his alchemy equipment. The mortars and the delicate glass tubes with swan necks surrounded the machine, which would rule the world. The legend of Lord Bufonite's Box had come alive. He had made it, and he was no legend, but he soon would be.

He turned the gas lamp off and was sure he heard Mr. Chadwick whimper. Levi closed the basement door behind him and went to search for his breakfast.

1

GOING HOME ISN'T AS EASY AS ONE MIGHT THINK

hey say science makes the world go around. Some argue it's the people who do the final pushing and shoving, but even they, the others, have to agree that science is a terrific tool. Science is the culmination of human predictive power, enabling them to shape nature.

Here under the sun, above the molten core, the thumping of an engine made a cart sway. The steel wheels of a locomotive propelled a monstrosity unlike anything the continent of Jadero had ever seen before. Sigourney Perri squeezed her hands against the wooden seat and hoped the motion would stop. Her lust for speed had dissipated when the first loud screeches had filled the air. She wasn't the only one afraid of the steel machine, but she was the only one of her companions.

In front of Sigourney, Siarl Ellis, Harriet's former secretary and freedom fighter and now her... something... looked at the changing landscape. He let out a long exhale. Undoubtedly he was dreaming about something. Not even noticing the unnatural speed at which they were going. Siarl was always dreaming, following fantasies one after another. Inventing things. Or at least he wished to create things, but their constant travel left no room for that. Sigourney, Siarl, and the Rabbit god of luck—who also sat in front of Sigourney in his human form—had been zigzagging the continent for the past four years. Not leaving any stone unturned. Sigourney was the only one who wasn't tired of the constant flux.

The Rabbit was drunk, as always. He nursed a drink in his hand and followed Siarl's example, gazing out of the window. Sigourney still found his appearance odd. He was like any other man in his sixties, with gray hair and soft features. The Rabbit could have chosen any appearance—as handsome or as young as he wanted—but he chose to be as indistinguishable as possible. The right word might be harmless, as he'd explained one night. When people thought nothing of you, you could do as you pleased. Be young and handsome, and you'll always be observed, and not only by humans. There are other gods to think about. Not that they'd pestered the three of them, since Harriet Stowe, the Prime Minister of Leporidae Lop, had defeated the gods. No one had seen them since. Cornelius AKA Crit had to still be teaching them about impulse control through the secrets of meditation.

Sigourney opened her mouth to say something, to stop the Rabbit taking yet another sip from his glass, but instead she shut it without letting out a sound. You could easily think that after all these years together Sigourney would be more at ease with Siarl and the Rabbit, or with anyone else. That she would be capable of saying more than five words. But while you can ease uncertainty, you can never take it out of someone like Sigourney. Not if they are trapped by the constraints of their mind. Agitated around others. Afraid of doing or saying something silly. Most definitely still averse to loud noises and crowds. The list was endless.

"This will be our doom," the Rabbit said and gestured with his hand at the cart's interior.

"The locomotive?" Sigourney asked, her voice clinging to her throat. She couldn't believe what she'd heard. Only a moment ago, the Rabbit had affirmed that the machine was a miracle he would never have imagined that humans could come up with. That he couldn't wait to get in and see what the steel thingy did.

"Yes," the Rabbit lamented, waking Siarl from his dreaming.

The boy said, "This is perfectly safe. The speed at which we are moving is harmless and has no effect on your innards. That's pure superstition—"

"Of course it can't harm my innards. Who would even think that? I'm in control of them. But that's beside the point," the Rabbit cut in before Siarl let loose with one of his ramblings.

"Then what is it?" Siarl asked, looking alert and ready to argue. That was another thing Siarl had been doing lately. When he wasn't rooted in his thoughts, he was moody and argumentative. And the Rabbit liked to add fuel to the fire by joining in.

"The gods!" the Rabbit said, louder than Sigourney cared for.

Here we go again, she thought and noticed other passengers shooting glances at them. She wanted to hide, but there was nowhere to go, and disappearing was out of the question.

"What have they got to do with anything?" Siarl asked.

"Can't you see that if this goes on, there won't be any gods left?" the Rabbit said in a lowered tone. While his disguise was perfect, consisting of all ten toes and ten fingers along with a perfectly average nose, two light brown eyes, and a mouth to speak with, it still didn't shield him from judgment. Humans' minds were full of reasons to despise fellow humans, or at least they thought they should harbor such thoughts.

"Is that such a bad thing?" Siarl asked.

Sigourney wanted to draw her green jacket's hood over her head and hide the conventional way, as her usual way was out of the question. This was one of Siarl and the Rabbit's constant disagreements. Siarl had started to dislike the gods after the war, and sometimes Sigourney thought that extended to the god of luck himself, who insisted he wasn't a god but a deity, a personification of pure luck. Siarl didn't see the difference. Not that Sigourney did either, but it was uncalled for to attack the Rabbit, who'd helped to save them and the whole continent from certain doom. Who was always kind to them. His luck worked its magic even now, keeping them fed and sheltered.

"Please," Sigourney said before the Rabbit could collect enough momentum to respond. Sigourney knew the cart full of people wouldn't prevent one of their full-blown arguments from starting, and any careless words would live on until the next opportunity presented itself to be used as ammunition. With those two, an argument was always lurking around the next corner. Maybe it was time they went their separate ways. This wasn't the first time she'd thought so. But she didn't care for such thoughts.

"I'm sorry, Sigourney," Siarl said, reaching for her hand.

Sigourney withdrew it. There had been closeness between them, more often than she cared to admit, but there were times when she'd rather not be touched. Now, Siarl's mood and the fact they were getting closer to the shoreline made her choke and shy away from any human connection. All she wanted was to be left alone, even when she saw she'd offended him. Going home was much worse than one moment of resentment.

The Rabbit turned his attention back to the landscape and took a sip of his whiskey.

"Why are you like this?" Siarl asked.

"Leave her alone. You have said enough today," the Rabbit said.

He had to know, Sigourney thought.

Siarl clearly wanted to reply, but he chose not to. He took a book out of his worn-out black sailor backpack, which looked gray and tattered, and settled to read.

The locomotive moved on across the continent of Jadero, passing small towns and kingdoms whose citizens came to gawk at the steam engine. If you were sensitive enough, like the Rabbit was, you could feel the machine's influence spreading. The Rabbit was right. It would change everything. Yes, it might be the death of the gods, at least some of them, but not the death of belief. People needed symbols, meaning, ideas. They needed something. Whether it came from the saving power of science or the solace that God or gods could bring didn't matter, as long as there was something to anchor humans to the world and to each other.

But Sigourney's mind wasn't occupied with gods or any arguments. She was anxious. They were traveling to the shoreline town where she had been born. It was the only place they hadn't visited in their travels, and Siarl and oddly enough the Rabbit had insisted they go, as the maiden voyage of the locomotive would run from Leporidae Lop to Threebeanvalley. She'd protested, but as always too weakly, and as always not telling them why. She looked at the ever-changing landscape from under her eyebrows. She was sure this time even the Rabbit's luck couldn't save her. Going home was the most terrible thing anyone could do. It unleashed all that had been kept perfectly hidden in the darkest reaches of the human mind. Things that should never see the light of day. It's just that heroes need to make compromises, even the shy and anxious ones, to vanquish the evil[2] and make the world a sunny place again. And heroes definitely have to know how to face their brothers.

Calling Sigourney's hometown a town was an understatement. The city was bigger than the kingdom of Leporidae Lop and growing even as the locomotive docked. Threebeanvalley's population had exploded after it became the biggest import and export harbor between continents. The invention of locomotives and the tracks in would speed up the process even more,[3] as the coal and new innovations traveled in and out of the city with ease. Also, the citizens had been wise enough to stay away from the war that had shaken the other kingdoms and republics in Jadero, giving them a tremendous economic advantage over their neighbors.[4]

This was the first time in a decade that Sigourney was back in Threebeanvalley. The place didn't look anything like she remembered. Buildings had risen from one story high to the skies. Their roofs and chimneys pierced the heavens, which

---

2   Of their mind, or the physical kind like overlords, mad scientists, and greedy brokers.

3   Making some of the natives wonder whether this was the same city they went to sleep in last night or whether they had been transported somewhere else, as new additions had risen in the houses next to theirs, and they were pretty sure the wall that split their bedroom wasn't there when they went to bed, and neither was the family living in it. Oh well, as long as they paid the rent.

4   Which was always nice, as putting one over on your neighbor was the sole purpose in life. Things didn't get better than that.

were cloaked with thick smoke. But the fresh breeze from the sea made the air almost breathable at the steps of the new station. Everything around it was clean and polished and decorated with small patches of trees and flowers, inviting the visitors deeper into the city.[5] But you could barely see anything through the people pushing past Sigourney, Siarl, and the Rabbit, who'd stopped to marvel. Other passengers didn't come here to sightsee. They came here to make money.

A wail rose to Sigourney's lips, but it never came out, as Siarl wrapped his hand around hers and drew her closer.

"In and out," he whispered in her ear. "I'm here. I'll never leave you."

Sigourney squeezed his soft hand.

Everything was too loud. Too crowded. Too smelly. Threebeanvalley had once been a small seaside town. Life here would have been perfect and peaceful, if you excluded her horrible family. Now everything was ruined. The city was monstrous.

"Where and what now?" the Rabbit asked, looking around, not appearing pleased about the crowds either, even when his luck pushed people farther away from them.

"We get to know the city," Siarl said. "Before that, we should find a place to eat and sleep."

The Rabbit nodded. He took a step forward and shut his eyes. Soon enough, a young boy running up the stairs with a stack of fliers collided with him. His leaflets scattered all around them, slowly floating down.

The boy dropped to his knees to gather his papers.

"I'm sorry, sir," the boy said, looking up in horror at the Rabbit, who had kept some of his godly height.

"It's all right," the Rabbit said, offering the boy his hand. The boy took his hand and pulled himself up.

"What you got there?" The Rabbit nodded towards the fliers.

"Oh," the boy said. He collected his thoughts and flashed a huge smile. "My papa owns the finest hotel in the whole of Threebeanvalley. We even have an in-house restaurant and suites you can stay in for weeks and clothes-washing services. Everything you could dream of. There are still a couple of rooms left if you need a place to stay," the boy finished. He

---

5   To waste their money.

couldn't be more than thirteen or fourteen, and he had mastered the art of selling. The boy had a dark head of hair and an honest face. It was the kind of look that would get him in trouble later in life, but also get him out of trouble with one huge, dimpled smile. And sell stuff, lots of stuff.

"May I?" the Rabbit asked.

"Yes, of course," the boy said and handed him the flier. "Say Lucas sent you and they'll give you a discount."

"Thank you," the Rabbit said.

"Be seeing you." The boy left them alone on the steps, making his way through the crowd, pestering others with his fliers.

The Rabbit turned to face Sigourney and Siarl. "What a marvelous human child." The Rabbit flashed a smile. "And here, that's taken care of." He pushed the paper into Siarl's unwilling hand.

Siarl took it forcefully, snorting loudly.

"Why can't you be happy about anything I do?" the Rabbit asked.

"The world shouldn't work this way."

"Then how should it work?"

"With logic. Not just because you want something."

"Isn't it the same with you humans? Want something, get it?"

"Not that easily."

"Can we go now?" Sigourney asked, peering at the people hurrying past them. While the crowd had eased, there were still more people than she cared for. Where was the homely fishing town she had grown up in? Not that she had ever done any fishing. More like throwing rocks and wishing to be far away from here and from their rented family farm further inland. Just outside all the hustle and bustle, so to speak. As far as she knew, her parents still lived there, taking care of their chickens and vegetable garden, scraping by. That was all they had ever done, scrape by.

"I'm sorry, Sigourney," Siarl whispered in her ear, letting go of her hand.

She knew he still loved her, and she loved him too, yet it wasn't enough. He wanted more than she could give, not only from their relationship but from life in general. He wanted to be something. She didn't. She was already Sigourney, and that was more than she could handle. To add something more to that was like inviting Calamity for a cup of tea.

The Rabbit and Siarl more than willingly obeyed her request, equally put out by the constant flow of people. They left the station behind, searching for the hotel the boy had pronounced to be the best. Sigourney guided them efficiently despite the newness of the streets and the buildings. If nothing else, she had a good sense of direction and spatial recognition. You could drop her almost anywhere in the world and she would find her way home like cats and dogs do —only if she was in the mood for it.

Sigourney had to admit the new Threebeanvalley was a beautiful city. The architects had kept trees around to ease the stress of urban life and to provide hiding spots for people to take refuge from the ever-scorching mid-afternoon sun. Sigourney stepped from one shadow to another, trying to avoid other pedestrians, as the morning sun was already burning bright. But the beauty was only half the truth; you only had to look up at the thick black smoke covering the sky. There was more to the city than the trees and magnificent houses. This was a place where the new innovations and consumer goods got made inside huge brick buildings with steam engines screeching all night and day. Here in the carefully planned newness and enchantment, you could forget what fueled the city. What made all the people pour in.

With Sigourney's uncanny ability, they arrived at Hotel Earl in no time. The hotel tried to appear old and distinguished, but it was newer than a newborn baby. And it was indeed the finest hotel in town. Huge open doors welcomed them in. Next to those same doors stood a concierge whose frown deterred anyone unsuitable from approaching, which was the true mark of a fine place. Those high in society always wanted something different than the common folk had. And when the common folk played catchup, it was time to move on to something new. And so the chain continued. Here, the concierge knew to keep out ruffians like the Rabbit, whose ensemble didn't impress kings and queens, and Sigourney and Siarl, whose inbreeding had clearly gone wrong, as you couldn't see the common side effects of blue blood, to protect the hotel and his yearly income.

"Maybe we shouldn't," Siarl said.

"Hogwash, this is just the place. Trust me," the Rabbit

replied.

"It's not that—"

"We stay here," the Rabbit insisted in a tone that left no room to argue back.

The concierge was ready to disagree. He lifted his hand to stop them from entering, but as soon as he was about to ask them to leave, a voice barked an order from inside.

"George, come here this instant. What do you think you were doing, chatting like that to Sandy," the voice said.

The man hesitated, but if there was one voice you wouldn't mess with, this was it.

The Rabbit, Sigourney, and Siarl walked into the hotel lobby, where they were instantly welcomed in by a huge, wall-high painting of a noble-born man—an earl, presumably.[6]

Sigourney glanced over her shoulder when they passed the concierge. He was being berated, most likely by his supervisor, who was several feet shorter than the man and looked like he knew the army book of tricks inside out.

They'd gotten what they wanted, but with a wake of casualties. Luck was never free. Someone always had to pay.

Sigourney turned her gaze back to the god, who led them to the front desk without sparing a thought for what had happened.

A jovial-looking man hovered over the front desk, peering at the guests nervously. Sigourney was sure it would be the hotel owner who happened to be open and friendly. Most likely Lucas was his favorite son, and whoever befriended the young boy would be welcomed with open arms by his father. This had happened time and again wherever they went with the Rabbit. The actors changed, but the script always went pretty much the same way. When they left, people went back to their normal lives, confused by the sudden change of character and angered by the loss of income. Sigourney had kept a diary about the effect. It had a clear structure and pattern, happening with precision. These favorable occurrences didn't happen only to the Rabbit. His luck had rubbed off on Sigourney and Siarl, making the universe more cooperative.[7]

"Welcome and good morning," the man who tended the

---

6 Not an earl, but there to give the illusion that there ever was one. The owner of the hotel was several steps ahead of his time when it came to branding and marketing.

front desk said cheerfully. He forced a fake smile onto his lips. Anyone in his position would have a strong desire to glance over his shoulder for confirmation from the hotel owner, but the man resisted the temptation.

"Morning," the Rabbit said. "My children and I would like a room." A sharp-eyed front desk manager would have noticed the so-called children looked nothing like each other. One dark and one light. That they looked more like trouble and should be thrown out. But the manager was too busy acting the right way in front of the owner to care about the Rabbit's lie.

"We might have one economy room—" the man offered.

"We can do better than that. Lucas promised us the best," the Rabbit said.

Siarl sighed.

"You know Lucas?" the hotel owner asked, pushing past the manager. Just on time to play his part.

"Yes, what a wonderful lad. He heard we needed a place to stay and instantly offered his help. He said his papa would look after us," the Rabbit continued, spinning his tale and playing his part.

"I'm his papa, and any friend of his is my friend," the hotel owner said, tapping his chest with his massive hand, a broad smile on his face.

Poor deluded man, thinking he was getting some great deal, and instead, he would be stuck with the bill when the curtains fell and everyone had gone home, Sigourney thought. Some in his place even sang and pulled out a few dance moves. She guessed the man had more sense than to break out into full-blown glee.

"Nice to meet you," the Rabbit said, and offered his hand to the hotel owner.

The man shook it eagerly. "Mathew Regan at your service. How about we find you the best suite in the hotel."

The Rabbit flashed a smile.

"At the price of an economy room," the hotel owner added.

"That's so kind of you and too much. We'll pay the full price," the Rabbit said.

---

7   Which you could easily consider a blessing, but not Siarl. He thought it was unfair, illogical, and downright rude, hating every one of the perks he got. Not that he ever gave them back.

"No, I insist. You are friends of Lucas, so you are friends of mine."

The Rabbit let go of the man's hand. "Who am I to argue against your kindness," he said.

The hotel owner laughed.

Sigourney was pretty sure the man would have liked the Rabbit to argue against such kindness. It was more than customary. The Rabbit didn't care about what was considered proper. If the man hadn't meant what he said, he should have kept his mouth shut.

"How about you show me where a man can have a drink and leave the kids to handle the rest?" the Rabbit asked.

"Sounds like a good plan." The hotel owner made his way around the front desk and guided the Rabbit across the hotel lobby, leaving Sigourney and Siarl behind with the front desk manager, who had a deep wrinkle on his forehead and was about to realize this wasn't the way the world worked.

Sigourney nudged Siarl, who was sulking next to her.

"The room key, please," Siarl said.

"But—" the man replied.

"Do you want them to come back?" Siarl asked.

No one who got caught in the net of the Rabbit's luck wanted to experience the confusion again. It was like sobering up after being drunk, with an understanding they had been fooled, but there was nothing they could do about it, leaving them only one choice—to pretend nothing had ever happened, preventing them from going insane.

"I'll get you that key," the man said and left Sigourney and Siarl alone.

"I hate this," Siarl said.

"I know," Sigourney mumbled, keeping her eyes on the flowerpots next to the counter. They smelled lemony.

"Why do we need him? Couldn't we..." Siarl didn't finish the sentence. He knew as well as Sigourney that they wouldn't be here without the Rabbit. That they had a good life because of him. And there was the fact they owed their lives to the god.

But it wasn't all the perks that convinced Sigourney to stay with the Rabbit. She loved him. Not the way she adored Siarl when she let her heart feel, but in the way you love a friend or a father. The Rabbit was the family Sigourney had never had. The one who protected her despite the cost. The one who loved her despite her weaknesses. And the one who wanted the best for her. Not that Sigourney's mother and father had been horrible people. They'd been just indifferent towards her. It was her brother, Levi, who'd had a twisted mind. He'd tormented Sigourney her whole childhood, being violent towards her in the name of curiosity. He had never been reprimanded by their parents, who saw their firstborn son as perfect and a miracle, unlike Sigourney. She was a burden. One extra mouth to feed, and the most despicable sort: a female.

"He means well," Sigourney said eventually.

"Yeah, and the road to damnation is paved with good intentions," he replied.

Sigourney left Siarl's response unanswered. What could she say? Yes, no, maybe? Or, who cares?

The manager came back with the key. He kept it close to his chest and refused to hand it over.

"I need your name," he said. His face shone with triumph.

Siarl and Sigourney exchanged meaningful glances.

"Ellis," Siarl offered.

"A full name, please," the manager snapped.

"Siarl Ellis," Siarl said.

"And is that your or your father's name?"

"Mine."

"It'll have to do."

Siarl and Sigourney were not kids in any sense. The front desk manager had to see they were well past the sixteen or even the eighteen marker, but there was nothing he could do. The manager reluctantly handed the key to them.

"Room 502 is up the stairs on the top floor to the right. It has an ocean view and twin balconies." He gave his rehearsed speech.

"Thank you," Siarl said and took the key.

Sigourney and Siarl left the lobby and climbed up the stairs to their room before the man could change his mind. Neither of them thought to look for the Rabbit and inform him where they were staying. His luck would guide him wherever he needed to go.

Sigourney couldn't wait to get to the room and put her feet up and have a nap.

2

IT'S NICE TO BE IN THE NEWSPAPER

ose Pettyshare thrust, ducked, and swirled as her opponent came at her. She was trying to take her mind off her work. There was only one thing that usually took the edge off, and that was fencing. Not your usual rules-riddled fencing; the real kind, with sharp rapiers and dirty fighting. Rose had noticed it took a life-altering incident to realize that rules were a figment of general imagination and nothing more. You could follow them if you wanted or for fear of punishment. But there were always those like her who were willing to look past the fantasy and submit to a beating if the risks they took didn't pay off.

Rose kicked her opponent in the stomach when the woman let her get too close.

Her opponent stumbled backward.

Rose didn't wait. She continued her attack, moving forward, tearing the woman's white garment from her shoulder. If she'd used more force in her attack, she would have drawn blood. Seeing the other woman bleed would have given Rose satisfaction like no other.

She basked in the glory of her small victory. The other

woman didn't. The slight scratch had been just that, a tear. The woman thrust her rapier forward, and this time there was blood. She stepped back, giving Rose time to breathe. If the other woman had wanted, she could have killed her.

Rose lifted her hand against her neck, letting her rapier's point fall. She could feel the blood on her fingers. She nodded to the woman, giving her permission to relax.

"I'd better get you a handkerchief." The woman slid her rapier into the sheath on her hip.

"Thank you, Abigail," Rose said and sat down at the edge of the mat.

Abigail left her alone in the vast attic, pressing her hand against the wound. It was only a scrape, but they weren't taking any chances. You didn't know what you could catch. Rose watched through the huge windows as the morning sun rose behind the city skyline. She'd needed this to drive away all the tension before going to see the bureaucrat, who would decide the fate of the banking branch she was opening here on Threebeanvalley's soil. So much depended on this morning going right. She tried not to think about it.

Finding a woman as a fencing partner had been a stroke of luck in itself. Abigail fell into her lap by pure accident. A day after she had gotten off the boat, she'd found Abigail in the strangest place you could ever acquire a teacher: a gambling house. Rose wasn't entirely sure in what capacity the woman worked there, but she did. Abigail had introduced Rose to Justice, who ran the place. The thought of the other woman made Rose's stomach twist. She was in pretty deep. Most of her own money was gone, so she'd dipped into some of the bank's, praying Percy, her assistant, wouldn't notice. Last week had been a bad one. Bluff the Prime Mover was no game for fools.

"Here you go," Abigail said, giving her a white handkerchief.

"Thank you," Rose said and pressed the cloth against her neck.

The woman sat next to her. "You are getting better. We'll surely beat out those rigid rules they taught you back at home. They won't save you if things come down to a show of strength."

"I guess not," Rose replied. "I just can't help but feel disappointed."

"Normal. If you had not let yourself be blinded by the opening your kick created and gone on without thinking, there might have been a different outcome. Me sitting in your place... Let me see." Abigail leaned over.

Rose could smell her as she studied the cut. Sweat combined with something flowery underneath. Rose bit her lip.

"Not too bad," Abigail said. "Deeper than I thought; I'd better bandage it. And you should clean it with water thrice a day to keep the infections away. If you can, add some salt to the boiled water after it has cooled."

"I'll ask the hotel staff." Rose shifted away from the woman.

"Good," Abigail replied.

They sat there without saying a word for a while. Rose looked at her black shoes, trying to come up with something to say. What Abigail was musing was a mystery.[8]

"Have you thought about what Justice suggested?" the woman asked after a long pause.

Rose's whole body stiffened, and she felt an instant fake smile rise to her lips.

"It's a good offer, and you should really see it as an investment in your future. Justice is a powerful woman to have as a friend, not to mention wealthy. Her fortune and mine in shipping and gambling will make up all the losses you might suffer," Abigail insisted, not reading the distress she was causing. Or if she did, she didn't care.

"But that would be like shooting my own leg off," Rose said, after searching for something neutral to say and failing even in that.

"Money is money, wherever it comes from. Think about it." Abigail stood up. "I'd better get you the bandage I promised and some water."

"Abigail," Rose said, reaching for the woman's hand and feeling it slip away as she rose to her full height. Abigail turned to face her. Rose couldn't decipher what the other woman was thinking now, or what she thought of her.

---

8   A mystery so easy to solve with one simple action: asking. But the logic of social conduct dictated it was better to play guessing games just in case... Why, no one really knew. Maybe the ground would open underneath them and swallow them whole, as that was always a possibility when embarrassment was on the cards.

"Rose, this is serious. You owe us, and a lot. Justice and I have kindly offered you a way out, not only by forgiving your loans but as a way to make money. Consider this a miracle and an opportunity."

"I can't promise you anything. The bank isn't even running yet. We need today's approval to go through." Rose withdrew her hand, which she'd left there to hang between the two of them in vain hope.

"But people have already come to you with their loan applications, with their business proposals. And I know you have hired brokers to look into potential companies to acquire. You only have to look them over and give us names and places." This time Abigail seemed angry.

Rose folded the bloody handkerchief, not knowing why. She just had to do something.

"Let me think about it," she said.

"You have a week before..." Abigail didn't finish her sentence. She didn't have to. She left the room to get the water and bandages.

Rose finished the sentence for her. "...we send our goons after you." Rose knew the drill. It was the same everywhere where you had money dancing on the edge between what's yours and what's mine. Some just had the government behind them and others took matters into their own hands.

Justice, Rose snorted. What a name to have.

She hadn't made a fresh start away from Necropolis as she'd planned. Not that she believed in plans; she was more the type to follow her intuition and impulses. They usually served her right. Now, the first and only mistake she had made was to step inside the gambling house. But in her defense, things had ground to a boring halt for months. Getting through the city's bureaucratic procedures was like drowning in quicksand. Slow, knowing perfectly well you were going to suffocate in the end. There was no point in struggling; you would only bury yourself quicker. Hence the distraction.

Rose unfolded the handkerchief and pressed it hard against the wound, letting the pain wash over her. She was here to open a banking branch, trying to fill the shoes of a tedious managerial position. Cursed to suffer just because of a similar failed mentality at the gambling house back at home. She didn't care about forms like 67d. She needed more, as she'd needed more and more back in Necropolis, never satisfied. At first, she'd worked as a bank teller for the Worthwrite Bank of Necropolis Ltd. Then she'd climbed up the ladder to be a broker, where the real banking lay. The rush when you took a risk and won big time was a feeling like no other. But then without warning she'd lost her clients' money and her own. At first, everything had gone splendidly. She'd made more money than any common fellow would dare to dream of,[9] but then... the politics had changed, and the markets had started to fluctuate. She had fumbled.

The thought of failing made her nauseated. She could hear her father scolding her, "Real banking is done in five-to-ten-year segments. The future is what matters, not now."

Rose shut her eyes, ignoring the image of the old fool. She truly had known how and what risks to take, but how was she supposed to foresee the leadership in Necropolis or in her own bank changing so quickly? Both positions were for life. She was lucky she had taken management and business courses at the University of Necropolis at her father's request, making Kitty Worthwrite bend enough to send her here to open the new branch and hide until the dust settled. Mrs. Worthwrite had had no other choice; no one else had volunteered. Even the thought of Threebeanvalley's hot and nourishing air hadn't convinced others to take the assignment. Necropolitans considered their city to be the greatest and the only place worth living, never having the original thought to venture out and see the world.
A bit close-minded, in Rose's opinion.

Initially, she'd felt the same. Now, she saw the upside of being abroad, and not only because of the weather. It was the colorful landscape and ever so open and positive people. In all this time, she hadn't heard a single sarcastic word uttered. At first, she'd thought all the kindness was a way to get under her skin and get one over on her and Percy, but nothing could be further from the truth. The people were nice here. Abigail was nice. She could be nice here too. If only—she never should have stepped into the gambling house. Then there was Percy. Rose grimaced.

Percy Allread was a witch who knew the power of hexes, sprinkling them behind him like investments for money and

---

9   Robbery, really.

reputation. As he had done when he'd gotten them in a local paper only a week after they'd gotten off the boat. Rose wasn't sure if she resented the man because of his powers or because of his appearance and manner. There was something wrong when a beautiful person wasn't joyous, open, and warm. Instead, Percy was all about schedules and proper protocols.

He would be waiting for Rose downstairs to take her to see the financial counselor. A quick courtesy call to leave their petition to open a new bank, or so their lawyer had assured her. Then they could get into the nitty-gritty, finding the right kind of connections, taking out the competition, securing a building and staff. Before that, Rose had to get dressed. She had taken a skirt suit with her to the fencing parlor. She preferred trousers, but they were not an option here. Back in Necropolis, men and women were equal. No one questioned a female banker, and female scientists were far from unknown. But here in Threebeanvalley, things weren't as liberal, which was funny if you took into account all the technical advances the city had to offer. All this meant she had to wear skirts and let Percy escort her around.

Her lawyer had urged her to buy a whole ensemble, including a corset and petticoat. She had done just that. At least the color of the skirt and the matching coat was to her liking: a deep purple.

To rebel a little, Rose had left the corset and the petticoat back at the hotel. She hated the feeling of anything pressing against her ribs. If anyone complained, she could always threaten to go bare naked. It wouldn't be an empty threat. She was known for her boisterous dares back at the university, with betting involved and lots of money won.

Rose headed to dress once Abigail had cleaned her wound and bandaged it. She hid it with her coat's neckline as best she could. Soon there was a knock on the door.

"Yes?" Rose asked.

"Your assistant is here." It was Abigail, sounding nervous. No wonder; Percy wasn't exactly known for his friendly chats. Most likely, he had stared at Abigail solemnly until she did as asked or fled.

"Are you decent?" It was Percy. She would recognize that prosaic voice anywhere. "We should be going," the man added.

Rose wanted nothing more than to say no, but she would be ready as soon as she got her coat on.

"A moment, please," she said and took the fencing clothes and the rapier into her arms and pushed out of the dressing room.

Percy loomed behind Abigail. He was indeed a pretty man, but his handsomeness came out of this brooding seriousness, making him mysterious to some. At first, Rose had entertained the thought, but the more time she spent with the man, the more she didn't want to cross that line.

"Morning, Percy," Rose said, trying to sound cheerful the way people did here.

"I thought we could go over today's tasks." Percy glanced at Abigail.

"Mhm," Rose let out. "Thank you, Abigail. I'll book another lesson later."

"See to it," the woman replied as if she was happy to see the back of them. But before Rose left, she stopped her. "Think about it. You have a week."

Rose hurried after Percy without replying.

Levi was hunched over his work desk in the basement. The fragments of a Bufonite's heart were scattered on the surface, illuminated by a string of gas lamps he'd installed all over the place. Quiet noises came from over his head as Otis and the maid, Evelyn, made a racket for the sake of breakfast or something else just as absurd. The necromancer had grown more interested in what went into his stomach than getting the new apparatus started despite the victory with the gold coin. Also, from the look of it, more interested in what Evelyn thought of him.

Levi found his hands shaking as he tried to attach a small cog to the wheel with his pincers. The gear dropped from his grasp, and he slammed his fist against the desk, making his open notebook snap shut.

He suppressed the urge to shout from the bottom of his organic heart and instead smoothed his curled hair behind his ears and began taking long breaths.

"It's only the day getting to you," he said to himself. "Soon, it'll be time to open the shop, and all will be well. The money will float in, and you can finish this new box."

"Did you say something, sir?" Otis' voice came from behind him.

Levi glanced at the man. Otis stood in the doorway, holding a tray.

"No," he replied. "I mean, yes. We need more money. We can't wait for months to get the machine to make enough coins to buy what we need. It'd be foolish to build the machine to the same size again. We need to make it bigger. As big as a printing press."

Otis lowered the tray onto the table, moving the gears and tools aside. There was porridge. Levi hated porridge. But there was also freshly squeezed orange juice, tea, and a croissant filled with what looked like apricot jam. And a newspaper.

Levi pushed the tray away.

"You need to eat if we are going to make it as big as you want," Otis said, sounding annoyingly patronizing. "And we could substitute the gilded plates with cheaper material so the coins it produces would make a profit rather than—" Otis didn't get to finish his carefully toned suggestion. Levi glanced at him and he fell silent.

"As you wish. It's your artistic process. But there's something you need to see that might solve everything." Otis handed him the croissant and then a newspaper. Pointedly, in that order, to force him to eat. Levi had nothing against eating. It was only that there was a time and place for it, and that was not when he was thinking. But to please the necromancer, he took a bite before unfolding the newspaper.

On the front page, in huge letters, was written: EVIL AMONG US! READ THE EXTRA!!!

Levi hated when they used exclamation points. They underestimated the reader.

The evil they were talking about was that people had gone missing. Humphrey Chadwick, the great clairvoyant, was one of them. NO BODIES FOUND. NEW DETECTIVE... said the subtitle.

"What of it?" he asked.

"We can't go on like this. We can't slowly burn our resources and hope you'll strike big somehow. We need funding, and fast."

"It's not like we haven't tried. We have sent our proposal everywhere, and they all see what I do as purely academic and unachievable," Levi groaned.

"But now we can make gold coins," Otis replied.

"Yes, and that took years of work, and damned if I'm going to give some investor a bigger share of my profits and my business just because they have the resources. If they wanted in on this in the first place, they should have helped to fund the research."

Otis shook his head and sighed. He sat on the high-stool opposite him, took the porridge from the tray, and began to eat it. Both of them knew Levi wasn't going to touch it, not in the mood he was in.

Levi hated the fact that Otis was right. Behind him rose the empty lockers where his supplies used to be. The custom-made plates, the gears, and the glass tubes weren't cheap. Not to mention what fueled the machine to make something out of nothing, the souls of the soon to be dead. Those took room in the little closets he'd built in the basement. Everything piled up.

Levi opened the newspaper, and on the next page there was a full spread about the Luddites. How the attacks had continued for weeks straight. Every night a new factory had been targeted, and the workers had been harassed. People were afraid to go to work. Levi had made a note last week. This had been front-page news, and now it had been moved onto the second page.

"How can people be this moronic?" Levi groaned.

Otis looked up from his bowl as Levi showed him the headline: MONSTER MACHINES OR A BLESSING FOR THE ECONOMY? LUDDITES STRIKE AGAIN!!!

"They have lost their jobs and they have nothing to fall back on. It's not like there's a system where the government aids them. The lucky ones have their wives and children doing odd jobs at the factories to put food on the table." Otis set the empty bowl back on the tray. The man was always ravenous. Levi had come to think it was because of the use of his powers, necromancy and shapeshifting. It was only natural that contorting reality consumed energy.

"I get it, better than you think," Levi said, and he did. He came from poor circumstances, where everything you did was to secure your survival. His parents' farm had been small and rented from the local landowner. They'd scraped by. He'd worked in the fields as soon as he could walk and carry his weight, and still it wasn't enough to secure a good living for his mother, father, and his little sister. He had sworn, after his lucky escape to become a clockmaker's assistant and then to study physics at the university, never to let such a travesty happen. The farm had been the worst kind of slavery: seemingly free. "But what they are doing won't change a thing. Yes, it might be a hindrance for the factory owner they targeted, but that won't stop the new inventions being made or the science behind it. The world will change, and it's the policies that need to keep up with the injustices happening."

"What about us?" Otis asked.

"They don't consider an alchemist and his shop a threat. More like a welcoming blast from the past, or how does that saying go? But I gather this isn't why you brought the paper to me?"

"No. Can I see it?" Otis held out his hand. When he got the paper back, he searched for the right page, handing it back to Levi.

There was a call for new inventions getting loans from the Worthwrite Bank of Necropolis Ltd. It was welcoming all new customers. Next to the rerunning ad was a picture of a quite attractive woman and an even more handsome man. The bank hadn't actually opened yet, but the ad explained how Miss Pettyshare and Mr. Allread had set out to bring competition to the markets and open possibilities for overseas trade.

Levi snorted. "You want me to contact them?" he asked.

"Yes. No, not them. Better not to associate with anyone coming from Necropolis. But anyone else will do. If a new bank opens up in the city, it'll start competition, and we might get a good deal to fund the machine and make it bigger and better. I have plans to retire rich and happy. This has already taken six years. I took a huge risk coming here. One that might cost me my life, if you remember. The more years pass, the shakier my holding on my dear life gets. On our own the process could still take an eternity. Or we could always sell the prototype and be done with the whole damned affair," Otis offered.

"They won't let them settle in the city. You know what they are like. The old families will drive away any competition at any cost," Levi said, rubbing his beard, not hearing a word his assistant had said.

"Yeah, but—" Otis insisted.

Levi shrugged to silence the man after translating the remark as "you dismiss me because it comes from my lips." He might be right.

"I have to open the shop," Levi said and pocketed his notebook. He took the orange juice and tea with him. "You need to feed the two others, too," he added before he forgot.

"It will be done, but think about it. We are running out of money. Your shop is an attraction. You are an attraction, but the ladies still spend pennies compared to what we could make if this works." Otis took hold of the tray. "And before you ask why again, I want money and power so they can't hunt me down. I can do what I want and be what I want, and they can't touch me."

"You keep saying that. Get Miss Illes, and we'll see where this leads," Levi said and closed the basement door behind him. He made his way up the stairs, past Evelyn, past the living quarters to the dark shop.

He lowered the juice and teacup onto the counter and took a deep breath in. Otis was right. They needed outside money. The parts weren't exactly cheap. Early on, he'd learned that the golden plates had to be forged well. Not passable, not mass produced. Individually cared for and loved, including all the joints, pumps, and gears. Even though what he made came out of nothingness, it didn't tolerate sloppiness. It was like the machine had to be tuned into perfection to be one with the universe.

Maybe he should contact the bankers again. Not just yet; the machine had to be just right.

Levi left the counter to open the shop door to let the already queuing ladies in.

3

COULD YOU DIM THE BEACONS OF THE PAST?

igourney lay on the suite's couch. She had her feet up against the golden-green backrest, her eyes shut. She wasn't sleeping, more like pretending she was. Listening to everything Siarl did. He'd spread a map of the city over the coffee table and was making notes. Sigourney wasn't sure where he found the map, but him having it didn't surprise her at all. While Siarl was a dreamer, he was also a doer, and a painfully organized one at that. He liked schedules, lists, structure, and waking up every morning at the same time and going for a jog. Something no one did in this day and age. More than twice the Rabbit had saved him from unwanted attention from police officers who couldn't wrap their heads around the fact that some people liked to run for no reason, health not being considered a good enough excuse. Once, the officers had sent for a doctor to assess Siarl's mental state before releasing him to the Rabbit's custody. The doctor had said Siarl had a particular case of determination and obsession, which in some cases might cause severe health problems. After that, the man had prescribed rest for Siarl. When those little moments of embarrassment stacked up, Siarl got moody and mumbled about the backwardness of modern man, believing in folklore and old wives' tales, and then he would snort, and Sigourney knew to keep out of his way.

Despite the incidents, Sigourney kind of liked his orderliness. It was a safeguard against the chaos of life she'd experienced when alone. She would never admit that to him. It was too fun to tease him about his nature. Sometimes he took it well and laughed along with her. Then there were those times that Sigourney didn't care to talk about.

"What do you want to see?" Siarl asked.

Sigourney opened one of her eyes and glanced towards him. Siarl sat on the armchair opposite her. He smiled and twirled a pen between his fingers. When he saw her looking at him, he smoothed his hair, which was now short. It made his ears pop out and exaggerated his narrow, sharp features. Another one of his modernization ideas. At first, Sigourney had hated the haircut, but now, if she was honest, it kind of suited him.

Sigourney shut her eye and thought about those quiet moments when she dared to let her guard down and be relaxed around him. She could feel his thick hair between her fingers. Not now, she thought, and said,

"I don't know. Nothing."

"You must want to see something. Maybe the sea? You love the sea. Or the lighthouse? I bet it's haunted. It's at least two centuries old. Can you believe that?"

Easily, she thought.

"Mhm," she let out. Her brother had loved that lighthouse. So had she. She'd spent endless days looking out to sea as the ships vanished into the horizon. If there was something she missed from Threebeanvalley, it was the ocean and its never-ending light blue water on a clear, bright summer day. Even now, she could hear the seagulls squawking as they swooped overhead.

"We could go there first if you want?" he asked carefully.

He knew her better than she thought; he didn't press her even though Sigourney was a hundred percent sure he wouldn't let her stay inside the hotel. So, it was either the lighthouse or some other place. She loved the lighthouse, assuming that her brother wasn't there.

Sigourney swung her legs down and sat up.

"What about Lepus?" she asked. The Rabbit god of luck's full name was Lepus Cornutus Bonnee, but they rarely used it, as there was something sacred and scary about saying a god's name aloud.

Siarl shuddered, but when he had shaken the name away, he said, "It'd be nice if it was just the two of us for a change. He's perfectly happy at the bar. I'm sure by now he has gathered a crowd around him to listen to exaggerated accounts of his travels."

Siarl was right. The Rabbit would surely have a following if he was in the mood to be admired. Also, Lepus was fine on his own. And if Sigourney spent a day alone with Siarl, it might cheer him up and ease the tension between the three of them, which had been building up for too long. Ever since the little arguments had started.

"I'll leave a note." It wasn't necessary. If the Rabbit wanted to find them, he could. But sometimes it was nice to pretend.

Sigourney stood up and walked to a desk next to the windows overlooking the city. Like in all the hotels in the known universe, there was stationery with the hotel's crest laid on the table. Then again, in some universes, the paper was replaced by a living organism with an impeccable memory and sludge-like shape, but here, the paper was made of wood pulp. Sigourney tore the first page off and left a note for the Rabbit. For a moment, she hesitated, wondering whether to close with warmly, sincerely, or yours, but in the end she decided to leave it open. It felt more personal that way.

"I'm ready," she said.

Siarl folded the map and grabbed his knapsack from next to the door. Sigourney glanced at the map in his hand.

She hated to appear like a tourist. When she was alone, she let her instincts guide her. That was impossible with Siarl. He had to know where they were at any given moment or else he felt naked. Sigourney had explained to him several times that they were where they should be and nothing was wrong, but he wouldn't listen to reason. She'd eventually given in and let him take maps with him and to be in charge of where and when they went. It was one of those small adjustments required to make a relationship work, she'd told herself.

Relationships were full of those small adjustments, she knew that now. She also knew that was fine as long as they shared their underlying beliefs. The minor things like what a good human life consisted of, how to treat others, and which side of the bed to sleep on. She always chose the right side and was always kind to animals, children, and the elderly. The rest of the humans were too much of a hassle for her liking, so she left them alone.

She followed Siarl out of the hotel and onto the streets laminated with missing person posters. Sigourney shrugged them off as the downside of city life and followed after Siarl. She wondered why Siarl always had to try to control everything. Sigourney had no grand illusions that she could be the master of her or anyone else's fate. What happened would happen, and she could only do her best in those situations. Not that anything terrible had happened in the four years they'd been together. Only minor incidents that turned into grand adventures. They'd spent months with the monks in the mountains after their cart had broken down. The monks had tried to teach Siarl inner harmony, but the bugger had refused to be at peace. He'd said there were too many ideas to explore. After that, they'd chased down a snowman with the monster hunter expedition from Necropolis, but only after the Necropolitans had arrested them for trying to steal their supplies.[10] They had only seen glimpses of the elusive snowmen, which possessed stronger juju than the Rabbit's. And on a peaceful canoeing expedition, they'd come across a white whale with a harness and a label saying, "Property of Ishmael." They'd gone on a quest to find this Ishmael, but the man had played hard to get. So they had set the whale free.

Sigourney liked to leave room for chance. It made life more interesting. But there were certain occurrences that she'd avoid at any cost. Here, it was running into her family. She looked around, trying to spot familiar faces. She wasn't sure if she'd recognize her parents or even him upon meeting. It had been years since she had last seen any of them. Now every face they met reminded her of someone she had known. A friend. A foe. A neighbor. But none of the faces she saw was her brother. Or her mother or papa.

---

10   Which was a false accusation, of course.

The more people she saw, the more confused she got, and on a few occasions she almost lost Siarl in the crowd. She was glad when they finally got closer to the shore and past the long, narrow bridge to the lighthouse island. There the houses turned older and smaller and more familiar. Sigourney had the fondest memories of the old fishermen's huts. More than once, she'd sneaked inside to have a look for all the treasures the men pulled out of the sea. Broken bottles. Wooden torsos of women. Seashells. And pearls.

Fishing had once been the only noble profession the city had known. Along with smuggling, of course. Then there were people like her parents who'd set up farms, but fishing had been what defined Threebeanvalley. Nothing else. Not anymore, though. Even here on the shoreline, Sigourney could hear the quiet buzz of people, the wheeze of steam engines, and feel the thick smoke coming out of all the new inventions that had taken over the once peaceful city.

Behind the fishermen's huts, the lighthouse rose majestically against the cliffs. A soothing breeze blew between the houses, bringing in the cooling sea air to ease the hot afternoon sun. Sigourney shut her eyes and let the briny air wash over her. Home, she thought. Tears welled up. Determined not to let them out, she bit her cheeks.

"You know, I've been thinking," Siarl said and hesitated. He took her hand and stopped her from moving forward. They stood there, silent on top of the dark, rough stones, under the watchful gaze of the lighthouse.

"Yes?" Sigourney asked carefully, opening her eyes. She tensed up after realizing he had been planning this. Whatever this was.

"That we could settle down. Find a nice place to call our own. What do you think? Threebeanvalley has a good university and economic prospects." He softly squeezed her hand.

"I," Sigourney started. She felt the words get stuck in her throat.

"You don't have to decide now. Think about it," he said.

They walked the rest of the way to the lighthouse in silence. The soothing sound of the sea washing against the shoreline and the seagulls' calls faded into the background as she tried to understand why he'd asked that question. It felt unfair. She couldn't stay here even if her heart would always be entwined with the city's landscape. It would be a prison sentence.

She let go of Siarl's hand, pretending she needed to use it to balance on the rocks to get to the lighthouse.

She peered at the towering building, which had deteriorated over the years. The paint had chipped, and its windows were smashed.

"Isn't that amazing? To think it was built hundreds of years ago. The sheer effort they put into this building and operating it is a testimony to human ingenuity," Siarl said, and with the same breath he added, "Let's go and see if the door is open."

He ran up the stairs, trusting his full weight to the metallic frame. Sigourney had a tight feeling in her stomach, but she followed him up, running as fast as she could. The steps groaned underneath her.

Her heart was pounding as she caught up to him at the top of the spiral stairs.

Siarl stood at the door, waiting for her. "It's locked," he said. "Can you?"

Sigourney nodded. She walked to the door and knelt down, taking a cloth bundle from her jacket pocket. She opened the parcel and selected the first tool from her lock-picking set. It looked like something a dentist would use. It had a small handle and a long, narrow, flat blade with a hooked tip. She pushed the pick inside the lock and wiggled it, trying to find a groove to lodge it in. When she was satisfied, she took another pick of similar length and narrowness but with a broader tip. She pushed it in, and soon there was a click. Sigourney turned the door handle, and it opened. They were instantly welcomed by still, musty air.

Siarl went in. Sigourney tried to grab the sleeve of his jacket to stop him, but it was too late. She stood up and peered inside before following him in. The place looked abandoned. There were no deranged brothers lurking around. Actually, the lighthouse looked spookier than she remembered. Or all the dark shadows, the marks on the walls, and the broken glass reminded her that she should have come clean to Siarl before they'd stepped into the locomotive. He wasn't stupid; he knew something was wrong. She didn't know if she could tell him that this was her hometown, that she had family here, that she had an actual past. Past and responsibilities she had cruelly abandoned. It felt like too much, even how silly it sounded. Letting someone fully in was the scariest thing she could ever do. What if...?[11]

This is just a lighthouse and another adventure among the many, Sigourney reassured herself and shut the door behind them.

❧

As Rose and Percy made their way down the stairs to the coach, he didn't offer to take her fencing clothes. He clutched the black diary he carried everywhere.

"You have a meeting with Page Briggs at ten o'clock," Percy began immediately.

"Yes," she replied, thinking how easy it would be to make the man uncomfortable.

"After that, I have scheduled you to have a lunch break. At half-past twelve, we will meet back at the Hotel Earl and go over the sites I have visited and assess whether any of them meet your standards. Then—"

"Then we talk over what comes next, unless you want me to be late to meet this Page Briggs." Rose cut the man short and hurried her steps before he made her endure the minute-by-minute description of the day. She was sure Percy had done just that. The only reason this morning was somewhat relaxed was because the man didn't know about Mr. Briggs' working habits. He'd tried to find out, she was sure of that.

"But—" Percy began.

"One task at a time, and you should be concentrating on the building sites you are going to visit. Securing a building is imperative if we want to succeed," Rose interrupted him again. They didn't have an address for the bank in the forms, but the lawyer had reassured them that they could fill in the detail later, as the licensing process would take at least a month. Still, this could be one of those endless debacles of chickens and eggs.

"I have been thinking," the man began.

Here we go again, Rose thought.

"Mr. Cumberbatch said I should escort you around. Is it wise to divide our attention this way?"

---

11   The cursed what if, the root of all good or the start of misery and unlived lives.

"Divide and conquer, as our late leader Oliver the Great used to say," Rose replied automatically.

"He's dead now," Percy jabbed back.

"But not because—"

"Because he went to face Minta without an escort," he cut in.

Touché, Rose thought, but instead said, "All according to the laws of necromantic battle. And if we don't want to end up in a fix, find me a good site to build our bank." This time she said it in a proper Necropolitan tone, full of command and severity without any foreign cheer.

"As you wish, madam."

"Now, did you bring me breakfast and my briefcase?" Rose asked.

"They are in the coach as you requested."

"Good." Rose was sure Percy would be the death of her. She hated schedules, she hated protocols, and she hated paperwork; banking was about gut feeling.

A driver opened the coach door as soon as they stepped out of the building. The man took Rose's fencing clothes automatically before she got in.

"Where were you last night?" Rose asked as she took her seat. She watched Percy squirm. As always, he wore a long black overcoat, black suit trousers, black shirt, and a black vest. The only light was the real bird-skull necklace tied around his neck with a plain string. "I came to see you, but you weren't in your room."

Percy distracted her by offering her a parcel containing a bagel with lettuce and cottage cheese. Not anything she had eaten back at home. In Necropolis, food was made to fatten you up and keep you warm against the damp, cold sea. But here it was made to delight you. She'd noticed that the warm, healthy sea air along with the exercise had made her appetite grow. Rose bit into the bagel happily.

"So?" Rose asked between bites. She wished Percy had brought a cup of coffee with him, but there was only cider to wash the food down.

"When was this?"

"Around nine p.m."

"I couldn't sleep, so I took a walk around the block." The way Percy said it made you think the words held true to a point, until you started poking your finger at all the moving parts and small details. Then it came apart like the petals of a dried flower.

Rose didn't believe him for a second. Was he going behind her back? Was he spying on her? Of course he was, but this could be about his skills as a hexer. The Necromantic Council sometimes sent people like him overseas to do their bidding, but Rose highly doubted the Worthwrites would let them do that on their penny. And Percy didn't seem the adventurous type. He was the accounting type, the type to stay cooped up indoors with his schedules and diaries and long columns of numbers that made humans manageable.

"The front desk manager handed me this." Percy offered her a thick brown envelope with her name scribed on it.

Rose licked her fingers and opened the letter, setting her food on the parcel on her lap. There was a note inside from Justice and a list of businesses in the area. It seemed like she didn't even have the week promised, nor the freedom to handle the matter according to her standards. If she were alone, she would shout and curse Abigail for ever introducing her to Justice. She calmed her nerves instead and pushed the envelope into her briefcase among the pre-filled forms for the local and international banking licenses.

"Anything I should know?" Percy asked, waking Rose from her thoughts.

"Oh, it was nothing. Just a survey I asked Mr. Cumberbatch to acquire. We need to get to know the city's businesses better," Rose lied. She would read it later when Percy wasn't looming over her, occasionally glancing at the bandage and frowning. What Justice had sent was useful. Information was power. If she wanted to crack Threenbeanvalley, she had to be aware of everything happening, even beyond the companies. The frivolous things like who was having a ball mattered more than anyone wanted to admit. She would have to get herself into one of those fancy parties, along with visiting the right museums and cafes. The trouble was that she would have to take *him* with her and keep Justice off his radar.

For now, none of that mattered. She watched as the coach moved through the bustling city. People had woken up to a sunny morning, rushing out to invent new things, invest in new ideas, and altogether make the economy go around and around, making people like her rich.

Rose got out of the coach at the City Hall. Her mind automatically jumped to going over the licensing papers. She had enough forms with her to drive any sane person to the brink of madness.[12] Luckily the lawyer they'd hired was good and efficient. The man had even gone over the city's laws and legal structure, political entities, how the economy worked, and how to conduct oneself in the City Hall to smooth the process. It didn't include bribery. The lawyer had been clear about that. Here the employees of the bureaucratic machine took their jobs seriously. She had to get this right. Then she and Percy could go full steam ahead, as they said nowadays, to get the bank up and running, picking out the right kind of brass, marble, decor, staff, and the rest to show that the Worthwrite Bank of Necropolis Ltd was here to stay.

Outside in the front garden, Rose noticed that people were glancing at her. Vexed by her poise. Vexed by her long steps. A lady never hurried. A lady never had a purpose. And a lady was always accompanied by other ladies or a chaperone, and she had none. To think that they thought she, Rose, a Necropolitan, came from the land of hobgoblins and trolls, yet there she held more respect than here. Back there, no one questioned her intelligence, mind, or capability to conduct her own business, and least of all her freedom. But here, in the industrializing, modern Threebeanvalley, she was just arm-candy with a dizzy head. That was an unfortunate minor detail everyone back home had missed when they had prepped her. Percy had *graciously* promised to take the lead.

"For the look of the thing," he had said.

Over her dead body.

Rose walked past the men and women judging her. In the past, she would have stuck her nose up and brushed them off, but Percy was right: appearance was everything. So, she gave a little nod and a smile spiced with a hint of submission. There was confusion, but at least they couldn't spit in her face.

Rose stopped to look at the map of the City Hall complex, sensibly drawn and immortalized at the park entrance. There were more wings than in any adulterous aristocrat's palace. The place she was looking for was named after one of the founding fathers, Rowbottom. Rose thought it was a regrettable name. Then again, who was she to criticize

---

12   Not Percy, though. But Rose had come to think there was nothing sane about
     the man.

—Pettyshare wasn't exactly a name to brag about. She finally found the right place. It was the next building over. She headed there, this time with a composed posture. She might pass for a governess, a fancy one maybe. Governesses were allowed to be out and about.

Inside the Rowbottom building, behind a desk in the lobby, a smallish woman attentively guarded the place against any unwanted visitors. She greeted Rose with an unsure smile. A smile that hovered between "what are you doing here?" and "welcome, our pleasure." This time, the scale tipped more to the what rather than the welcome.

"Good morning," Rose said as she approached the secretary.

"Good morning and welcome to the City Hall's financial department. How may I assist you today?" the woman asked. She had a squeaky voice. The kind that made your teeth ache. A proper guardian then.

"I have a ten o'clock meeting with Page Briggs. Where can I find his room?" she asked.

"Her room is up the stairs to the left. Third door from the right, number twenty-three." The woman frowned. Rose surmised that she wasn't making a good impression.

She had assumed it would be a man who she was to see. Maybe the modernity had crept in more than she'd expected. "Thank you," she said and rushed off before the woman could say anything else.

Page Briggs' room was easy to find. Like the woman had said, it was up the stairs and to the left. There was even a name on the door, etched with bold black letters on a brass plaque.

Rose knocked on the door and waited for a reply. The reply took longer than she'd anticipated. She was about to knock again when a rough voice stopped her hand in mid-air. Page Briggs, presumably, said, "Enter."

Rose pushed the door open and stepped in. A broad-shouldered woman stared at her, measuring her from behind a desk covered in papers and ash.

"Take a seat," Page Briggs said, sounding more like hollow earth than the high shrill of a mouse on helium.

Rose took a seat opposite the woman's desk and laid her briefcase on the floor. She tried not to breathe in the smoke-filled air. Rose leaned forward to shake hands with the counselor before sitting down, but the woman had taken a cigarette out and lit it, refusing to engage.

"Do you mind, Miss Pettyshare?" the woman asked, leaning back in her chair.

"Not at all," Rose replied. It would be pointless to protest in a room that already smelled like a chimney. Rose sized the woman up. You could say the financial counselor was stocky. She had short brown hair cut just underneath her ears and bangs. There were deep lines around her mouth that deepened further as she took a drag from the cigarette.

"How can I help?" Page asked.

"Oh yes, I'm here to apply for a permit to open a banking branch. I have the necessary papers here," Rose said and leaned towards her briefcase.

"Then let's have a look at them," the woman stated between inhales.

Rose took the papers out and handed the forms to the woman, who took them without looking at Rose and began to read them immediately, holding the cigarette between her fingers. Occasionally ash dropped onto the table and onto Rose's papers. The woman brushed it off and continued reading.

Rose opened her mouth to explain, but the woman lifted her hand to silence her.

The woman flipped the front document over and moved on to the second form, 2b.

"I and my lawyer—" Rose began, but the woman silenced her again with the same hand gesture.

Rose was feeling distraught. She'd prepared to exchange a few words of pleasantries before moving on to the papers like the lawyer had instructed. She'd planned to explain her bank's noble purpose, history, and how they were long-established in Necropolis, how they could benefit Threebeanvalley and the inhabitants. She had even prepared to add in a smile and a line about the vital work the financial council did in the city. She'd also been prepared to flirt when she'd thought she would be meeting a man. But all that was thrown away by the rude woman who made Rose's cheeks heat up. She wanted nothing more than to storm out, but it wasn't an option. She was stuck with the machine on the other side of the desk, made out of organic flesh yet alien to the concept of human dialog.

"You are missing an address," the woman stated when she'd flipped the form over.

"My lawyer told me it could be added at a later date with appendix form 5c."

"Your lawyer was wrong." The woman shut the folder the papers were in and handed it back to Rose. "There's no point in me going over the rest. Come back when you have an address."

"But—"

"I'm afraid this is insufficient."

"No—"

"That's all, Miss Pettyshare."

Rose felt her face get hotter. She counted to ten to calm herself down, as anger was a useless emotion to let out. Rose took the woman's annoying stare with ease as she composed herself. She seemed to have forgotten who she was and what she could do. Fooled by the city's open and positive people into thinking that a smile and kind words were enough to get ahead in life.

"I'm afraid that won't do," Rose said. "I need to have the permit before I go and commission a building. My lawyer instructed me that appendix form 5c could be added within six months of the initial review and receiving a temporary license."

The woman stared back with her lifeless eyes. "Under new guidelines, we need your residence before we can proceed."

"But—"

"Come back later when you've secured a permanent address."

"That is unacceptable!"

The woman reached for a black book on her desk and flipped it open. "I have an opening in a month, the seventh of June. Will nine o'clock suit you?"

"You cannot do this!" Rose raged. She instantly regretted her carelessness and composed herself. "When were these guidelines changed?" she asked in a friendlier voice.

"Yesterday," Page said and took a drag of her cigarette, eying Rose.

Rose bit her lip. She could argue back and say this was unfair treatment of foreign investors, but there was no point in arguing even when she was right. Page Briggs was like a mountain that wouldn't budge. Rose needed to be on the woman's good side, or she would be stuck forever.

"Nine o'clock is fine."

Rose watched the woman pen her name into the diary. She frowned when she saw Rose still lingering there.

"Have a good day," Rose said and left.

Rose was boiling with rage as she shut the door behind her. She wanted to slam the door, then go back in and shout at the woman about how outrageous this was. How the city council and the woman were trying to make it difficult for new banks to enter the market. But she knew it was pointless. She had seen her fair share of the same tactics back at home. She would have to find a loophole or a way around the new guideline rather than declare a full-on battle against bureaucracy. It was a rare hero who won against the machine.

Rose snorted. She knew the guideline wasn't even a proper law. Page Briggs had looked like a woman who'd follow instructions to the letter, but Rose was wrong. Page Briggs was a woman who liked to piss people off. It gave her sadistic pleasure. Rose's apparent frustration was just what she had been looking for to start her bleak morning. It was the little cruelties in life that gave her a sense of self.

4

ALL THE UNCOMFORTABLE THINGS
OTHERS LEAVE OUT

evi pushed the door shut after the last customer. He wanted to torch the place and be done with it. Not that he wasn't proud of the shop he'd built from the ground up after they'd forced him out of the university. His former colleagues had laughed at the alchemy part, but the shop had kept him, Otis, Evelyn, and the rest fed and clothed. It wasn't that either. Nor was it about the customers who came here when everything else had failed, or often enough, for a resupply of pigments for their fabrics or to buy his little mechanical sculptures as gifts. No, he liked the adoration and the charm he could put on to sell the customers more than their hearts desired. Commanding a room full of ladies was easy. Controlling a room full of gentlemen was another thing entirely. It was just that there was more he could do. The Bufonite was real, and so was quintessence. Keeping the shop open was wasting his time.

"All settled?" Otis asked from the back door.

The man was too silent for his own good.

"Yes," Levi said and turned around after he'd flipped the

closed sign to face the street.

Otis looked different again. This time he had extra hair.

"You forgot something," Levi said.

The man patted himself, and when he finally noticed he had a layer of fur covering his neck and part of his face, he said,   "Oh."

The fur disappeared.

"Has Miss Illes arrived?" Levi asked.

"She's in the basement. That was what I came to tell you." Otis shifted his weight and leaned against the counter. The necromancer took the newspaper from the table and glanced at Levi. "Have you thought about what I said?"

Levi didn't reply. He drew the curtains, preventing any unwanted attention towards the shop. There had been incidents. Dares. Robberies. The word "alchemy" made people think funny things about gold and even about animated corpses. If only they knew. No one had ever gotten too far. It was handy to have Otis around. A huge black wolf with murder in its eyes made people reconsider their decisions. Levi wasn't sure if the necromancer could rip open anyone's throat, but as ever, appearance held more sway than substance.

"I'm still not sure what you are proposing. To sell the Bufonite to the highest bidder?" Levi groaned.

"Why not? We would be rich beyond our dreams and could leave this godsforsaken city. There's a wide, bizarre world out there."

"The highest bidder wouldn't let either of us leave. They would still need a necromancer willing to go against the Necromantic Council and someone who understands the mechanics of the machine. Do you want to serve under a master?" Levi walked to the counter.

Otis shuffled to his left, saying nothing as he made room for Levi to get to the cash register. There was no need to say anything.

Levi opened the cash register and took out a stack of banknotes.

Otis raised an eyebrow, which was more luscious than the one he'd had this morning.

"For Miss Illes, as a down payment," Levi said, despite having no reason to explain to his assistant what he did with the money. Sometimes it was just easier than to bark and bite.

"Are you sure we need more souls? Aren't the remaining two enough?" Otis folded the newspaper in half and then one more time for show. Levi should do something to improve the necromancer's humor, but he wasn't in the mood to pamper the man's delicate ego. He should be, as he couldn't do this without him.

Before Levi could come up with anything to say, Otis pushed forcefully away from the counter and changed his frown into a smile. "I'll head out, if you don't need me."

Levi waved him off. It was better if he went and did whatever he did to ease the tension. Most likely something involving someone's wife.

Levi stopped in the kitchen, took the plate Evelyn had left for him, and made his way to the basement. Miss Illes was already waiting for him, sitting on the stool next to the work desk. The Bufonite, or maybe Perrinite—no, something else— was hidden under the rags.

"You wanted to see me?" Margaret asked. Her expression was deadpan under the eyepatch. It wasn't like her voice or any other part of her demeanor ever gave away what the woman was thinking.

"Ah, Miss Illes, such a pleasure to see you," Levi said.

No reply. Not even a facial tic. Just a piercing stare, waiting for him to stop playing social games.

Oh well, he never was that fond of all the silly things humans needed to interact with each other. Nonetheless, they did work. Except with people like Margaret. Before you even made your move, they had stripped you naked and filed you into the category of either dangerous, useful, or to be ignored.

He was evidently useful to the woman, otherwise she wouldn't be here.

"I need more," Levi said as he stepped down the stairs into the basement.

"Already? It's not exactly easy to find them. Most of them don't broadcast their talents as number five did—or their whereabouts," she said, taking a pair of pliers from the desk and playing with them.

"They wouldn't, would they? But there are disturbances, things other people report. And it's not like it's a secret. It's common knowledge that some people are born with extraordinary talents, like Otis and Humphrey. And some learn. Did you know that you can study to become a necromancer overseas? A witch too." Levi lowered the plate to his work desk next to Margaret.

He saw her glancing towards the food hungrily. The only true expression she had ever let slip in front of him.

Levi pushed the plate towards her. She hesitated but accepted the offer without saying a word.

"Yes, but we have already exhausted those here in Threebeanvalley, who are easy to get and don't cause that much concern," she said, her mouth full of asparagus. "Number five was a huge risk. They are still searching for him even though I spun a story that the dead took him as revenge. And my favorite, that he's fleeing with his lover from her rich husband. People love that kind of romantic nonsense. I've heard a play is being written."

"Risks we can take. Risks I pay good money for," Levi said, ignoring the rest, how Margaret got things done. Though he had to admit she was brilliant.

She said nothing.

As if she knew he was running out of money for his expensive materials—that what the shop produced wasn't enough.

Then the unnerving woman shrugged. "I might have one, Malvina Corran. She's a patent clerk. But I'm not completely sure if she has the extra you need; she hides her talents well. Of course, there's always your sister," Margaret said, wiping the side of her mouth with her sleeve and continuing to eat.

Somehow the woman had been able to fish that information out of him, and she hung on to the fact like a parasite to its host.

"We have already exhausted that option. It's like she never existed. Last record of her was in Leporidae Lop, and nothing ever since." Levi took the authenticated gold coin from his jacket pocket and fiddled with it. He was uncertain whether he wanted to meet Sigourney, let alone kill her. Yes, she might answer the question of why one person was as plain as he was and the other one possessed the ability to hide in plain sight. And yes, she might be the key to explaining why the Bufonite worked only through specials' souls. And yes, he was still angry with her for abandoning their family, leaving him stuck at the farm. Of course, he'd made his exit, but that didn't change the principle of it all. But to take his own sister's life. There had to be a complex disorder named after such a desire.

"We have someone who might know where she is." Margaret kept her attention on the plate.

"Who?" he asked, watching the woman eat the last of the asparaguses and move on to the steak. He made the coin move from finger to finger.

"Number five, if you have forgotten. He's clairvoyant, the genuine deal, as his posters claim. I imagine he's finally ready to talk, or have you already used him?" Margaret flashed a smile.

"I'm not sure if that's such a good idea. Just get me the woman," Levi said, annoyed by how unnecessarily cruel Margaret could be. To rob someone of their name and render them into a mere number was like denouncing their humanity. Despite what others might think, he didn't care for cruelty. Morally dubious things had to be done sometimes, yes, but there was no need to be an asshole about it. There was a line between torture and necessity, which should be carefully stepped upon.

"You mean Miss Corran?"

The coin dropped from his hand, clanging as it hit the floor. He stopped to pick it up, pocketing it.

"I guess there's no harm in asking. Will you join me?" Levi said, gesturing deeper into the basement, where there was a row of doors. A casual onlooker would have thought them closets, where an alchemist held all his miracle cures, dyes, and gold. But they were not. There was something more valuable in them. Souls.

Margaret didn't have to be asked twice, even when there was still food left on the plate. She jumped off the stool and followed Levi as he made his way to the second door on the left.

Levi stopped and took a keyring off the hook next to the door.

"Mr. Chadwick?" Levi pronounced as he pushed the door carefully open. Thus far, the man had been cooperative and hadn't tried any funny business, but you could never be too careful. Sometimes being cooped up inside a little room did funny things to your head. Often enough it started with anger, then withdrawal, and later they began speaking to themselves while rocking back and forth in the middle of the room. It wasn't a pleasant sight. If there was any other way, he would do it. Let them mingle with each other. But that would be a volatile cocktail. Isolation was the solution that would do the least amount of harm to all. And he needed more than one. A few of the souls they had put into the machine hadn't taken.

The older man was curled into a ball on the bed. He didn't even glance towards them.

"Mr. Chadwick?" Levi repeated.

There was no response from the man, who had lost some of his pomposity along with weight since he had gotten here. Not because Levi didn't keep him fed. He did. Maybe it was because he wasn't able to be up and about. Smell the roses and so on. Levi had written that in his memos. The small observations about what confinement did to the body. If only there was another way.

Levi coughed.

"What do you want?" the man asked. There was spite in his voice.

Good, Levi thought. At least he still had his spirit intact. Those who lost their minds were difficult to work with.

"I need you to help me find someone," Levi said.

The man refused to face Levi and Margaret. "What makes you think I would do that?" he asked eventually when the alchemist didn't react to his silent aggression. Curiosity had won. It always did, even over terror.

"It's in your best interest," Levi stated. Not a threat exactly. No. He didn't like violence, and torture was ineffective despite what the legends said. A friendly chat went a long way[13] compared to a needle stuck underneath a fingernail.[14]

The man sat up on the bed and turned to face them. He grimaced when he saw Margaret standing beside Levi.

"If you want me to find someone, I need something of theirs," Humphrey said.

"Is a toy good enough?" Levi asked. A bunny rabbit was the only thing left of his sister's.

"I won't let you kidnap a child," the man protested. He

---

13   Around the universe and back.

14   The surest way to hear exactly what you want to hear, truth and information be damned.

lay back on the bed.

"Not a child; my sister. She's quite grown up," Levi said. He might disagree with what he said if he knew his sister and what had become of her. He had standards, and those included taking life seriously and having aspirations. There was something concerning about people who didn't want anything from their lives. Even children dreamed of becoming this and that, onions included.

"Then you'd better get that toy of hers, or if you two share blood, your hand is fine. Connection is all I need," the man spat out and sat back up.

Levi was okay with his indignation as long as he cooperated. He went to the man and sat next to him on the bed, offering him his hand. Levi noticed Margaret tensing up at the door, readying herself.

The clairvoyant shut his eyes, and soon he began to tremble a bit. "Name, please," he said.

"Sigourney Perri," Levi answered and clenched his teeth together as Humphrey squeezed his hand tighter.

He began to chant her name, then suddenly he fell silent. The hand relaxed around Levi's fingers but did not withdraw. His breathing got slower.

"Can you see her?" Levi asked.

The man shook his head. "Not her. Through her."

"What do you see?"

"A changing landscape. I hear a slurp. A whistle."

"That could mean anything."

"There are mountains."

"Ferrum?"

"I'm not sure."

"When is this?"

"Not sure about that either. It's the strong feelings I get. This could be now. This could be tomorrow, or way back. But I know I'm in a locomotive."

"Good, that would surely mean close to the present. Can you see where she's going? A ticket? Something?"

"No, but she's in the presence of two men, an older and a younger one. They seem to be arguing."

"Can you fast forward to the future? Maybe to see a station?" Levi asked, wondering if that was possible. And if it was, would it mean their path was already determined from their birth? That he was only an observer, going through the motions, with no say in what was going to happen? Formed energy, never ceasing, always in flux from one shape to another, always with the same destiny, cycle after cycle, from one bang to the next.

"It's hard to tell. The future is a questionable concept. It never stays the same. It can. Sometimes people are set in their ways and their paths don't change, but your sister isn't one of them. What I get is this snowy image with flashes here and there. I see a head of hair being touched. I see a lighthouse's spiral steps. Then there's fire," Humphrey said and opened his eyes.

"Fire?" Levi asked.

"Could be," Humphrey said.

"Where?"

The other man shrugged and let go of his hand. "Who knows. But the lighthouse felt familiar. She went there with the younger man with short brown hair."

"Could she be here?" Levi asked more to himself than the clairvoyant. They'd spent endless hours there, up in the lighthouse at the shore. She would hide from him and he would try to piece together how everything worked. There was a whole world inside those walls, and a whole ecosystem to observe beyond the compound.

"I wouldn't know where to begin guessing. Now, if you could leave me alone, I was back at my daughter's wedding, giving one of my famous speeches," Humphrey said, going back to lying on the bed, not giving a rat's ass about Levi still sitting there.

Levi left the man to dream. If it was what kept him functional, who was he to stop it. He locked the door behind him and Margaret.

"You know the lighthouse in the city?" he asked as soon as they were back at the work desk.

"No, but I can find out," she said.

"Visit it. If she doesn't show up there, look for other coastal towns with a locomotive connection. But first, get me Malvina Corran. This doesn't change anything. And if you do find my sister, let me know before you act," Levi ordered.

When Margaret departed with his money, he sat on the stool and pulled the rags off the Bufonite and its skeleton friend. They needed a bigger one. But should he make one with several connected apparatuses or one huge one with multiple souls? Levi drew the half-eaten plate of food towards him and began to nibble the leftovers while he looked at the parts. He flipped open his notebook and began to write down calculations. The huge one would cost him years of income. Why did everything in life have to come down to money?

Sigourney and Siarl stood in the musty octagonal room inside the lighthouse. The walls were made from wood paneling, and in the middle of the room, a metal staircase led to the upper floors. The first floor was empty except for the stairs. The place looked abandoned and sad. Its history hung in the air like an obtuse guest who refused to leave.

Sigourney bit her lower lip. The place's atmosphere and Siarl's closeness made all her worries ever so present. She wasn't sure if she could stay. Or even stay with him. The mere thought made her chest feel tight. Siarl seemed to have forgotten what he'd asked. He was too enchanted with the place.

"Can you believe this?" he uttered, touching the wood paneling, which was painted light blue and scratched with carved initials. "To think every single board is smoothed from a tree trunk and hand-carved. In a way, it's beautiful, but a waste of time, as modern machines can do it faster with their sawmills and without the need for so many men. Everything is getting cheaper and more accessible to people like us. We could have any kind of house we want. You and I."

Sigourney swallowed and shrugged, concentrating on what was rather than what could be. Somewhere on the panels, her initials were immortalized in the wood. She wasn't proud of what she had done, but that was youth for you. The need to leave an impression in the most peculiarly ineffective ways.

Siarl moved on, paying attention only to the lighthouse. Sigourney was glad. Siarl stepped onto the stairs going to the upper floors. She followed after him. The second floor was also empty. There was only an empty shelf on the wall and a window looking out, keeping an eye on the sea, made from tiny panels of harlequin-shaped glass. The walls were covered with writing, but Siarl had lost interest in the pointless scribbles.

"This is amazing. I can't believe the rooms are this lofty.

Of course, the lighthouse looks tall from outside, but this is something different. I could live here," Siarl said.

Sigourney froze, listening to Siarl's quiet breathing and trying to understand whether he'd said it seriously or whether it was just one of his dreams. Soon Siarl moved back to the steps and said,

"I want to see if they used wood pyres here or if they had a mirror system with candles and oil lamps or lenses. Could they already have used lenses as they do in the modern lighthouses?"

Sigourney could breathe again. It was just a passing thought.

Sigourney loved the idea of the solitude the lighthouse offered, but she could be as alone on the road as she could here, and at least then she would be in constant motion, never growing old, never collecting moss.

She followed after Siarl to the third floor. It was the lighthouse keeper's abandoned quarters. There was a low wooden desk covered in a thick layer of dust and bird droppings. Next to it stood an armchair and a bench, which didn't look welcoming; the opposite, in fact, with the dirt that had piled up there. The window had been nailed shut with a wooden board, and there were no signs of any dinosaurs' descendants with their majestic wings and sharp beaks. Behind the staircase was an old bed, which lay under an intact window. Next to it was a cabinet with "Library" carved on the doors. Sigourney knew it was empty, but Siarl had to peek in. He sighed and shut the doors and moved on to examine the darkened edges on the wall where paintings had once hung. Of what, Sigourney didn't know. They'd been taken or stolen a long time ago.

"I can't understand why this isn't still functional. It's not like the shores have gotten less dangerous," Siarl said.

"The route changed," Sigourney replied automatically.

"It did? But still, there's a need to show where the shore is. The waters are still shallow and rocky," Siarl insisted.

"There's a newer lighthouse on the little island off the coast," Sigourney said, looking out the window.

"I didn't know that." Siarl frowned.

Sigourney could feel Siarl's eyes upon her.

"We'd better go up," Sigourney said, and half ran to the stairs.

"Hey, wait up," Siarl shouted after her.

Sigourney didn't stop. She hurried up the metal stairs past the fourth and fifth floors, which were part of the lighthouse keeper's quarters, with huge windows to observe the activities on the water. On the fifth floor was an abandoned work desk with a hidden journal that Sigourney knew was cached in a secret panel in one of the drawers. Maybe she should offer it as a distraction to Siarl? Perhaps then he'd forget what she'd said? But she didn't dare to stop. She pushed the last door open, to the room that held the lighthouse's heart. There they were, the lenses and the lantern. Siarl had been right—the lighthouse was modern despite its age.

Siarl came up behind her, panting a little. Sigourney knew how to run fast in uncomfortable moments. She had always been good at putting distance between herself and her problems. Now she debated whether she should go past the lenses and the enormous lantern to the observation deck and hope the view would take Siarl's full attention, but she didn't have to. The lenses were working their magic already.

"Oh," Siarl exhaled, fascinated by the sizable geometrical structure made of glass and a metallic frame that held the lantern inside, amplifying the light the flame usually cast. By some miracle, the framework was still intact.

And Sigourney was safe.

She relaxed and made her way around the room, peering out through the vast windows to the sea as it surged against the shore. Somewhere in the distance, a white seagull swooped over the blue water accompanied by loud cries.[15] She listened to Siarl's steps, dancing around the lenses while muttering under his breath about mass, curvature, and force.

"How can they have made the middle lens so spherical, and how did they carve all the circles into the glass? Did they carve them by hand, or was it a mold? Or... Or...?" Siarl muttered.

There was no need to answer, as it wasn't a real question. It was just him rearranging his thoughts. For Siarl to become what he should be and use his curious brain as it should be used, he couldn't continue moving from one place to another. Sigourney understood that. He needed similar minds

---

15   To think seagulls' great, great, great, great... great grandparents were once as fearless as velociraptors. Okay, they have kept some of that spunk when it comes to things like ice cream cones and other unguarded food. Good.

to cultivate his thoughts, and he needed a passion to sink his time into, and it wasn't traveling and seeing the elusive yetis or great white whales with harnesses, or even zombies in the land of the living dead. His whole essence was something he could dream inside his head.

Sigourney left Siarl alone to inspect the lenses, going in and out of the cupola containing the lantern. She pushed open a glass door leading out to the observation deck. The wind whipped against her as she made her way to the railing. She closed her eyes and let the sea air wash over her, wiping away all her sorrows as it ruffled her hair and her clothes. She had known for a long time that she couldn't keep going on and on and keep everything bottled up; she was just afraid to let anything out. The truth might crumble her, and she wasn't ready. Why couldn't she keep living in the moment? What was wrong with that?

Siarl stepped out carefully next to her, not wanting to spook her. "I think we need to talk," he said.

Sigourney hadn't heard him approaching. She didn't reply.

"You keep things from me, and I accepted that a long time ago, but something is different here. You are different here, and it's affecting you more than before. I'm here if you want to tell me what this place means to you," he said, leaning against the railing, watching the sea and its diverse life. If he let himself, he would get lost cataloging and understanding what he saw, but not this time. She came first. She knew that.

The wind and the waves hit against the lighthouse, bringing with them a cold drizzle. Siarl turned around to hide from the worst of it, but he didn't leave like Sigourney needed him to.

"I'll always be with you. I'll follow you to the end of the world. You have to know that." Siarl sighed. The words sounded more like a burden than a declaration of eternal love.

"I think you should leave," Sigourney whispered.

"Is that what you want?" Siarl asked.

"No... yes... Siarl, I don't know," she mumbled. "But you should live your life, not mine," she added when he kept standing there next to her like an unmovable force. Sometimes it'd be easier if he didn't have deep convictions about how the world should be and how a man should act.

Siarl was the only man who had any honor left. Not the stupid kind of chivalry with rigid rules about who walked into a building first, but the real thing, with compassion, understanding, fairness, and respect. He was too good for this world, which didn't work the way he thought it worked. For him to survive, he needed to be a bastard. A selfish man with enough aggression to make his needs heard and fulfilled. But he wasn't. That was why the Rabbit put up with him, and that was why Sigourney couldn't let go. He made her feel safe, and not because he was a man. It was because he was the only person in the world she could trust. Yet she couldn't say aloud anything that was bottled up inside her. It was stupid. She was stupid.

Without a word, he drew her into his arms and turned to face the sea again.

The Rabbit god of luck, Lepus, sat in the Hotel Earl's bar with his new friend, the hotel owner. It had taken him a long time to get the hotel's bartender and the owner to understand what a cocktail should look and taste like. Now he nursed his carrot drink.[16] Despite the cocktail, the Rabbit was feeling unusually bored. The hotel owner, Mathew, was a docile creature, eagerly wanting to fulfill Lepus' every wish. He was even willing to sack the bartender, but the Rabbit had put a stop to that, not wanting to alter the course of human lives... too much. Not, at least, for the worse. He'd learned that lesson back in Leporidae Lop with the wars and all that. He wasn't exactly proud of how he'd let Harriet Stowe, the Prime Minister of Leporidae Lop, use his luck to control all the citizens' lives and happiness. It had left a bad taste in his mouth and a great distaste for cages. He shuddered at the image of the "birdcage" where the Prime Minister had kept him for years. Cruelty. Freedom and one's own body were sacred.

---

16   Which had taken an eternity to make. The Rabbit was sure the bartender was a bit thick. But he was wrong; the man had something called professional dignity, which included taking into account the client's health. This was why he'd refused to be involved in making a cocktail from jam mixed with a deadly amount of vodka. But he had yielded. There was something about the older man that made you do as you were told.

But this constant travel and staying out of human destinies wasn't what he would call a life. All this seemed to make the small human female, or Sigourney, as others called her, happy, and he went along with it. He didn't know how to leave her, despite being sure she was stalling her life by staying with him. Lepus had become more than her god; he had become a friend. From the fragments of her life that she'd disclosed, he'd gathered she hadn't got many friends, or a family for that matter. He would change that. It was the reason he'd brought them here. Siarl might argue that it'd been his stroke of genius to travel to Threebeanvalley, but it wasn't. Lepus had made sure the locomotive tracks were built and the city had enough luck to prosper.

The Rabbit god of luck took a sip from his drink and looked out of the huge windows to the hotel's garden. Colorful flowers, vibrant green trees, and beautiful metal benches and tables formed an oasis outside.

Mathew slurped his cocktail, sounding both eager and unwilling to drink the alcohol-infused carrot jam. The man looked dizzy and alert. Ready to anticipate the Rabbit's next wish.

"Do you think Threebeanvalley is a good city to live in?" the Rabbit asked.

"Definitely; you couldn't pick a better place to settle down. Everything is growing and blooming, and then there is the nature and the sea," Mathew said, slurring his words a little. The man pushed the cocktail farther away from him.

"Hmm," the Rabbit replied.

"Are you thinking about moving here? If you are, let me know. My wife's brother is..." The man hesitated. A look crossed his face, as if he wasn't sure what was real and what wasn't. "...is a real estate agent." Again, the man had a pained look on his face.[17] "He can help you," the man added.

"I'll keep that in mind," the Rabbit said and took a sip of his drink. "Now, what can a man do to have fun around here?"

"What would you like to do?"

"Something where you can wager your livelihood for a

---

17   He was sure his wife had a brother, but he'd always thought he worked in catering. He had to be mistaken. Why else would he say what he'd said? But somewhere in the city, a man became who he had never been and always been, feeling confused enough to have a lie-down in the middle of the street.

quick profit," the Rabbit said and grinned.

The hotel owner didn't grin back. He was experiencing more discomfort than bright realizations. His brain was trying to work out why it was crept out. Why his instincts kept saying to him, "Run!" The man swallowed and said,

"I think there's a place, but I have to warn you, gambling is illegal in the city."

"I don't mind. There's always someone to police even the most innocent fun," the Rabbit replied.

"I... Neither do I," Mathew said and tried to grin. It didn't suit him. His mouth was all tight, and if you paid close attention to his lips, they seemed to curl downward and not up.

The Rabbit gulped down his cocktail and wiped his mouth on his sleeve. "Show me the way," he said.

"I..." the man let out. He tried again. "I... I think... they open only later. It's a bit early for gambling." He said the last words with more confidence. "We have lovely bathhouses. Also, the central garden is a w—"

"Oh, it's always a good time for gambling. Take me there, and I bet you this hotel that they are open and packed with people," the Rabbit interrupted him.

Mathew had lost all his color. He looked like he was going to faint. Something inside him insisted that if he wanted to live another day and secure a future for his offspring, he should choose his next words carefully.

"I'm sure you are right. I've never visited such a place and couldn't even begin to imagine how it functions," the man said and sighed with relief.

"Then it's high time we change that," the Rabbit said.

Almost.

The hotel owner's words had started well, but the ending had kind of screwed him over. Then again, if the Rabbit had his mind set on something, there was seldom a way out of it. Not for mere mortals, at least.

5

ALL DREAMS FOR SALVATION LEAD TO
KINGFISHER ROAD

Levi woke up as his head hit the desk. Gears clattered away from him, some ending up on the floor. For a moment, he looked at them, unsure what had happened and where he was. Then he remembered. He'd begun to dismantle his previous attempts to construct a Bufonite, feeling like a butcher and a grave robber all in one. But he had no other choice; he needed the parts to make a model as big as a Hilderberg's printing press unit to see if that was even possible. Somehow, he would have to acquire more materials for it.

He had sketched out how the framework should go together. It would be a stunning work of art and a display of the best craftsmanship he could manage. Still, it might not work. The Bufonite might end up like everything nowadays—a thing appearing to have substance rather than actually having it. Moral corruption through the superficial. Yet he had to admit, looks mattered. Anything social was a show. And if you got the showy part right, you could rule. Why else would humankind pursue aesthetics? Investing extra effort in the surface made it easier to impress. And quintessence deserved a fitting casing. But what if the souls combined together would destroy the whole fabric of creation? It was a risk he had to take.

Levi got up from the stool and began to gather the parts and set them in their rightful slots. Chaos was not acceptable in his workshop. Everything had its place, time, and function. A life with machines dictated that. When mechanics took over, there was no need for the chaos of nature. Human or otherwise. Everything was rationalized, sized. Everything had a function, a pattern to follow. No gravitation, no decay; nothing would intervene with the proper course of his or anyone else's existence. All planned, all calculated. Not hindered by circumstances. Yet he felt like there was a but, something he was missing.

When Levi was done, he glanced at his pocket watch. It was best to call it for tonight and catch some shut-eye before morning came and the shop had to be opened once again.

He turned off the gas lamps and closed the door behind him. He walked up the stairs to the kitchen and from there to his private quarters. As he passed Otis' room, he noticed the lights were still on. He paused to listen. There came a giggle, which sounded a lot like Evelyn. He would recognize her child-like laughter anywhere.

Not lucky outside then. Otis' insatiable thirst for conquests had gone too far. Levi had ignored such behavior thus far, letting him do as he pleased, but Levi would prefer it if the man didn't shit where he ate. Evelyn knew too much for both of their good to allow her to slip off into the night of her own accord. Also, she was a nice kid, and Levi didn't want anything bad to happen to her. Though, one could argue she had taken the risk and should bear the consequences. But there was no point embarrassing them now. He would talk to them tomorrow morning.

He moved on, not wanting to hear the rest.

Levi welcomed the warmth of his room. Evelyn had lit the furnace in the corner for him hours ago. The fire inside its belly had already weakened into a cinder, but the heat had stayed. The room wasn't much to look at. A bed, a small writing desk, a wardrobe, a washing bowl and pitcher, and a considerable mirror standing in a frame, and that was about it. One or two of his own drawings on the wall. But no other decor or rugs as they preferred in high society. He didn't have the time or the interest.

Levi removed his jacket, lowering it onto the wooden frame of a mannequin, which looked like a stick figure. He took off the rest of his clothes and folded and smoothed them on the rack, then slipped into bed naked. A luxury he never experienced as a child. A small indulgence he allowed himself.

For a while, he tossed and turned, listening to Evelyn giggle more and Otis groan. The last time he'd made a comment to Otis about his love-life, the man had inquired after Levi's affairs. He hadn't demeaned himself by answering such questions. What was the point? There were always ladies circling him, fawning over him, and he could have any one of them. They were drawn to his tormented artistic genius, ready to burn their fingers. But he didn't care. Sex was pleasant and got the body going, but he seldom needed such a release. He had other things on his mind.

Levi took another notebook out from under his pillow and began to write down all his thoughts from today about the Bufonite and the alchemical recipes he should tinker with. There might be a way to improve the cure-all he'd come up with, make it taste sweeter and lighter for the kiddies. That would open up a whole new market and show the apothecaries, the pill pushers, that he still had it.

He fell asleep, the notebook resting on his chest. It would be nice to say he dreamed about the machine, or even about some grand adventure. Levi dreamed about nothing, or so it would feel when he finally woke up. As soon as his eyes closed, he was greeted with darkness. Sigourney would say it was because of his corrupted nature. She would be wrong. The darkness had nothing to do with his character. It was a mystery why some dreamed and others couldn't recall a single image from the night before. Maybe it was the sheer tiredness that always accompanied Levi to bed, making nightly visions elude him. Then again, it could be the fact that he wasn't paying attention to the hidden power of dreams. The creativity he could unleash through them. Maybe he thought of them as pointless, failing to understand that even animals dreamed, sharks included. That dreams served a function, sleep as well. It was no hindrance cutting his day short; it was a gift.

Whatever happened in his mind throughout the night was cut short as the curtains flew open, enabling the harsh sun to shine straight into his eyes, leaving him squinting against the brightness and a dark, blurry figure of the female persuasion.

"Good morning, sir," Evelyn said brightly, taking away any gloomy thoughts.

As his eyes focused, he could see her better. She was holding a tray. That was not what caught his eye. It was the extra blush she had on her face against her softened, welcoming features. Her brown hair was tied back, making her high cheekbones stand out. There was something chaste about her, yet there was a tease and a chase behind her huge, innocent eyes. It was no wonder Otis fancied her.

"Morning," Levi grunted and pushed himself up to lean against the headrest.

"Otis thought it was best if you had your breakfast in bed. I made eggs and a salad. There are extra berries and fruit in the cup as well. I thought you might prefer coffee this morning," she said, still sounding cheerful.

"Hm," Levi managed to say. He wasn't that keen on mornings. He hated them, in fact. Just when he had gotten the hang of this thing people swore by, he was yanked back into reality more tired and sluggish than before.

Evelyn set the tray on his lap and looked around. "Do you want me to wash your clothes?" she asked when she noticed the outfit he had worn yesterday neatly folded on the rack.

"Do you like working for us?" he asked instead of answering and took a sip of the coffee. The bitter, full taste spread inside his mouth, welcoming him back to his usual self. The one who knew where all the beans were buried.

"Yes," she said hesitantly.

"And you are aware of what's expected of you?" he asked.

Those huge, watery eyes, so innocent a moment ago, glazed over. "Y-yes," she stuttered.

"Good. And you know who pays the bills and who owns the house and the shop?" Levi asked. Now he was tasting the berries and fruit Evelyn had ever so carefully chopped into a small bowl. Strawberries, blueberries, grapes, apples, and oranges. Everything one might require for a perfect morning. She nodded, not able to get even the pathetic "yes" out of her mouth.

"Excellent. I would hate to see your reputation ruined and your family abandoning you. Your father is a good man, and his poor heart couldn't take any scandals," Levi finished his speech. What she made of it was her own choice.

She looked remarkably gray. Still, there was some sense in her. Instincts took over, and she nodded and curtsied.

"And before you go, take the clothes and wash them. I think this is an excellent day to wear one of my best suits," he said.

She scurried away.

Levi finished his breakfast. Otis had been right; it had done wonders for him. But he knew he had been unnecessarily cruel. However, it had to be done, or so he told himself.

He got up, stretching his naked body.

An elderly lady from the other building was watching him. He gave her a smile, and for a moment, she looked confused. Then something kicked in, and she smiled, not looking away.

He did his morning stretches, push-ups, and squats under her watchful gaze. The next time he glanced out of the window, the woman's son, presumably, was hunched over the old madam, shouting at her.

What a pity.

Levi dressed in his best suit. It was black, cut to his form, and made of the finest cloth there was. The suit was made to impress. He brushed his dark brown curls, making them fall just so. When he was satisfied, he tied them back with a ribbon to get most of them under control, leaving a few to frame his face. That always made the ladies fawn all over him. He took the pocket watch, glanced at the time, and was sorry to see that he had no time to go down to the basement. He would have to open the shop. Levi put the pocket watch in his vest pocket and took a last look in the mirror. He was impeccable.

Before heading out, he glanced out of the window. The madam's curtains were drawn shut. He could sense the disappointment and anger oozing out from behind the beige drapes. What a pity. People had too many funny ideas of what was and wasn't proper. They shut their eyes and minds to the things that could make their lives a little more exciting.

His body might not be pushed to its limits, but there were muscles, there was tension, and there were things that made anyone turn to putty in his hands.

Humanity. Sometimes, he wondered why he even bothered.

The first customer of today proved the point. A noble lady, no more than eighteen, stepped in with her aunties and friends, and she sure looked as if she was going to melt onto the floor if he only gave her a smile. He did.

There came a nervous giggle from the group.

"How may I serve you fine ladies today?" he asked, stepping past the counter.

More nervousness, even from the aunties.

But one of them had enough courage to speak up. "We are looking for the right dye for a dress for an outing. We were thinking along the lines of indigo," the woman said.

"And will this be for you or...?" He let the rest hang in the air as he glanced at the young girl clearly at the center of the party. Maybe courting or presented. No, not presented. That happened at the age of sixteen and in a white dress, and she was surely past that.

"For Mirabella here," the aunt said, laying her hand on the young girl's back.

"Then," Levi stated, lifting his hands in the air in defense, "I cannot, in good conscience, sell you that."

They looked shocked.

"Don't get me wrong. It's a fine color. Lovely, in fact. Royal indeed. But you, milady, are a spring flower, one of a kind, and you should be as fresh as a breeze and as light as a feather," Levi said, bowing to her and offering his hand.

She gave her hand to him almost lethargically, as a high society lady should, and he kissed it as lightly as polite social conduct dictated despite having already stepped over the line. But this was what they expected of him. He would play the part and get the money.

"If you have blue in mind, may I suggest cerulean? No, no, no," he said, shaking his head. "That would darken your complexion. It has to be arctic, or maybe daffodil. I know you said blue, but hear me out. Saffron or canary would make you flow through the crowd. Yellow is your color. Blue is too conservative, even in the shade of arctic. You want to shine and show who you are. So young and so fresh and so alive!"

He was already bored. From the look of it, they were sold. And he didn't have to go on listing all the advanced colors he could make unlike anyone else in the city. That was why the ladies came to him. That was why the dressmakers, the cloth factory owners, and the rest groveled at his feet. Thus, it would be easy to believe him to be wealthier. Many did. And he encouraged that belief. The truth was that the materials cost a fortune. Yes, he made a profit, but there was more to be made.

Soon Mirabella and her party departed from the shop, the canary dye with them and a few other items like a love potion[18] and a cure-all medicine. At least he hadn't lied about the dye part. Yellow was the color of youth and exuberance, and many shied away from it.

When he'd counted the money and noted it in his ledger, he collapsed behind the counter to wait for another customer to come in. He took the notebook out and began to scribble down calculations. If only there was a way other than the ghosts in the machine. He'd tried, but nothing else seemed to work. The legend of the Bufonite never mentioned necromancy. Then again, it was unwise to trust the myths. They left out a lot and included a dash of mystery in everything they touched.

The shop bell rang again, and he had to once again push the notebook back into his jacket pocket and put on a fake smile.

Rose left the City Hall behind. Her heart was still racing from meeting Page Briggs. She was infuriated. She was ashamed. Percy would have a field day after she told him, and he would report back. She was sure of that. A month more?! They couldn't have that. There had to be another way around it. She sat on the first public bench she found outside in the park. She had to breathe. Rose regained some of her strength and her anger receded in the coolness under the shade of the Coast Live Oak.

Yes, the delay in getting the bank set up would reflect poorly on her. Worthwrites weren't known for their

---

18   Which causes the cheeks to bloom like a rose. Levi always made sure there
     was an effect.

understanding. Yes, she'd let herself get soft under the welcoming words that riddled the city. At least back in Necropolis, you knew the sarcasm and attacks were real. Yes, Rose had an urge to stand up, storm back into the woman's office, and demand a review, but it wouldn't help, not with someone like Page Briggs. She had to have more finesse with Percy, the permit, the bank, the city, Justice...

Could she commission a building or even rent one without a license?

In either case, it would be a significant risk. More so when trying to keep up with the Worthwrites' standards. They had said that the building had to be a statement.

And Percy?

What if she just escaped? Even for a short moment. Maybe she could go in just for a quick game of Bluff the Prime Mover. No, that would be foolish. Even more so as she hadn't decided.

Rose took the envelope Justice had sent out of her briefcase. In it was a list of all the registered businesses in the city and a request to find those specialized in technology. This was about the Luddites. How had she missed that? Or the fact that Justice was the queen of the rebellion? What about Abigail?

No, she couldn't associate with any of this. But there was no way to come up with enough money to pay her back in such a short time. That was the point. They knew her hands were tied, and she had to yield.

She understood why they had chosen her. All this made her wonder whether the games had been rigged.[19]

Anyway, the point was that there was no walking away from this. All that was left was to bluff and survive until things weren't so dismal.

She tried to make out from the company names what they produced, but it was impossible. Like Acing—who would choose such a name? Rose continued scanning the names. Or

---

19 Oh, it would be so much better if it was so. Then at least she would get to save face and go on thinking she had some great intuition when it came to card games, risks, and knowing one's odds. Such lies made it easier to function. And there was nothing wrong with positive and self-preserving thinking; it was part of a healthy mental state. But there was a thin line between necessary lies and absolute delusion. One day, the lies might play catchup, especially with the great deceivers. Although they never seemed to catch up to those who did the dreaming and deceiving with other people's money.

there was the Alchemist's Shop. Okay, that was not so obscure. Dyes, cure-alls, and philosopher's stones. When was the last time she'd visited one? It had been ages, as the alchemists in Necropolis called themselves chemists, dropping off the "al" part and the baggage that came with the two letters. They had stopped pursuing transmuting gold, viewing it as a silly fantasy. There was no shortcut to making a quick profit.[20]

Visiting the Alchemist's Shop would be a good way to bide her time and to show she was cooperating, yet it would do the least amount of harm. And Rose couldn't deny that alchemy piqued her interest. There was something romantic about the idea. A view she clearly shared with many in the city. More so now, as the new trend of picking up old things and putting a mystic pin on them had made dabbling in the etheric realm lucrative. Rose had seen signs for fortune tellers, tarot card readers, clairvoyants, spiritualists, and the rest both in the city streets and high society parlors. Not something she would invest in as a banker. Too flimsy.[21] But even so, it was a good distraction.

Rose tried to mentally locate where Kingfisher Road would be. She couldn't. She had a map with her, she was sure of it. Rose opened her briefcase to flip through its contents and found what she was looking for. She took the map out and opened it on her lap, moving her fingers against the black street lines. The city was made of straight lines and grids, making it easy to navigate. Only in the older part of the town and around the gardens did the streets curve, forming an impenetrable barrier for a foreigner.

"Kingfisher Road," she repeated aloud as if it would manifest the street from the bottomless Kraken sea to help her escape the screwup others called her life. Rose smiled as her finger landed on the right name. *There you are, you sneaky little demon,* she thought.

The road was hidden in the older part of the city, fittingly near Blue Songbird Park. She would have to travel across

---

20   Something she habitually liked to forget, especially when it came to her own actions.

21   You might argue that the odds of a result were similar to gambling, but one was rational and the other… not so much. And rationality would always win, no matter how irrational it was.

Threebeanvalley to get there. She had the coach and the driver Percy had hired. But the fact was that it was Percy who had hired them, and money skewed loyalties and confidentiality. Even doctors spilled the beans in a tight spot. She had the option to resort to the public transportation system. To a horse-drawn carriage with fixed routes. She would bet her life that there was one going from the City Hall to the park. The two main attractions. But public meant public, packed in like sardines, as the locals would say. It would be an experience, to say the least.

Rose folded the map, put it into her briefcase, and stood up, leaving the comfort of the Coast Live Oak's shadows. She wanted to open her coat and let in the cooling breeze, but that would have been improper.

Rose glanced at those she passed, seeing their discomfort. All the women she saw wore tight corsets and petticoats with layers upon layers, even in this weather. There was something distorted about having to fight to obtain freedoms, and the fact was, it took a lot for the women to fight back. Not because they were weaker; the opposite, in fact. They could endure almost anything.

But it had always been in her nature to rebel. She loosened a few of her buttons, swimming against the tidal wave. It could be suffocating at times, but asphyxiation tended to make you feel more alive. She smiled as the other women glanced at her menacingly or rather held their heads high, making sure Rose understood that she was nothing and would always be nothing. The men just frowned and moved on. The thing was, it was often the women who held tightly to the old customs, passing them on to their sons and daughters even if the rules bit into their own pampered asses. Rose turned her gaze away and headed out of the park.

As expected, Rose found a public transport line just outside the City Hall. There was a lamp post lookalike with a schedule attached to it. She glanced over the omnibus chart and was confused, to say the least. The table looked like a jigsaw puzzle where all the pieces were borrowed from Monopoly. Rose couldn't make sense of which omnibus went where. There were too many different carriages, all competing for the same customers, and following Kraken only knew what paths.

She could trust her luck and jump into the first one that

came by and hope for the best or go back to the carriage Percy had hired.

"May I?" a man's voice asked behind her.

"Yes, sorry. I didn't mean to hog the chart." Rose stepped aside.

"Of course not. But I mean, may I assist you? You seemed lost," the man added.

He was an older, relaxed-looking gentleman in a second-grade business suit.

"Oh, yes, sure," Rose said and felt herself blush, unsure why. Maybe it was the man's smile.

"So, where are you heading?" he asked.

"Yes, that too," Rose said, hating to appear like an idiot. The man had taken her by surprise, sneaking up on her and altering her world without permission. "To the Old Town, near Blue Songbird Park."

"Then the number three pascal of Hobart and Sons will get you the closest. As a matter of fact, I'm heading that way. If you like, you can ride with me," the man said. "You can call me Aurelius Pond." Aurelius lifted his floppy brown hat and inclined his head.

"Rose, Rose Pettyshare," she said, offering her hand to him.

He took it, and instead of shaking it, he gave it a light peck.

"Charmed, I'm sure," Aurelius said. "Shall we retreat under the trees to wait for the pascal? It will be arriving in ten to fifteen minutes, and I, for one, would like to be out of the scorching sun."

"Sure, and you are sure the omnibus I should take is the number three?" Rose asked, squinting her eyes and trying once more to make some sense of the transportation schedule. Or the pascal chart, as the man had called it, after its inventor.

"I give you my word of honor," the man said.

Rose followed him under the nearest tree. All she wanted was to stand there in silence, look at the passers-by, and amuse herself imagining their hopes and fears but ending up estimating their net worth as always, but it was impossible. Aurelius chatted away as she watched the new rich make their way through the town among the old rich. The Worthwrites had been right to send her here, to this perfect bubble of

Threebeanvalley.

The new rich had that extra pompous attitude to make up for their lack of history. They wore luxurious clothes and carried around expensive status symbols like beautiful parasols and delicate brooches. The men wore designer hats and leaned against polished black canes as they walked. Everywhere else in the world, the economy was limping on, but here it galloped in a luscious field of mind-blowing inventions.

It took ten minutes for the carriage to get there. In the meantime, the pascal stop had filled with people seeking refuge in the shade with her and Aurelius. Rose and about twenty other customers climbed on board the carriage, paying a penny for their travel.

The older man assumed he would sit with her.

"Do you mind?" he asked. If it'd been anyone else being so shameless, Rose would have gotten angry. But Aurelius had an innocent and joyous way about him. He looked mostly harmless with his roundish, kind face and shabby brown suit. He was the kind of old man who'd get away with robbing you because of his massive smile and dimples. Most likely, you would feel so bad for him having to stoop to stealing at his age that you would give him a ride home and ask if you could help him in any other way. Luckily for Rose, the man wasn't aware of this side of his charm, or else she would have lost not only her personal money but the deed to the bank as well.

"Not at all," Rose said and scooched over, holding her briefcase on her lap. She was feeling uncomfortably hot and, for a moment, wished she was back home in the damp, cold, gloomy weather. There was something to be said for the marshlands, the openness of the hostile sea, and the dead and decay always reminding you of your mortality. Rose was surprised to find how Necropolitan she was.

The man continued jovially chatting away about his restaurant and what he had been doing at the City Hall, which was getting a liquor license. He spoke about the hot water fountains and the spas built around them—about the tourists, about business travelers, about her and how lovely it was to meet her. Rose's ears were bleeding by the time the man got up, tipped his hat, and bid her farewell.

As soon as the man was gone, Rose started to miss him.

He had been surprisingly good company. It was a brief longing, and she forgot all about the man and their conversation when she saw Blue Songbird Park at the end of the street. As soon as the carriage stopped, she got out to survey the vibrant display of flowers and green trees. They were more than welcoming, and the air felt a lot more bearable here. Rose had read from a brochure that the garden had pavilions, small bridges over its reservoirs, and waterfalls to give the citizens hideaways. Maybe she should lose herself in there for a couple of hours, but Rose knew she wouldn't.

She took out the map once more, folding it so that it showed where she was and Kingfisher Road. She navigated her way through the streets, getting a bad feeling that there was no going back—that she'd started something she might not want to finish.

6

ALL THIS EMPTY CLATTER THAT SEEMS TO COME OUT OF PEOPLE IS MAKING MY HEAD SPIN

The engines turned, and the excess hot air whistled as the machine reached its maximum speed. The operator, a small man in his fifties, ran around the device, making sure the gears were running smoothly, the trinkets came out the right shape, and money got made. He was proud of what he did. He knew the language the machine spoke, how it sang to him when they were in trouble and hummed when all was good. Now the whistle was like the purring of a cat in front of a cozy fire. It did what it was meant to do.

He took one of the small parts of the fish out of the assembly line and inspected it. Everything was as it should be. He nodded to a little boy who was waiting for his approval. The boy took the parts the machine had made and hurried with them to the women sitting at their desks, ready to assemble the silver fish from their moving joints. From there, the products would reach the markets, where there was an ever-growing demand for the small trinkets that kept bad odors away. The industrializing and ever-expanding city with its diverse population was nothing but an assortment of smells, ranging from pleasant gardenias to acrid sweat and rank sewers, which even the most accustomed city dweller could smell on a bad day. The silver fish containing the fresh scent of orange, mint, or rosemary kept civic peace at any family dinner table.

There came a loud knock on the large wooden factory doors. He didn't bother to look over his shoulder. It had to be one of the vendors, or one of the refill runs for the stock. This was not the usual hour, but maybe the boss or the lady always trailing after him had changed the schedule and cut a better deal. He took a monkey wrench in his hand and knelt to loosen one of the machine's bolts, the one he always had to loosen when the engine had run for an entire hour straight. If he didn't, there would be a cough, and the parts came out all wrong.

He liked the little fish they made; he'd bought a pack of them for his entire family to celebrate the Winter Solstice. The boss had been gracious and given him a considerable discount, or else he would have had to leave the grapefruit oil out and buy three fish to be shared, and then there would have been endless bickering over empty vessels without substance.

He loosened the bolt, and the machine let out a quiet fizzle, but the speed stayed the same. The engine was a marvel. He knew the boss had designed it with those bright fellows at Hilderberg Factories of All Technologies. The ones who revolutionized the printing press, making news and books affordable for almost everyone. At least the news. There was a newsboy on every corner selling truth and possibilities for pennies. Now mornings and afternoons weren't the same without a cup of hot coffee and a paper full of daily gossip about what happened yesterday and what was going to happen tomorrow. A wonderful concept he didn't know he'd needed. He inspected the blades, cutting the silver foil to the right sizes, and was satisfied that the parts were still coming out as they should.

He lifted his gaze to see where the boy had gone. Young people, he thought, no respect for punctuality. He expected to find the boy chatting with one of the women assembling the fish, or curled up in the corner, taking a nap on one of the rag sacks, but the boy was busier than that. The boy was dodging a huge man grabbing him by his collar and yanking him up. He dived underneath one of the tables and crawled speedily away, avoiding the stomping legs of the workers and attackers.

The room was filled with men wearing red masks over their faces and swinging metal pipes and other equipment. They hit the machines and threatened the workers, warning them to stay away.

A man was heading his way, and he looked on in horror as another attacker behind him jammed a pipe into the machine operated by Huge. The engine screamed in agony as the gears came to an unnatural halt.

He screamed in agony too, lifting his monkey wrench high and stepping between the approaching attacker and his machine.

"I'll hit you, boy!" he shouted as the man kept coming.

"Move over, grandpa, or I'll hit you," the man answered back.

He barely heard the man, but he read the words from his lips and responded, "How dare you threaten me in my place of work! Go away, you... you... hooligans!"

"This is for your own good, grandpa. So step aside," the man replied in a calm tone. But he didn't hear the calmness. Only the threatening words.

"Over my dead body. I won't let you touch my Betty. That's the last thing you'll do," he said.

"You are crazy. One day your Betty will take over, and there'll be no need for you any longer. If you think she cares about you or your boss, you are mistaken. So let me pass and do what's right. That monster of yours is taking jobs away from good lads and gals, and if you protect it, so will you. Move, or I'll hit you, and I'll do it without hesitation or regret," the man cautioned.

He stared at the attacker in disbelief. How could he think that? Yes, there had been troubles, and yes, he was one of the lucky ones who knew the machine through and through, but Betty taking over, or her being the reason why the man in front of him had no job, was nonsense. His wonderment turned into a scowl as the man kept coming.

There was no other choice; he charged and swung his monkey wrench at the misguided youth. The next thing he knew, he was on the floor, and Betty let out her dying wail, spewing out the last fish parts she would ever make. They clattered to the floor as he tried to get up, but there was extra soreness in his backs, and his leg seemed twisted. He had taken a tumble when the attacker had evaded his attack and punched him in his side and pushed him off.

He searched for someone to help him—the boy or someone else who could drag him to safety—but his gaze stopped on a woman who'd jumped on one of the work desks. She was commanding the attention of the attackers, wearing a similar mask to those of the attackers, but what separated her from the others was that she did it with style. She had high-heeled boots on and wore a long, dark sailor jacket with a little black number underneath. No better than an undergarment.

"There has to be more than these machines. Search the upper floors and find out what they are hiding here. Find someone who can tell me where they keep the blueprints," he read from the woman's lips. If he hadn't lost the better part of his hearing to the machines, he would have heard her alluring voice and be swayed by her.

"Yes, ma'am," one of the Luddites nearest to her said and took a group of men, and now, as he looked more closely, women as well and headed to the upper floors.

He whimpered. Too loudly, as the woman on the table fixed her attention on him. He tried to crawl away, but the pain in his back was too much, and he winced. He wouldn't have been able to flee anyway, but his basic instincts had taken over and overwritten any logic.

"Bring him to me," the woman said.

He swallowed.

Two men hurried to him, carefully lifting him to his feet and supporting him as they steered him towards the desk. The woman had gotten down and was now assessing him.

"Are you hurt?" she asked.

He didn't say anything, only looked back, horrified.

"Are you hurt?" she asked again.

No answer.

The woman's calm face was twisting into an angry pout. So unfitting to her beauty. But before she could repeat her question, the young boy stood up and said, "He can't hear you... ma'am."

"Why not?" she asked.

"None of them can. It's the machines, ma'am. What's left of their hearing is this ringing and muffled sounds," the boy replied.

"And you?"

"Young still, ma'am, only been here three years," the boy said.

"And how old are you?"

"Quite old, ma'am. I'm nine," he said proudly.

"Nine and you work here?" she asked, lowering herself to the boy's level.

"Yes, this is a good job. Better than what my brother does at the cotton factory. It's the lungs, ma'am," he replied.

"I see. Then how does..." The woman nodded towards the machine operator—him.

"Arnold," the boy supplied.

"Then how does Arnold communicate with others?" she asked.

"He can read lips," the boy said eagerly and only then noticed what he had done.

"Thank you," the woman said to the boy, who had already dived back under the tables.

She turned to face Arnold.

"You are hurt, I can see that. I'm sorry, that should not have happened. Abigail there," she said, pointing at a woman standing casually next to her yet looking like she was on guard duty, "will get you a chair and a glass of water."

The woman grabbed the nearest stool and helped him onto it.

Arnold winced once again from the ache but was glad he didn't have to stand any longer. The pain in his ankle and back was excruciating.

"Now, you might tell me a thing or two about what you do here and where the owner of this shop is, or at least where the foreman is. Also, about the blueprints," the woman stated.

"Ma'am, with all due respect, my lips are sealed despite the kindness you are showing me," he replied.

"Are you a fool, Arnold? Tell them and they will let us go. The boss and the lady don't give a rat's ass about what happens to us, so why should we?" his coworker hissed from under the table, waving his hand to attract his attention.

Miller, he thought. All mouth and no backbone. Also,

he had no clue what he was talking about. He, Arnold, had always gotten along well with the master. The lady was another matter. She gave him the willies. She was not right. So hard. So uncompromising.

"No one says anything," he announced and crossed his arms.

That didn't seem to bother the woman. To his horror, she was smiling at him. She kept measuring him, or more like looking into his innards, into the nooks and crannies he wanted nothing to do with. She was stripping away his humanity and mocking him. There was nothing of it left inside when fear and basic instincts took over.

Arnold gasped.

The woman got off the table and knelt next to Arnold. "Have you heard about justice? What is right is right, and what is wrong is wrong, and what is due will be paid in full?"

He leaned away from her. If he leaned any farther, he and the stool would tip over.

"Mr. Miller," the woman said. "You seem to have a firmer grasp of this situation. How about you help your friend Arnold here and ask when was the last time he ate a good meal with his salary? Or saw an increase in bonuses as the price of the little fish skyrocketed since the other factory closed thanks to us? Now he sees it as his duty to guard the master and his lady, calling it justice, and us... what would he call us, Mr. Miller?" The woman kept her attention on him.
She was some sort of witch. She had to be, despite such nonsense being no more than a superstition those folks in the countryside believed in. Arnold was a man of science, and he knew the woman was just messing with him. With all the looking into his innards and... and... and making him hear her better. The tones of her voice were soft despite being harsh. The alluring promise of passion was hidden there when she demanded justice. The demand for him to tell her everything.

He heard Miller clearing his throat. What a traitor, Arnold thought. He would get the man thrown out of the union they had been talking about with the other lads. Such a machinist was not welcome in their midst. There was a thing called loyalty and knowing when to keep your mouth shut. The last being the vital part. Then he noticed he'd heard what Miller had said. Also, he'd let his gaze shift to the backroom, where the blueprints and the rest of the relevant papers were kept, and where he expected the boss and his lady were hiding.

Miller never got a word out as the woman once again stood up and said, "Thank you for your cooperation. Now, Abigail, would you be so kind as to gather the workers and take them to the roomy supply closet at the back with enough food and water to last a day."

Arnold clutched his chest.

"You are not dying, Mr. Arnold, or Mr. Freedman, as would be more appropriate. There are no monsters in the darkness. I promise my friends will leave you an oil lamp to keep you company. It will only be a couple of hours, or in the worst case a day. Someone will surely miss you. Your wife, perhaps, has already come back home from visiting her sister and her sick kid..." the woman said.

If she said a word after that, he didn't hear. He passed out.

At the lighthouse, Sigourney listened to Siarl's gentle breathing and felt his warmth against her skin. It was now or never. Yet even though she knew he wouldn't judge her or say any angry words, she choked. She looked at the sea one more time to take in the strength of the ocean and the calmness of its being. She could be as strong and as serene as the sea, despite the constant motion making the waves crash against the shoreline. If the sea could survive and be as ancient as it was and still always be in flux, so could she.

"Siarl," she started.

He said nothing, careful not to spook her. She knew it, and he knew it, that she would stop if he said anything.

"I have been thinking..." She was stalling, trying to find the right words to say. How she hated words. They were so hard, and full of meaning, but they didn't always mean the same thing to everyone. Take, for example, a word like "fine."

"I'm fine!" Are you?

"You look fine." Do I?

"That's fine by me." Really?

Words were so treacherous, they were harmful, they were spiteful and hateful, but they were the only way humans could convey their needs and wants to others.[22] She had no other choice than to try and find the words for him to understand.

Sigourney took a deep breath in and struggled free from his embrace. She couldn't do this if she was pressed against him. His closeness always made her feelings complicated and her thoughts scrambled. She knew her mind better when he wasn't around.

He let her go without resisting.

Another thing he knew about her.

She hated that he understood her so well. That he saw who she was better than she did.

Sigourney laced her fingers around the lighthouse's railing and squeezed hard.

"I'm from here," she said and waited for the world to shatter.[23]

It didn't. Nothing broke. Siarl didn't say anything. He just stood there waiting for her to fill in the rest.

"I grew up not far from here on a small farm my parents rented from a local landowner. I used to come to this lighthouse every day to get away from home and from my older brother. I have never been back here ever since I left," she said, surprised how the first three words made the rest come out more comfortably than she thought possible.

Siarl still stayed silent. But this time, she needed him to say something. She wasn't sure if she could go on. But she did.

"I hated it here. My brother was horrible to me, and as soon as I could, I left. It wasn't like my parents cared. We had a huge argument. They wanted me in the fields, and I couldn't. I just couldn't. I felt like I was suffocating here, despite knowing that what I ate and what they ate depended on every single thing we did at the farm. That didn't seem like a life anyone should lead. Not when nothing was ever enough. Not when the landlord took more than half. I wanted to see the world and not get stuck between the cabbage patch and the carrot patch. But me leaving might

---

22 We blatantly seem to ignore all the other methods.

23 Things seldom shatter. That's only our minds playing tricks on us, thinking and fearing the worst and painting unpleasant pictures. You could say that consciousness is kind of a dick. But it's the only game we have.

have driven them into destitution, and... and..." Sigourney swallowed the rest and looked out to the horizon, feeling the urge to disappear into it.

"I'm sorry, Sigourney. I shouldn't have asked you to come here. Do you want us to leave?" he asked.

She was sure he didn't mean those words. That he wanted to say something else. That was the thing with words—you could also use them to mask your true intentions. She knew what he wanted to say. Siarl never ran away from problems or from the past. He went in headfirst and asked questions later, unlike how he was with everything else. How could two contradictions live inside a person? It was like caring for the environment and at the same time satisfying every whim one had, starting from clothes and moving on to fast-moving machines powered by horses with bright red paint on them.

"I..." she started. Sigourney squeezed the railing so hard her knuckles turned from red to white. She wasn't thinking about horse-powered machines or clothes. She was thinking about motion and running feet and how the cold railing felt good against her skin. It felt more real than the world around them or the conversation they were having.

"I..." she started again.

"Should stay." He finished the sentence for her.

"Yes," she whimpered.

"Then we stay and search for your brother and parents. Then you can decide if you want to meet them or not. You don't have to. I can do all the searching and meeting if you like?" Siarl stated.

Sigourney nodded.

"I think we'd better go then. And maybe find something to eat before we start our quest," Siarl said.

"Yeah," she replied weakly. Sigourney followed Siarl back inside the lighthouse and down the stairs. She couldn't help but wonder about the old saying, *"the words will set you free."* That if you say things aloud, they won't have a hold over you any longer. Then why wasn't she feeling any lighter? Quite the opposite, actually. She was sure that nothing good would come out of this. Nothing ever did when it came to her brother. But she couldn't let the past define her anymore.

But now, with truth and openness, there came expectations, and Sigourney didn't handle expectations well. She concentrated on her feet as she went down the stairs, keeping her in the present, not mulling over the past or fearing the future. She listened to the echoes their feet made. There was an extra beat beyond theirs. She was sure of it as she became more aware of the world beyond the blood vessels rushing underneath her skin. They weren't alone. It was almost like she'd wished for this distraction. As if the Rabbit's luck had sent it forth. Not that she saw the possibly uncomfortable upcoming social situation as a positive. Still, she welcomed it with open arms because Siarl might soon request more. Names, dates, times, her imprisonment... something she hadn't told anyone.

Sigourney reached for Siarl's sleeve, stopping him from moving onward. He gave her a quizzical look. She nodded down towards the steps. He clearly got the message. It was not as if someone was masking their ascent.

"I'll—" Sigourney started.

Siarl interrupted her. He said, "No, we go out like normal people would."

"But—" Sigourney tried to reason with him.

Siarl didn't listen. Her ability to hide was another thing that had started to annoy him. Once, he'd loved how she had taken them to places closed to the ordinary public. The libraries hidden inside the universities, monasteries, the private art shows in aristocratic mansions, the holy places forbidden to him or to her, and watching a wolf pack hunt its prey under the nonjudgmental full moon. They'd shared all that and more. Then suddenly, he didn't want any part of it. He wanted to be a normal boy, as the Rabbit would snort when Siarl was getting under his skin.

"We'll be fine. If it's the authorities, we can talk our way out of any trouble, saying we had to see the lighthouse before we left our home city for good. That this is a special place. They'll understand," he said.

"You want me to lie?" she asked, a bit shocked. Yes, Siarl had lied before, but never without good reason. Every time he did, a piece of the decent guy who believed in rules, morals, and doing the right thing died.

"It's not a lie. We'll leave at some point. Maybe not tomorrow, but we won't stay, that much I'm sure of," he said. "And before you protest, saying it might be someone else. What then? They are breaking the rules as much as we are. In that case, we do what normal people do—we greet them, exchange pleasantries, and go on our way. It's not that hard."

Sigourney leaned against the staircase wall and fought against her whole being, which screamed, "Hide, run, flee. You'll never learn to say the right thing. They will hate you.[24]

"Okay," she said instead, knowing the person inside her was a moron, unlike the one Siarl carried within himself. She would have preferred some wise fellow guiding her, soothing this thing people called existence. But no, she hadn't gotten a strong moral mentor, only a hurt animal who never made good decisions, even in the face of death.

He offered her his hand for moral support. She pretended she didn't see the gesture. Both of them knew she did. Sigourney saw another small piece of Siarl die. Not illusion. Not love. He accepted her as she came. If she was a better judge of character, she would know it was hope, trickling away. A leak that one day would need something more significant than a bandage to cover the gaping hole.

Siarl led the way down the stairs. Sigourney followed close behind. The steps they'd heard a moment ago stopped, clearly hesitating, unsure what would be behind the next corner. Sigourney wondered whether the visitor would be like Siarl or like her or someone else. A bit more adventurous, unruly, socially graceful... A whole new breed of person. Sigourney loved to look around and picture the inner voice guiding the people she saw, wondering what it whispered to someone with such a sad, tormented face or the one who seemed to be smiling not only from their lips but from their eyes as well. Or the ones deeply immersed in their thoughts; did they hear some great plan that the universe had bestowed only upon them?

Siarl slowed his pace, getting caught up in the mood that had taken over the lighthouse. It was something between caution and curiosity that lay underneath the wind battering the outer walls, bringing with it the sound of the sea and the seagulls. The note that had once been soothing had now turned tense. He seemed to shake off the sudden change and carried on, open to what might be waiting for him. There was that hope thing going on again, seeing life and all the opportunities in a positive light.

Sigourney only saw a haunted shadow painted on the

---

24 Yep, consciousness. What a dick.

walls. Something that looked like the monsters from her nightmares. Not with big teeth. That would have been too easy. A creature she could have fought off. This one had clingy claws, an oppressive, sluggish aura. Evil as she saw it.

But the shadows didn't belong to a police officer or some thug. It was an average-sized woman with an eyepatch. She wore trousers and a long coat perfect for being outside all day. Her black moccasins rested leisurely on the steps, ready to take a leap forward or back if necessary, in no way intending to look threating.

"Hello there," Siarl said.

"Oh, hello," the woman said. "I was wondering who else had found their way here. This place is so often empty when I come to watch the sea."

"Not this time." Siarl let out a nervous chuckle.

"Are you two alone? Or should I expect more company for my bird watching?" The woman pushed her full weight onto the tips of her toes.

"We are alone. Only visiting the lighthouse and reminiscing about the old days," Siarl said.

"Good. As much fun as it is to share the birds with someone, there's something to be said for opportunities to be alone with one's thoughts," the woman said pleasantly.

"True that. We'd better be leaving then." Siarl stepped aside to let the woman pass them.

"Oh, don't go on my account. I wouldn't want to intrude on your exploration if you are only visiting? I'm sure we can share the space. I'm more than sure that this is one of those days when I have this false notion of solitude and truthfully I crave company. And you can call me Margaret." She leaned against the frame of a small window, which let in soft light through the milky-white glass.

"Nice to meet you, Margaret. I'm Siarl, Siarl Ellis, and this is Sigourney Perri." Siarl faced Sigourney and continued, "But I have to say, we were already making our way out. So, it's no bother."

Sigourney tried to think of something to say, but the exchange was going faster than she could keep up. Also, none of the words meant anything to her. They were this empty clatter that seemed to come out of people who, for some odd reason, felt like speaking was as necessary as blood circulating around the body. But she was sure the woman had said something about watching the sea at first; however, she knew it was impolite to point that out. That much she'd learned thus far. Never show you have an impeccable memory. Not at least when the other person had contradicted themselves. Never point out, when they say something like, "We haven't met before," and you have, "Yes, actually, we have. Here and here." That's the same as spitting in their faces and calling them a rude name. Or at least that's how they usually acted. It had taken a long time for Sigourney to understand that you couldn't do that. The world was full of these weird social norms like how long to maintain eye contact. And no, people didn't like it when you counted—one clockwork, two clockwork—when you gazed into their soul-mirrors. It crept them out.[25]

"Oh, good," Margaret let out.

Sigourney was sure she detected a hint of disappointment.

"It's windy out there," she said, trying to appear part of the conversation and ending up regretted her words instantly. What a moronic thing to say. Couldn't she have gone with something more obvious? She could have said something about her moccasins. But the moment was gone.

The woman peered at her and gave her a smile.

Sigourney felt the small animal inside her burrow its head deeper into the sand.

"Occasionally, that means a good day to watch birds. Other times, I come home empty-handed. From the ground, I wasn't sure which one of those days this would be. The skies seemed to be empty except for the seagulls, but to catch a rare bird, you have to be patient. I have been sitting and watching the sea for the better part of two hours on the rocks, and I thought I might have better luck if I came up, seeing as you opened the lock for me," Margaret said. "I thought about following you in at first, but then I thought better of it. I thought I should let you have that solitude I was so keen on a moment ago."

"Aah, then it was a good thing we decided to visit the lighthouse today. There were so many other choices we could have gone with." Siarl jumped back into the conversation.

"Are you visiting Threebeanvalley?" Margaret asked.

"Yes, we arrived today, actually," Siarl said.

---

25 In a bad way. Just saying.

"Lucky me then." She was smiling again. That same kind of smile that had made Sigourney's inner animal do funny things previously. This time it was dancing some sort of weird dance, as if it was standing on hot stones.

"Where are you staying? If you don't mind me asking. I have heard getting a room can be nightmarish. All the people coming and going," she said.

"Siarl, I think we'd better go and leave her to her birds," Sigourney interrupted him when he was about to reply, trying to tug his sleeve without the woman noticing. Impossible. So, she settled for letting the words do the speaking.

"Yes, forgive me. I have been taking up your time. She's always complaining that I talk too much. We'd better leave. Have a good day, Margaret the birdwatcher," Siarl said.

Sigourney was glad he was playing along.

"I'm as much at fault here. Yes, you must go and enjoy our lovely city. If you wake up one day with a sudden desire to watch birds, you can find me here most days. Have a great day," she said and passed them, moving up the stairs.

Sigourney pressed herself against the wall a bit more than necessary to allow the woman to pass comfortably. When she'd left them alone, Sigourney hurried Siarl out, not letting him stop to marvel at anything or comment on the encounter or anything else.

Sigourney glanced over her shoulder once they were out of the lighthouse. If the woman, Margaret, had followed them down, she didn't see. Sigourney lifted her gaze up, trying to spot whether the woman had already made her way to the outer circle. If she had, there was no sign.

"What was that all about?" Siarl asked as they were making their way through the rocks and to the bridge leading back into the city.

"I had a funny feeling." Sigourney bit her lip. She was sure Margaret had said she hadn't seen them and then suddenly she had. Again with the contradictions. Okay, the human mind was like a drawer full of mismatched socks. Keeping track of them was close to impossible, and Sigourney wasn't any better. She wasn't even sure if she owned a drawer, let alone matching socks. But still, Sigourney was sure the amount of holes in the woman's story was beyond normal.

She glanced once more at the lighthouse before the view disappeared fully behind the fishermen's huts. She didn't see the woman. Maybe she had overreacted?

"Sigourney, sometimes I wonder what has happened to you to make you distrust every person you see. This is not me putting pressure on you, but she was just an ordinary woman, interested in birds, and you instantly saw her as an enemy. Of course, there's the eyepatch thing, but you can't judge people on their exterior. You know that. I'm sure of it. Let it go, and let's find something to eat." Siarl took her hand.

This time she let him, in spite of her mind insisting that it would have been better if he'd allowed her to hide them. That sometimes people were exactly what they seemed to be. And it wasn't the eyepatch, or the contradictions, not that they helped Margaret's case at all. It was the smile and the way she'd looked at Sigourney. The small animal inside her had done more than whimper; it had frozen in terror.

7

IF I GAMBLE IT ALL, WILL YOU PROVIDE?

The Rabbit god of luck gulped his sweet cocktail down from his travel mug. He'd made the bartender at the hotel prepare it to go. The hotel owner, Mathew Regan, followed miserably after him, mumbling something about books to go over and a quiet dinner with the missus and sighing at how nothing made sense anymore. The Rabbit could release him, as he didn't need the man to show him around, but he didn't want to be alone; nor did he want to disturb Sigourney and Siarl on their way to their destinies. The lighthouse would be just the start.

The Rabbit was sure his mood was getting lousier, and the hotel owner was there to keep the worst of it at bay. If he fell deeper into this desperation, he wouldn't be responsible for the consequences. In a way, Mathew's misery was a cheap cost to prevent his devious mind from coming up with something worse. Gods' minds could think up thousands of funny things before they'd even had their breakfast cereal.

"Mr. Lepus," the hotel owner said. "We have to turn left here."

They were standing on a busy street, people rushing past them, their feet rapidly beating against the paved walkway. Behind their eyes was fear. The city was heating up. The Rabbit could taste it.

The Rabbit didn't react at first, letting his name wash over him. It felt like tiny particles[26] all over his body coming alive, tingling and vibrating as belief poured in. It was dangerous to get too attached to that feeling. To hear more than one person say his name. That had been the case with other gods and the war he'd prevented. Belief was like a drug. It gave you a sense of importance. An imploded ego, you could say. Telling you there was nothing you couldn't do and nothing you shouldn't do. You deserved everything you wanted. Every whim you had should be fulfilled, and who cared what followed. Who needed self-control and second thoughts? Or third. Lepus stopped the sensation from going any further. That was all he needed now. Megalomaniac thoughts. Not in the mood he was in. Not when he needed things to take place on their own, without his luck intervening. At least, not too much.

He followed the hotel owner to the alleyway. The street was narrow and dark, if that was even possible in the mid-afternoon sun. But there it was. Shadows lurking everywhere, making the place seem ominous, with a funny smell that made you think of a dog who had taken a bath in a gutter of piss and vomit. It was the kind of alleyway where you could expect to die at any second, as behind every corner a mugger or even a murderer waited for an opportunity to jump out with their wicked thoughts and sharp knives. That was what Mathew was thinking, eyeing every shadow suspiciously. Not as bad as it sounded, because at least his destiny would be his, and not the Rabbit's.

If any evil thoughts were lurking around, they kept to themselves as Lepus made his way through the alley. You couldn't really jump out at a seven-foot-tall rabbit with well-formed muscles and hind legs that made even the burliest legs look like those of a chicken, to put it mildly. The odd thing was that the Rabbit appeared like a harmless old man if you looked sideways. The robbers, the murderers, and the other madmen turned around and fled to different alleys in search

---

26   Those things that scientists said the universe was made of.

of easier targets, and the Rabbit and Mathew traveled with ease to the gambling house.

A house like any other house except unsavory characters hung around the entrance, eying all who passed by, thinking evil thoughts and expecting the worst.[27] They were those kinds of characters any sane person would stay away from, but the

Rabbit marched over to them.

The hotel owner let out a quiet whimper.

The Rabbit pondered whether he could make the man's mood change if he let him win, but he suspected a man like him might get too obsessed with winning and end up losing it all. That seemed to be the case with most humans with delicate egos. The Rabbit would ensure the man had a moderate win. Enough to pay off his time, but not enough to make all this worth the trouble.

"Evening, gentlemen," the Rabbit said, nodding to the two unsavory characters by the doorway. To him, the men looked like schoolboys, their clothes too oversized to be taken seriously.

"Move along, old man," the one nearest to him replied. He was a tall man who thought all his muscles were in the right places. He would run back to his mother crying if the Rabbit cared to show him what real muscles looked like.

"As soon as you care to step aside." The Rabbit flashed a smile.

The man staggered, but some people are immune even to the charms of gods, and he recovered quickly, frowning.

"You have no business here," the man said.

The Rabbit reached for his pocket. The two men tensed up but relaxed when he took a stack of banknotes out of his pocket.

"I think I have a meeting with Lady Luck inside. She's waiting for me with a cocktail and a deck of cards." He chuckled.

"Yes, you shouldn't keep any ladies waiting. They don't like that," the one who hadn't spoken thus far said and stepped aside, opening the door for the Rabbit and Mathew. For a moment, the hotel owner had entertained the thought

---

27   The thing about expecting the worst is that you often enough get the worst. People deliver. In this way, the men who hung around the door often enough got a whiskey bottle catapulted at them and obscene insults about their mothers thrown in their faces. Just another typical night, in their opinion.

that they couldn't get in, but no luck.

The Rabbit folded a few of the notes and slid them to the bouncer before he left them alone in the alleyway.

As soon as he stepped into the building, he could smell luck in its rawest form mixed with desperation and last chances. Not to mention broken dreams. This was the dark and jolly side of how his powers worked. If his fur were showing, all the hairs on his body would be standing up. He watched the endless rows of tables covered with green fabric and wheels of fortune. The distinctive pattern of cards shuffling together and marbles clicking against wood made him hum while luck from those miserable creatures who'd been foolish enough to come here this afternoon returned back to its source. To him.

"Time to play," he said aloud. He had grown several inches taller, the hump on his back had straightened, and his face had turned years younger.

Mathew moaned. Not very loudly, but anyone with ears as acute as the Rabbit's and the habit of picking up fear, having an underlying concern for anything loud and with pointed teeth like his brother Tamtue's[28], heard even the slightest sound. He patted the man on his upper back and handed him a stack of banknotes.

"But..." the man said as his eyes went wide. "I..." he managed to utter.

"Don't spend them in one go," the Rabbit said, already ignoring the man and scanning the room for his first target. When he found one, he smiled.

In the corner of the room, there was a card game going on, and at the table sat a man with tobacco on his lips. He'd pushed his thumbs underneath a huge belt buckle with a cow's skull on it, which sparkled in the dimly lit room.[29] The man leaned backward, fielding a smug expression. Just the kind of man the Rabbit wanted to teach a lesson to. Not that he was keen on making humans any more intelligent. They

---

28   The snake god birthed from the superstition of his people, the gainsborians. They believed Tamtue to be the source of immortality through continuous renewal and as the bringer of water.

29   If you asked the Rabbit, something like a penguin would have been luckier and more intimidating than a cow. There was something suspicious about an animal wearing a tuxedo. But humans had always gone with size rather than essence.

were annoying buggers already, with enough tools to blow up the entire planet. More so now, as the steam engines took over the world. It wouldn't be long before they learned to harness the power of the tiny particles governing the world, and then he and his fellow gods would be gone.

The Rabbit shook his head and lost those inches he'd gained earlier. The slight hump came back along with deeper wrinkles on his forehead.

"I think I'll try that game," he said to Mathew, but before he limped to the table, he scanned the room once more.

It was a massive room with the usual smoky, dark feeling of any place where something illegal was happening.[30] Now the area was occupied with the typical characters and not some glamour puss who wanted to have some excitement. These were men and women who were serious about getting ahead in life by betting against the odds and the house, hoping Lady Luck was looking over their shoulder. They would be devastated to know that instead of some fancy woman in a green costume, there was a hairy rabbit. Which was, in a way, a more logical step in the evolution of the human idea of what luck was made of. You didn't get much luckier than a rabbit, who'd mastered the art of multiplying and knew when to run away.[31] Any ordinary, sane rabbit wouldn't even consider gambling in a place like this, knowing that the odds of survival were stacked against them. Still, the Rabbit god of luck was made of human minds, and he'd inherited their somewhat questionable traits, such as the habit of self-destruction. But the Rabbit wasn't scanning the room for an easier target; he was seeking something to make the hotel owner's heart race. And he found it.

Near them, a roulette table with two men and a woman waiting for the chance to win big welcomed in anyone keen on marbles on black and red.

"You should try your luck there."

"But—" Mathew said.

"Go on. It's just a wheel. While they are capricious in nature, they are governed by the laws of nature and not by

---

30   It was like the law of the cosmos.

31   Which was always, increasing the chances of survival.

man,[32]" he interrupted the hotel owner and nudged him to move to the table. If the man thought to protest, he said nothing and did as the god told him to.

The Rabbit instead made his way across the room, warding off anyone wanting to distract him. A few women had tried to approach him, either offering their luck to him or inviting him to drink his troubles away. He had no time for them now. The Rabbit was here on business. Pleasure would have to wait. He hunched his shoulders when the pompous man looked towards him and dragged his feet that much more. Not enough to appear irreparably pitiful, but enough for the man not to take him seriously. He had always said the mind games should start before you even entered the stage.

"Is this seat taken?" he asked, looking at one of the empty seats at the table. There were already five players in.

The dealer looked at the Rabbit and then glanced at the pompous man.

The man nodded, and the dealer said, "Take a seat. I was just dealing the cards in."

The Rabbit groaned as he sat down, holding his back. "I haven't had the time to change my money into chips. Can you do it here?" he asked when he'd found a comfortable position.

"House rules are to change them at the door, but as you are new here, sir, I'll make an exception," the dealer said. He was a young man. In his early thirties or late twenties. There was nothing special about him except a relaxed nature that welcomed others in, making him appear harmless. The Rabbit never thought anyone harmless. Everyone was capable of doing the most horrendous things if the circumstances pushed them to. Even a saint could kill a man with electric shocks. Especially if someone was peering over your shoulder with a clipboard.

"Thank you, young man," he said and took the stack of banknotes out of his pocket. "Do you think this is enough?" he asked.

The dealer held his breath. The man with the belt buckle corrected his posture slightly, and there came a few other gasps from around the table.

---

32   He was lying. Anything manmade should come with a warning sign: "Might turn dangerous." That was faulty logic for you.

The Rabbit pretended he didn't hear or see any of those.

"It will do," the dealer said, taking the banknotes with shaking hands.

The boy's eyes widened even more as he counted them and turned them into chips. When he was done, he motioned for one of the women to come and collect the money and pushed the Rabbit his chips. It was a tall stack of greens, reds, blacks, and blues. The Rabbit dragged them closer to him to inspect them, pursing his lips as if trying to make sense of what he was holding. He dared a glance behind him to check that the hotel owner hadn't slit his wrist opens. Mathew hadn't. The man had sunk his head into his hands and was looking at the wheel as if it was his greatest enemy. Good, the Rabbit thought. He twitched his nose and turned back to his own table.

"So, what's this game called?" he asked, looking innocently around at the other players.

Suppose you thought of a city as a living thing. In that case, you could say Threebeanvalley invited people from all over the world in with shiny promises of jobs, opportunities, fun, anonymity, gambling, money, women, and anything else it could use to power its belly. But the people brought more with them than carcasses to move things around; they came with parasites others might call the mind. That tiny thing made them do funny things like smile at one another, or tell a lie to gain funding for their political campaigns, or the all-time favorite, massive-scale marketing to convince people they needed this or that. That was a real mystery for any sentient being.

The cities had to endure those little quirks that came with humans in order to feel the pulse and see beautiful buildings and leisure areas built on their backs. If there was no constant movement, babies crying, then the cities were in trouble. Then they were dead. You didn't want past. A magnificent civilization had to be remembered at any cost. What history had shown was how easily the mighty fall. Sometimes all that was left was a single stone that marked the presence of what? The living didn't know.

But inside the cities' bellies lived those who knew how to

navigate the waters to make their lives their own. To use the towns and their laws to their advantage by pulling all the little strings that connected things to bring them resources, admiration, love, and services, to name a few. Rose Pettyshare thought she was one despite the setback with Page Briggs. So did Justice. Levi too. They all saw that they could shape the world to their liking, manage the chaos. Sigourney didn't. Maybe she was the least delusional one or the most tragic.[33]

Now, Rose Pettyshare wove her way through the old town streets to the Alchemist's Shop to find out how she could twist its peculiarity to serve her purpose. The shop was only a couple of blocks away from the park, in a high building with apricot-colored walls and white decor. She pushed the front door open. A bell chimed as she entered. She half-expected it to be empty, but there were five customers inside. One of them was talking to a man in his thirties standing behind a counter, measuring something on a scale. The man was stylish and had a charismatic way about him. Rose looked away, peering around the shop.

The shop looked like a modern apothecary. There were dark wooden shelves with all sorts of bottles on them. She spotted the man's selection of dyes, noting the royal purple, crimson, and scarlet among the containers. She wondered whether they were synthetic or made from real snails and madder plants.

On the other side of the room were shelves stocked with little mechanical creatures and statues. They were a delicate and perfect gift for someone who cared for the wonders of the new.

Farther away from the door on the right-hand shelves, she wasn't too surprised to find dark green bottles labeled cure-alls, full of alcohol and herbs, promising good health and other miracles. She moved away from the section, glancing over her shoulder. The man, presumably Levi Perri, as the roster had said, was chatting to a younger lady now. The girl's face was red, and she listened to the man intently. She nodded her head along with his words as if spellbound.

---

33 A tiny amount of self-delusion might make you more immune to life's troubles. The outspoken realist might have it wrong. But then again, the realist might do the least amount of harm, as you couldn't rob them of their delusions or force them to defend them at any cost. One of those eternal damned if you do and damned if you don't curses.

Rose should have guessed the man was a charlatan. She sighed and made her way to the door. Maybe this had been a mistake. She could take the cure-alls and the mysticism that came with the shop and the man, but she drew the line at charming young girls, although she wasn't sure why. No doubt it was a lucrative way to make money from the high society ladies. As a banker, Rose should encourage her clients to use their strengths to make their businesses work.

Still, part of her upbringing or some other foolish notion she carried inside her insisted that no one should use someone else's naivety and youth against their better judgment. That there was a dirty and a more righteous way to make money. She knew exactly how silly such a statement sounded in light of her own habits and failed endeavors. All those whom she'd cheated and lied to had known the game was rigged. The girl here in the shop believed in the illusion, and suddenly, Rose felt uncomfortable with it. She hated it. Either being away from the fast money-making pace of Necropolis or the city's friendly atmosphere or some other lousy reason had made her grow a conscience. Such a thing only got in the way of making money.[34]

"Miss Pettyshare, if you could, please wait. This won't take long," the man said before Rose could slip away.

She turned around to face Levi and saw both him and the lady staring at her. While he looked at her in a friendly, open way, the girl glared at Rose.

"I'll wait," she replied. She was not sure if she said it to spite the younger woman, who suddenly looked a lot less naive, or to satisfy her own curiosity about the man knowing her name.

The alchemist soon ushered the lady and her companions out. They made their distaste towards Rose known as they left, mumbling snide comments and giving her glances that would make a lesser person whimper. Rose smiled. That was the thing about pretending to be nice—it had its cracking point. Or Rose had gotten better at reading the faces of

---

34 Others might beg to differ. Some saw money could be made with good intentions, morals, and noble ideals. It could be. But the question was on what scale. Also, was it foolish to uphold morals against the background where people generally cheated and lied to make money, and everyone expected you to do the same? Even customers. It seemed like people had stopped caring. Funny old world.

Threebeanvalleyans, and knew a polite smile could mean a lot more than it seemed to.

"Good riddance," Levi said and flipped the sign to closed.

"Now, Miss Pettyshare, how can I assist you?" he asked, facing her.

Levi Perri, the alchemist, was a handsome man. He had the unusual charm of someone who didn't quite fit the conventional image of handsomeness but made up for it with beautiful peculiarity. He had brown curly hair that came down to his shoulders and a thick beard, which Rose was sure he meticulously styled to look artfully unkempt. What made him distinct was his slightly crooked nose, thin but wide mouth, and a left eye whose eyelid drooped slightly, making him appear impish... in a good way. The way he held himself made Rose feel drawn to him. Not like the earlier customer had been. Not her. But on an intellectual level. This man knew the secrets of the world. He was going to take her there with him if she let him.

There was money to be made here, even if there were no machines beyond the cute little statues.

"As introductions clearly don't need to be made, I'll get to the point. I found your name on the list of businesses in the city and was curious about the thought of alchemy. I had to come and see it. I'm a banker from Necropolis, searching for investments." Rose let her gaze wander away from the alchemist, back to the shelves and to the beautifully drawn symbols and forms framed on the wall behind the shop's counter.

When her attention returned to the alchemist, the man smiled, and Rose's heart skipped a beat. She ignored her first response, as she knew that smile. She had seen it several times in her line of work. Smug but trying to be friendly.

"I like your bluntness, miss, and I have seen your advertisement in the *Threebeanvalley Daily News*, but I wonder what my little shop might offer you," he said.

Distraction. "Alchemy is an interesting profession, but if we are honest about it, most are more akin to chemists and apothecaries—"

"Yes, most are, and yet here you are. Let me be audacious, dear Miss Pettyshare. Nowadays, people look for spirituality and have a need to go back to the old days, feeling discomfort among all the new apparatuses and sciences which, don't get me wrong, are marvelous. I don't deny that. In fact, I approve of it. But alchemy has a mystical appeal to man's primitive nature. We find it easier to believe in elements and that we have a soul rather than in steam. And while the image of mystical alchemy might come in handy, I assure you, madam, that what I do is practical chemistry and nothing more. But might I offer you a cup of tea, so we can discuss it further?" he asked.

Before Rose had time to answer, an otter waddled through the back door and let out an *iik* sound, taking its place next to the counter. It tilted its head, looking with its back eyes at the alchemist.

"And I might as well show you after the tea what an alchemist can do," Levi added, ignoring the otter.

"A cup of tea would be lovely, sure, but..." Rose glanced at the creature.

"Don't worry about him. He's the greatest friend you can have. But now for that tea. Shall we?" Levi offered his arm to her.

Rose took it, darting a quick look at the otter. It seemed friendly enough.

"You know, the old wives of Necropolis believed otters to be tree people who deceived humans to steal their souls."

The alchemist laughed. "An apt description of my Otis. The great soul devourer."

Rose raised her eyebrow.

The otter let out an *awk-awk* noise.

"Always bossing me around and demanding others' attention," Levi explained and closed the shop door behind them.

He took her to a backroom parlor. It seemed like the alchemist lived where he worked.

There was a dreamer quality to the man, but some dreamers were worth the trouble—those who changed the world just by glancing at something. Mr. Perri had such an aura. She would have to be careful with him and not jump into deep water with both feet without looking. But it had been such a long time since she'd had a passion project, and the alchemy shop and the alchemist could be one. It might also be a great way to get Justice off her back for a while and maybe make extra money to hide the differential in the bank's chest.

Yes, more and more, as she observed the man with the unique pet, she saw salvation.[35]

---

35 The trouble is that a seeker will always find a reason, salvation, or excuse. Such is the power of perception, hope, positive thinking, and the ability to deceive even oneself. (Yep, that again.) It was a power like no other and could be used for good or disaster. A mother might say that this was the man who would save her and her children from destitution and an uncertain future. Yet all the outcomes were possible. The same went for an entrepreneur or a painter on their last nerve. But what else was there to do when there was no hope? Would the valley of despair with dead trees, rotting corpses, and hatred-filled monsters take over? No one truly understands what a paradox it is to exist, making one conclude that either the planners of all things are nutters or that chaos reigns, as always.

8

ALL OUR DREAMS IN A NEAT LITTLE BOX

evi Perri observed Rose. The banker quivered under the soft light of the backroom parlor. Ever so slightly, trying hard not to. She took a sip from her flower tea as her gaze traveled around the room. Levi cursed; he hadn't invested in the room's decor. It was still in its original state, with orange wallpaper with beige lilies on it, which had half-faded, and while the armchairs and tables were functional, they were not built to impress. He was unsure if he could even charm his way into the woman's subconscious. She could be one of those women who were only dazzled with facts. One thing was true—his usual charm hadn't worked yet. She needed intelligence behind the words said rather than a lowered tone and a lean forward, which had worked for the previous customer. But the girl had been just that, a customer. Rose could be more, or rather her bank could be more. A partner. The silent kind.

Past him, Otis balanced his weight on the armrest next to Rose, occasionally shooting sideways glances at Levi. The banker had quickly gotten used to the enormous brown otter. Maybe a familiar sight from back home?

Levi wondered how eager the Worthwrite Bank of Necropolis Ltd was to have its fingers in Threebeanvalley's booming economy. Were they trying to corner the market with the old, or were they truly interested in the new as the woman had claimed? Would she listen to him enough to understand that what he was proposing was magnificent and not a mere concept? Levi didn't know if he wanted this, but it would be foolish not to see where this might lead.

"Miss Pettyshare, I have to be honest... I'm flattered by your bank's interest in my little shop, but I'm not sure what it has to offer you," he started.

Otis let out a low *iik*.

The woman with raven hair and royal features stiffened a little. Then she scrutinized his face, searching for words. The fraction of a second when she said nothing felt like an eternity. In a way, it was an eternity. In that precise moment, hundreds were born, hundreds died, thousands upon thousands fell in love, and others spiraled into desperation; new inventions were made and lost, nothing would be the same, but nothing had changed. None of that mattered here and now. The only thing he yearned for in that moment was sound.

"A franchise maybe. Your shop has a charm about it that could be transferred all over the world, starting in Necropolis, which would welcome the nostalgia of alchemy and those wonderful mechanical sculptures you have made," Rose said eventually in a calm tone.

"Hm," Levi let out. "Would necromancers care for cure-alls and toy soldiers that can be wound up to move?"

"There are common people like me who have nothing to do with necromancy, the undead, or witchcraft. Times are changing, and the old customs must go. Or..." Rose laughed. "Or in your shop's case, be brought back with a twist."

Levi joined in the laughter; it would be rude not to. "A twist, indeed. Maybe a bigger one. I promised to show you what I can really do. There might be more." Levi left the words hanging to pique her curiosity.

"What more might that be? Have you alchemists finally worked out how the philosopher's stone works and made gold?" Rose smiled and leaned over to set the fine porcelain cup back on the saucer, making Otis shift his balance.

"You might say that. But if you would permit me to

prepare a demonstration for you to see what I can do, we won't need to bother franchising my shop for amusement and curiosity like some circus trick. We could revolutionize the world together." Levi got up from the chair he had chosen, looking for Rose's approval.

She gave it to him.

"Come now," Levi said and patted his side.

Otis lazily rose up and jumped down to take his position.

When they were out of earshot in the hallway, Levi asked, "Are you sure about this? Is she common, as she states?"

"I can't sense anything extra from her. If she is a witch or a necromancer, she hides it well," Otis replied. It was always disconcerting to see an animal use a human voice.

"Then we go ahead with it." Despite what Levi had said, he hesitated. There were so many what ifs.

"We'd better. Shall I go back and guard her?" Otis asked.

No, Levi wanted to snap. It was clear enough even in his otter form that the necromancer fancied the banker, but it wasn't like Otis could turn back into a human and drive the woman away with his moves.

"Sure," Levi replied and headed to the basement.

Behind him, he heard Rose say, "Oh, you came back. Aren't you a cute one?"

Otis *awked* happily. The awk sounded more like a human pretending to be an otter than an otter being its lutra ancestor.

Levi headed to the basement past the kitchen, where Evelyn was immersed in baking. As fast as Levi could, he grabbed the working Bufonite and laid a cloth over it before carrying it up. He patted his chest pocket to make sure he had the notebook with him. He danced around Evelyn, whose calmness had turned into a dash around the kitchen to get the timing right with one of her lavish dinners. From the smell of it, she was stewing meat and vegetables in the masonry oven. Levi's stomach growled in response. Basic bodily functions would have to suffer, as there was no telling whether Otis had found a way to charm Rose even in his mammal form and ruin everything. Maybe the woman would propose that he should become a circus director and devise a show with well-behaved otters. That would be a sight. Him in a red jacket and puffy trousers and Otis forever in his otter form, being petted by ladies. He better hurry before the woman thought up another scheme to make money out of him. She'd seemed oddly keen to turn his alchemy into enough profit to satisfy a huge bank. Either she had a hunch about the changing markets for alchemy, which he highly doubted, or she had something personal going on. With personal, there was no telling whether it would be a blessing or spell his doom.

As Levi stepped into the parlor, he found Otis had taken his place on the woman's lap, resting his head against her arm. He had taken a very liberal interpretation of the concept of guarding. Levi glanced at the necromancer as he composed his posture and walked towards the darkly varnished coffee table. He laid the Bufonite there and sat next to the banker.

"Let me explain first, and then I'll show you," Levi said and took the notebook out of his pocket. He flipped it open.

Rose looked confused. Maybe she'd expected him to come back with an actual philosopher's stone, never expecting something as simple as a notebook. But it was more effective than gold or a gun could ever be, if you asked Levi. A tool for dreamers and world-changers.

"I'm not sure what I'm looking at," Rose said, squinting as she examined the drawings of the Bufonite. The schematics. The calculations. "You want me to help you build a machine?" she added when Levi had given her enough time to take in the schematics, not drowning her with his thoughts.

"Yes, you could call it a machine, but it's more." He paused. Now or never. This was the first time he was presenting the machine to someone other than Otis, and he'd jumped in without too much forethought. But as he'd noted, the banker was more than eager to make this work.

"As an alchemist," he began, "I can make dyes beyond mortals' dreams. I can turn glass into gems that look like the real thing—diamonds, emeralds, rubies, you name it. And we could debate forever about natural and manmade and how they compare to each other. We both know the markets would praise the natural and criticize the shine of manmade despite the value being arbitrary. Something we decide. It goes to show how foolish we humans can be. That something dug from the ground with hard labor and blood has more value than the gems I could make without deaths, and still they would look and shine the same. But appearance doesn't count when calculating a gem's worth. It's the deaths that add value, even as talk about labor unions and workers' rights is growing louder. They say it's a way for the masses to take the reins back from their masters. A delusion, I say, when the other side has all the resources at their disposal. The war would never be fought on equal ground.

"But that's beside the point. I sometimes get carried away; do forgive me. This machine does more than turn one thing into another or make something that can pass for real. It can make you anything you want out of nothing, and I don't mean fake gold or fake diamonds: I mean substance. Years ago, I stopped pursuing the thingamajigs, the worthless fulfillments, and truly learned the potential modern chemistry and machinery have to offer. You know, coming from Necropolis, that the compounds hidden in nature can be made to serve us. They can even animate the dead. That's what I have done. I have discovered a way to turn lead into gold, so to speak, if you prefer the old alchemical symbolism. Still, I'd rather say I have discovered the power of the universe, which itself was breathed out of nothingness and yet is full of life." Levi ended his speech.

Rose said nothing for a while. For good reason. Her head was spinning as it tried to wrap itself around Levi's speech and find the necessary information.

This time he took in the silence, letting her have her moment.

Not every second had to be filled with noise. There was an advantage in allowing the other person to speak as there was an advantage in not letting them get a word in edgeways, let's say, with a customer. Levi had always been good at controlling the mood of the conversation in the shop. The trick was stepping out of the situation, not being fully invested, and being able to toy with everything said and done. But here, his heart was racing, and he had to really concentrate so as not to drown Rose in another avalanche of concepts.

"This all sounds... amazing and confusing, I have to confess. Mr. Perri, I'm truly impressed, but..." Rose searched for rest of her thoughts.

Levi closed the notebook. "But you don't have to believe

me. First of all, I don't need you to fund me to test and see whether the machine works. It works. I can make grains of wheat, gold coins, you name it. But the thing is, it's a slow process now, taking months to produce a single coin. I need to make the machine bigger and better in order for me, us, to take over the markets. You and I could change everything with it. Change how production is done. How profits are made. Most of all, with the machine, we could bring prosperity to many and not just a few. You don't only have to take my word; I'll show you." Levi leaned over the coffee table and took the cover off the machine with one swift pull.

"Oh," Rose said, and her words were followed by silence. The golden Bufonite with detailed ornaments, magnificent gears, and aesthetics to put any masterpiece to shame gleamed in front of her eyes. Levi didn't dare to stare too long.

"Can I?" she asked.

"Of course," Levi said.

Rose lifted Otis off her lap and lowered the otter to the floor. She moved forward and touched the machine with shaking hands, maybe afraid it might break from a single touch.

"It's a thing of beauty, I have to say. Did you make everything yourself? The carvings, the construction, the science, and the design?" Rose asked, shifting her attention from the machine to Levi.

"Yes, but I can't take full credit. This is an apparatus dreamed up by Lord Bufonite."

Otis let out an *iik*.

Levi glanced at him but continued, "If you are familiar with our local legends, Lord Bufonite was a noble-born man, a prince, who abandoned his duties to help the needy, and the only way he could do that was to dream up a machine that could feed and clothe the poor. And he did just that. But what became of the machine is forgotten. There was a great war, which destroyed not only him but also his entire family. There were rumors about a fair maiden and treachery, as there always are with stories. Nevertheless, the machine is and was real, I'm sure of it," Levi finished.

"And you did this based on..." She searched for the word.

"On a myth. Yes, the story has always fascinated me. How this mortal man could have built something so transformative without the help of gods or the supernatural. But as I said, the machine was real, and so is the science behind it. I have a background in physics and chemistry. If that helps."

"And you want to feed the poor and the hungry?" Rose asked.

"Yes and no," Levi replied.

"No?"

"Not out of the callousness of my heart. If there's something to learn from the legends, it's that a machine like this has to be controlled and guarded. One careless action might cause a war and destroy not only the machine but civic peace, with or without any fair maidens in sight," Levi said, clearly intending the last comment to soften the mood. As Rose didn't comment, he went on, "But that would be the end cause, yes. Only after a good system was in place, so as not to collapse everything and cause more destitution."

"Hm," Rose said. "And it works?"

"Let me show you," Levi said, kneeling next to the table. He opened the lid of the Bufonite, showing Rose that there was nothing inside but mechanical cogs and pulleys and the glass tubes with a pale blue-green liquid in them. Then he shut the cover and turned the levers, and soon the room was filled with a gentle humming.

"For now, this thing can make two things. Wheat and gold." He spoke softly over the machine. "But I'm sure I can make the bigger version do more than that, and faster. I was thinking something the size of a printing press—a dozen of them for starters to get things rolling. For both of our sakes, I adjusted the machine to make wheat, as for now the gold takes too long," Levi said.

Rose opened her mouth to reply, but her words were lost when the machine began spewing out wheat grains. The humming got louder, and soon the table was filled with a cupful of wheat.

Rose got to her knees next to Levi to inspect the grains. She took a grain and rolled it between her fingers.

Otis jumped up on the table.

Levi switched the machine off. "You might want to taste them. I assure you, they are completely harmless. Evelyn, my maid, has baked me more than one loaf out of them, and I'm still alive and kicking, so to speak." He pushed the last lever downward, and the humming gradually died down until the room was quiet.

So quiet, in fact, that Levi found he had been breathing heavily. He steadied his breathing, not wanting to appear oafish.

"Yes, sure." She seemed unsure but followed his example as Levi took a grain from the table and put it in his mouth. Otis also licked up a few grains until Levi shooed him away.

The grains had the usual nutty, earthy flavor.

The process had gone as it should. The quintessence worked.

"Hmm," Rose said.

"If you like, I can bag you a sample, and you can show it to an expert and get them to assess what it is. It's supposed to be wheat, and it is. I stand by that, but I assume you want to double-check. Also, take this," Levi said and took the gold coin out of his vest pocket and handed it to the banker.
Rose automatically reached for the coin.

"You might as well find an expert to have a look at that as well. It took me and the machine weeks to make, but I'm sure we will be able to make the process faster with multiple machines. So, what do you think?" Levi leaned slightly forward to meet her eyes.

"That you will give me until the end of this week to get my octopuses in a row, and we can make this legend of yours alive and bigger," Rose said.

❧

Sigourney and Siarl had gotten back to the hotel. She'd glanced over her shoulder the whole way there from the shore. There was this extra feeling of being hunted. The sunny city with the open, welcoming streets had suddenly turned into a horror trap. She saw the posters of the missing persons, the little trinkets with skulls and bones the people carried with them—the symbols and knickknacks of the superstitions of past eras. Until now, she had only seen the abundance: the new gadgets, the jewelry, the fashionable clothes that had put hers to shame. But there on the skirts' lace patterns were pentagrams, eyes, and other stitched wards to keep the evil away. None of the symbols had been there when she'd lived in Threebeanvalley. The city was changing, for worse or for better; she couldn't be the judge of that. Also, maybe they were right; maybe there was some evil lurking behind the polished exterior, and not just greed. Such a thing would always be there, whatever form it took. It was something else.

Siarl kept smiling next to her, missing all of the signs. Always off with the fairies. But what if the fairies had pointy teeth and talons that could shred you into pieces?

No, Sigourney was sure he didn't want to hear her warnings. He would say she was overreacting. That Margaret the birdwatcher had gotten her spooked, and her mind had reacted by creating monsters where there were none. And she would end up believing him. He was only being reasonable, as there were no monsters.

But Sigourney wasn't ready to let go of what she felt and saw. That not everything was as it appeared. That the city wasn't as open and jovial as people thought. Why would it be?

There were no exceptions to the rule.

Sigourney had seen enough cities, enough places, to know there was always a dark side to everything. Even Leporidae Lop, governed by luck and Harriet Stowe, had had its miseries. Those who would do anything for their next bite to eat. No houses to go to. No one to care, or if someone cared, they carried suffocating burdens with them. Then, there in the shadows of the human mind lurked demons, the ugly ones. Not just figuratively, but the real deal. People pretended they weren't there, but they were. She had seen them. And she was sure she saw them now, behind the human masks.

Why would they be any less real than a giant rabbit or elusive snowmen or the monks on the mountain with their secret voodoo? Or her? What she possessed was not normal. You didn't break the laws of nature just like that if you were part of the physical world. She had never before thought about it in such a way. Maybe that was why she had never felt as if she belonged anywhere. Perhaps she didn't. Perhaps she was a fluke who shouldn't exist.

"Sigourney," Siarl said, taking her hand in his and stopping her from walking past the hotel's front steps. "We are already here, at the hotel."

"Oh. I..." she mumbled, not knowing what she'd planned to say.

"Let's head to the restaurant and eat something, and then

we can go over what else you want to do," Siarl suggested.

"Shall I call him?" Sigourney asked.

"Let's not. Let him enjoy his ways." This time he said it softly, where in the past there had always been a tone of disapproval.

Yes, *his ways.* Sigourney looked away when the Rabbit got into those moods that Siarl called "his ways." The Rabbit could be heedless, to put it mildly. Then again, it was his nature, and who was she to deny him that?

She followed Siarl inside the hotel and to the restaurant. It was packed full of people. A waiter stopped them from going any farther, eyeing them from head to toe.

Sigourney said inside her head, *"You would think better of us if we were wearing skulls and bones. There they are, under my skin. Can't you see?"* But she never said those horrible thoughts aloud.

"Good day," the man said. "I'm afraid we are packed this fine late afternoon, and we are prioritizing those who are staying at the hotel. Would you like me to recommend another restaurant?"

"We have a room," Sigourney said to everyone's horror, hers too.

"You have?" the waiter hurried to ask.

"Yes, we are staying in suite 502," Siarl said when Sigourney went mute as the waiter tried to stare her down.

"But—" The waiter stopped himself when he saw the look Siarl was giving him.

Sigourney called it his friendly warning face. The one that indicated there would be kind words involved with a lot of embarrassment, and later there might be shouting from the manager. Siarl could do wonders with a simple smile, opening his eyes slightly and tilting his head.

"Yes, sir. I think I might be able to squeeze you in. As I said, we are having a memorable day today. Famous new cook, and the word has gotten around. You know the newspaper article," the waiter said, stepping aside, letting them farther into the restaurant.

They followed him through the dining hall.

Sigourney felt all the blood from her brain flee to her stomach, which loudly growled as she passed soups, grilled salmons, garlic pasta, vegetable surprises, chocolate puddings, vanilla cakes, tiramisus, and the list went on. The remaining functions in her head were plotting what to order, or more like what not to order, as her stomach was sure it could fit in all the dishes her eyes landed on. She had forgotten how hungry she was.

The waiter found them the most secluded table he could, far away from the windows and other prominent guests. If the waiter thought he was doing them a disservice, he was simply wrong.[36] While Siarl might be a front row sort of fellow and didn't mind being on display, he appreciated privacy and respected the fact that Sigourney was not only the back row sort, she was the out of the room and under the stars type. She knew that, and she was thankful for all the ways he put her first. And despite what the waiter intended, this was the perfect spot to observe the entire room.

Sigourney watched the man go after reluctantly leaving them a menu. She'd learned to endure the social situations, the restaurants, and the formality that Siarl and the Rabbit seemed to prefer. But a picnic at the lighthouse would always sound better to her.

"Do you think I should get myself a suit?" Siarl asked while Sigourney pretended she was looking over the menu. She had already decided. It was the soup first, then the vegetable surprise, then the ice cream with cookies and strawberry sauce.

"If you like," she said carefully, keeping all the rest to herself.

"It could do us some good. Not always being thought of as ruffians. While such an image has its romantic charm, I would like to be taken seriously." Siarl lowered his menu.

Sigourney wasn't sure if he was waiting for her to argue back or agree with him. She settled for staring back at him. She wanted to look away, maybe pretend there was something in her eyes and rub them, but as soon as her gaze was caught in his, she relaxed. It was Siarl looking back at her. The one who made her heart beat faster every time he touched her. The one who could make her whole body relax if she only let it.

"Then we should get you one," she said.

That seemed to be all there was to say on the matter.

---

36   The nasty, wicked little release he got was only poison for himself, and he would never realize that. There it sat, forever inside his guts, this black, shapeless gop, though whether he deserved it was up for debate.

The waiter came back after an awkwardly long time. Long enough to start wondering whether you have been forgotten and should make your presence known, or in Sigourney's case, slip into the kitchen and steal a plate for yourself as a way to balance out the situation. All fitting in the moral realm of Hammurabi, a man who was very keen on retribution and cutting off hands.

"What will it be today?" he asked, still uncomfortable dealing with the two of them.

"Soup, vegetable surprise, bread, butter, and ice cream dessert," Sigourney let out before the waiter could take a breath after his initial question.

Again, he looked towards Sigourney, a bit shocked. Usually, that only happened when she disappeared, not when she tried to engage like an average person would.

"That sounds good to me as well, except instead of the ice cream I would prefer tea and a slice of dark chocolate cake," Siarl said, handing back the menu.

"And to drink?" the waiter asked, collecting his composure quickly, having done this job long enough not to question a somewhat lucrative order. Not at least until it came time to pay the bill.

"Ale and water," Siarl said.

"Water for me," Sigourney confirmed.

"I'll be back with your soup," the waiter said and disappeared back where he'd come from.

"Too bad we are staying at the hotel," Siarl said. "Otherwise, we could have dined and dashed. It would serve him right."

Sigourney smirked. "If the Rabbit were here, he would insist we did it anyway."

"Aye," Siarl said and laughed.

It was good to hear him laugh. She had forgotten what his laugh sounded like, and only now did Sigourney realize how much he was hurting. How much he had given up for her and the Rabbit with the constant traveling. Why hadn't she noticed before?

She cursed how wrapped up she was inside her own mind. She had been ignoring Siarl wholly. And what had he done? He had been there for her. Helped her over all the minor obstacles that felt like mountains, and had she been thankful? No! Even today, she had run off rather than listen to his wants and needs. Such a child.

Siarl's laughter turned into a frown. "What's wrong?"

"Nothing. I mean..." Sigourney shook her head. This was silly. "I'm sorry, Siarl. I just can't help myself. You are always there for me, and finally, when I make you laugh, I steal it away instantly. Why am I doing this to you?" Her posture sank, and she began to play with the fork on the table, moving it around, pushing it with her fingers, shoving it as if it deserved to be bullied. As if it would wipe away everything.

"Sigourney?" Siarl looked confused. He reached for her hand.

She let him stop her from playing with the fork and met his gaze.

"You were laughing there, having fun. And I realized that you haven't done that for a long time. That's my fault. Then I didn't even want to tell you. Siarl, I don't deserve you. You could have anyone in this room. They would be kinder, not as childish and stupid and stubborn and closed off as I am."

As she said all this, a tiny voice inside her screamed again that she was making this about her. What she wasn't. Was she seeking pity? Was she expecting him to say, "no, you are not"?

And there they were, the words. Sigourney could see his mouth starting to form them.

"Siarl, you want a life here or somewhere else, don't you?" She cut his words off.

He once again looked confused. She couldn't blame him. This was the first time she was trying to speak with him. Go deeper than the surface, beyond the painted dreams where they could be anything and ignore reality.

"Yes," he said, squeezing her hand. "With you."

"I'm not sure that's possible. If I'm ready or not. All the demons are after me, and I have been hiding from them thus far, thinking that if I can run, I can outsmart them. I know how stupid that sounds and how naive I have been. But that's not someone who you should settle with. You want someone who can offer you the same kind of care and help as you have offered me. I have been self—"

"No, you haven't. Sigourney. Don't say that. I love you." His eyes were shining, and Sigourney wanted to look away. He was going to cry. Because of her. The once tough freedom fighter who'd kidnapped Harriet Stowe for his own country, to save his people from a slow, agonizing death, and he was going to cry because of her and her words.

Sigourney swallowed.

"We don't need to talk about this now," Siarl said.

"Then when? You asked me a question back at the shore, and I ran away, like I always do. Not able to face what's inside me or what you ask." Sigourney's whole body tensed up. She needed to escape. Everything hurt. Every muscle. Every joint. Every bone. Still, she sat there.

"Tomorrow," Siarl said, his voice sounding thin and hollow. He had been waiting for this to happen. Maybe not now. Possibly years from now. "Let's have this day just for the two of us. Get me that suit. See the bathhouses, the gardens, the old town, the factories, and all the rest. We can even see a fortune teller. The city is famous for them. What do you think?"

Sigourney bit her lip. "Sounds like a plan." For a moment there, she was sure she saw Margaret from the lighthouse enter the restaurant. She shook her head, and the woman was gone.

"What's wrong?" Siarl asked.

"Oh, nothing. Just my mind playing games for dis..." That was as far as she got before the waiter came back with their starters.

Outside, people pressed their noses to the windows, starving to death, unsure whether there was even a future for their malnourished children who ate poisonous food knowingly, as there was nothing worse than an empty belly. Gas lamps and new steam engines had yet to revolutionize the farming industry. It was the wealthy and noble who ate the way Sigourney and Siarl were doing now, and only the men. Women were expected to fast and look ghostly thin.

Sigourney was going to eat every bit of her food and steal some for the others. There had been a time when she'd pressed her nose against the glass and dreamt that one day she could afford to eat. Maybe it was high time she started to pay forward all the good she had received. Possibly the Rabbit's luck could be used for more, and maybe that was what Siarl had been talking about all along. To have meaning in one's life beyond oneself. First, she would get her past fixed and forgotten, then she would do something about her life. She promised.

Sigourney slurped up her soup, to the horror of the other

guests. And she enjoyed every second of the small social infringement. You could say it added salt to the soup.

9

CAN YOU HEAR THE DICE BEING ROLLED? DO THEY ROLL FOR ME?

The Rabbit god of luck scooped the chips he'd won into his lap. He heard the pompous gambler with the enormous belt buckle exhale loudly. The rest collapsed into their chairs. A few rounds ago, he'd turned the game around. Instead of bleeding money, he'd gradually increased his winnings. The Rabbit was being evil, and he knew it. It wasn't fair; his talents far outstripped those of the humans. But the man and the rest of the people at the table had to learn a thing or two about luck. Or so he reasoned.

The Rabbit glanced over his shoulder and saw most of the room had stopped gambling and had come to follow the game of cards. He spotted the hotel owner in the crowd, not looking pleased. But not sad either, as if he'd lost his whole fortune. The Rabbit's luck had been doing its worst and best inside the gambling house. He could easily distinguish those to whom he had been favorable. They didn't look like they were ready to push their granny under the bus, but if things kept going the way they were, they might reconsider.[37]

He turned back to the game, Bluff the Prime Mover, and saw the dealer sweating. Someone else had joined in observing them, standing behind the dealer. From the look of it, she was the owner of this place.

The Rabbit frowned but shook the thought away.

He wasn't sure why he was drawn to these places. Maybe it was because he felt fully alive here. Loved, feared, cursed, and worshiped. Everything a god, a deity, could ever want. This might be the last temple on this continent where humans still truly believed in a higher power. Okay, they had to. When playing with luck, there was only ever the illusion of talent.

The dealer dealt another round.

The Rabbit lifted the top of the cards with his thumb, keeping the rest against the table.

He smirked. Some of the participants sighed and hit their cards on the table, saying things like, "I'm out." "I hate you." "She will kick me out."

Not that his smirk had meant anything. His cards had been a miscellaneous collection of humans, gods, and cats. Gods, he loved playing Bluff the Prime Mover. The gods always won, but too many in one hand and they destroyed everything. Then the cats won.

"Place your bets," the dealer said.

The Rabbit scratched his head. His cards wouldn't get any better no matter how much he toyed with his opponents. He had four gods, a cat, and three humans, and none of them worked well together. He was sure the pompous gambler, whose name he intentionally kept forgetting, saw through his smile, even though the Rabbit had been erratic with his expressions throughout the game. There was always the option of folding, but the other players still had more money to be unburdened of. The Rabbit had always thought having money was a burden. Look at anyone who had it. They seemed to be disillusioned about life... and luck. It was his moral duty to set them free of such misconceptions.

---

37   No god wanted contentment among his or her subordinates. You didn't know what contented, devious minds might come up with when they got bored. There were already such horrendous ideas in the air, like equality, general well-being, public healthcare, and free education. The world could only go downhill from there.

The Rabbit smirked again. The next three cards the dealer dealt on the table would define everything, and the Rabbit had a feeling luck was on his side. He pushed a mountain of chips into the middle of the table and waited for the others to react.

The pompous man stiffened. The Rabbit's sensitive ears could hear the man's teeth grinding together. The man couldn't lose face. Not if this was his regular joint. Not when his identity and reputation hung on the card game. Oh well. The Rabbit tapped his fingers against the table. That seemed to increase the teeth grinding.

"I raise," the man said and pushed all his chips in.

The room gasped.

The owner of the place folded her arms and locked her eyes with the Rabbit.

"I match," the Rabbit god of luck said, pushing in more chips.

"I fold," a woman next to the Rabbit said, causing an avalanche of similar responses from the rest of the players.

The Rabbit barely heard her. He had his full concentration on the pompous man.

"The bets have been placed," the dealer said. He took the first three cards from the deck and laid them on the table, picture side up. They were three different humans.

The pompous man hit his fist against the table, making the chips fly before they could change their cards with the dealer and before the Rabbit showed his hand. The man launched himself over the counter, coming straight at the Rabbit.

The Rabbit leaped up from his chair and scooted backward. You could say he was a tad too fast for a man of his age.

The pompous man fell face down on the floor He got up faster than the Rabbit expected, but he never landed his punch. Not because the Rabbit got out of his way but because the security guards seized him and pinned the man down. He wailed and tried to struggle free.

"If you could follow me," the owner of the place said. Somehow, she'd appeared next to the Rabbit without him hearing her footsteps. The woman had a sweet, melodic voice. To be accurate, a seductive voice, which made even the Rabbit god of luck's skin form goosebumps despite the species difference.

He was about to follow the woman, but then he remembered who he was and stopped. Also, he wanted to kick the pompous man when he was down... to keep teaching him important lessons. That was why he was here. No one else got to call themselves Mr. Lucky.

The woman misread him. She said, "My staff will bring your chips. Now, if you could come with me."

The Rabbit toyed with the idea of saying no to the woman and seeing what happened, as he still had unfinished business here. There were still chips to be won, but then again, he was getting bored. He could sense the mood of the room changing from hope to melancholy. The incident had changed everything. That was often the case with violence. The only question was, was the change for good or ill?

The Rabbit knew the answer. He said, "Then lead the way. But before we go, I didn't come alone." He motioned for the hotel owner to come with him.

Mathew reluctantly pushed through the confused crowd, who didn't know whether to leave or to stay and gawk in hope of something exciting happening again. More often than not, nothing good followed an outburst of emotions. Or, in this case, after the violation of self-image. The usual route of fists flung, smashed beer bottles, and knife wielding had been prevented, and now it was as dull as drowning your sorrows at the bar.

"This is Mathew Regan, the owner of Hotel Earl. A splendid fellow altogether," the Rabbit said, patting the man on his shoulder.

The hotel owner flinched. He looked like he was ready to flee. The hotel owner knew when there was a possibility of being used as a tool: left with the bomb when everyone else was already running away. And this was it.

The Rabbit twitched his nose, forgetting that he was a human male, making the gesture somewhat vulgar. Nevertheless, it made the hotel owner's agitation wash away as the Rabbit's powers poured in.

The reach of his godly powers didn't extend to the woman. She said, "Then you two had better follow me." Coldness had crept into her voice, reminding the Rabbit how lucky he had been to never go down that rabbit hole and acquire a walking-talking-moralizing "inner voice" in the form of a female partner. Now, as he thought about it, Siarl had somehow ended up filling that space in his life with his constant complaining.

The Rabbit again twitched his nose. He would have to get rid of the two humans, and soon. All the traveling and whatnot had been fun thus far, but you could only repeat the same thing for so long without getting bored.

"Lead the way," the Rabbit said and chuckled.

The woman nodded to her security guards. They followed after the Rabbit and the hotel owner.

"So, fellows, what have you been up to?" the Rabbit asked his escort.

He was met with silence.

"Do you think I'm in trouble?" he asked and winked.

Again, he was greeted with silence.

"I'll take that as a yes. You know, I have done nothing wrong. Just playing the game as it should be played. No cheating. No counting cards. No nothing. Just pure luck working in my favor. I think there's been a huge misunderstanding here," he said and held back laughter.

It had been a long time since he'd been threatened with violence.[38] All this was making him feel alive. There was nothing like the possibility of dying any second. Not that the humans could kill him the usual way, but at least they could try.

Still no reaction from his escort.

Except for the hotel owner. He whined, "Please, shut up. You are getting us into trouble."

"Don't worry. Trouble and I are good friends. We have nothing against each other," the Rabbit said.

Mathew whimpered.

They followed the woman through the gambling house, past the tables and roulette wheels. The place was surprisingly huge; the dimmed lights must have played tricks with the Rabbit's perception. The trouble was that he was growing bored with his surroundings and the souls who occupied the tables. He was tired of all the walking. If he had known the woman would take this long to make her point, he would have walked out of the door and found something more

---

38 He had already forgotten the pompous man, who was nothing but a fleeting memory. The pompous man would beg to differ. To him, meeting the Rabbit was a life-defining moment, the worst kind.

invigorating to do. But he hated to admit that this was the most fun he'd had for ages. What with Siarl's planning and Sigourney's disappearing acts, their travels had been predictable despite all the snowmen and assassins sent by the gods and the rest. They had been child's play to him.

The woman pushed a door open, leading them into the back room of the house.

Here we go, the Rabbit thought. His heart skipped a beat.

The place turned out to be your standard office with a dark desk and cabinet, a huge sofa, and a red rug over the wooden floor, along with the rest of the things you could expect to find inside a manager's office. Except there were no windows.

The Rabbit was disappointed. He'd expected a dark alleyway where the security guards would beat and kick him, or a torture chamber with spikes, or at least some kind of interrogation room with bright lights and metal tables to make everything seem cold and impersonal. The Rabbit shuddered at the last thought. Impersonal was the surest way to evil. At least with kicking, there was bodily contact. For someone in isolation, that was better than not being touched at all.

The woman made her way behind her desk.

"Do sit down," she said, indicating the sofa.

The Rabbit took long strides and sat down.

The hotel owner followed him sluggishly.

"If you aren't going to beat me into a pulp, then what is this all about?" the Rabbit asked.

The woman let out a soft laugh, which managed to take over the whole room.

The Rabbit's fur felt electrified. Which was odd, as the Rabbit was sure he was in his human form. But there it was, the feeling of his fur vibrating and anticipating another lovely sound issuing from the woman's cherry lips.

"There won't be a beating tonight. I'm sorry if you had such a misconception. This is a friendly chat. You and your friend can relax," the dark-haired woman said.

Next to the Rabbit, Mathew sighed.

The Rabbit leaned forward instead and smiled. "Then what do you want from me? Money? The chips? What?"

"Dear Lepus, I have all the money I could want. Don't

you recognize me?" she asked.

The Rabbit squinted his eyes. She was right. There was something familiar about her behind the beautiful mask she wore. The woman currently had almond-shaped eyes, which were lined with black eyeliner and mascara. Her huge cherry lips accentuated her diamond-shaped face. Her almost pitch-black curled hair framed her face, making her the most stunning woman the Rabbit had ever seen. More beautiful than Gertrude, who had for so long made sure she was the fairest of them all. But behind all that was a feeling the Rabbit couldn't shake. That he and this woman had been there when the stories were told, sitting around the campfire. When the nations were formed.

"Justice?" he asked.

A smile spread across the woman's face. "It took you long enough," Justice said.

"But..." the Rabbit began. The woman looked nothing like the Justice he knew. Justice wasn't drop-dead gorgeous with a petite frame.

The Rabbit shuddered. Justice's body under her tight black dress made his animal instincts wake up. But that didn't use to be the case. She was like a sister to him. Shaped from the same mind. From humankind. And she used to look like a sturdy woman whose boots were made for kicking men and gods into obedience. Now those same legs were crossed, and the feet wore black velvet high heels, making the Rabbit scratch the back of his neck.

Oh, boy, he thought. He had gotten himself into a bigger mess than he thought.

"What are you doing here?" he asked when he'd recovered from the initial shock. What he truly wanted to ask was, "*what have you done to yourself?*"

"Times are changing, my darling Lepus, and one has to keep up with the times. I'm here to survive the next revolution of the human mind." Justice crossed her legs the other way. Those long, narrow calves of hers. The Rabbit had to do everything in his power to remind himself that there were rules about touching sisters. Rules that had reached even the gods, which made no sense—there was no escaping the fact that he and the rest of them were formed from dreams.

"But—"

"No buts, Lepus. You must sense it already. The old gods

are dying, and new ones are being made. But you and I will survive. Humans need to believe in justice, mercy, love, luck, stories to make them work together. If they forget those things, all they have achieved will burn to the ground. But that doesn't mean things don't change for us. You have to already feel that our bodies will fade. That we are turning into abstract concepts. If that happens, we will turn into a basic instinct, and there won't be an 'I' any longer. And Lepus, I don't want to die," Justice said.

He could hear the desperation in her voice. No, not hear. More like feel the despair inside his own mind as well. He had known for a long time that he had at best a century to go until there was no Lepus. There was only Luck. And men like the one with the belt buckle would have free range to call themselves Mr. Luck or Mr. Green without fear of the oldie-but-a-goodie punishment—smiting.

"But why here, and why looking like that?" he moaned.

"I had to keep up with the times. This is what sells. This is how I get them to notice me," Justice said. She gestured to her body with her hand.

"But inside a gambling house? There's no justice here. There's just me, and I'm not fair," the Rabbit insisted.

"There's more justice in here than in a modern courthouse," she replied.

The Rabbit twitched his nose. He dreaded to ask what she wanted him to ask. He could taste those words on his lips, but he wasn't willing to let them out. The last time he'd associated with gods, there had been a continent-wide war. A war that Justice hadn't taken part in, now that he recalled. But that didn't make things any better. When it came to gods and their need to stay alive and in power, madness followed. He was at peace with his inevitable demise. The Rabbit had had a long, happy run around the planet. He had seen and done everything. What more was there to want? Carrots wouldn't do it for long, with or without vodka.

Things don't come out of nothing. They come from somewhere. Even the rain doesn't magically appear. Evaporation and the formation of clouds are involved in the birth. So, here Rose was, listening to someone explain that the universe, the planet she stood on, the stars, the moons, the sun, and whatever else was out there, the cosmic monsters like Kraken, had come out of nothing. All the reason inside her said the man was lying, but she believed him on some level. Not because of silly words, but because of the passion and conviction in his voice. He lacked doubt. What an alluring and dangerous cocktail.

If only she could leave it there, but she couldn't. As a money-minded woman, she had to question everything.[39] She questioned the clouds, the rain, the cosmic radiation, and Kraken itself. She questioned her flesh, her skeleton, and what she saw and heard. That was her job. Risks had to be measured against reality, yes; however, the secret was that sometimes facts didn't matter. Sometimes the fairy tales and rumors won and were more lucrative. It was like the cure-all bottle. A promise of hope, a better life, a fix, beauty, and simplicity packaged in one. Could the machine do the same? If it did, it was a risk worth taking. And if she didn't, her competitors would get dibs on the new technology of making something out of nothing, and that would leave her and the Worthwrites on the shore like an abandoned bride.

If only the crystal balls worked. Oh, of course, she knew they did. It was just the future had so many different paths it could take. Everything had already changed before you sat on the bench and the madam had taken her ball out. As common as it was, she and other decision-makers had no other option than to trust the human power of prediction, which everyone knew was as useful as a sieve on a sinking ship.

Levi offered her his hand to help her up from the floor, where she had been staring at the machine in silence for longer than necessary. She took it and was astonished to find it coarse.

"You surprised me, Mr. Perri. I never thought to find something like..."

"The Bufonite," Levi offered when she searched for the name.

"Yes, the Bufonite, inside an alchemist's shop. I came here out of curiosity and found... I don't know what I found. Still, we are going to make your machine bigger and better, if the

---

39 Something money managers didn't do enough. You could say faith made the world go around.

gold coin is indeed gold and the seeds wheat." Rose added the last sentence carefully, not wanting to promise too much before she could wrap her head around the facts.

The alchemist's otter let out an *iik* sound.

"You too astonish me, Mr. Otter." Rose laughed.

"I trust you to keep this between the two of us before we get into the fine details of how we should proceed after you have your proof," Levi said, cutting Rose's joy short.

She'd let the excitement sweep her in and had forgotten to question and poke holes in everything and everyone for a moment there.

"Of course. And if we decide to proceed, everything will go through our lawyers. But before that, you have my word that nothing said and shown here will go beyond these walls."

"Thank you, Miss Pettyshare. One has to be careful with these things." Levi gently guided her out of the parlor and deeper into the building. Rose glanced into the shop through the open door and saw customers peering inside. The alchemist indeed had this odd aura around him, and she was sure it wasn't because of how composed he was with everyone. It had to be his eyes. Something coming from inside.[40]

They passed a maid as they went through the kitchen. She gave them a nervous smile amid all the baking. The room smelled like a home should. Something she had never had. Only cold nights at the dormitory. Magda crying her eyes out above her, and the others not doing so well either. Rose never cried. Not then, and she wasn't going to start now.

She smiled back at the maid, ending up making her even more fidgety. Rose had always found it silly how many different statuses could be inside any given room. It was like ranking cattle by their beef quality, except the state of health had nothing to do with it when it came to humans. That ship had sailed a long time ago. Rose felt a sting of sympathy towards the maid. She wished to say to her *"never hunch your shoulders. Show the world who you are. Hold your head high. You belong here as much as I do."* She didn't say any of it, despite having learned the hard way what status and class meant at the boarding school. Instead, she followed Levi to the back door,

---

40 A mistake too many made. Attributing things to an inner state when there was only outer action. It was a beautiful thought about substance and soul. What if there was none?

where he let her out, blinded by the light.

The otter had followed them, and it let out an *iik-iik* when Rose said her goodbyes and stepped onto the street.

"Mr. Perri, this was educational, to say the least. I'll contact you as soon as I have the assessments ready. In the meantime, I would highly recommend finding a good lawyer and getting your financial statements up to date. Only then can we move forward." Inside her briefcase, a bag full of wheat grains and a golden coin weighed heavily.

"I'll get it sorted out. Good day, Miss Pettyshare, and it was my pleasure to make your acquaintance." He kissed her hand.

Rose's mind jumped to all the possibilities open to you if you had an endless supply of gold as soon as the back door closed after her. She headed onto the streets, intending to find her way to the hotel. But as she had a devious mind, one that could calculate all those risks and other doom and gloom scenarios, she found herself up against an error message composed of one word: flood. Markets couldn't handle this kind of machine; it would break everything. Levi had been right about that. It had to be controlled and guarded for the sake of civic peace. Not to mention the sake of profits. But Rose was sure she could do that.[41]

And how had the alchemist ended up in the position of having to share everything with her and the bank? The usual reason was not having initial capital in the first place, which made her wonder about the Alchemist Shop's finances. Before she could even dream of going into business with the man, she had to know that he wasn't some hopeless romantic who would waste her resources pursuing idealistic notions.

But the rest of her thoughts evaporated into the cosmos or got lost in her synopsis when Justice's men stepped out of the shadows. She had never expected the woman would have her followed. There were two men—one looking like he could stare down an ox and the other like he could read your every move. There was more muscle to the men than a single person could ever need.

Rose squeezed the briefcase tighter against her side.

"Miss Pettyshare, won't you come with us? Justice wants to speak with you," one of the men said. The one with a long

---

41   They always are.

scar visible under his white shirt collar. He wore a blank expression under his wool cap—a hat with razor blades hidden inside the seams. Rose made a mental note.

There was no way she could argue back.

"Of course, it would be my pleasure." She let them guide her to their open cart.

She kept squeezing the soft leather briefcase the whole journey to the gambling house. This was... the miracle she had been waiting for, and she couldn't, *couldn't* let it be taken from her. People like Mr. Perri were the reason why she loved banking. Not only because they provided lucrative opportunities to make money, but because they were exciting to be around. Some of their passion and excitement about their creations always spilled over to her. But innovation wasn't her job; it was to secure funding and ensure the legal framework. Moreover, now it was to play Bluff the Prime Mover with the real world. She had to cheat her way out of this situation by hiding her true intentions from Justice and Abigail, and the money from Percy. Then she would have to bribe, extort, and twist Page Briggs' arm to get that license. Then there was getting the necessary funding for the machine. Maybe even swiping it from under the Worthwrites' noses and making them pay for it. Making something out of nothing would make her filthy rich, especially if no one else had the technology. That was another thing she would have to check. But she couldn't exactly send rumors flying around the city. Too dangerous. What an exciting mess; better than gambling.

She was back.

The last thought was wiped away by the sight of Justice surrounded by her lackeys. She had been ushered into her office through the gambling house, which had been quiet and melancholic, as if someone had won big time, and everyone knew all the luck was used up for the day. Superstition, but as a gambler, she recognized the feeling. If she was honest, she partly believed in it. Odds just didn't feel rational. They felt like they were tied to each other, as if one dice roll had history and connection not only with her rolls but all the rolls made in the vicinity.[42] Now, she felt like someone had

---

42 One of those fantastic biases the brain came equipped with. But not all is lost. You can teach it to know better.

taken her dice away and was threatening to roll it for her.

"Rose," Justice greeted her.

"Justice." Rose tried to keep a pleasant smile on her face. The other woman looked a little disheveled and out of breath. So did some of her men. Rose made a note of it as she moved past her initial irritation and fear to read the room to make sure she got her dice back and was the one doing the rolling. "You wanted to see me."

Justice blinked.

Rose was sure the other woman had forgotten she had been summoned here. That something more significant had passed before she was ushered in.

"Do sit down," Justice said as she collapsed into her own chair, looking tired.

Rose made her way to the sofa. She laid the briefcase carefully next to her feet, trying not to appear too protective, yet keeping it close.

"How can I help you?" she asked.

"Yes, help. What a clever way to put it." Justice began to look slightly more like herself. She corrected her posture, and her eyes were again sparkling the way they always did, letting you know you were screwed, but you just didn't know how yet. "I had a surprisingly busy morning, but a good one. Fortune is truly smiling on me and our cause. Has Abigail told you what we do?"

Rose shook her head. "Not as such. But as far as I can tell, it has something to do with the Luddites they write about in the newspapers. And do forgive me for calling you such."

"I don't mind—it's a name we have come to accept. One always has to have a label in order for others to see you better. Wouldn't you say that the word 'banker' next to your name spares you a lot of confusion you might otherwise encounter here in Threebeanvalley?" Justice gestured to her men, and they nodded and left them alone.

Rose watched them go. "Yes, it can sort out the confusion, but it's a curse word to others. Not everyone associates bankers with beneficial terms."

"Goes to show, you can't please everyone with your cause, just as I can't. But not many people say there shouldn't be bankers. You serve a function, and so do we. Luddites is as fitting a name as any. To some, it means justice. And as always, to some, justice is a bogeyman who'll come and get you if you close your eyes. There's no pleasing everyone. That doesn't mean there's no merit to our cause or that it's not a noble one. Can I ask you...[43]

Rose smiled.

"Do you think the new machines will make the world a better place? The future more secure?" Justice crossed her legs.

Rose looked away from the woman. "Do you want my honest opinion? Or to hear your words echoed back at you?" She glanced back.

Justice laughed. "The moment I saw you, I said to Abigail that there's a woman to be reckoned with. I like you, Rose Pettyshare. And yes, I want your honest opinion. We can't call many things ours, but at least we can do so with our opinions, and it's a shame if others smother them into oblivion."

Rose wanted to snort. Wasn't that what she and her Luddites were doing, and with violence to boot? She didn't say that. Instead, she replied,

"They will make the future a better place. Everything is easier, faster, and cheaper to produce; more people can have luxuries and information. The printing press has already given us so much. Books and newspapers accessible to all of us. And the information will set us free, equalize us."

Justice leaned forward. "Sometimes it feels like I have lived thousands of lives, seen new inventions come and go, heard so many speeches about new revolutionary ways to live, and yet I have seen no improvement in human nature, happiness, or quality of life—quite the opposite, in fact. After every generation of new machines, people start to cater to the machines' needs instead of their own lives. I have seen a procession of lost and tormented souls who wander aimlessly on the streets, feeling lower than a bug among their kind. So do forgive me if I don't share your optimism. But I also understand that you can't help but to believe. That's always been the way. But you need us to warn you of the dangers. To point out that your great equalizer, the printing press, hasn't actually done what you say is in its spirit to do. Who controls the machine and the product it produces, I ask you to

---

43   As always, not a real question. The time you say no and refuse to engage is the time you show how empty words and gestures can be. And feel yourself get kicked in the social nuts, as the other person will give you the stink-eye and more.

consider."

Rose wondered who was kidding themselves here. Justice, who was no older than her, claimed to have witnessed all this, not seeing that it was just her getting too caught up in her ideology to assess the situation objectively. Of course the woman would see the men who were lower than a bug, because she searched for them to confirm her world view.

"But what about the rise in life expectancy or freedom or education? Centuries ago, men couldn't dream of individuality, let along enjoying their golden years or having rights to call their own, and now women can ask for the same. To be considered more than child-bearers; to be considered human. The same goes for the ghouls, undead, werewolves, and the vampires, you name it. You say there's no progress, no change. I think you are not looking hard enough at what the printing press, among other innovations, has done to improve our lives. I can't deny that the power hasn't shifted as much as we want. That the same families hoard all the gold. Yet things are not as dismal, because all you have to do is come to me, show me a good business proposal with an alluring product, and I'll help you make your dreams come true. That's what I have done with the alchemist today, and that man can shape the world..." Rose stopped herself from saying more. Damn her and her big mouth. She had gotten too caught up in the debate. She resisted the urge to glance at the briefcase.

"Yet humans are as miserable as ever, more so. The same human lurking underneath the surface, robbed of valuable input, reduced to no more than a cog in the machine," Justice replied.

Rose could breathe again. But she better not push this further. "Yes, but as a banker, I am also just a cog in the machine—"

"Indeed. That's why you are here. You must have received my parcel, and I hope you will look at it and pass me the necessary information. But that's not why I called you here. I heard you were not as lucky as we wanted you to be at the City Hall. That's not acceptable. I planned to propose to move all my assets into your bank, and that will be impossible if we can't change the circumstances. Was it Miss Briggs you saw at the City Hall?" Justice stood up. "Before you answer, might I offer you a drink? You look like you need one."

"Sure," Rose said, feeling the color drain from her face. The woman had been spying on her. How much had she seen? Again, Rose had an urge to take the briefcase into her lap and hold it tightly. She kept her eyes on Justice, who opened the desk drawer and took out two crystal glasses and a bottle of something brown and sturdy.

Justice offered her one of the glasses, and she took it. Soon the heavy, aromatic smell of sweet alcohol reached her, and Rose was sure the mere scent went straight to her head.

She took a sip of the rum offered and felt warmth spread through her chest. It was the good stuff.

"Now, was it Miss Briggs who rejected your application?" Justice sat down on the sofa, putting the bottle next to the briefcase.

Rose flinched.

"I'll take that as a yes," Justice said.

She let her. Better that than knowing the truth. Or this could just be another game the woman was playing to see if Rose coughed up.

"We'll have to see about this. I have friends at the City Hall, and they might see to it that you have your license by the end of this week." Justice took a sip of her drink.

Rose nursed hers and wondered how to reply. "I—"

"Sure you can," Justice replied as if she'd read Rose's thoughts. "So, what was the problem with her this time?"

Rose straightened her back, trying to stop feeling like some pitiful charity case, or better yet, a trapped animal.[44]

"They needed a residence for the bank to even start the procedure."

Justice shook her head. "Bureaucrats. Always inventing new ways to torment us. But luckily, you have me, and this issue is easily resolved. I have a couple of empty buildings in the city, or empty-ish. I'll let you pick the one you like, and we'll have your bank up and running in no time." She sounded cheery as she said the last point.

And the woman had said she was for the people, Rose thought.

"I can't ask you to do such a thing—" Rose tried instead.

"Hogwash. Consider it done. Miss Briggs will learn what

---

44   The one Sigourney always felt like.

her duties are, and all will be right with the world again. Now, Miss Pettyshare, do you want me to set a private table for you?" Justice asked ever so innocently.

Rose couldn't say no. She had to pretend everything was as it should be. She drank the rum in one gulp and heard the dice being rolled.

10

LADIES DRESSED IN BEIGE AREN'T PUSHOVERS

ules, regulations, mechanics, bureaucracy, and categories make the manmade world controllable, easier, except for two chaotic variables—the humans and the rest of freaking nature. Levi sometimes entertained the thought that he knew humans. That their wants and needs were simple. It all boiled down to nurturing their ego.[45] He had done just that. Rose wanted this. He was sure of it. She'd left with the coin and a bag full of wheat grains. The Bufonite would finally come to be. Now he only had to master nature, the trickier one.

How many years had he worked to unlock the full use of quintessence? He'd lost count. It had to be at least seven years working on the concept and mechanics. Seven years of agonizing about how he could power the machine. And the solution had been as simple and annoying as spirits and the etheric realm that Necropolitans used in the glowing skulls. Hence Otis had entered the picture. The necromancer had

---

45 Kind of a restricted view. But everyone needs a survival strategy when it comes to all things social.

worked for him for three or maybe four years now, after they'd smuggled him to Threebeanvalley. Three years and the man still feared the Necromantic Council and their retribution for disobeying their ultimate rule about everything necromancy, feared that they would send hunters after him. But they'd faked Otis' death, and the lengths they'd gone to should prevent anyone from looking into the matter. Levi had mixed a cocktail of chemicals to make Otis appear dead. There hadn't been a heartbeat and he wasn't breathing when the doctor pronounced Otis deceased. Then there was the corpse they'd put into the coffin and the death certificate for the Council.

Levi glanced at Otis, who was still in his otter form, parading around the room. The necromancer was right. Money from a bank would change everything. Still, the otter would have to be reprimanded. As much as he appreciated Otis and his talents, the man treated this as if it were a game.

After Rose had left, Levi turned to face the necromancer. He was begging food from Evelyn, who was giggling nonstop now the banker was gone. Levi wondered if he should remind the maid of their conversation, but even he could see they were enjoying themselves, and he wasn't a complete bastard.

"When you're done here, I want to talk to you. I'll be in the parlor," Levi said.

The otter licked its paw. "I kind of like it this way," Otis awked.

Evelyn let out a giggle and then glanced at Levi and suppressed a second laugh. She hurriedly wiped her hands on her apron and went back to tidying the kitchen.

"Only because she noticed you," Levi said, meaning Rose. "Don't you go playing with her. She's too important."

He heard Evelyn snort.

The otter blinked, jumped in the air, and suddenly there was a man in its place, doing a somersault before landing on his feet.

"But you can't say I wasn't useful," Otis said, his voice still sounding hoarse. "But yes, let's talk in the parlor." He glanced towards the maid.

"Yes, useful indeed. But we are playing a dangerous game here. She might not be a necromancer, but she's from your neck of the woods, and she knows necromancy when she sees it."

Levi instinctively reached for the gold coin, which was no longer in his pocket. Instead, he massaged his beard.

"Don't worry about it. I'll let you keep taking all the glory," Otis jabbed back and indicated that if Levi insisted on airing this all out in front of Evelyn, he was going to play dirty.

"I was planning to. Safest that way." Levi walked past the man, making his way to the parlor.

Otis followed him.

Levi wanted nothing more than to forget what they were talking about. While the social stuff was important, or at least other people made it an imperative part of existing, he would rather consider far bigger things. To stop the useless argument, he asked,

"What do you think, a separate process for everything we want to make, or should we train the spirits to make it all?"

"For the bigger machine?" Otis graciously jumped in, knowing Levi better than anyone else in the world.

"Yes." Levi took his notebook out and drummed his thumb against it. "These separations seem arbitrary for me. We only need to teach them to do everything we—"

Otis interrupted him. "Yet they have to know the compounds beforehand. While what you said to Rose is true about making things out of nothing, they still need a model to do it from and a command from us to do so. If she looks carefully, the wheat seeds are exact copies of each other. No weather has affected the growth pattern. They are like the ultimate design."

"Yes, I know that—" Levi sat on the couch and pulled the Bufonite closer to him.

"People, or should I say rivals, will question if there are too many exact copies floating around. Then what? They'll make sure they are seen as fakes and then forbidden," Otis said, sitting on the couch's armrest.

"Then we teach different machines to alternate the patterns. That's not an issue. The issue is getting them all to do what we want." Levi flipped open the Bufonite's cover and peered inside to wait for inspiration to strike.

"I don't think it's a problem. When I was building the glowing skulls, the trick was to program them to react to all the different possibilities by giving them enough information. The same could be done with the Bufonites. We teach the spirits to do it all by giving clear instructions on how to process what we give them. We start with the simple and move to the more complex. Gold is simple. It's a basic raw material. But wheat, that's another thing entirely,[46] and we have already mastered it. Ada's spirit can make it faster than before," Otis said.

Levi frowned. He wasn't as comfortable as Otis was with the spirit world. The glowing skulls tapped into the general etheric world, but they'd tried that with the Bufonite with lousy results. It seemed like the machine needed something more. Otis had suggested using spirit to tap into the creative part of the cosmos. Spirit like Ada's. The empathic old woman with the ability to read your emotions like an open book. Levi could still hear her quiet sobs when she realized she was going to die. Again, Levi felt a twinge of pain, but it had to be done.

"Are you sure we can't use the already dead and the common?" Levi held his breath, wishing again that the answer would change.

"No, the forgotten are diminishing and the angry are uncontrollable. We need a stronger connection to whatever we are tapping into, and the specials seem to do the trick. I'm not entirely sure why, but I have been doing some experiments with our failed projects, and I think it's something to do with passion for life or the ability to change the physical world. Ada's empathy could shape all of us. She could manipulate those she saw—"

"Not Margaret, though." Levi cut his words short, thinking back to when they'd had this same conversation years ago, when the working Bufonite had been only a distant dream.

"No. She's... I don't know what she is, but she's not normal. She gets past their barriers. And I'm sure she enjoys the hunt and the killing part." Otis shook his head in disgust.

"Yes," Levi managed to say. Margaret's unique skillset was necessary. There was no denying that.

"What are you going to tell her?" Otis asked.

"Margaret?"

"No, Rose."

"About the specials, and you? We'd better not. That's too

---

46   Wheat has more genomes than humans do, just to be clear about who is more
      perplexing here.

risky. They wouldn't invest in a stolen patented technology." Levi was sure they would if they could get away with it. Loopholes about overseas laws and so on. Good lawyers could work miracles with regulations and their wording.[47] Chipping away their integrity a bit at a time. And one day, the whole house of cards would collapse, and what was left behind would be civil disorder or some form of slavery where those with enough money and power could dictate everything to their liking. Levi was going to be a winner in that game.

"She'll want to know how we do it. I'm sure she and her associates will make a connection to the skulls. That's how our minds are made. We know the dead power everything we come across. There's nothing else in Necropolis except death and the undead. It took me years to understand that we necromancers are nothing but slaves to cater to their needs the way the Necromantic Council demands. I wouldn't be surprised to find an undead sitting at the head of the organization. A hushed-up secret," Otis hissed.

Levi searched again for the coin and had to content himself with rubbing his beard again.

"Not here. All Rose witnesses here on my home soil is science making progress. The weaving machines, the newly found compounds like dynamite, the scheduled buses; the list is endless. She'll be blinded by all of this, and I can give her a detailed account of the mechanics. If what you say holds true, they are ever more willing to believe science will triumph over necromancy. They will have more leverage."

"Then you'd better add steam to the mix to make it look like the usual progress and not the old she already knows. You are right; that's why they have sent her here—to profit from the rising conflict of manmade or undead-made to machine-made. Yes, she and the Worthwrites know the machines will win. They want their own Bufonite back on their home soil. But when necromancers have a look at it, they'll sense the dead," Otis warned.

"Then why did you insist on going along with her?"

"To be honest, I didn't think that far ahead. I'll find out whether the man she came with is a necromancer or possesses other powers we don't necessarily want around the Bufonite..." Otis let his thoughts trail off.

---

47 Worse than witches casting curses.

"And the Necromantic Council won't want anything to come from here to their home soil. It will dilute their power and rule. It might even shake the core of the whole government. The ultimate rule of necromancers." Otis began to smile slightly as he said that.

"I would think that would be a bad thing for you as well?" Levi stated.

"Oh, yes. A bad thing, indeed. If you don't mind, I'll leave you for now. I just had an idea of how we can amplify the spiritual power in the machines. I need to test it. You'll find me in my room," Otis said, jumping up from the couch's armrest, not waiting for a response.

Levi had underestimated the man's desire for freedom. He had been more than willing to run away with Levi and get out from under the rule of the Necromantic Council. How far would he go to hide from them? Levi couldn't let the man flee, not with his secrets. Levi needed his necromantic expertise, but Otis needed Levi's mechanical and chemical understanding. He might as well tinker with it, having closed the shop early. Also, in his heart, he knew that the original Bufonite was fully mechanically forged from the laws of physics and chemistry. Not spiritual. Not magical. No maidens and their blood involved. Just pure science from the secret formula of the universe, that one mathematical pattern to explain everything. It had to be there. Maybe hidden in the nuts and bolts of the human soul. There had to be a reasonable explanation for why Otis could alter the balance between life and death, and what he was and wished to be. Or why his sister could hide in plain sight.

Levi flipped his notebook open and dropped to his knees next to the coffee table. He turned the Bufonite over and opened the panel underneath, revealing a closed system of blue and green liquids made out of his chemical cocktail, with the spirit trapped inside. The spirit was forever in flux inside the tubes, governing the pulls and pushes in the belly of the device. A perpetual motion machine, as he'd intended. Itself a miracle. Mechanics he wouldn't share with the rest of the world. Levi smiled and leaned over the device. If the universe was made out of nothing and yet had come to be, then how? The world and everything in it either was, or it wasn't. The two stages that governed everything. But what if they weren't mutually exclusive? What if he, Rose, Otis, or his sister was and wasn't at the same time? What if the barriers their skins were made of weren't as solid?

No, Levi thought. Now he was rushing onward, not stopping to assess any of his statements. Leaps, that was why he was stuck with Otis and would share the profits with the bank. Leaps were the surest path to a wrong conclusion and destruction.

Go back to the basics, he thought. Energy was the source of everything, yes. Without it, there were no humans, no life. For plants, there was photosynthesis. To the naked eye, part of them came out of nothing, but that was a lie. There was an interaction with sunlight, and sunlight was something.

The spirits were like that sunlight. To replace them, he needed another source of power.

Levi began to scribble in his open notebook. Later, he would have to make a supply run to see if an order could be placed—a big one.

"But what is quintessence, which seems to govern the whole of creation?" Levi muttered to himself.

Life can be unbearably silly, frivolous, light, and yet heavy, like a stone dragging you beneath the current, drowning you when you are looking away—one occurrence at a time. Life doesn't have to match reality; it can live in imagination and be as real as a small pebble in your shoe and as annoying without contradiction. The same could be said of societies, both the original kind and those that laid their eggs in another bird's nest and expected them to take care of their offspring, or like a bird that steals everything and takes care of nothing. But this was not about societies.

This was about Sigourney, who hadn't told Siarl when they'd retired to their hotel room that Margaret the birdwatcher had been there again. She tried to push the thought away, but it didn't leave her. Not even the next morning. She could still see the eyepatch and that smile. Sigourney had a sickening feeling in her stomach. And the Rabbit hadn't come back either. Usually, the Rabbit found them after his excursions, but not last night. Then again, he was a god, and he should be fine as long as there were no other gods or Harriet Stowes around.

She shouldn't worry. Her paranoia was just on overdrive. Sigourney corrected her posture on the couch, watching as Siarl moved around the room, doing his morning chores. Push-ups here and there. Washing after his morning exercises. Getting dressed. Muttering something about luck and how it never left him alone, how it was still pulsing through his veins. Something had happened during his morning jog, and Sigourney wasn't sure what. He'd refused to say, or more like avoided giving her a straight answer.

Sigourney clasped her hands around her knees and rocked back and forth. After eating her breakfast of blueberry waffles and cleaning herself up a bit, she had been ready ages ago. It had taken her fifteen minutes.

"What do you want to do today?" Siarl had stopped his pacing and interrupted her thoughts. "Do you want to see your family?"

Sigourney took a tighter hold of her knees, stopping the rocking, gazing out through the open windows at the sunlit rooftops.

"No," she said. "I'd rather do what we discussed and do the rest tomorrow or the day after."

"Are you sure? It will—" Siarl began.

"Yes, we can let luck guide us through the day and forget the rest. Who knows what we'll see and hear," Sigourney interrupted him.

"Sigourney," he warned her, seeing past her words.

She looked at him from under her eyebrows. "I'm sorry. That was a cheap shot, I know. But I promise I'm not saying this to avoid anything, only to take a moment for just us, as you asked for and as I want. Everything will change when I see my family, and we won't have time for just the two of us."

"If that's what you genuinely think, then yes, let's find me that suit. Actually, I would prefer to be wearing one upon meeting your folks."

Sigourney gave him a funny look, and he looked away.

"Are you ready to go, or do you need to..." He let her surmise the rest.

"I'm fine." Sigourney released her legs and stood up. "Let me just get my jacket."

"It's a warm day—"

"I'm never without it." And she wasn't. There wasn't a day she hadn't worn her moss-green jacket. It was worn out and patched in so many places it was hardly even the same jacket any longer, but she couldn't let it go. Not when it had been with her up on freezing mountains. It had been under all the layers of fur, but with her nevertheless. And the last time she'd washed it, she'd sat there waiting for it to dry, watching as the river flowed by and dreaming about the clouds, the birds, the soft sunlight, and inner harmony. The Rabbit and Siarl had gone to the nearby city to get supplies, daring for once to leave her alone.

Sigourney put on the jacket over a short-sleeved white blouse, matching her grayish traveler's pants.

"Here," Siarl said and tossed Sigourney her greenish cap.

She snatched it and pulled it on. Then she followed him out, noting that Siarl had dressed in his best travel suit, which made him look like a street thug. Something better than workman's clothes, but not good enough to make him part of this society.

On the way down to the lobby, they passed a fancy couple. The woman's confident poise and briefcase made Sigourney wonder whether life would be a lot simpler if she was like her. The woman held herself like someone who never doubted her own existence. Never thought she was a phantom of someone else's imagination.

They made their way to the front door, Sigourney occasionally glancing behind at the woman, hearing her talk with a posh accent. Sigourney lost her train of thought when the outside world greeted her with a harsh reality—the eyepatch woman was back. She leaned against the corner of the opposite building. Almost hard to spot, but not to someone with a seventh sense for danger. The woman was no longer wearing trousers. She wore a beige traveling dress. Clearly, she wanted to blend in with the crowd. No one would choose such clothes to make a statement.

Sigourney seized Siarl's arm and nodded towards the corner.

"Okay, maybe you are right," Siarl said. Nothing else had to be added.

It was too late to hide; Margaret had spotted them. They moved across the street. The woman smirked at them and pushed herself off the wall, heading to the alleyway away from the hotel.

Sigourney squeezed Siarl's hand, and he responded. They

would follow her for now and see where Margaret was leading them. The responding squeeze also meant, *I should have listened to you earlier. I'm sorry, Sigourney.*

They sped up their steps as Margaret took longer strides. She knew they were behind her, but the eyepatch woman didn't run, didn't zigzag through the street erratically. She moved with calm determination, taking them deeper into the city, away from the more clamorous parts. The shop windows turned into lodging houses, and here people wore everyday clothes. Some of the factory workers had missing fingers, while others had nasty scars on their faces. The signs were there—everything was going to be taken over by two words: faster and cheaper, latching on to all systems like a parasite. Even to nursing homes, driving people to early graves.[48]

Siarl sighed next to her, and Sigourney knew why. He wanted to stop to chat with the men and women they had seen and figure out how he could better their lives and further the progress they worked with. That was Siarl for you. He was made to solve problems, and not only to please people. But Margaret was pushing deeper into the narrow streets. Siarl kept turning his head, undoubtedly taking everything in. Sigourney didn't care to look around. Her chest already felt tight, because some time ago, the neighborhood had gotten familiar. They were heading to the older part of town. Something bigger and nastier than a family reunion was transpiring in front of her, and luck had made sure it would come to find her. She was sure of that. She wasn't sure whose luck this was. Maybe something had happened to the Rabbit. He hadn't come back, after all.

"Sigourney," Siarl said in a low tone.

"What?" she snapped. She hadn't meant to. It was just that her mind was too occupied, and when that happened, she wasn't always able to control what came out of her mouth.

"I think we are being followed." He glanced over his shoulder. "Those four men have been tailing us ever since we left the hotel. I'm sure."

Sigourney dared a quick side glance. Siarl was right. There were four men after them, and they weren't even trying to hide the fact. The men kept their eyes on them. Sigourney

---

48   Both the patients and the nurses. If that even has to be pointed out.

turned her attention forward again, watching Margaret slow down, and only because their steps were slowing down. Somehow, they had ended up in a weird limbo, where they did the hunting while they were being hunted. Sigourney began to chew her lower lip. If they hid now and headed away, they would lose the birdwatcher woman and possibly fail to rescue the Rabbit from whatever sticky situation he had gotten himself into. But the four men looked like they meant business. Sigourney had lived on the streets long enough to know when there was a concealed pipe inside a sleeve. Why would anyone want to rob them? But sometimes people were desperate enough to do stupid things.

"Do it," Siarl whispered.

And she did. She tugged him into a side alley to make it appear as if they were fleeing from everyone. She heard the men start to run, and she guessed Margaret had also spun around. But when they were out of view, she hid them, and they pushed themselves against a boarding house's wall to wait.

In no time, the men rushed in, with Margaret not too far behind. She was the reason why the men didn't run past Sigourney and Siarl. She made them spin around to face her.

"Who are you?" one of the men said as Margaret blocked the exit.

"I could ask you the same," the woman said cautiously, a hint of scorn in her voice.

"What did you do with the girl and the boy?" the man spat back, clearly not that clever.

"I'm the one who got here after you. So I could ask you the same question." Margaret sang her words out.

"Don't play clever with me," the man growled. The others next to him stiffened, and one of them let a carved pipe drop down from his sleeve to his hand.

"Oh, we are going to play this game. I like this game." Margaret laughed.

That made the men nervous. It wasn't supposed to go this way. The woman should have coughed up and run. Then there was the fact that logically, she couldn't have done anything to the girl and the boy, because she was the last to arrive. But sometimes, logic was only a distant notion when immediacy and emotions took over. Now those same emotions were saying *flee, the woman is crazy*, but such an idea was swept away by their sense of self-worth. No one was going to make a fool out of them. Let alone a woman in a beige suit.

One of the men took a step forward. Margaret didn't budge.

Siarl was about to let go of Sigourney's hand and go to the woman's rescue, but Sigourney squeezed harder and shook her head.

It was a good thing, because as the first man swung his pipe at Margaret, she quickly took hold of the man's arm and slammed it against the wall. There was a loud crack, and the man wailed. He dropped the pipe, which rattled against the cobblestones and clattered away from him. Margaret drove her knee into the man's crotch, and all will to fight left him.

He collapsed on the ground.

His friends had been looking on thus far, astonished at how things had gone, but now they were shaking themselves out of it. They were still set on that same path of maintaining self-esteem at any cost. But they weren't as stupid as their friend, who had attacked alone. They came together, which later, when their brains played catch-up, might dent their sense of self-esteem.

Margaret pushed her right arm into the air as a stop sign, and the man coming from that direction froze. Her smirk seemed to say, *"You wait there. I'll come to you soon enough."*

The first one to reach her felt her left hand tighten around his throat and found himself being lifted. Margaret crushed the man's windpipe, and his legs began to kick rapidly underneath him. He gurgled.

The third of the attackers was wiser than his companions, and he turned around and ran.

Margaret dropped the man to the ground. His throat oozed blood where her fingers had punctured the flesh. His body twitched, but it was clear enough he would soon be dead.

Only then did Margaret release the remaining man. She bashed his head against the wall. The bone cracked against the bricks as if made of porcelain. The man slumped against the wall. If he survived the incident, he would need more than a miracle to make him functional in a world without modern medicine or rehabilitation plans.

Margaret stood there, admiring her handiwork.

"I know you are here, my little prey. My little sister. But we can play games if you like. As you see, I like games. But don't worry, I don't plan to kill you. Oh no, I don't. I have much better things planned for you. But as I'm a lady, and in the name of good fun, I'll leave you for now. I'll find you later. Maybe tonight, maybe tomorrow. But I will find you, now I have gotten your scent. And how sweet it is, my little prey, my little sister." With those words, the woman spun around and ran out of the alley.

Soon enough, the city's finest poured into the street. More people than just Siarl and Sigourney had witnessed the incident, and they had alerted the full cavalry. There were six men in blue uniforms.

Sigourney tugged Siarl's hand, wanting to leave, but he refused. He dragged her to the first man, whose hand was broken in several places. But it wasn't him Siarl was after. He knelt down and took the pipe, which no one was paying any attention to. Then he nodded to indicate that they could leave. When they were out of earshot, he said, "I recognize this. The Rabbit is in big trouble."

11

THE SEEDS OF CHANGE IN THE
UNCERTAINTY

he Rabbit god of luck waited for Justice to say *it* aloud. To say what she wanted of him. Deep down, he knew why he was here, sitting on the couch in front of her, being measured, challenged, and probed to act the right way. He hated acting the right way. The Rabbit didn't believe in the right way. Such a concept seemed to vary from one person to the next. A little bit of chaos and chance was what made life exciting. Not that he liked this part of luck, when once in a blue moon it favored someone else's needs over him. Okay, it made life interesting, but gods and interesting were a volatile cocktail, which always left behind a headache and the big question: why.

Mathew took in shallow breaths next to him. The Rabbit was sure the hotel owner was seeing more than a mere mortal should, and his tiny brain wasn't sure what to make of any of this. The Rabbit felt lousy. His moral duty was to save the human from all this and get him back to his reality.[49] The Rabbit opened his mouth.

Justice interrupted him. She said, "It will start from here in full force, and if we stop the industrial revolution now, the flight might not spread onward for decades. It's our duty to stop the change for the humans' and our sake. Think about how the world would be without spirit. Without belief! With just money, power, and mechanics governing humans. They will kill each other and themselves, maybe not tomorrow, maybe not in hundreds of years, but one day there will be none, and everything will be bare and dead, and you and I can't escape to other realities, as we are nothing more than the memory of these creatures. We'll linger here as a past curse on a dead planet. You owe it to humans to act. Lepus, with your powers, we can alter the future. The key is in your veins. It always has been; you just refuse to use it for anything bigger than a card game."

Yep, she'd collected her momentum and gone insane.

"Justice, you can't know that. Humans have surprised us time and again. They might make something beautiful." He opposed her out of spite, not quite believing his own words. But humans did surprise. Sometimes they were more than they could be, demanding better from themselves as a collective and not only as individuals, and things changed. Sometimes for good, occasionally for the worse, not seeing all the webs the social connectivity was made of.

Justice snorted. "I can feel the wrongness being done here in my bones."

And they say Justice is blind, the Rabbit thought.

"We shouldn't intervene. Humans have a right to do as they please," he tried again.

"No, we are gods; our nature is to intervene," Justice retorted. "Or have you forgotten what it is to be powerful, living all these years here among the humans, fulfilling the wishes of that... that... girl, Sigourney?"

"Leave her out of this," the Rabbit growled. Rabbits could do that too. If you think of a soft, cute version of the creature and combine the picture with the strength of a forest king and the spite of a wolverine, there's the growl the Rabbit was making.

---

49   If he was in the mood to be noble. Moods are important; they can make armies march.

But Justice didn't flinch. She had heard worse. She had been there when the lands roared and drowned under the blood of men; she had been there when the cries of a child went unheard, and the wail of hunger filled the air. One modest growl from an individual was nothing.

"That is entirely up to you," she replied.

"But you are Justice! You wouldn't do that," he persisted.

"Haven't you heard what I'm capable of? According to humans, I can punish, torture, and kill, and it's all fine if it's in the name of ideology. In the name of righteousness. As far as I'm concerned, I have free rein to do whatever I want." Justice stood up, her high heels clicking against the floor.

The Rabbit shuddered. "You have changed."

"You have to change with the times," Justice said.

"No, you don't. You could rally against this revolution of yours. You have incorporated so much of it inside yourself, and I don't mean in a good way." The Rabbit twitched his nose. Justice was right, though. The change was happening, and this pimped-up version of herself was proof of that.

"Sometimes you have to be bad to get the desired outcome, especially when they are trying to build it again," she replied and snapped her fingers. A group of men rushed into the room.

They had pipes in their hands, and to the Rabbit's horror, he recognized the items. He'd stared at those same carved metallic bars for longer than he cared to remember from inside Harriet Stowe's birdcage.

"Those should have been destroyed," he gasped. "She promised."

"They weren't. And when you look long enough, what you need reveals itself and plans get formed," Justice said.

"You planned this?" the Rabbit asked and jumped up. There was no doubt anymore that she had led him here, and he had let her. He should have smelled her handiwork from miles away. Gods were not subtle. Far from it. They were pampered kids fulfilling their every whim, convincing themselves that it was for the good of others. There were always arguments to advance any side. A way to twist even torture and murder to serve a purpose, wiping away the evil.

"Sit down. I have to insist. No, I didn't plan to get you here or make you come. While you and our fellow gods were invested in that pointless war, I was concerned with bigger things, seeing to it that I took care of all the loose ends. You included. There's no point in fighting, Lepus. If you help my Luddites and me, you'll see the world will again be a good place to live. There's no reason to harvest the humans for their blood and bask in that glory for another decade while doing nothing and bickering with our sisters and brothers. So in a way, you are right about being here among the humans and living inside their thoughts and hearts. But Sigourney's love for you won't be enough. She will die, and she's just one person. Join us, and there's no need for violence, and you and I can go on." Justice offered him her hand.

The Rabbit laughed aloud. His voice filled the room as he changed from an old man to a towering rabbit that hovered above Justice's men. The hotel owner took cover and leaped behind the couch.

"You're choosing the wrong path, and if you think luck will help you, think again," she said, grimacing as the laughter rang in the room.

"Why wouldn't luck help me?" he snorted.

"Don't kid me. I can sense you are tapped out. You have been using it irresponsibly. Such a rare commodity, one that can make a difference in the world, and you use it for what?" Justice asked.

"That was just some small-time gambling back there," the Rabbit said.

"I don't mean that. You have harnessed it to mold the lives of others to help Sigourney and the other human. I imagine that took a toll, so sit down, and there's no need for this," she said, waving her hands at the men, who stood menacingly with their pipes.

The Rabbit could remember the electric shocks that made his whole body freeze, the pain, the fear, the hatred, and the control the metal entailed.

He looked at the couch, at Mathew crouched behind it, at the men, and then at Justice. The Rabbit hated doing what others asked of him.

He leaped at the closest man, planting his hind leg against the man's chest. The Rabbit caught him by surprise, making the henchman fly into the wall. His pipe dropped to the floor, clanging as it went. The Rabbit wanted to dive at the pipe and take the weapon, but it would only zap him and keep zapping him until he let go. He turned around instead to face the approaching men. He made a quick calculation and arrived at the number fifteen. The unfortunate unconscious man had been number sixteen.

The men blocked his exit. He glanced around to see if there was another way out, but there were no windows.

He glanced back at Justice. She had taken out huge handcuffs and leg irons made from the same inscribed metal as the pipes. The Rabbit felt mortified by how low Justice had stooped.

"Stop this, and we don't have to use these," she said, dangling the torments from his worst nightmares in the air.

If she thought a threat would motivate him to cooperate, that was a lousy miscalculation of any sane living person's thought process. Such an act would only make him want to fight more. As happened to be the case with so many who came before and after him.

The Rabbit brushed his paws against his arms to feel the remaining sparks of his luck and lifted them into fists, covering his face and waiting for the men to make their move.

The first two who dared to part from their colleagues stumbled over their own feet, whose shoelaces had oddly enough got tangled by themselves. The men hit their heads against the pipes as they went down, passing out.

Justice laughed in the background.

Mathew gasped.

The next men weren't as unfortunate. This time five men left the group and rushed towards him with their pipes. No one tripped. No one hit each other with their pipes. Not at least until the Rabbit darted into the fray and got underfoot. When he did that, three men were struck by their coworkers, but the others managed direct hits, and he could feel the powerful electricity jolting his muscles.

They spasmed.

The Rabbit stumbled but got away without additional contact, searching for his balance. But his flight was short. The remaining eight men were still between him and the door, and behind him were the three other men who were already highly excited about the contact they'd made.

Finally, the men got the hang of this attack thing and decided that for the protagonist not to flee, they'd have to pile on him together and not go in as easily defeated twos and threes.

The Rabbit felt seven simultaneous blows all over his body as he took out four men with one swoop of his right paw, knocking them over like bowling pins.

The first two went down instantly, but the two others staggered, trying to get a sense of what had just happened and go back to doing what they were doing, which was a bit hazy now. They looked at the pipes and then around the room and then at their feet and finally at each other. One of them collapsed, his sensible brain deciding enough violence had been done. The other rushed back in to attack the Rabbit. So did the remaining seven men, who kept hitting the Rabbit repeatedly.

The Rabbit swung around to make his huge paw sing some more, as he didn't have enough room to kick the men with his sturdy hind legs. But as he landed another punch, he heard a click underneath him and felt a slight electronic zap. The leg irons snapped around his ankles. Justice looked up at him, giving him a sweet, seductive smile. The Rabbit staggered under the momentum of his swing. He fell against the floor, accompanied by a loud thud.

"Now get me the humans," Justice growled.

"I'm not with him," the hotel owner wailed.

"Not you, silly. The girl and the boy.

Rose heard the cards shuffling against each other, dice rolling, and the rest of the cacophony of the gambling house. Her mouth felt dry, but she didn't dare take a sip from the drink she'd nursed for the better part of three hours. She wondered whether she should glance at her cards again and try to read the mood of the room, ascertain whether the other players had gods, cats, or humans in their hand. It would be too much of a giveaway, she decided, and kept her pose the same. There in the middle of the table was a big pile of chips, and among them was the alchemist's gold coin. She wasn't sure how it had gotten there, but... there was no excuse. She couldn't take it back. Not according to the rules of the game, her own dignity, or because of the fact that Justice's men were looking at her. Abigail included. Rose felt alone, unsure, and her world was spinning out of control.[50]

Yet she had a pretty okay hand, and there was a chance she could win this round. It comprised three cats and four humans with feline affiliation. No gods, or the system's servitude would collapse. But if anyone had one god with six of the right kind of humans, it would top it all. She massaged her left wrist and instantly regretted it. The woman opposite her made a note of it. She had to own it. Rose continued massaging her wrist. She had been losing rounds, bleeding money, but now she could feel the win. It had to come. It would get her in the black.

The man next to her was stalling the game. He was debating whether to go all in or fold. People were getting restless.

Why from the bottomless sea had she put the gold coin in?

The answer was painfully simple. She'd had full trust in her cards a moment ago.

"For gods' sake, choose already, man." Another player hit his fists against the table, making the chips clatter.

Novice, Rose thought.

"I'm all in," the man who had been stalling said. He put his cards on the table and pushed in a stack of blue chips.

The other player stared the man in the eye.

"I'm out," he said.

Rose felt ready to puke. But this was no time to let her emotions cut in. If her cards weren't going to do the talking, then it was going to be bluffing that got her out of this.

Rose relaxed her body, gazing around the table to see what the others would do. All her chips, along with the coin, were in.

Two other players folded instantly after the man's declaration. There were only three of them left. The man next to her, the woman who'd seen Rose massage her wrist, and her.

"I double," the woman said.

"It's all in or..." the dealer said.

Rose was sure the woman snarled.

"Out," she said, and got up from her chair, not even wanting to see the result. She stormed out of the room with

---

50   The usual human experience, especially if you kept everything to yourself.

her remaining chips.

"Two cats, three cat lovers, and two gods," the man said, showing his cards.

Rose shut her eyes and took a deep breath in. "Three cats and four cat lovers," she said, opening her eyes and flipping the cards face-side up.

The whole room fell silent.

Rose dared to glance at the man.

He nodded to her, and she stooped in to scoop the chips towards her. Ever so casually, she pushed the gold coin into her vest pocket. She stood up and said,

"I believe that's it for me. Next time, gentlemen and ladies. It was a pleasure." Part of her wanted to continue—this might be the beginning of a winning streak. But the gold coin burned in her pocket, and the usual wait for reward and the dopamine rush were replaced by the bigger gamble: Levi and the machine.

Abigail stopped her before she left the room.

"Drink?" the woman asked.

"I'd better not. A raincheck? I have to get back to the hotel." Rose let the woman open the door for her.

"Of course. I'll send one of the boys to go to the hotel with you. You can't be too careful." Abigail trailed after her.

The rest of the gambling house felt odd, as if it was full of energy. The earlier feeling of desperation and used-up luck was gone, and people were more than eager to spend their money and test their fortune.

"That's unnecessary. I can manage," Rose said.

"Don't be silly. This is not about that." Abigail took hold of her arm, stopping her next to a roulette table. "Is something wrong?"

Rose shook her head. "I'm just tired. I had a long day."

"All the more reason to let one of the boys take you back to the hotel. Let me do this for you."

Rose wasn't in an arguing mood. She left Abigail behind after exchanging the chips for money. At the hotel, she tried to stay under Percy's radar to give herself room to think. But the man finally found her. She was eating a slice of apple pie with ice cream when he made his ambush at the hotel's restaurant. He looked flustered as he sat down opposite her. Rose wondered how long she could delay starting a conversation with him and how long it would take the diligent man to explode. She had blown up all their carefully laid plans, and now she was enjoying her dessert. It had to be killing him. Not the dessert, but the silence. Percy was the kind of person who didn't eat sweets—the kind of person you should think twice before trusting, at least in Rose's opinion. Desserts were an important part of life. The little enjoyments that made it worth your while.

"I have—" Percy began.

"All in due time. Do you want some?" Rose pushed her plate towards him.

He got that horrified look on his face when someone goes against all conventions and offers them a plate of germs.[51]

"Never mind then. More for me." Rose took the plate back and resumed eating.

"Stop—"

Any moment now, he would explode.

Rose wasn't sure why she tormented him so much. An act of revenge for the long voyage here? He'd made her suffer through tedious hours with him as he'd laid out the rules. The endless rules. And she couldn't ignore that at every turn he'd showed apparent readiness for backstabbing. Sure, it could be her mind playing tricks on her, but she'd rather be paranoid than be sorry later.[52] Or maybe it was just the only entertainment she could enjoy to wipe away all that had happened today. She had to lash out at someone, and Percy was the only one who might be able to endure one of her moods. There was so much pent-up energy inside her from carrying all the responsibilities on her own.

"Toying with you? No, I'm just collecting my thoughts on where to begin. I had an eventful day," Rose said, sounding apologetic, or as apologetic as she could make herself appear, which would sound false to someone who wasn't as emotionally cold as Percy.

"You should have come to see me as soon as you got back like we agreed. I could have been doing something useful instead of worrying that you had been robbed and murdered." Percy's features softened, and his stiff shoulders relaxed a little. Not much, but enough for Rose to be sure

---

51 Those things that make you think, what if humans are nothing but massive vessels for their parasites? And so it goes.

52 Two words: self-fulfilling prophecy.

they were sailing in safer waters when there was the thought of murder and mayhem. Such things brought up familiar and warm feelings to any true Necropolitan.

Yet Rose didn't think for a second that he had been worried about her dying. More like about not being able to control the situation combined with the suspense of not knowing.

"I should have, but..." Rose couldn't quite figure out what to tell him. She was still trying to piece together the odd encounter with Levi. Was he what he professed himself to be, or a charlatan perhaps? But she had the proof, didn't she? Then there was Justice and her offer. And gambling, and the money in her briefcase.

"How did it go with Miss Briggs?" Percy interrupted.

Of course he knew the bureaucrat had been a she and not a he. Had he told her? No. He'd let her go in unprepared.

"Not well, I'm afraid. It seems like she needs a lease or a building permit before she can start to process our papers. A permanent address, so to speak."

"How—"

"New guidelines, and she's one of those fastidious kinds of civil servants. There was no going past her or bribing her," Rose said before he could start a litany of questions. Should she add that a new friend was looking into it? That would make Percy even more suspicious, and maybe he would even report back to the Worthwrites. She couldn't go home, not now. Not when the city might be full of people like Levi.

"And the hotel address wasn't enough?" Percy asked solemnly.

Rose hadn't even thought about that. She should have. Kraken shit. It might have gotten them past the clauses and into building a bank. She was sure it would have. And the woman had surely left that out purposely. Rose kind of wanted to tip her hat to the bureaucrat. She'd had Rose's number pegged and played her like the pied piper guiding the rats to their doom.

"Not an option," Rose said, her stomach feeling tight. It could be the apple pie, but she highly doubted it.

"That gives an unfair advantage to those already established in the city," Percy snarled. He laid his diary on the table and flipped it open. "We'd better contact our lawyer and have him look at the new guideline and see if there's a way past it. Did you get us a new time slot?"

"On purpose, no doubt. Our new time to request the permit is a month from now, nine a.m.," Rose said, carefully pronouncing every syllable.

She watched as Percy penned the date and time into his diary. Everything would be much easier if the man were on her side.[53]

"Tomorrow, we will go and see Mr. Cumberbatch. He will sort this out. There's no way they can treat us like this. Should we go over the buildings I visited?" Percy lifted his gaze and laid his pen on the notebook. Where Levi's notes had been beautifully descriptive, written in cursive, decorated with all the ornaments and details the machines would have, Percy's were methodical, full of charts, dates, and times, composed of short sentences.

"Yes, of course. Tell me that there's some good news, at least! That there's a place that's up to the Worthwrites' standards." Rose finished the last forkful of the apple pie and regretted it instantly. She couldn't order a new one, not when Percy was there. She deliberately left out Justice's offer, not trusting it in the first place. Feeling it was an offer she should refuse. The woman would have too much control over her, especially since she knew her secrets. Rose wanted to scream, or at least order that second pie and make sure she could momentarily forget everything. Sometimes it was better just to eat pie, run, sleep, binge-watch something—birds, maybe? Their flight soothed the senses.

"There are two possibilities, and that's why I needed to see you instantly—to have your input and put in an offer. The rental market is heating up. All the available buildings and spaces in the inner city go in a heartbeat," Percy lectured.

Rose couldn't quite believe that, but then again, Percy never exaggerated. Never during this trip had she heard him stating anything other than the facts. The man truly had a stick lodged somewhere deep in his innards. Even a thorough shaking wouldn't make it fall out. Maybe she should share with him all that had happened today, as it was lonely to fight alone. And as a bonus, it would surely evoke some sort of emotion inside the man. Also, she *did* have an obligation to share the news with him, there was that, but...

---

53 Not that she had ever let him be on her side.

"We won't leave here without a working bank. But we can't put down an offer on any of those locations yet. I have to check a few things first," Rose said, trying to stay as vague as she could yet offer him something. Risky, she thought, but it was high time she started to make executive decisions. The first question was, should they add a floor for Levi at the bank? A secure place to hold him and the machines. Under their control. Levi might not agree, but they could make him sign a contract in the name of safety.[54]

Instantly, Percy's face became solemn. Those severe eyes of his squinted, as if he was trying to understand what was going on inside Rose's head. Not a task she recommended to anyone. *She* didn't know what made her tick half the time.

"Shall I reserve the locations anyway? The markets are what they are, and if we don't act, we might end up with nothing," Percy said.

"I trust your judgment. Start the negotiations for those with enough space. Not as grand as the one in Necropolis; more like the branch at Northen Yslands," Rose replied and waved the waiter over. "And Percy, a heated market isn't a good enough reason to make rash decisions. We don't want to end up with anything that will jeopardize our future, so no promises. Only due diligence."

"Hm," the man let out. "As you wish. The one at Chick Pea Avenue would be ideal both location and size-wise."

"If you say so."

"But then again, the other ones are on Back Alevin Road. They are smaller but closer to the other banks, with a higher asking price," Percy continued.

"How much smaller? And are we talking about vacant lots or buildings?" Rose asked.

"Buildings. The plots I went to see were almost out of the city compound, and while the city center might migrate in the future, it'll be a long time from now. Also, I believe it's four thousand eight hundred square feet smaller, and it's missing two additional stories," Percy said.

"How many floors are we talking?" Rose asked.

Percy was interrupted by the waiter, who had finally noticed Rose.

"Was everything to your liking?"

---

54   You could get away with anything in the name of safety.

"Perfect. I'm finished and happy. Add my food bill to the Worthwrite account," Rose said and stood up.

"Of course, madam," the man said and wrote something in his open notebook. "Will there be anything more?"

"Thank you, but I'm good," Rose replied.

The waiter soon hurried off.

Percy took his diary and pen from the table and followed Rose out of the restaurant.

"Four," Percy said behind her.

"Four is not bad; it might prove difficult later, if and when we get the bank running, but the additional two could make a difference, as I have exciting news," Rose said. She had decided. She needed to confide in someone or else she would burst. Back at home, it had been her girlfriend Magda. Here, she was all on her own, and Percy was the closest thing to a girlfriend she could find. Abigail was no help. "But I'd better share it with you in my room. And we can always buy the neighboring buildings if necessary." She was feeling a lot better. It had to be the pie.

"Yes, of course."

They made their way to the upper floors. Rose listening to Percy's quiet, almost absent breathing. He was fit, and despite considering herself in perfect shape for her age and size, she was breathing laboriously as she moved up the five flights of stairs. What did she know about the man anyway? That he'd started working at the bank just before he got this assignment. That he had been in accounting and was moving to the banking side of the business when he had been assigned to go with her. That was almost all she knew about him. Except that he lived alone and was in the prime of his life, twenty-four years old. That much she had been able to fish out.

Rose opened the door to her room to let Percy in. He looked uncomfortable, fidgeting in the doorway as if he was committing some heinous act. Rose couldn't help but sigh for the waste of such a handsome face and nicely formed body. He stepped in nevertheless, taking his place near the exit, letting Rose make her way to sit at the foot of her bed.

She shrugged the thought off.

"Yes," he replied and was about to open his book again.

"Put that away," Rose ordered.

He stopped and glanced at her from under his eyebrows.

"You can remember it. I'm sure of that. What I'm about to

say needs your full attention," Rose said. She could feel her heart thumping against her chest. But she knew she couldn't do anything without Percy, and she needed Levi's contract secured as soon as possible.

"Yes?" he groaned.

"I found us a potential client. I believe he deserves as much money as we can spare straight away. You remember the parcel you gave me this morning? It had the complete roster of businesses in the city, and one caught my eye," Rose said. "I know what you must be thinking, but to me, this is more than we expected. The Worthwrites didn't only send us here to set up a branch and expect our clients to march in. They wanted me to find worthwhile investments in the new technology, and I have done just that. What would you say about these?" Rose reached for the gold coin in her vest pocket and tossed it to Percy.

He caught it with ease, even though she had thrown it too high and fast.

"What about it?" Percy asked, opening his fingers and looking into his palm.

"What is it?" Rose asked.

Percy frowned, surely trying to work out how Rose was trying to make a joke out of him.

"It's your common gold coin without any markings. The weight is right and the texture as well, if I'm not mistaken."

"No, not at all. What about these?" she asked and took the bag full of wheat from her briefcase, where she had ever so carelessly left it. This time Rose took it to him.

"Seeds? My agricultural knowledge is too limited to tell what kind of seeds they might be," Percy answered after opening the bag.

"It's wheat. What if I told you the same machine made both of these out of nothing?" Rose asked.

"Then I would say someone took you for a fool," Percy stated.

"I would say that too if I hadn't seen it with my own eyes at the Alchemist's Shop," Rose said, still gazing into his eyes.

"Impossible," he snorted.

"My first thought as well. But I was mistaken. This is true, and we are going to invest in it after we have made sure I wasn't played. It's even more pressing to get the bank licensed so we can claim Mr. Perri's invention as ours. His machine will change the game, and we are not going to let it pass through our hands."

"Too good to be true," Percy insisted.

"Probably. Still, it's better to see it through. So, get me a meeting with Mr. Cumberbatch and find me an expert," Rose said.

Percy made no move. Not towards the door or to open his diary.

"Do I make myself clear?" Rose asked.

"Yes." With those words, Percy left her alone.

She made her way back to the bed and collapsed on it. The room was spinning, and Rose with it.

12

WHAT IF THE UNIVERSE WAS IN A TEACHING MOOD?

Any pursuit needs dedication, that single-minded determination. But others often see it as obsessive, destructive, silly... The thing is, when the person succeeds, the tone changes. "Oh, I always told you to carry on. You will get there." But before that, it had been, "Do something reasonable. Stop dreaming and get a job." "Get a better job." "You'll never make it, so stop being so bloody single-minded. Get that head of yours out of the clouds and be like the rest of us."

Levi had never been like the rest of them. But he had been one of those lucky ones no one had bothered with. He had done it all alone. Contrary to what Sigourney thought, their parents had never given him a second thought. They might have taken his side in arguments, but he was treated with the same lack of care, love, and attention. "Useless extra mouths," as their father had once said. All this had forced him to see that money and independence made a huge difference. Alchemy had secured both these things, up to a point.

Once again, he woke up sprawled on top of his work desk. The house was quiet, and the gas lamp was glowing faintly, about to go out. The Bufonite lay on its side in front of him, and Levi watched the bluish light of the tubes flicker. The light of Ada's spirit, as he liked to remind himself sometimes. Ada's death had been unfortunate but necessary. Maybe all the machines should be named after the dead... no, too obvious.

Levi pushed up from the table, and his stiff back reminded him that he wasn't young any longer. Everything started to go downhill when you turned thirty. The little aches didn't go away as easily. They preferred to nestle inside the body as a constant reminder of your mortality, in case you happened to forget. Would immortality make man's life less cruel? Would he be less self-indulgent if there was no need to worry about death and dying?

Others might see what he did as evil. They might say that he took lives for his own purposes, seeing souls as an instrument. Levi knew there was no ethical way around it. But it would be unreasonable to answer the question of the greater good and whether the end justified the means too easily. Sometimes people had to be sacrificed so everyone else could move forward and survive. Also, a very twisted mind might argue that specials received an unfair grace from the universe, and still they wasted their talents. Think of Humphrey Chadwick—or number five, as Margaret called him. He could use his clairvoyance for good, yet he was a showman, a charlatan, after money and fame. He could have bet on the future and won, and at the same time invest the money in small business, creating more jobs, increasing the general well-being. But what did he do? He took messages from the great beyond, told tales about tall, handsome strangers, and what else? Repeated over and over again that Aunt Nelly is looking after you, so there's no need to worry whether Lance is a good husband or not. Aunt will make sure nothing goes wrong, and soon there will be kiddies running around named Nelly, Cinnamon, and Lance Jr.

What a waste.

Yet it was his life to have and misuse, even if he could use his talents to improves the circumstances of others. Think of a world where everyone had their independence. A time where it didn't matter if you were born into a good family, on a resource-rich continent, and at the right moment. He could equalize it all during his lifetime. A personal Bufonite for all. He would be forever remembered. He who spared lives, he who corrected the injustice as he wiped away the resources game that the rich played at the expense of men and women like his father and mother. A game that was random, illogical, and destructive.

Think of his alchemy business. He sold expensive dyes for those with enough money to throw it at arbitrary things. But they were not arbitrary—the right kind of color, demeanor, and showiness ensured positions, favors, power. Never in his youth could he have dreamed of spending his hard-earn money as a farmhand on a bottle of dye that cost more than a week's worth of food and a book every now and then. That extra money someone spent on color could feed and educate the poor. The world was unjust. And he wasn't even thinking about the number of resources allocated to guns and steel. Germs, he understood—those needed guardians. Even plants and animals got sick. But what if his machine could cure all of those? The possibilities were endless.

Levi woke from his thoughts. The back door opened and closed. He jumped up from the chair and headed to the kitchen. He was alarmed for nothing. Otis made his way through the room, making more noise than he usually did.

"Otis," he said, stopping the man. The necromancer looked startled. "Where have you been?"

"At the Hotel Earl, finding things out."

Levi moved past the doorstep to the kitchen.

Otis shook his head. "It doesn't look good. I should have stopped you from talking to Miss Pettyshare. The man she's traveling with isn't normal. I followed him through the night, and he has been busy, trying to find the hidden necromancers and witches to send them home, not to mention the nasty werewolves and vampires who step past the boundaries. I thought I was careful, but he sniffed me out. I'm not sure how and what he is, but he managed to see past the spirits I sent to check him out. He made no move to do anything about them, but I'm sure he felt them."

Levi wanted to ask, are you sure? But Otis knew his Necropolitans and their dark arts, so he didn't.

"Did he follow you here?" he asked instead.

"No, I don't think so. I was careful. It took me..." Otis fished a pocket watch out of his vest. "More than five hours to make sure the tracks wouldn't lead him here."

"Hmm," Levi said. "Useful special, or something else?"

"Definitely something else. He's powerful."

"A necromancer?"

"No, that I'm sure of. I can detect one miles away. Hexer, witch...? Banks use them, but so does the Necromantic Council, as hunters. Kraken shit, I hate witches." Otis pulled a kitchen stool out from under the table with his foot and slumped down.

"What now?" All this was beyond him.

"Now we make sure he'll never see the machine and me. He could be just a common clerk, but he might be more, and he might be willing to report back to the Council. Every Necropolitan knows you don't have necromancers overseas. It's bad for business. You might get a loan necromancer, but only if a government asks, and with a hefty price. You wouldn't find them working inside an alchemy shop." Otis snagged the basket Evelyn had left on the table. He flipped a beige cloth off and reached for a loaf of bread. He bit in, munching away under Levi's gaze.

All this was like something from those Penny Dreadfuls people loved. The whole idea of werewolves, vampires, ghouls, undead, gargoyles, witches, and other monsters was amusing. A figment of an overactive imagination. But then he'd sailed to Necropolis, and there they had been, up and about in the daylight, going about their business like any living, breathing human being would.

"There can't be werewolves and vampires here," he said, more to himself than for Otis' sake.

"Why not? They are their own people and can do as they please." Otis shrugged.

"But—"

"They are not under the Council's jurisdiction. I don't think they would dare to try to control them." Otis had a smug smile on his face.

"I thought they were restricted to Necropolis. That your monster hunter force sought and fought any fugitives? Or so I heard," Levi stated. They were getting off track, but he couldn't pretend this didn't interest him. The whole concept of Necropolis was insane, and it shouldn't exist.

"Only those who misbehave, and if you ask me, who are they to forbid werewolves or any other 'monster' for that matter to act as their nature dictates. But it's a silly urban myth that werewolves hunt down humans to eat. We smell like spoiled meat, or so my friends tell me. Also, vampires are not interested in virgins. Something to do with the fainting, and they're too young and frivolous for their liking. A woman or man in their eighties, now there's someone to have a conversation with." Otis still had that smirk on his face.

The man was toying with him. Another thing he'd noticed Necropolitans did, treating you like an imbecile just because you didn't happen to know the local customs.

"Anyway, it might be better if I left town for a while to wait for the dust to settle." Otis changed the subject after reading Levi's mood.

"Out of the question. If we are going into full production, I'll need your expertise. And we have the specials to look after."

"Then what? We need to sort out this fellow Miss Pettyshare is traveling with." Otis had finished eating. Now he was looking back at Levi with heavy eyes.

The man was scared. It was disturbing; Levi had rarely seen him this concerned. Even when they'd faked his death, Otis had been jovial about it. Now, there were deep wrinkles on the man's forehead at the thought of having to go back and face the Council.

"Could Margaret handle him?" Levi asked.

"I honestly don't know what the woman is capable of. She might be. But—"

Levi finished the sentence for him. "But we don't want to kill the man. That would raise too many questions. Still, I think we'd better send her to figure out who the man is. Better her than..."

He never got to finish his sentence as Margaret came crashing in through the back door, and she wasn't alone. On her shoulder, she carried an unconscious bald man.

"A welcome committee just for me?" Margaret smirked. Before Levi or Otis could piece together the situation, she continued, lifting the man's head so they could see. "This here is Barnabas Wyat, number six, or Barny among friends. He was a sneaky little devil to find, hiding inside people's dreams and heads, playing peeking games through others' eyes. But you can find all sorts when you have time and are taking a stroll around the docks. Unfortunately, he sniffed a little too much to be present at this lovely gathering. Where would you like me to put him?"

There was a tight knot in Levi's stomach, and he felt the need to puke, but he kept himself under control.

"There's a free room in the basement. But I thought you —"

"Miss Corran can wait. Extra presents are always fun, and our Barny here is powerful and docile. You'll like him."
Together they went down, Otis helping Margaret to carry the man. Levi kept his distance.
They lowered the man onto a straw mattress. Margaret pushed a metal bowl next to the bed with her foot, anticipating the effects of the narcotics she'd used.

"All nice and delivered," she said as Levi locked the door behind them.

The wood on the door and the walls around them was carved with symbols to lessen the specials' skills. Otis had tied spirits into the markings to make them effective. The necromancer had fished the wards out of one of his books, and Levi couldn't deny their effectiveness. Ada's empathetic waves had been confined in her room. So had Edith's hallucinations. Edith was the third person Margaret had taken.

"Did we really need another one? We already have two," Otis stated when they had made their way back to the work desk where the Bufonite lay open.

"Ada might have been a fluke, and we have failed before. We need to get this right if we are still trying to get Rose Pettyshare to fund us."

"No, I have the process pegged now," Otis groaned. "It's a bit different compared to the computing skulls, as they don't need a power source, only connection to each other and to the mainframe. The Bufonite needs to tap into their life-force to produce new data and not just read the existing data and speculate from that. After Ada, I can repeat the process blindfolded to make any soul run in the mechanical circulation and follow simple commands."

Neither of them heard Margaret say, "This one is free of charge. I needed to blow off some steam and have fun."

"What about the expanded supplies? Do you think we

can make the process work on that scale?" Levi asked.

"Commands are easy. We are already past the hard part. We only need data input with clear, readable instructions, and that's your department. Switches don't work. It has to be a more complex input system. But whatever you come up with, I can teach the spirit to read and produce."

"Like yes and no?" Levi said aloud, more to himself than to   Otis, who frowned.

"I–" the man began.

"Not yes and no. More like ones and zeros that form a wider sequence that will tell the reader what is requested. Like zero, zero, zero, one is a gold coin. Zero, zero, one, zero could be an ingot or something along those lines. A whole new language with pre-existing symbols and syntax." Levi didn't notice, but Otis was shaking his head.

"Whatever floats your boat. Go for it," Otis said. "I'd better head to bed."

"So," Margaret interrupted the conversation.

"Yes, the payment, of course. I'll get it, and yes, Otis, go to bed."

"Sure thing, boss," Otis answered. Before he left, he asked,   "What about the man?"

"I'll deal with it. Sleep tight, Mr. Thurston."

When Otis was gone, Levi asked, "And Sigourney? The lighthouse? What did you find out?"

"Waste of time. Number five must have seen the past or the future and not the present." Margaret took a seat next to the Bufonite and played with the minuscule screwdriver, tapping her eyepatch.

Levi sighed with a mixture of disappointment and relief. He reserved the right to be indecisive and irrational, just like any other human being. Not that he allowed such a luxury to others. In them, it irritated him. A lot.

"Do you mind me hanging around for a bit after you get my money?[55] I could use one of Evelyn's home-cooked meals." She flipped the tool in the air and caught it before it hit the open machine and its delicate glass tubes.

"Be my guest, as long as you do it upstairs. And before I get you the money, I have another task for you. Our possible investor has an associate called Percy Allread, and he might

---

55   Who was she to say no if they offered to pay?

turn out to be problematic. I want you to find out everything about him and contain him," Levi said, doing his best not to snatch the screwdriver from the woman's hand.

"Sure thing, *boss*. So, light torture and then off with the head? Or..." Margaret didn't finish, leaving Levi to imagine the rest.

Levi was sure he heard gaiety in her voice. The overly helpful and light tone she always used when she had something nasty in mind. Of course, it could be because this was the easiest way to make Evelyn cook for her. The woman could eat a horse if someone let her. And Levi was sure the woman had no other place to call hers.

"I'd prefer the or. Just the information for now. Then we can revisit those thoughts. But I'd better get you that money now."

"Take your time."

Decisions can be impossible. You could go after the running lady or follow the steel. There Sigourney stood, watching as the officers collected the men Margaret had murdered. Unsure what decisions she, they, had to make here. If Siarl was right, the men had something to do with Harriet Stowe and the cage she'd used to keep the Rabbit imprisoned. But it didn't make sense that Harriet would send her men after the Rabbit and them. Harriet knew she could always ask if she needed a favor. They were friends, after all.

Truthfully there was no actual decision to be made. Margaret was gone, but she would be back. Sigourney was sure the woman hadn't lied about having her scent and the ability to hunt her down with it. If someone who could crush a man's windpipe says they can do something, you believe them.

"How are we supposed to find him?" Sigourney asked.

"Let's get out of here, and you can do the usual trick." Siarl took hold of her hand and pulled her back towards the hotel.

They made their way to the busy street without saying a word. A solemn atmosphere followed them around. Both of them had seen their share of people dying, but the brutal murders were not quite what they wanted to witness.

"I'm sorry, Sigourney. I should have believed you when you said something wasn't right."

"Don't worry about it. How could have you known?" She gently squeezed his hand. Sometimes she wondered if it was a blessing that the only way to hide others was by touch. It was such a perfect excuse to feel the warmth of another living being. She liked holding hands with Siarl. His were like alien hands that felt familiar, like her own, yet not attached to her.

"I—" Siarl began.

"Please, don't. You don't always have to be so perfect and correct all the mistakes made by you or others. Everything is fine."

They made it to the hotel's street corner. Past that there was a little opening where they sold vegetables, cakes, fruits, drinks, you name it. Sigourney bought a massive stack of carrots from a vendor, an older lady with her grandson. They were kind enough not to try any chitchat, just money and produce changing hands. Siarl insisted on buying a couple of nectarines to ease the hot weather. It was the right call. As soon as Sigourney bit into the flesh, the sugary taste was a welcome relief. It stopped her body from shaking. She hadn't noticed it was doing so.

"To the rooftop?" Siarl pointed at the hotel's roof.

"Better not. What if there are more of them?"

"Okay. You choose one then."

She chose the one over a barber's shop. They climbed up the ladder attached to the building's wall. The flat roof was secluded, but someone had built a flower garden among the chimneys, and little bees and butterflies were busy at their work. It was a pleasant place to finish their nectarines and set up for the Rabbit's summoning.

Summoning sounded as if there was chanting and complex rituals involved, but it was quite simple. Sigourney lowered the carrots onto the roof's surface.

"Lepus Cornutus Bonnee, I bought carrots for you. We'll wait here for you. Please, come. This is important."

That was it. The Rabbit had superhuman hearing, and he'd insisted it was tuned to detect Sigourney and Siarl speaking anytime they needed him. In the past, it had always worked.

They made themselves comfortable and sat there to wait. While the Rabbit had superhuman hearing and, in his godly form, could outrun any locomotive, he still couldn't manifest himself if asked. He was quite sorry about that, saying that in truth, it was the humans' fault, because of what they thought a rabbit or luck could do. If he could, he would. When he was in one of his moods, he would joke about starting a religion to right the wrong.

Usually, it took a few hours, and he would be there, never stalling too long. The carrots always did the trick. He couldn't decline, and Sigourney had become an expert at choosing the juiciest ones. But there was no sign of him. The day was turning into evening, and Sigourney had dozed off. Siarl woke her up.

"He's not here."

Sigourney rubbed her eyes, trying to adjust herself to a reality where the Rabbit didn't come to the rescue.

"Something must have happened to him. Do you think...?"

"No, this won't be Harriet's doing. She vowed, and I believe her. This is something else. We have to find him. And... and I think the only way to do that is through luck." He looked sheepish when he spoke.

Sigourney didn't press him. She was too riddled with her own faults to be brave enough to point out the ones others had. Also, it wasn't nice when you had to do something you detested or refused to do with all your heart, especially when others were as gracious about it as a herd of elephants on a rampage. You had the urge to stomp your feet, scream, and let your fists do the talking when people saw fit to point their fingers at you and laugh, "See. See. You are swallowing your words. We always knew you would have to," or something along those lines. That was just plain nasty—the everyday evils that ate away the spirit.

"You are right," Sigourney replied. "So?"

"We should find scarves and then go from there," Siarl said, looking away from her, still uncomfortable with the situation. Nevertheless, he was doing it.

When they got down from the rooftop, the carrots with them, they decided not to head to the hotel. There might be more men with pipes waiting for them, making this whole situation even more awkward. What had the Rabbit gotten himself into?

They found the marketplace on Oastwich Square, which

was busy and crowded. All around them, the people spoke different languages. Siarl instantly went into a dream-like trance and began observing the bustle. Sigourney instead took deep breaths, trying to survive one ordeal at a time. She reminded herself that this was only excitement she was feeling and not anxiety, but the market was too much for her to believe in her reprogramming attempt.

They continued down the path past the booths, where you could buy almost anything machine or human-wise, but not produce. That was sold down at the harbor and in other smaller markets along the streets. This place was for the extra. Meant for those with abundance, who could buy something new and not wear hand-me-downs. Most people in the city relied on second-, third-, and fifth-hand goods. While the machines were making everything faster and cheaper and money was making its way into broader use, it wasn't yet to the point where the world was a parade of mass-production and consumption. That would come later, changing the concepts of freedom and individualism, and offering hedonistic pursuits as the meaning of life.[56]

Sigourney noted that there were no beggars on the streets. This would be the ideal place for them. This was where she had been just before leaving home, collecting enough money to buy her freedom. Now, as she thought about it, she wasn't sure if she'd witnessed anyone begging in the city. Not even at the locomotive station. Maybe things were truly getting better with all the new, shiny things she saw. But the unfortunate truth was that she was mistaken; she was only seeing very clever policing. Then again, you could argue about the cleverness part, and the policing as well. So it went. Out of sight, out of mind, or how did the saying go—see no evil, hear no evil, speak no evil. All doable by following the first rule: turn a blind eye. But the thing was, it wasn't only the poorest of the poor who got dealt a bad hand, who were missing legs and arms or were deformed, either from birth or from malnutrition. It was also the workers, or should it be said the ex-workers. Life was the ultimate price to pay, and when your lungs were full of dust, it was only a matter of when the old fellow in the hood came calling your name. In the meantime, you had to eat.

---

56 Don't mind the gaping hole where the sense of belonging would have been.

Still, everyone—the police officers and the good, law-abiding citizens—was mistaken. The people were there, but unseen. It was like the man with deep wrinkles, greasy, messy hair, maybe one or two teeth missing, and dirty jeans and a dark blue jacket leaning against a darkened doorway—barely noticeable, yet there. One person makes your heart squeeze into a tight ball, but then suddenly there's a release, and only a fleeting memory as a woman in a luscious beige wool coat and too much perfume brushes past you and you are caught up in a new sensation.

But Sigourney saw both of them twisted up in her sensory input. The downside of her anxiety. She saw everything and couldn't put anything behind her. He breathing became more laborious, and she took a tighter hold of her green jacket. This was why she preferred the woods, the mountains, the little brooks, and the vast oceans. There, life seemed to be rooted in a nostalgic reality, in the so-called basics. It was easier to remember what life was all about when the birds sang their mating songs.[57]

"Breathe," Siarl said.

Sigourney followed his command and let the air out. Only now did she notice that he'd produced a map in his hand and was navigating the streets towards another awkward, anxiety-riddled moment. For the Rabbit, she thought.

"Siarl," she exhaled.

He took her into his embrace, and together they found a vendor who sold scarves, bags, shirts, and everything one could hope for relatively cheaply. Siarl bought her a green scarf and himself a black one. Not the ones the vendor tried to push on them, but the more refined ones from the back. When he showed the money, the disbelieving vendor gave up and sold them the beautifully woven scarfs.

If they had paid closer attention to the vendor, they would have noticed that he wasn't your ordinary immigrant. He had pointy fangs. So did some of the customers in the market, along with pointed, hairy ears. Threebeanvalley, to Levi's horror, had indeed started to draw in vampires, werewolves, gargoyles,[58] and ghouls, but the latter stayed out of the

---

57   Not that Sigourney was that keen on the mating part herself, but good for them, the birds.

58   People just thought someone had terrible taste and were too happy about the

humans' way, knowing they wouldn't be welcomed, not when even the beautiful and muscular peculiars had to hide their true nature. Then there were the banshees, the winter folk, all of whom could be considered humankind. The peculiars were drawn into the city for the same reasons that humans came there: for work and money. Unfortunately, even the immortals needed capital to keep trotting on. But Sigourney and Siarl didn't pay attention.

A palm reader tried to lure them inside her tent as they stood there, trying to figure out their next move. Siarl politely shook his head.

"Maybe another time."

"Shouldn't we..." Sigourney began. She looked around and tried to force out the rest of the words.

A slender woman brushed past her, and Sigourney was filled with the sense of death and dying. For a moment, she saw all the humans having numbers, which seemed to tick away. The woman clicked her tongue as she walked away from them.[59]

"We can do it here. This is as good a place as any." Siarl offered the green scarf to her.

She took it and tied it around her eyes. He helped her to secure it better. Then he put his black scarf around his and took hold of her hand.

They swirled around, and when their feet chose a direction, they headed that way, letting the world guide them. Siarl had taken the lead, keeping them securely attached.

"Lepus," he kept mumbling under his breath, as if to make sure the capricious luck delivered something close to what they were looking for. The least they could hope for was a clue. The best outcome would be the whole Rabbit.

They tried not to let their bodies determine their way over the cobblestones. Luck had to be the one doing all the talking.

Sigourney's feet were already getting tired. They had left the market a long time ago and were on the quieter streets, from the feel of things. They heard snickers and shouts as they moved. There had been several attempts to rob them and even shove them under the upcoming traffic, but luck kept

missing pigeons to notice the gargoyle migration.

59   To prevent herself from letting out the death scream her nature insisted on.

them safe. The blindfolds stopped them from trying to intervene, thus causing calamity. Now, the universe would take care of everything. The robbers got run down by a carriage or one of those new steam-engine vehicles, which could be categorized as some form of mini-tank—without turrets, of course. The mockers got pooped on by the passing birds. Others got their dish served cold, so to speak. You could say luck was in a teaching mood.

The world went quiet as they took a left turn. Sigourney was sure they were in a narrow alleyway pressed in by walls on both sides. Nothing seemed to move. The air was somewhat clean, without the city's characteristic odors, but heavy, as if something untoward waited for anyone daring to venture farther. There was no turning back. Luck had guided them here, and here they would find where the Rabbit was.

"Watch where you are going," something huge and soft snorted as they ran into him.

Siarl winced next to her, and Sigourney guessed that someone huge and soft had laid his enormous hands on Siarl.

She took her scarf off, ready to kick the man, but opted out. The man was indeed huge and soft. Sigourney stared at his belly button, or where it should be under all the dark-gray clothing. Close to what the men who had attacked them had worn. Something between a gentleman and a street thug. And he wasn't alone. There was another man, and they were guarding a green door.

"Siarl," Sigourney said.

He took off his scarf. "We are ever so sorry. I had no intention of stepping on your toes. It was the universe guiding us to them, and I'm sure it should have warned us before such a travesty happened."

The man looked at Siarl the way people did: deciding whether to hit or laugh.

This time the man chose the third option, which was some form of snarl combined with a frown.

You could say Siarl was non-threatening, as the man was at least three times his size. No one ever took Siarl's muscles and straight back seriously. They too often thought he could be snapped in half with one swift movement. They would be surprised, as so many had been before them.

"Can I ask what this place is?" Siarl continued in his jovial tone.

The other man, behind the one whose toes had been crushed, shrugged.

"Gambling," he said, as if to explain everything, and it did.

They had come to the right place.

"Any chance we can go in and have a look-see?" Siarl gave his best smile.

"Not without capital." The man smirked back as if he'd won this round. Again, he was unsure about what it was a round of, but there was no mistaking that somehow the smaller man was having him.

"Would this help?" Siarl took a stack of banknotes out of his pocket. With luck on their side, money had become somewhat superfluous.

The men looked at each other. Sigourney was sure they were wondering if they should rob the tiny man. One of them pushed the door open, letting them in, having concluded that whoever was paying for them to stand there on the street for hours upon hours shouldn't be pissed off by foolish actions.

Sigourney and Siarl went into the gambling house. The door banged shut behind them. The whole room tingled with raw luck.

The Rabbit was here.

13

WHEN THE WORLD WAS FORMED

The Rabbit had been dragged across the gambling house's wooden floor and into the basement to be fattened like some prize pig. Not the kind of pig like the two kids who had not been able to distinguish sound construction from confectionary walls that would disappear at the first sign of rain. Anyone with half a brain would have known better than to enter. Mushroom houses the Rabbit could condone. They could be the next evolution in house building, at least in impoverished areas. Something to do with floating abilities and fire resistance. But gingerbread? Only an evil person would come up with something like that.

But here he was, trapped like the children had been. But Justice wasn't planning to fatten him with sugary delights. No, it was worse.

There came a quiet hum in front of him. He sat on an altar next to two golden bowls full of juicy, juicy carrots, where he could see the worshipers. At this precise moment, he hated Justice around the universe and back.

He felt the chanters' love and devotion pour into him.

Every hair on his body stood up and vibrated. Every cell felt like it was on the brink of exploding. It felt like that shake after holding a wee in for a long time and finally getting the anticipated release.

This was no way to treat a brother.

He could lose himself in the chanters' words. Be there forever and ever, thinking he deserved all the admiration. He would explode soon if all the powers in him didn't get a release. But he couldn't, not when he was trapped inside the chains that Harriet Stowe had so carelessly forged. Humans never thought through their plans and the ramifications. They always thought they were in control. What was the harm in making something destructive that was capable of wiping out entire civilizations? Because they knew they were the good guys, using it only to advance some divine plan their small brains had come up with. But no, humans and their self-entitlement never were much good at prognosticating what the future truly held.

The Rabbit half-wished to be back in Harriet's cage. Because while humans were insane and adept at putting their plans in motion, they were small-timers compared to the gods and their megalomaniac plans. At least humans couldn't fill a planet with living creatures that had competing motives and see what came of it while they prodded and used Pavlovian responses to add fuel to the fire. Perish the thought when humans found a way to do just that.

The Rabbit glanced over his shoulder. The hotel owner sat behind him, looking as hopeless as before. He had been muttering for hours straight about doom and impossibilities and bad luck. The last part was clearly addressed to him. It was the first time the Rabbit had been considered the harbinger of misery. Granted, he couldn't kid himself about it anymore. He and his powers were no good to anyone. That was why he had never been part of human lives or the gods' games. He was unreliable in every possible way and he knew it. Chaotic, you could say.

Past the chanters, who came and went in shifts, never leaving him alone without the resonating love, were the serious men who'd gotten a kick out of beating him and shackling him. They held the pipes in their hands, waiting for the Rabbit to make one mistake. He watched them with one eye open and the other concentrated on meditating.[60] The Rabbit knew he had to get out of here along with Mathew, but Justice had made it more than difficult.

The Rabbit opened both his eyes and heard a chanter in the first row gasp. He stood up to his full height and saw how the guards tensed up, ready to move. The stupidity of individual heroes was gone, and all the men and women looked at each other, nodding to indicate a plan, if and when the Rabbit acted.

He wanted to tear the shackles off, to release the power they kept pumping into him and wipe that smug plan off their faces, but Justice walked in at that same precise moment. Alerted in some cosmic way, or just her luck working against his.

Not fair, the Rabbit thought.

He watched the woman walk towards him, her perfect hips swaying from one side to the other. In the past, she'd stomped, not swayed like a canary.

He wasn't sure if he had ever despised anyone before. Feared, yes. An image of Gertrude, Tamtue, and Harriet Stowe popped up. The three standing shoulder to shoulder, looking at him and smiling at his downfall. Yet he'd pitied them and the actions they took to get what they wanted. But what Justice was doing was worse. Not because of the violence, no. Gertrude had threatened to cut off his huge velvety feet and use them as a conversation starter. Tamtue had wanted and would always want to eat him, as the snake god was his mortal enemy.[61] But it was only natural for the prey to think there were ways to co-exist with the predator. For some odd reason, predators never seemed to desire laws or taxation or any other guarantees against randomness with pointy teeth. Then there had been Harriet Stowe. She'd locked him inside a cage and kept him there for decades. If he weren't a deity, he would have gone mad, losing himself inside that tiny space, but he hadn't. The light beating that Justice had put him

---

60   Animals were better with split brain things. The right side of a pigeon's brain, for example, didn't tell the left what it saw.

61   Despite the Rabbit not seeing things that way. Mortal enemies were so last century. They had the United Gods (UG) constitution that Crit had come up with. A new step in the evolution of social affairs. Not that anyone wanted to use it. It was so much easier to force others into submission.

through in the office was nothing compared to what he had already experienced, but the thing that made this worse was what she had become, and that was what he hated. Her new personality would seep into the rest of humanity. Not that he cared to think about how it had gotten there in the first place.

The Rabbit saw the future, and he didn't like the picture it painted.

He smiled, creeping out his captors, even those with pipes in their hands. Now they'd joined their master, their queen, their god, trailing after her.

He had always thought if you can't beat them, join them. But this time, that little bit of madness, that dance between a joke and tragedy, was not something he would do.

"Justice," he said.

"Lepus, I see you are doing well." She gave him a smile. He did look good, didn't he? The smooth white and gray fur was slightly shinier. The aches in his bones were gone. And he felt like he could crush his enemies—which he didn't happen to have.

The Rabbit wanted to kick the orange silk cushions aside, which still bore his butt print, but such a small act of defiance was pointless. He kept his eyes locked on hers.

"You know why I have come," Justice stated.

He knew. It was the same story told over and over again. Who he was and would be was defined by what he could do for others. Justice, like Harriet Stowe, wanted him to stick out his paw for her and release luck into the woman's veins, so she could get what her heart desired.

"To have a chat." The Rabbit pushed his shoulder blades together, extending his height by a few inches.
There was a sigh of awe coming from in front and behind.

The Rabbit stopped himself from glancing back to see Mathew. It was a pity the mortal had gotten caught up in all of this. If the Rabbit had known, he would never have forced the man to come with him.

"So be it, if that's what it takes to get you to do as I want," Justice said, repeating the same argument she had used yesterday.

"You know my answer to that. I'd rather take the beating than give you an ounce of what's mine," the Rabbit said and meant it. Despite being shackled by the goddess of justice, he still had a say in where his luck went and didn't go. And he wasn't going to let her have it. If she'd asked nicely, sent him a polite letter stating her predicament, then maybe he would have loaned what was his to her, but now—not a human's chance in an apocalypse.

"There are worse things than a beating." Justice grimaced.

"Should I be saddened that my dear sister is threatening me with torture? That you have stooped this low?" The Rabbit made a move to sit down.

The whole room tensed. They watched him slowly make his way back onto the cushions and try to fold his legs into a lotus pose, having to abandon the idea due to the shackles.

"In times of war, we must call upon our courage to do what is necessary to secure the survival of those who matter, those who know what has to be done and are willing to do it for the future generations," Justice said. Behind her, the henchmen bobbed their heads along with her.

"Don't give me that bullshit. You are corrupted by their thoughts—you must see that, dear sister. When we sat around the campfires, you spoke about nobility, the sanctity of life, and not succumbing to evil. But here you are, speaking about what exactly?" the Rabbit asked.

"No one needs to get hurt; that's why I need your luck. Something is working its way out from this city, changing the fabric of humanity, changing our rule to the rule of machines and mechanics. And you can stop that without lives being wasted if you just give me your paw." Justice's beautiful face turned ugly from hatred and anger. All wrinkled, all red.

"So, it's me who's doing this? I'm the evil that stands in your way, giving you an excuse to do as you please. Send your men forth to light up their billysticks in that nice blue and purple. I can take the electrocution, I can endure the pain, but what I can't stand is the sight of you." The Rabbit lifted his chin, daring Justice to do what she so easily did—mix war, torture, and the thoughts of righteousness into one big mess that corrupted her soul, causing her to serve the path of hatred and anger instead of law and integrity.

Her henchmen stepped forward. She lifted her hand and stopped them from moving to attack him.

"You are mocking me. Once again, I beg you to see reason. Do not be blinded by humans. When they are done with you, when they have won, you'll be nothing but a furry little rabbit who'll die in one to two years. Is that what you want?"

"This is not about what I want. If you hadn't lost sight of who you are and why we came to be, you would see that as well." The Rabbit shut his eyes. He was done with her.

"Then have it your way. This is what you wish for. This is not me doing this to you; this is you doing it to yourself." Her tight words reached his enormous ears. He refused to open his eyes and look.

The first blow to his shoulder made him fall to his side. He curled up, covering his head with his great paws, and whimpered, to his own annoyance. Every time a carved pipe hit him, a shock made his whole body shake and then stiffen. His muscles trying to fight off the unwanted invasion.

He wasn't the only one whimpering. The hotel owner cried in pain a moment before each billystick hit the Rabbit's body, making things more painful. Anticipation was a killer.

All this felt odd, as the chanting never stopped. The Rabbit's name echoed through the cellar. And oh boy, did he see the irony of it all. He grinned, but soon it turned into an agonized grimace.

"Lepus, Lepus, Lepus..." they chanted, and the Rabbit wanted to kick the men down, leap up, and tear his sister's head off. He wasn't sure if he would have done it if the shackles weren't in place. He had never liked violence. Such a pointless way to use dominance to get what you wanted. There were easier ways, but a brutish soul with a damaged mind and low self-esteem might not see those subtle ways.

"There's a far worse destiny than this. My men have been following those two pets of yours. What if it was her instead of you feeling the blows?" Justice asked.

The Rabbit tried to force the words out past his tensed jaw muscles. The only sound he was able to make was a louder whimper.

"I thought as much," Justice said. "Step aside," she commanded her men.

The beating stopped.

"So, what do you think?" she asked, moving up the altar steps and offering her hand to him.

The Rabbit lifted his paw, and it slumped down hard on her hand, making her lose her grip on him. The paw smashed against the floor.

Justice said nothing. She knelt down and stroked his paw.

With one last effort, the Rabbit made sure he controlled his luck glands, giving her only a tiny sparkle. Still enough to make Justice feel the elation that always followed when luck poured into you.

When the transaction was over, she looked like she'd snorted a bag full of cocaine. She pushed up.

"Bring me the list," she shouted.

The Rabbit kept his eyes shut, thinking about being dead in one to two years. Not such a bad thing after all. At least no one could ever use him again. The conversation from yesterday looped inside his head.

"Since the dawn of time, the other gods and deities have wanted to use me for their own personal gain, but never you. I remember you telling me that such a thing was beneath your integrity. That when you have to stoop to use others to gain what is right, there's no reason to live. Have you changed your mind, dear sister?"

Justice had snorted. "I was an idealist back then. I know better now. The world doesn't work that way. To get your own justice, you have to do whatever is necessary for the outcome. And don't forget for a second, I'm doing this for you as well. You just don't see how much we have to lose." She had sounded sad more than angry.

A tear rolled down from the corner of the Rabbit's eye. He wondered whether this new Justice was formed from the minds of men or whether the men were formed from her mind. This was not a world he wanted to live in.

"What now?" a henchman asked.

"You'll see," Justice said. He could hear the smile in her voice. She'd found a target to attack, and the Rabbit hoped it wasn't the place where the change would begin. It was high time the gods were gone if this was what they were reduced to.

He listened to her heels click against the basement floor. Her men followed.

"Lepus! Lepus! Lepus!" the chanting continued.

"Are you okay?" A hand touched his shoulder.

The Rabbit cracked open his swollen eye and saw Mathew crouched next to him.

"I'll be fine. We'd better get you out of here."

"Lepus, Lepus, Lepus, Lepus..." The ostentatious love made him feel worse, especially as behind it, he heard the one who truly mattered call his name, and he could do nothing.

Rose had been trying to shake Percy off all morning, but he refused to leave her alone. She was sure he was more paranoid than usual. Always glancing over his shoulder, waiting for something. For what, she wasn't sure. The world to come to an end? There were those kinds of people who expected the worst all the time. She should have noticed that Percy was such a fellow, who expected the rich, layered cake in front of him to give him some bizarre disease and kill him on the spot, or the sunny morning to turn into a devastating storm that would wipe out the entire city and all that he held precious. But as she thought about Percy, who was brooding next to her, watching Threebeanvalley's university garden rise in front of them, she realized that the image she'd conjured didn't fit the man's personality. He wasn't hysterical, and he didn't hold anything precious. If he did, he hadn't cared to disclose it to her.

But he had been fidgety ever since they left the hotel and ever since they saw their lawyer, who promised to take a look at the new amendment and sort it out. He hadn't even left her alone with Abigail, eyeing every move they'd made. The whole fencing lesson had been a disaster. Percy had twitched every time Abigail's rapier had come close to Rose. So they'd cut the lesson short, and Rose hadn't got the chance to properly talk to the woman about Justice and the buildings she'd promised. She'd left her a handwritten note along with part of the roster, where she had struck off random names to indicate that they were of no interest to Justice and her merry band of brothers and sisters. The Alchemist's Shop was among them.

Percy once again glanced over his shoulder as they walked down the paved road.

"What is it?" Rose snapped.

He clearly didn't want to answer.

"Tell me. You can't keep clinging to me like this the whole time we are here. That will be disastrous for our mission." Not to mention to her side activities.

"There's something familiar working here. Something from back home." Percy was as stoic as he always was. Rose wanted to shake him. To mess up his perfect haircut. Something to make him less like an empty shell and more like a human being.

"I'm not sure what you mean. Has someone sent a competing bank here?" Rose took Percy by his arm to make him face her, but she instantly let go when his eyes met hers.

"If they have, they are playing dirty and going against the Council's rules." His eyes narrowed a little, and Rose wanted to look away. At least there had been emotion, no matter how unwanted and poisonous it had been. Rose didn't care much for the Council. Without it, she would be freer to make money.

"Stop being cryptic. What does the bloody Council have to do with anything?" Rose asked. She was fed up with all the power games the man was playing. If he was their lapdog, then she'd prefer him to be out in the open about it. All the hiding was unnecessary.

"Well—someone is using necromancy. I sensed something at the hotel, but whoever they were, they masked their trail well." Percy didn't look pleased. "And there was an attack last night. My room was ransacked, but they weren't expecting hexes or a witch. So they fled. I didn't see who they were. If I had to guess from the size, a female of some sort."

"Are you okay?" she asked, instantly worrying about Justice and her men. It could have been their doing, but why would they attack Percy? There was no reason. And why would they use a necromancer or someone similar?

He nodded.

She said more to assure herself than Percy, "It could have been a local with raw talent. Some do slip through the cracks."

There were such people. Rose knew that not all the necromancers they had at home were local. Many came from overseas to study there. Most likely coerced and pressured by the Council, although some came willingly. Raising the dead was a nasty business, and she was glad to be here, playing with the mechanical rather than the great beyond. Who knew what Kraken and other gods thought about the whole matter. The dead should stay dead. She had always thought that, but there was no reason to go declaring it out in the open. Not in

Necropolis, not if you wanted to do business. The dead were a highly profitable commodity. The most secure way to make money was through taxidermy. She guessed that it was the same with the living. But instead of stuffing parts that were flat and stitching parts that sagged, the doctors took care of sore throats and runny noses, cuts and broken bones. But who knew what lengths the living would go to when fixing cosmetic faults became possible for them as well. Humans were the vainest species she knew. Vainer than vampires.

"I highly doubt it. Not when they sent spirits to check us over and used the dark arts to attack me." Percy's voice shook her from her own thoughts.

"Who would be that foolish? Out in the open. But I didn't—" Rose began.

Percy glanced around. "No, you wouldn't. But this is not the time and place to talk about these things. People are already looking at us."

Percy was right. There was an extra pair of eyes on them, and not only because of Rose not wearing a corset and petticoat under her emerald dress, but also because of Percy. The man refused to wear anything other than black clothes. A white shirt would make a huge difference, but no, he was a witch, and there were standards when it came to his clothing. Also, his bird-skull necklace wasn't helping matters at all.

"Then charm them," Rose said out of spite, knowing the man wouldn't display his talents. Not here and not now. Only after an approval had been processed and double checked.

"We'd better move on. The specialist in material physics I requested has a short window to see us." Percy turned back to face the large building.

"Lead the way," Rose said, practicing the cheery tone of the locals.

They made their way through the campus. It was bigger than she'd thought from the outside, but nothing compared to Necropolis' university. There was also a considerable age difference. Everything shone with newness here.

It would be easy to think that all the marvelous inventions and thoughts kept people distracted enough not to be bothered by Percy and Rose, but that was too much to ask from humans. People kept staring at them everywhere they went. It was distracting her. Several times Rose glanced at her clothing, and gradually it began to dawn on her that she didn't fit either. She should have gone with meek. A fashion and mindset that will inherit the world, according to some. The general mood in the place of thought and novel ideas clearly agreed. Again, Rose was taken aback by how backward Threebeanvalley was. Was it that modern thoughts hadn't yet followed the booming economy and innovations, or was it the way of the land?

Clearly, she should dial down her continuous rocking of the boat. It was bad enough that she was a woman in a man's business.

If Percy minded the stares, he didn't let it show.

"Here we are," he said, stopping behind a door with a nameplate on it that said "Horatio Arlington."

Rose smiled and braced herself for being bored to death as Percy knocked on the door. She hoped the man inside was livelier than the exterior—a brown door with a milky-white glass window.

"Yes?" a hesitant voice asked.

Percy pushed the door open and said, "Good morning, sir. We have a ten o'clock meeting scheduled."

"Yes, yes, yes. Do come in," a man's voice said.

Percy pushed the door open wider. A man was doubled over a desk with measuring tools and an apparatus that looked like some elaborate version of a microscope. Rose half expected the man to be as ancient as the fossils she'd collected as a child on the seashore near her aunt's summer place, but Mr. Arlington was only ten years older than her, tops. Still, he bore that ancient look and voice as if they were second nature. As if the bones in his body were already creaking, and as if he was going through life in slow motion beneath the youthful mop of black hair and bright eyes that shone with keenness. Not the keenness of the company, but passion for the image shining through the microscope.

"Ah, Mr. Allread. I was waiting for you," he said. "What an interesting case you have brought in front of me. I have the samples you gave me here." The man became animated, and the years fell away.

Horatio Arlington looked concerned when he saw Rose stepping in.

"Good morning, Mr. Arlington," Rose said and tilted her head slightly as she had seen the noble-born women here do.

"And you might be?" the man asked bluntly.

"Let me introduce you to my boss, Miss Pettyshare. She's the one who secured the samples you are looking at," Percy said.

Rose wanted to kiss the man for that.

"Ah, yes. Interesting specimens you have here." Horatio turned back to look into the microscope's lens.

"But are they what they are meant to be?" Rose asked.

"That is a question we all seek to answer, and it is one of the most difficult. We can always entertain the thought that our perception is guided by our wishes and wants or that we only get partial glimpses of the world. That is why rigorous measuring is necessary. Then there is the school of thought that claims everything is fantasy, maybe an error in the cosmos or a dream or to some a nightmare sent to torment us by some great being that even measuring can't..." Horatio went on.

Percy cleared his throat.

"Yes, yes, yes. But the way you look at the matter, they are what you think them to be in a most peculiar way." Horatio lifted his head and gazed towards them.

"Fake?" Rose asked. Her chest felt tight.

"No, I wouldn't go that far. They are what they appear to be. I have tested the gold, and it acts like gold should. All the measurements are perfect. Perfect indeed. The purest gold I have ever come across. Like it was the mockup for all the other gold deposits. I am not sure if you get my meaning. It doesn't matter. I would be highly interested to know where this gold was dug up," Horatio said.

Rose smiled.

"Oh, yes. Silly me. Of course, you cannot disclose such secrets. But if you go back, you have to let me study the ground. Or at least send me a sample of the other minerals found in the area," Horatio said.

"May I ask why?" Rose asked.

"Yes, indeed, you can. To some, such a finding, or a place, might be the spot where our planet, world, creation began. Highly improbable, but worth a look." Horatio leaned forward.

"Based on the gold coin?" Rose asked.

"Not the coin alone. If the wheat grains are from the same area as well, maybe growing above the gold deposit, then we have a combination of a fascinating sort." Horatio smiled. It was that baffling kind of smile that came from deep within his inner life and was not meant for the onlookers.

"Why?" It was Percy who managed to ask before her. Until now, he had been immersed in taking notes in his diary, letting her lead.

"To the careless eye, the grains are grains. They are indeed wheat, as you instructed me to determine. They are. But what is remarkable is that they are all identical. Not a single mark on them is different. While nature makes copies—even humans can birth copies of themselves—it is rare. Very rare indeed, but possible. But this magnitude of copying without environmental markers and at this stage of the life cycle? Interesting. Also, they are perfect specimens, just like the gold coin." Horatio got up. "Now, was it Miss Pettyshare? Yes, I think it was. These are amazing finds you have made, and I must find out why and how they came to be in order to answer your question about their substance."

The man was making his way to her, slowly but steadily.

Rose felt like a slow-motion locomotive was coming at her, yet she couldn't jump out of the way. Not because she was petrified. Far from it. It was more like the locomotive was this strange creature, maybe a tortoise, and she had to see what would happen next. Would she indeed be injured when their orbits collided? Soon the man was next to her and had linked his arm around hers despite Percy stepping closer protectively.

"Let me take you to the cafeteria, and we can discuss how I can be helpful to you with your next step." Horatio patted her hand.

Rose wanted to laugh aloud. The fossil was more cunning than a past relic of a tortoise. She should have guessed. To survive academic life, you had to be more Machiavellian than those who loved science and progress cared to admit. A language she knew how to speak, but the thing was, the man had served his purpose for now. There was no way she was going to tell him how the items came into her possession.

Rose swallowed her laugh. "All in due time, Mr. Arlington. We have a tight schedule today. Money doesn't go around without some aid."

"Are you sure? I heard rumors that Mrs. Dacher made a batch of her famous fruit cake this morning." Horatio was trying to appeal to her nature as a woman. Rose was sure of that. One part of her wanted to agree. Saying no to cake was sacrilegious on so many levels that the social insult of the deed was the last thing on her mind.

"I'm afraid I'm sure. But we will keep you in mind when things progress." Rose disentangled herself from his clutches.

"Yes, yes, good. Would you mind if I kept the specimens?" the man asked.

"Again, I have to disappoint you. The items in question are the bank's property, and as a spokeswoman, I wouldn't be doing my duty if I let you keep them," Rose answered.

"I did not mean to put you in an awkward position. If you find more, please do bring the samples to me. There is so much hidden in them that..." Horatio sank into his own thoughts. This time, Rose wasn't sure if it was unintentional or for show. Also, she had a disconcerting feeling that the man hadn't said all he could say. That he'd found more in the mystery. But if she pressed on and she'd misread her hunch, it might embarrass her and him, or even worse, she'd end up boring herself to death when the man gave some sophisticated explanation of how material physics worked and why these samples made everything so exciting. Now that she thought about it, Horatio hadn't been wrong about the meaning of creation in a way. Levi might be tapping into more than technology and...

Rose was annoyed. There was the "and" just on the tip of her tongue, but she wasn't sure what that "and" was.

No, she would come back to this later. For now, they had to secure a contract with Levi before he showed his work to anyone else. This would make her rich. The Worthwrites too, of course. But she'd found the man, and she would make sure she controlled him, and no one else.

She was glad she'd lied to Abigail and Justice.

14

REWINDING LOOPS INSIDE THE
MECHANICAL DESTINIES

o Sigourney, the gambling house was like a dark pit of human fallacy. She saw despair and hope in the same faces competing for the light of day, all depending on how the cards lined up and the wheel span. Yet, like the Rabbit himself, for the other players, a rare win would be enough. They needed the high the anticipation gave them. It was never about winning. Okay, maybe initially, before getting sucked into this world, but afterward, the thrills came from the randomness of it all with a hint of possibility. Sigourney's stomach was already a roller coaster, so the extra ups and downs felt like her guts would burst open like some horrible alien creature. The Rabbit seemed to need this to feel alive. Maybe some people already had too much excitement and sought quiet places to calm themselves down, and those without that boost craved the rush of falling from a cliff with only a thin layer of fabric keeping them alive.

Dear Lepus, be alive, she thought.

At least the gambling house had dimmed lighting, hiding all the crannies and nooks, soothing Sigourney's sensors. Yet her hearing was amplified. Siarl breathed heavily next to her; the Rabbit had banned him from accompanying him to these places. The god had said that Siarl ruined the game. That counting cards and probabilities was cheating, especially when the boy took a rational approach to choosing the odds.

"Hm," Siarl let out.

"I can't see him," Sigourney said despite already seeing where this would lead.

"Yes, of course. Me neither. Let's split up and have a look. He's bound to be here, otherwise..." He didn't have to finish the thought.

They separated. Sigourney pushed to the back of the room, and Siarl circled to the left, away from the bar. Sigourney felt eyes upon her as she made her way around the place. She walked into a darkened corner, made sure no one was looking at her, and made herself disappear.

It was soon clear that the Rabbit wasn't in the front gambling parlor. Not in any of his many human forms. Sometimes he changed his appearance to fit the game's mood, from young to old, male to female, or anything in between. But there was one constant: his gray hair with white patches, as if he wanted to hold on to something that was genuinely him. Sigourney glanced around and noticed a heavily guarded corridor. It had to be where the private games were played. She searched for Siarl, spotting him sitting at one of the card tables.

She got angry—Siarl was taking this too lightly—and then she remembered he never took anything faintly. If he had his mind set on a task, he did his best to complete it, searching for the most logical solution. She hoped he was doing just that, and she left him alone, heading to the corridor.

The two huge men—who always appeared the same in whatever continent, city, universe they were in—didn't see her passing. They were busy eyeing the drunks, the unwanted, the poor, daring them to stay away. Sigourney tipped her green hat as she moved past them and smiled. There were times when she too could enjoy the little things that made you notice life was kind of silly. A whole lot silly, if you asked her when she had been singing obscene songs to lighten the mood and to remind herself that nothing was too serious; that all before her had lived and died, as would she and all those who came after her. Some were remembered past their eras,[62] while others faded away in a few generations.

The house, past the gambling parlor, was nice. There was a faint yellow light from the gas lamps. After the first two rooms, there were paintings on the walls and rugs on the floor that spoke of wear. Most of the pictures depicted the sea and ships. Very realistically, she might add.

Sigourney pressed her ear against all the closed doors, trying to hear if the Rabbit or anyone else was there. She heard card games being played, love being made, and people talking about serious matters, but as she wasn't that interested in politics, revolutions, and machines being destroyed, she moved past them. She had always thought people made a fuss about nothing most of the time. All problems could be fixed with a little bit of common sense and a whole lot of kindness. People just didn't do that. They wanted to have a bigger slice of the common cake, or preferably the whole thing. She felt more kinship with those who got theirs taken away, partly because her start hadn't been that great. Oh yes, she had had her cake, but it was one of those weird dried fruitcakes with all the leftover bits included, which no one dared to eat because it might choke you to death. Even that had been a very, very thin slice. But it was better than imaginary cake or one made out of gravel. Gravel that corrodes the intestines, so you gradually bled to death. But empty bellies ate anything, and they didn't have to fast to fit into the size-zero dress. This was why she hated humans and politics and anything social, really.

Behind her, she heard Siarl speaking in his overly friendly tone. He was being escorted by one of the employees. He had a stack of chips in his hands in a rainbow of colors.

"Where will this private game be? I must be lucky for you to suggest such an exclusive endeavor," he chatted away. Siarl could lie, although he liked to pretend he didn't.

They passed her. Sigourney brushed her hand on his sleeve so he would know she was there. He paused his chatter for a moment, but soon enough he picked it up and allowed himself to be guided through a door.

Sigourney peered behind them and was relieved to see an actual game going on and not some hidden torture chamber

---

62   Usually, those who dared to dream unspeakable things and change the world. A much easier way was to kill lots and lots of people while conquering the world.

for those who counted cards or were plain annoying, as Siarl could often be.

All along his plan had been to make his way to the high rollers table, knowing well that the Rabbit would be there, if he was here willingly.

Siarl mouthed, "I'll be fine," as the door closed.

Sigourney kept wandering the backrooms without result. She managed to find some sort of office, but a lot of good that did. The only thing she discovered was the flowery smell of perfume, making her remember Gertrude, the god who'd wanted to cut off the Rabbit's feet and make her a pet. But she couldn't be here.

She closed the office door behind her and made her way towards the basement. She froze as a stunning woman came up the stairs. She was surrounded by men and women who had masks on, and they were holding on to the same metal poles as before.

Not Harriet Stowe then, or Gertrude, but a god nevertheless. Sigourney could recognize gods when she saw them. There was a magical aura around them, and not because of their powers, no. The appeal came from their dyed-in-the-wool self-confidence. They knew their worth, they loved themselves, and they could make everyone obey their will. Or so they thought. But someone like Sigourney, with little love for the pompous and the self-serving, usually saw fit to stay away from such creatures and seek the company of those who didn't have that masters-of-the-universe attitude. The Rabbit didn't, and Sigourney was sure it was because he had been hunted all his life. Okay, if she was candid, there were times when the Rabbit liked to mess with the destinies of mortals, and she didn't much care for that. Siarl would do a victory lap if he knew she thought this way.

Sigourney pushed her back against the wall and held her breath as the god came closer. The woman suddenly stopped and looked around. Sigourney bit her lower lip, trying not to exist at all. Deep lines formed around the woman's eyes as she tried to piece together the odd sensation Sigourney's hiding left behind. The eerie sort.

The seconds seemed to stretch, turning into an eternity.

The moment was interrupted by Siarl walking down the corridor. This time he had a wooden box with him, which was full of chips. He was being escorted by two tough-looking henchmen, which in a way was an inaccurate description, as one of them was a woman. Her sex didn't lessen how tough she looked; quite the opposite. And despite Siarl's grin, this time around, they weren't taking him into another private game for those beings who saw all the cards and hands without opening their eyes or existing at all. They were taking him to meet the gambling house's justice, where counting cards was the highest offense one could commit. All clearly part of Siarl's plan; his grin told the tale.

When Justice's eyes met Siarl, she gestured for her masked men and women to move past her.

"You don't need me," she said. To the others, she added, "Take that boy to my office."

Siarl was manhandled and pushed towards the room where Sigourney had smelled the strong perfume. She could smell the same scent on the woman. A god indeed. They couldn't help but make themselves as alluring as they could. Sigourney was never one to care what was on the surface, especially now, as there was something nasty behind the god's eyes. She clearly had unseemly plans for Siarl and no doubt for the Rabbit too, which most likely included using luck.

"Where's the other one? The girl, Sigourney?" Justice asked as she walked towards Siarl. Her hips swayed as she walked.

Siarl held his breath.

Sigourney kept biting her lip. Not because the woman had called her name, but because when she and Siarl had met, he'd allowed himself to be spellbound by a divine beauty.

Siarl blinked. "She's not here. I'm all alone."

"You think I should believe that, boy?" The god crossed her arms.

"It's up to you what you believe. I can't decide such things for you."

"You are a lousy liar."

Siarl clutched the wooden box, managing to stop the chips from rattling.

"So, are you going to let him feel my wrath alone," she said scornfully, "or are you going to show yourself?"

Sigourney came out of hiding despite her whole body being petrified. The ache in her belly made her want to puke, but she couldn't let Siarl be taken. Not alone. There was nothing worse than being alone. She could see again the lightless prison pit where they'd kept her.

"There you are."

Behind the woman, Siarl shook his head. As always, he'd wanted to do the rescuing. His nature wouldn't permit anything else.

"Where's the Rabbit?" Sigourney asked, reminding herself that gods were people too in some perverted sense. And if you were bossy enough, you might get away with it all.

"Don't you worry about that. Now, would you two please step into my office and we can discuss the future together. I'm not an unreasonable person, and I'm sure we can find a solution we all can agree upon happily." She guided them into the office.

"Please make yourselves comfortable." Justice indicated the couch.

They sat side by side, Siarl laying the chip box next to him, already forgetting its existence.

"We would like to know where Lepus is, and to hear he's okay," Siarl began.

"The Rabbit means that much to you?" Justice sat on her desk, crossing her legs.

"Yes," Sigourney managed to utter. The idea of being bossy stuck inside her throat.

Siarl, meanwhile, was in the mood for one of his speeches. "Mistress, we can only guess what this is all about, but holding someone against their will and maybe using them for personal gain isn't a very noble thing to do—"

Justice laughed. "Oh dear me. Noble? Such a naive way to see things, but I will indulge you. This is about cooperation, and no one is going to grind him down, least of all me. I'm his sister, and I love that big-eared creature from the bottom of my heart. So I promise he's safe with me. You can call me Justice. Mistress sounds like something the cat dragged in and forgot."

"The Justice?" Siarl asked.

Sigourney couldn't help but notice his eyes sparkling.

"The one and only. You have heard about me, boy?" Justice leaned forward ever so slightly.

As vain as the other gods, Sigourney thought. Even the Rabbit.

"I have read about the personification of pure concepts like the Rabbit god of luck. It's such a fascinating idea that a being can come to life from all the wishes, dreams, wants, and beliefs bestowed upon them and use those to shape the world."

"Yes, there's that." Justice's eyes turned into thin lines, but as always, Siarl didn't pay attention. He was more of a word kind of guy compared to Sigourney, who was stuck in the realm of micro-expressions, over-analyzing every syllable.

"Do you change over time as human concepts alter? Can you control the concept of justice, or is it the other way around? The Rabbit refuses to speak with me about these things, saying—"

"That no mortal man should know the ways of the gods," Justice finished the sentence for him.

"Yes, that, but I truly see no harm, because if we can understand the dynamic between the mortals and the gods, we can use it for the common good..." Then he noticed what he was doing.

"What fascinating friends to die for," Justice remarked.

There it was, the truth. The Rabbit wasn't going along with his sister's plans. She, like all of them, was using him for his luck. That was why she had those pipes, billysticks. It was to hurt the god the only way she could.

"If you are hurting him..." Siarl jumped to his feet, about to add more, but Justice snapped, "Sit down," and he obeyed. There was something in the way the god said it. She had the backing of the whole book of law; all of them.

"I'm not hurting him any more than needed, and no one is killing anyone here. I'm not a murderer. I stand beside the victims. Nevertheless, he's willing to sacrifice his godhood for the two of you, for your kind. So, you see, it isn't me who is killing him. It's you. We can help each other there. If you love him, as it's painfully clear you do, convince him to help me locate Lord Bufonite's machine. It can't come to fruition."

Justice was clearly leaving something out. Too often people thought that because Sigourney was socially awkward she was either slow or snobbish. But she was actually quite a fast thinker, and if she had even an ounce of snobbishness, then maybe the social thing would go better. Moreover, she could smell the truth being bent here. It smelled like chocolate cake with arsenic. Yet the anxious part of her needed to ask, "What if she is right? What if it's me killing Lepus?"

Justice continued, "As I see it, you have two options. Find Lord Bufonite's machine and bring it to me and you can have Lepus back, or convince him to cooperate."

"What makes you think we can do that?" Siarl asked.

"The air around you tingles from his luck. It's pulsing through your body. Use it," Justice replied.

She was about to say more, but Sigourney interrupted her.

"Why can't you locate it then, if you are indeed a god?" Maybe she shouldn't have said that. The wrath the god had promised was closing in, from the look of Justice's expression. It changed from surprise to anger and then to amusement.

Justice smiled. "Come here," she commanded.

Sigourney shook her head, at a loss for words.

"I'm not asking nicely. If you want to understand why I can't locate one lousy machine and one lousy machinist, I'd better show you, mortal. Your kind too easily sees us as all-powerful. Able to conjure anything out of thin air. Some of my sisters and brothers can, but then they are rubbish at everything else. You imagined us with restrictions because you failed to imagine us clearly enough. We are more like a bogeyman lurking in your mind's darkest oblivion, clawing our way out into reality. So forgive me if I can't keep track of all of you. Do you happen to know how many living souls exist at the moment?"

"No, we don't, but let me go on her behalf." Siarl once again came to the rescue.

"Yes, you would. You would love it, too. But she will hate every single minute of what I'm about to show her. That will be her punishment for thinking she can behave as she pleases with the gods. So." Justice held her hand out to Sigourney.

She got up from the couch and went to the god. She let Justice wrap her hands around hers, and instead of feeling the tingle of luck, a wave of paralyzing fear poured into her. Her feet turned as heavy as the ground upon which the building stood. She was drowning under the weight of melancholia, anger, and a scream fighting to come out, but because she was the blind, mute embodiment of justice, all she could do was bear witness and remove herself from the horrors she heard and saw. Then and only then, when she'd gathered all the evidence, was she meant to deliver judgment. But how, when all she saw was life dying under the ruthlessness of others, from murders to cruel extortions to wars? There were so many faces. So many tears. So many broken bodies, which made hers convulse. When she bent double, Justice let go. Sigourney collapsed on the floor and felt Siarl's arms wrap around her shoulders.

"And you wonder why I can't see one individual among all that. I'm not meant to see the one. I'm meant to see all. I am justice. And past my convictions of what is good, I haven't seen anything beautiful since you dreamed me into existence. Did you have to make me? Yes, otherwise, you would have collapsed a long time ago into your own corruption. But who would have foreseen that you would find a way to bend the truths and laws, making a mockery of me and your systems. When I say I'm not a murderer and I stand on the side of justice, I mean it. So, which one is it going to be? The machine or Lepus?"

"Should we have taken the deal?" Siarl asked and stopped moving forward. They were back wearing the scarves and holding hands somewhere on the streets of Threebeanvalley. Neither of them knew exactly where. They'd left the gambling house an hour ago. Night had fallen, and it was nearing dawn. All the nasty people with bad intentions had been surprised to find that sometimes luck worked on the side of justice, using things like falling bricks and random heart attacks to aid the wheels of fortune. Actually, there hadn't been too many nasty people. Mostly curious onlookers wondering how two seemingly blinded people could make their way around the busy streets so effortlessly.

"What else could we have done? She would have used us against him," Sigourney replied.

"Yes, but... maybe, you are right. Justice..." Siarl searched for the right thing to say.

"Was a bitch?" Sigourney asked.

"Gods, no. I didn't mean it like that." Siarl took his and then her scarf off.

"But I did. I can say it. Maybe it's not a nice word to describe someone, and yes, her gender has nothing to do with any of this, but there was something wrong with her. She had lost it, if she was indeed who she claimed to be." Sigourney regretted her words instantly, remembering the sensation

Justice had given her. She massaged her wrist, where the woman's fingers still burned her skin.

"Judge none until—" Siarl began.

"You have walked a mile in their boots. Siarl, I know," Sigourney sighed. "Yes, I did that, yet I judged her because she wasn't what I wanted her to be. I know that too. But she shouldn't have taken the Rabbit, and she shouldn't be doing this to us. We shouldn't be on our way to find and destroy Lord Bufonite's machine. Destruction and justice shouldn't go hand in hand. Nor should we." She stopped as Siarl gave her one of his looks.

"Don't give me that. What I'm trying to say is that I shouldn't judge. That if it were me carrying the burden she showed me, even a fraction of it, I would be beyond repair. Siarl, I saw people dying, not good deaths. Then there were all the whispers of greed, and the speakers didn't see... they didn't see what their actions led to—the small and big cruelties. She saw them all. It's a miracle she has any integrity left. To witness the horrors people can do to each other yet find no laws to right the wrongs... it's maddening. Everything was just plain wrong, Siarl. Her, the world, this situation, us, me. How can anyone be happy? How can anyone go on?" Sigourney fiddled with the scarf hanging from her neck. She felt the woven knots between her fingertips.

"Because we have to. What other option is there? And no one can be happy all the time, but we can try. We can also try to change the world for the better, even just through our actions. There's always hope, Sigourney, never forget it." Siarl gave his usual speech. The one that never changed. The one he believed in wholeheartedly. The one that made the Rabbit snort and call him an idealist. "And I think she showed only one side. There has to be lawfulness somewhere on this rock, or she wouldn't exist at all. It's all the small things that matter. Anyone can start with something small."

And as always, Siarl believed so fervently that it made Sigourney almost believe. Still, she couldn't. While Siarl had grown up in an unjust situation, where Leporidae Lop and luck had destroyed the land he'd walked upon, and he had witnessed his kin suffer and die from malnutrition, he'd kept his hope for the good of humanity. She'd had her ribs kicked in just because of who she was. No one had come to her aid and talked about noble ideas or shown love or care. She'd endured neglect at the hands of those who should love her unconditionally. Life, humanity, and all the aspirations people fought so hard for, all of which Siarl considered a basis for everything, seemed like a mockery to her. But he had been loved. He had never missed the most precious gift parents can give their child, which made everything better. So she couldn't believe.

"How are we supposed to celebrate the small victories when Calamity keeps sending animals into extinction and serving mud to humans? Especially when there is so much ignorance." Sigourney clutched at the scarf.

"Ignorance can be bliss, especially when people create a bubble around themselves. We can't truly blame anyone for doing so. It's how they survive this world that none of us ever asked to be in. What I'm saying is that we should concentrate on the things we can and move on from there. That doesn't mean you have to shut your eyes or let what she showed you suffocate you—" Siarl began.

"But this is not right. None of this has anything to do with what's just," Sigourney interrupted him.

"No, I guess not. I can't argue with you there." He couldn't. "It's why I stopped you." He said the last thing accusingly, or so Sigourney took it.

"It's not me who is insisting—"

"Sigourney, please. I only asked to make sure we have thought through what's going to happen next. Someone has to ask the question. If no one does, then where would we be? Blinded by our situation, refusing to consider whether there are other options."

"What options? Go back and let her use us against the Rabbit?"

"No, that's not what I mean. We could always go to the police or..." Siarl let his thought fall short.

"The police against a god?"

"Yeah, I know. It's just that I don't like anything about this. Nothing we do will make it right."

"You know as well as I do that there are no simple rights. Perhaps it's better if we go and see what this machine is and what it does, and then decide what to do and how to do it. It's not like we don't have time to consider how to react after we get all the facts. That's one thing with gods—they know how to bide time." Sigourney lifted her scarf back over her eyes. The last image she saw was Siarl watching her with his sparkling puppy dog eyes. The same expression he always wore when she surprised him.

"You are right about the informed choice and her using us against him. I should listen to you more."

"I should try to speak more."

Siarl laughed, and it felt good.

They moved on, the good feeling lasting only for a moment before they both felt as lousy as before, but at least they were feeling lousy together. That was a whole lot better than anything cheerful or gloomy done alone.

The pulled-up scarves let them shield their minds from making conscious choices to ruin the universe's perfectly laid plans. Plans that had snuck up on them and had been waiting for them to step into their radar.

Sigourney was the first to notice something was wrong. There was an unusual and persistent echo behind them. And it wasn't someone who Justice had sent after them. They had been able to lose the not-so-subtle goons after four blocks. A quick turn around the corner, hiding themselves, and then returning to the street in question after the men had run past them had done the job. But this new noise continued despite their invisibility. They had been forced to go into hiding, as they didn't want to be responsible for all the casual accidents that followed after them. A vampire had tried to approach them, but luck had seen the potential danger, and the ropes on a passing timber cart had snapped, and the vampire nearly lost her life in a freak impaling accident.

"Someone is following us," Sigourney whispered.

"I know. They have been there for a few blocks already, if I have calculated it right. It could be a coincidence, but this time even I don't think so."

Siarl slowed his steps, meaning he did what he always did, intending to face the danger rather than run away.

Sigourney took the scarf off, and she instantly searched for possible escape routes up the houses' walls, in through the unlocked and locked doors, all the back alleyways, darkened corners... nothing missed. But that was just her first reaction. Even while calculating all the possibilities, she knew they would stop to find out who was following them. Not only because Siarl insisted, but because she too had to see who was able to detect them past her barrier. Not to mention the fact that whoever was following them had worked around the obstacles luck had put in their way. A worthy foe, or, in a perfect universe, a friend. It would be nice if there was an ideal universe for everyone, where all their beliefs applied a hundred percent, like a utilitarian universe for those who believed the rule of maximizing well-being. Of course, there would be a separate place for those who mistake it to mean hedonism. This wasn't the case, as for some reason all personal tastes got mashed into the same universe, leaving everyone to fight out which glorious idea would gain popularity in any given time and space. Around and around they went.

And as this was not even near to a perfect universe, Sigourney's hairs stood up as spooky action at a distance determined how this encounter would go.

"So, you finally noticed me, little sister." Margaret stepped out of the shadows. She had been a lot closer than Sigourney and Siarl suspected. She had her eyepatch off, and they could see the darkness in her blackened eye. It seemed to eat the remaining light the dawn had bestowed for those who weren't afraid of twilight.

"Now, little sister, I have one request. Will you come with me? I promise you'll like where I take you. I cross my heart and hope to die." Margaret made a cross against her chest, and added, "Shall we?" offering her hand to Sigourney, clearly seeing her although she was still hidden from sight.

"How—" Sigourney managed.

"It's a curse. It's a gift. But when you can detect corruption, madness, fear, hate, decay, and all the other fun things, you notice all the little things, little sister. And as I said, I can smell you even under the stink of the gods. You shouldn't go playing with them. They are nasty little parasites. They gobble you up whole... Let me guess your next utterance —what are you? Does that really matter? As fabulous as I am through and through, I'm flesh and bone, tied to this contraption." Margaret flung her hands in the air and spun on the spot. When she faced them once again, she bowed, looking up at the same time and locking her black eye on them.

Sigourney fought to get words out. She was drawing a blank on what to say. The eye, and Margaret as a whole, was too fascinating and magnificent. And present. She had charisma—the wrong sort, some might say. Margaret wore an all-white pantsuit, shining like the lighthouse's beacon. Either luck was pointing out with a bright, bright arrow where they should go, or this was a distraction sent by another godly influence.

"I'm afraid we can't do that," Siarl said. He had taken the scarf off and was wrapping it around his hand, having let go of Sigourney's hand and revealed himself. "Whatever your reasons or wherever you are supposed to take us, we have other engagements. Now, if you'll excuse us, we'll be on our way."

He didn't sound sure at all, knowing perfectly well that his words were empty. Walking away from someone who saw past the invisibility, knew about gods, and was beyond strange was like someone saying, "Come and see the unicorn poop I found" and you refusing. You knew it was silly to go and look at excrement, but another part said, "It's unicorn poop! There might be rainbows. What makes you think I'm going to miss that?"

Margaret laughed. "Oh, sweet, misguided friend, I don't need you. You can go wherever you like. I'm talking to the little sister here, or haven't you been listening?"

Siarl stepped between them. "You are not taking her anywhere."

"But I think I am. Here, little sister." Margaret flung a small cardboard cut-out in the air, and Sigourney's instincts kicked in. She couldn't help it. She came out of hiding and dived to catch the card.

Luckily, Margaret did nothing. She waited for Sigourney to have one of those aha moments, which are necessary for people to find new perspectives in life.

There in Sigourney's hand, she held a beautiful business card. On the bleached cardboard was written in calligraphy:

The Alchemist's Shop
Levi Perri
Kingfisher Road 28
94700 Threebeanvalley

As Sigourney had feared, facing the past was inevitable and not pretty at all. The color drained out of her face, and her whole body went limp.

"What is it?" Siarl asked.

Sigourney was sure he did, but she couldn't quite register what was said or find the stamina to answer back. The business card kept trembling, and she couldn't figure out why. It was like this alien artifact with a familiar pestilence you didn't want to catch.

"I..." she managed to say.

"What did I say? You'll like it." Margaret kept smiling, and undoubtedly she was fully aware of the turmoil going on inside Sigourney. It wasn't hard to see.

"My brother," Sigourney uttered when Siarl tugged the card free of her hand.

"Yes, little sister. A brother indeed. Isn't it nice, family reunion?"

"I can't." Sigourney shook her head. "This is cruel, bringing me here for this. How could he?"

Margaret frowned. "All me," she tried.

"Do there happen to be machines involved?" Siarl asked, handing back the card, making Margaret's frown deeper. If Sigourney were paying any attention to the woman and if she were the sort of person who enjoyed someone ending up the butt of their own joke, she would have been delighted about the power shift. But all she thought was that luck should be about kitties, gold, bright futures, and all cuddly and happy, not about brothers and the past. There she was wrong. With luck, you could never honestly know what random encounter or offer would lead to something good. All humans and, for that matter, gods were born with a restricted view of the future. Gods only had enough control over all the little things circling their orbit and others' orbits to give the illusion of authority. And there lay the weird paradox of inflicted misery. Everyone wanted to hoard nuts against uncertainty. Still, no one could know if they needed hazelnuts or pecans or other nuts, so it was better to go for everything, creating a tad more uncertainty for everyone. Okay, that was not the entire definition of inflicted misery, people were excellent at inventing new ways, but it was part of it.

So here, Sigourney was unsure whether following Margaret would lead to something good or not. Would it just make her loop back to the beginning? Despite herself, she said,

"Okay."

15

WHY I WAS INVENTED IN THE FIRST PLACE

The whole room vibrated from the voices of the chanters who came and went in shifts, never leaving the Rabbit god of luck alone. He could feel and see the city beyond the walls, hear his believers' questions and the munching of the hotel owner, who ate to collect the strength to escape. Mathew had earned his freedom in the Rabbit's book. Among all this, he had shown kindness even when he had every right to hate him.

The Rabbit concentrated his mind outside the gambling house, seeing Threebeanvalley, then the continent, and finally the whole planet from space, which some say curves like a donut and tastes like raspberry and rum. How irrelevant everything was. How trivial he was, and yet people mattered, with their deeds and misgivings. Moreover, if he wanted, he could alter their lives on this spinning rock. Justice never thought he could do that on a massive scale. They never did. Restricted by their narrow view because of their fettered minds. But he had never cared to control others to do his bidding. Freedom of choice was better. At least then you knew they cared about you, unlike the feeling he was now getting from the chanters.

Some pompous human being who fancied himself a molder of minds might think the meaninglessness he felt inside and the disinclination to intervene was caused by Thanatos, the drive for death in all its macabre glory, making him forget the significance of existence, the sparkle that made enduring life bearable. The thing was, there was no contradiction between the lack of universal meaning of life and purpose. Everyone made their own purpose. That was how it should go. Others be damned. But that wasn't why he opted out. It was the harm he could be used for and had been used for so many times.

The planet spinning with its blue seas and yellow and green valleys in front of his eyes was so small and full of want and "me first" shouts. He couldn't help but think, what if one wave of luck could change it all? But the feeling of tightness in his paws, the cold, electrified metal pressed against his skin stopped him from going forward. There was only one place to release his luck, and that was to Justice. This imperative was carved in his shackles.

The Rabbit sighed and let his view drop from space, closer and closer, to the mountains and then the oceans and finally to the trees, stopping over Threebeanvalley, which expanded across the horizon, filled with chimneys, smoke, moving mechanical wonders like the steam-carts operated by men wearing goggles, and among all of them, the tiny humans. The cursed creatures who knew their worth only in death, when they received that final judgment on whether the lives they'd lived had been worthy. How he pitied them. How he wished his kind could leave them alone with their thirst to be loved. It should be the other way around. Maybe not love, but guidance and solace because all of them, all of us, were tormented with the same questions. So there was no good reason to kill each other over the uncertainty of the future. If only they knew how to talk to each other.

Oh well, even a complex syntax that supposedly separated them from animals couldn't save them.

The Rabbit could still hear the chanters and their pleas. He wished they would stop, as at times, he would gladly have let them drag him into their desire. But now he laughed over their chants and the clack of Justice's heels against the stone floor. She was once again making her way to the altar to milk him for all he was worth. From the sound of her heels, the last outing had been successful. Progress had been stopped, for now.

Poor Mathew, though. His munching and his heartbeat sped up along with the steps. But that wasn't what held the Rabbit's attention. That would mean caring, and he didn't care about Justice, or about the hotel owner beyond his duty of freeing him. He was even less concerned about the chanters' faith, even when their love washed over him like nothing before. In the past, there had been whispers of hope to get his, luck's, attention, but none truly loved him. Rather, they feared and hated him. Not until he met the small human female did he understand what kindness and unconditional love meant.[63]

He concentrated all his efforts on Sigourney and Siarl. They were by her side, standing outside her brother's shop, staring the future in its face. But instead of the usual anxiety that had dominated her whole being for so long, the Rabbit was sure it was what kept her functional.[64] There was a change in her determination—now it was indignation. Maybe more time had passed sitting on the orange cushions than he'd thought. Yet it was still the present, not tomorrow or yesterday. What was the present but an observation of the mind and the combination of memories and reflections of self through others' passing in space. All very twisted and complicated, something only a human mind could come up with, and they couldn't blame the universe for it. The universe was multidimensional, and everywhere at once.[65]

Still, there she was, trapped without her permission, and here he was, feeling guilty for abandoning her. More so now, as the situation had turned complex—the other sister was there, and her kind never followed luck. They made their own. Maybe he shouldn't have insisted on this. Perhaps he should have guided them to a sunny beach with fruit plates and sugary drinks. But from what he'd gathered, Sigourney

---

63   Though it was not all fun and games. Responsibilities and all, which messed with your head. Love and caring was a game for the strong and brave.

64   The little neuroses fuelling her. Fuelling all of us.

65   Even with the dinosaurs. Especially with them.

wasn't a beach, fruit plate, or sugar kind of human.[66] She was one of those he would call perplexing.

How on the holy carrots was he supposed to help her get out now? Maybe luck could open up the ground she stood on and gravity would swallow her into some bizarre escape hole, or a law-abiding police officer could march in because of a routine inspection? But no such thing happened. Instead, Sigourney stood there politely, making no fuss, thinking it was a reasonable way to behave. It wasn't. He and any logical human would disagree with her.

"Ahem," the Rabbit heard a voice say.

He ignored the noise. It had happened several times already, there was no mistaking to whom it belonged.

"Your shackles are burning. If you don't stop trying to use your powers, your skin will only burn into blisters," Justice said.

Then he could feel it—the pain. The Rabbit opened his eyes and saw that his fur was scorched around and under the forged iron, and his skin was bubbling from the heat. To top it all, he could smell the burned skin. It smelled like game.

The Rabbit didn't reply. He continued sitting on the cushion, looking over his subjects in a way that would make any unaware person think he was basking in the glory. Not the case. He was searching for that one fellow who might be devoted enough to lack the usual selfish genes and release their god. It was hard to see who might fit the bill underneath all the hoods. They all looked the same, like ants from the skies. A perspective humans wouldn't appreciate, as they would like to think of themselves as people and would certainly like their gods to think along the same lines.

"Lepus." Justice interrupted him. In fact, she had repeated herself several times. He could respond or continue to ignore her. The latter made everything more fun. Maybe then he would see to what lengths she was willing to go. Not that there was any question about that any longer.

Mathew whimpered next to him. The man had stopped eating.

"What?" Lepus asked.

"You know what I want. Do we have to go over this every time?" Justice held out her hand.

---

66 Except with cookies.

The Rabbit looked past it as if it were made of glass, inspecting the floor very keenly indeed.

"Give me your paw," Justice snapped.

This again, the Rabbit thought. It was always the same. All he amounted to was his paws and feet, and nothing else mattered. He could accept this from humans, but Justice should know better. It would be the same if he tried to use her only as a measurement tool, forcing her to be weighed again and again to justify one idea over another. He would never force her to stand on a scale to validate her existence. Who would ever do that to another being?

Yet he'd ended up obeying her, sprinkling his luck in the hope that the universe might arrange things differently for him and the two humans he had grown to love. Now that he thought about it, he was the reason they were in such big trouble. Sigourney should have let go of her past a long time ago and not let it drag her under the depths of the deep black ocean. What was the past but a motion that had passed? The present was all that mattered, and in the present, she and anyone could be anything they wanted to be if only they didn't look behind or worry about the future.

"Lepus!" she threatened him.

The Rabbit gave Justice his paw and let her stroke it once more.

She did something he had never imagined she would do. Justice lifted her other hand, and the men and women joined her, forming a long chain. His luck moved from hand to hand, tingling as it progressed.

The Rabbit's whole body shuddered from the connection. He shut his huge black eyes and let the feeling sweep over him, trying to guide his luck where it should go.

"Now, dear Lepus, give us a point in time and place to halt the march of the steam engines. The one new invention that will alter the city and the world, Lord Bufonite's machine," Justice said, offering him a map of Threebeanvalley.

The men and women behind him looked expectant. They had disrobed, and instead of your garden variety humans, they were equipped with muscles, pipes, pistols, clubs, and swords. There was no mistaking their intention.

"Why do you need me? Didn't you just send them there on your behalf?" he asked.

"Who might they be?"

"Don't trick the trickster. I heard what you told them. You sent them to the machine. So why don't you let them bring it here as you asked?"

"Because they are working for you and your force, fulfilling wishes I have no part in."

"Then—"

"They'll be collateral damage to make you behave."

The Rabbit shut his eyes and let one of his fingers land on the map. She still didn't understand how luck worked.

"So, where did it land?" the Rabbit asked, keeping his eyes shut.

"Near Blue Songbird Park. That's all you need to know," Justice stated.

"Undoubtedly your future awaits you there," he said, his voice booming in the cellar. No one heard his words or the warning they carried.

He listened to Justice instruct her men on how to proceed with the doomsday machines once they found it; how to bring the progress of bright inventions to a halt; how to make everything right again.

The Rabbit wondered how she had gotten everything so wrong. You could seldom fight against change. It happened regardless. That was how humans worked. They invented things to help their lives become simpler and more convenient, bringing along the good and unconsidered consequences. That was humans for you, thinking no further than tomorrow. But who was he to prevent their chosen paths? Yes, he was their god in a way, but to go to war with the creations of their minds like Justice was doing was too much. Too much commitment, too much caring, too much seriousness for his liking. And too much death and destruction and tears. The tears were the worst. Every time Sigourney's eyes watered, he felt panic rise inside him. He didn't understand how humans could live with such a defect.

"Why stop there?" the Rabbit asked.

Justice glanced towards him, barely sparing his suggestion a second thought. It had to be the shackles that caused her to believe his suggestion might not be genuine.

She turned back to address her followers. The Luddites, as they liked to call themselves. The Rabbit thought Lepusians would have been more fitting if this was indeed about worshiping him, but he wasn't stupid. He understood that everyone except Sigourney and Siarl saw him as a tool to be used for their own ends.

The Rabbit wasn't done with suggesting.

"I mean it. If you truly want to stop the machines, why attack only one place that may or may not bring more wonders upon us? I arrived in this city by locomotive. Don't you think it deserves a whack? Carrying foreigners and their new bright ideas into the city? How about the other factories with their chimneys spewing out smoke to fill the lovely sky and smother the seagulls? Oh, and yes, how about the investors and the city's rulers? Don't you want to teach them a lesson? If you go attacking places one by one, it's just pointless terror. What you want is war. Wars change things. They break a lot more machines and people than one attack on one tiny house on an isolated street."

Justice crossed her arms, glaring at him, making the Rabbit wonder if she was morally against what he was proposing. Maybe he was stepping too far from Justice's ideals, or it might be because he was undermining her authority and being helpful and all that. Of course, it could be the fact that changing her actions from a rebellion to a war was too on the nose for her flawed logic.

"Your distraction won't help them."

The Rabbit lowered his paws and shrugged. He wasn't sure how this would play out for anyone. His luck usually took detours and insane jumps, but in the end, it always delivered everything to his liking, maybe. It wasn't as straightforward as Justice and others who'd used him liked to think. Okay, sometimes it was, but you had to know how it worked to harness it. Even Harriet Stowe, who had come close to controlling the capricious force to her advantage, had thought twice before taking leaps of faith to obtain the outcome she wanted. It had often been about the chicken and egg question, or more like the question of actions or luck. Often enough, Harriet had leaned on action rather than luck. At least you could control your actions.

"Just being helpful."

Justice snorted. "You want me to believe that? If you cooperate and keep out of this, I will deliver them to you. Wouldn't that be nice?"

"That's not for me to decide. They should live their lives

according to their own paths and not my wishes," the Rabbit countered.

"You can't seriously mean that. You let them loose in the city full of your luck, and you call their destinies their own? There's nothing about their lives that is their own ever since they met you. You think of yourself as an innocent bystander, but you are more involved with everything than you like to admit. More than any other god or deity. Every event needs a little bit of luck to bring it into existence. If you just harnessed what you have, you could make the whole world yours," Justice replied, her followers nodding beside her.

Again, she was mistaken. You make your luck and hope there's cooperation from the universe. You can't harness luck, only mitigate the risks. But she was right. Who he was had altered the lives Sigourney and Siarl should have led.

"No," he said.

"No?" Justice asked.

"I don't want them here. They should get as far away from me as possible. You do that favor for me, and I help you bring this city back to the dark ages," the Rabbit sighed.

"You care for them so much?" Justice asked, stupefied.

"That's the only thing in life worth caring about," the Rabbit said, refusing to engage with her any longer. He took a carrot out of one of the golden bowls and began to eat.

Justice looked at him, trying to meet his eyes.

He looked away. She would never understand what was valuable. Justice was blind in more than one sense.

"We'd better get going," Justice said to her Luddites.

And she left, trying to make the world a better place one whack at a time, forgetting why she was invented in the first place.

Progress has its victims. So it has always been. Those that cannot adapt will get trampled over, not to mention those unlucky ones. They march on the streets, some with anger, some with glazed eyes and numb bodies. All ignored and cast out of society. Others wonder where their fear, hatred, desperation, depression came from. Still, they disregarded the underlying cause and attributed all the symptoms to the people's nature, seeing them as evil, weak, rude, cruel, or ignorant—quickly moving the blame into the person when even they, the lucky ones who'd survive the new tide, were unable to control what happens next. So the fault must be internalized, making the world a safe place to be. Otherwise, they might be next. On and on goes the circle, with understanding and kindness falling by the wayside.

"Percy, this is wonderful, isn't it? And we have first dibs on it. We own it, and we'll own the world through it. The only thing we need to do is secure the machine," Rose said when she and Percy were outside the university building. "We need a contract, and now. We should get our lawyer and head straight to Mr. Perri."

"Miss Pettyshare—" the man began.

"Don't Miss Pettyshare me. You are about to say we have no clue how the matter comes to be. Yes, Mr. Allread, we don't, but we'll find out and make it ours. This is the greatest invention we could ever acquire, and I won't lose it. If it will keep you happy, we can go with an initial contract that leaves us room to walk away if necessary."

"Rose." Percy took hold of her arm, shocking her. Not with the touch. No, she didn't mind him holding her. His touch was softer than she'd expected. Almost apologetic. It was how he used her name. There was a plea mixed with the warmth of familiarity.

When she looked back at him, he shook his head and said, "Never mind."

Should she press him to reveal whatever had snapped him out of character or not? She chose not. Rose let him guide her through the garden to the coach.

Their walk was so safe, so proper, reminding her how she missed Necropolis and the shady characters lurking around every corner. Here the street tugs were altar boys compared to the Church of Kraken variety; their altar boys knew how to make you cry. A girl needed to dance on the edge of terror to feel alive. Maybe someone out there saw her as a tasty treat. But the truth was, they didn't. If there were any monsters in the city, and there were, they were drinking tea in tea parlors and exchanging pleasantries over the counter at the apothecaries, where the true terror lay.

People brushed past them. She could hear their feet echo as they got farther away. Rose squeezed the handle of her briefcase, which contained the gold coin and the seeds. Oh,

Levi, what a golden inventor you are. Not some average enthusiast, but a real single-minded creature. So alluring. More now, after the expert's keenness. In the fullness of his being, Levi tapped into the origin of creation, yet how? And could someone else figure it out? Was there another machine? Levi had mentioned a legend. Legends were public knowledge, and patenting them might be tricky, but Mr. Cumberbatch seemed like a man who could convince a court that blue was red and red was red at the same time. No one could force Levi to reveal how he came up with the concept or how it worked after the lawyer had worked his magic. One thing was for sure —they couldn't use any words associated with the legend. Or could they? It was a powerful marketing tool to tap into nostalgia, the better days. She could capitalize on the city's dislike of new inventions by making them think the Bufonite was something old, a legacy of sorts, and thus should be guarded against people like Abigail and Justice. Those two wouldn't let go. They would hunt Levi, her, and the machine to the edge of the world with their anger. She would have to hide Levi and the whole business until nothing could stop them. Until a private army could be built to safeguard it. This was all so much bigger than she could have ever imagined—a real gamble that she could win.

"Are you alright?" Percy asked, drawing her closer to him.

"Quite alright, thank you. Why do you ask?"

"You were weaving a little."

"Deep in thought, dear Percy."

The man handed her into the coach.

She swept up the hem of her dress with her free hand and sat down. She smoothed it when she'd found a comfortable sitting position. The coach jerked into motion after they instructed the driver to go to Cardinal Grove, where Mr. Cumberbatch's office was located. It wasn't too far from the Alchemist's Shop.

"Miss Pettyshare, can I be frank with you now, as we are indoors?" Percy looked straight into her eyes. He had that extra seriousness in him. His mouth was in a tight line, as if he was attending a funeral.

"Always, Mr. Allread." Not that Rose meant it. With someone like Percy, who kept his cards close to his chest and took life seriously, the news could only be agonizing.

"I have been dishonest about why I am here, what my

duties are. Because of those duties, I have kept a close eye on..." Percy explained.

Rose's heart began to beat. Her hands turned sweaty, and her mouth was getting dry. She watched his lips move as she concentrated on keeping a blank expression. She waited for him to tell her that he would contest her seniority over the irregularities in the numbers and take over. She came up with several excuses, from clothing expenses to dining clients, for why she shouldn't be judged. He would know she was lying. He was too astute to be fooled. And Percy didn't seem like the sort who would take bribes. He always sat like some royal executioner, delivering the king's justice. Always so precise. Always so proper. Always so right. There would be no getting past him. Then when the Worthwrites found out, she would be sent home. She couldn't go home. Not now. Not when the machine was hers for the taking.

Percy coughed. He'd finished his speech, and she hadn't noticed.

"What?" Rose cocked her head, trying not to show her agitation.

"I said I look forward to your instructions," Percy stated.

Rose went back over the man's words, realizing she hadn't heard anything past the first two sentences.

"As the acting head of the Threebeanvalley branch, I..." Rose began, but she stopped. Percy's face was twisted into an odd expression of masked confusion, like when someone tells you something personal and you reply by saying, "*Rule 975G dictates the previous sentence to be null.*"

Percy straightened the notebook on his lap while Rose tried to find those perfect words to propel her into safer waters. Truthfully, there were none. Some silver-tongued vaunter could have played jazz with the situation, spouting several perfect lines in a row that seemingly made everything better. Still, when you stopped to think, they were as hollow and useless as a chocolate bunny on a sinking ship. She gave up.

"Sorry, Percy, I didn't hear a single word you said. Could you please repeat yourself?[67]"

---

67   Rose delivered that small hurrah for decency so often lost, yet ever so necessary to make everything worthwhile. Not that Rose was happy to be standing on shaky ground at the mercy of others. But that was the price to be paid.

Percy collected his thoughts and exhaled. "My confession to you was long overdue. It was dishonest to take this post and expect my other obligations not to affect my performance as your assistant, but clearly they have. Last night's attack was proof of that. Then the..." He paused. "Never mind. What I'm trying to say is that I haven't been the best assistant and accountant for your needs. I should have been there with you, helping you with this machine and at the City Hall. The Council's business shouldn't be handled with smoke and mirrors. We, I, do an honest job. In all honesty, I was sent here to hunt down the defectors. The necromancers, werewolves, vampires, witches, hexers, and others like them who have no business setting up their shops to teach the dark arts away from Necropolis' shores. They should know better than to be lured in by the riches here. My performance as your assistant has suffered, and I beg you to forgive me."

Rose had expected her life to come crumbling down. For him to take over. But mercy and forgiveness had never crossed her mind. Of course, she'd thought a hexer like Percy could be part of the Council. Still, it was more likely he had been sent here to monitor her. The Worthwrites were not the trusting sort.

"And did you get your defectors?" Rose asked. At least this wasn't about Justice.

"Some of them, yes," Percy said.

"Are they in your custody? Will you be heading back?" Rose hesitated, not knowing why.

"No, they are dead."

She raised her eyebrow, making Percy uncomfortable.

"It couldn't be helped." He looked away.

He wasn't ready to disclose more, but Rose wasn't satisfied. Percy was associated with her, and the dead bodies affected her as well.

"I need you to tell me the truth."

"I was forced to fight. They refused to surrender and go back to beg for the Council's mercy. So they died. Curses can be dangerous." Percy straightened his bird-skull necklace.

Rose had a hard time picturing Percy killing anyone, least of all with curses. There were no killing curses, or so she was told. But who knew what the Coven of Witches taught inside their study halls, away from prying eyes. Yet he had killed, there was that. And there was the fact that Rose didn't see Percy having a single malicious bone in his body despite the rumors that hexers usually had a vindictive nature. He was a choir boy; the one who came into practice with a tuning fork.

"They forced you; you had no other choice." Rose was unsure whether she should lean forward and console him, but she was sure he would flinch away from any unnecessary closeness. She moved on. "But about the bodies. I have to insist they are not in any way associated with the bank." Rose heard the callousness in her own words.

"A body. I was sent here for a necromancer, Cathy..." He shook his head. "Better if you don't know the full details. All I can say is her body has been processed and is being sent back home. I have acknowledged my involvement to the city's authorities with a signed and sealed order from the Council. None of this should come back to haunt you."

"When?" Rose asked.

"Yesterday."

"Yesterday? When you went to contact the lawyer and the expert? And now you are telling me you were running around the city, hunting necromancers? Don't answer. Why are you telling me this? Are you asking my permission to leave?"

Rose wasn't sure that she wanted to lose Percy as an assistant now she finally knew he wasn't sent here to spy on her. Or maybe he was. Nevertheless, the man's idea of sloppy work was way beyond the standards anyone could expect. It was scary to imagine what the operose man would be like when fully committed. There would be no hiding from him anymore. And there was the fact he might be able to use curses to kill. He was dangerous, but he seemed to fancy her on some level. So he was *her* dangerous. Could he help with Justice and Abigail? His talents might allow the machine to stay hidden from prying eyes. Did he use plants, soil, oils, or candles as the base for his hexes? A soil bundle hidden inside her pocket might secure luck with gambling, and she could win enough money to pay back the debts she owed and sever her ties with Justice. She might even dare to try to win extra. Loose money always came in handy. Here they didn't realize that common seaweed accompanied by a hex would keep the cards on her side. And a dead man's noose could hold Justice off her back like a repellent. Perfect. She couldn't let him leave now. Damn the Council.

The tight line between Percy's lips stretched tighter.

"This isn't about whether I'm leaving or not. I told you because you have to understand who I am to appreciate the warning I am about to give you. I have been reading the mood of the city. It's my job. There's terror underneath the surface. Rose, I'm a witch, and through my curses, I can feel the present and future. Something vile visited us at the hotel, sniffing me out. I believe that same something is the root cause of the terror. It's hunting and eating people. There are more missing people every day. I have been putting my spells around, trying to get a better feel for what's going on. Extraordinary people are going missing and have been for a long time. I have searched for the culprits, those like Cathy, While she tried to make almost an honest go of it, others haven't. There's something that wants to shape the city and feed on it. I need to find out who, why, and what. This feels like the olden times in Necropolis, before all the rules. What if someone is foolhardy enough to try to raise the dead and rule the place? The Council cannot let that happen." Percy's eyes shone, and his body trembled from excitement or anger. Rose wasn't sure which one.

"What does this have to do with the bank and the machine?" Rose asked.

Outside, the coach slowed down and began to make its way through the narrower streets. The thick industrial smog was creeping into the city, or more like settling in from above, as the winds were changing. Soon everything would turn into suffocating darkness, and all anyone could do was hope to avoid a collisions or trampled feet as they made their way around the city. Making money didn't stop just because the world turned dark and bitter. It became the perfect opportunity for inventive gals and lads to pocket some coins.

"Everything, Rose. I'm cautious with my premonitions, as mistakes are possible, but Rose, I can't shake the image of the city burning and you being engulfed by the flames. And since you have brought the machine to my attention, I have no doubt that it's at the center of it all. Curses don't lie as humans do." Percy's tone had changed.

This was the most animated Rose had seen the man. She understood why. Who would be this invested in numbers and sheets? Okay, Percy might be, and she was sure he was, but this was an extra layer of spark he'd been missing before. A true witch then, not only a hexer to make the bank's books appear as they should for the bureaucrats—all the more reason to take his words seriously. Though Rose was sure there was always terror in a city. It was full of humans, after all.

The coach stopped, and the driver opened the door for them.

"Madam and sir, we have arrived at 79 Cardinal Grove." The man shuffled aside to let them out.

Rose got up from her seat, but she didn't get very far. Percy took hold of her arm and squeezed it tight. He drew her closer to say,

"You have to hear my warning. The whole city reeks of death. Not the good kind. It's better if you go back to the hotel and let me investigate the machine and its maker further before we get the lawyers involved."

"No, Mr. Allread. We will see this to the end." Rose gently extracted herself from his grip and headed out of the coach.

"This is not normal, Rose. This is not Necropolis. I fear you will get hurt. It's my duty to protect you." Percy stepped out behind her.

"No one is getting hurt. Not on my watch. I'm not completely useless or helpless. I am the master of the situation. We'll find out what this is about. There might be a reasonable explanation for your suspicions. If this is even the real cause. Nothing you can say will make me walk away from here. Not now, not because of your senses. I appreciate what you told me, but this machine is too important, Percy. So what if it leads the city to burn? It's worth it." She saw she had said the wrong thing.

Percy looked disappointed. "If you say so, madam."

16

THE HAUNTING MECHANICS OF THE PAST

The past is a funny thing, especially when it comes to family. It's like this chokehold where you could suffocate yourself with one wrong move. Or like a giant polar bear sitting on your chest when you think you have to face it. All families are dysfunctional in one way or another, but some are beyond repair. Their minds are too far gone. They don't want to see their shortcomings. They would rather blame everyone else for keeping their sense of self intact. They are too deep in their own orbit to care about others, even their children. Those who they are supposed to love and protect. They see others as tools and are willing to use them. And the innocent, the children, who have a built-in feature to love their parents, get their lives ripped apart, and reality kicks in before they hit their third birthday. Then someone, later on, wonders why that child is so dysfunctional, shut down, angry, destructive, depressed, or abusive themselves. Their minds, like their parents' minds, are too far gone, repeating the pattern, pushing their problems on someone new, hoping they will heal the so-called family curse. It's like this little cruelty that keeps on giving.

Sigourney knew what family curses were and felt their weight now as she looked up at the Alchemist's Shop sign. All the bad memories lurked behind it like some depressed goblin whose only amusement was to bite anyone who got too close. That goblin growled inside Sigourney's stomach as she stared at the shop door against the burnt-orange building. It was not only Levi she had got as much distance from as she could. Her mother had been one of those people whose love was a pretense with strings attached and laced with martyrdom, making everyone feel lousy about themselves and responsible for her mood. It was an endless pit of resentment and guilt, eating away at her. Sigourney's head felt like a wobbly jelly in a Sigourney-sized mold. She loved her mother, yet she despised her.

So, Levi was an alchemist. She couldn't wrap her head around the fact. She thought he would be a politician, a merchant, or a soldier. Or even a smuggler, following in their uncle's footsteps. He'd always yearned to make others do his bidding. How could an alchemist command others? And why would an alchemist have the machine of all machines, as Justice had called it? And what did her brother want from her? Everything had turned into quicksand, eroding her sanity.

In the background, Siarl was insisting on clarity, and Margaret was refusing to give it to him. But she wasn't really listening to their argument. She'd been transported back to that moment when she and Levi had last seen each other. The situation called for a dramatic departure, something later generations would immortalize as a great tragedy or sign of destiny. But nothing of that sort had happened. In her memory, there he was as a sixteen-year-old, sitting next to a ditch and eating his bread and soup before heading back to the fields. Their father sat next to him, watching her heading into town to sell the trinkets their mother's brother had brought to be sold onward. Not as much as a goodbye was shared, just a frown and a grunt, and she had never gone back. It had been her moment of escape, at the age of twelve, with the pennies she had gotten from selling those trinkets. The necessary pennies she had stolen.

"So here we are, little sister. Isn't it marvelous?" Margaret chuckled next to her, breaking through the barrier of the past.

Here again was the disconnection between the words and their meanings. "Marvelous" was far from the adjective she would use to describe the Alchemist's Shop sign or the door with her brother's name painted in bold letters. She was thinking along the lines of frightening, intimidating, shocking, bloodcurdling, spine-chilling, and pudding. She wasn't sure where the last one came from, but there it was, among all the other words, showing how personal meanings were.

"Maybe," she said.

"Shall we?" Margaret suggested, stepping towards the door.

Sigourney held her breath as she took a step forward.

"What is it you want from us? Her." Siarl stopped them from moving forward.

"Does it matter? You're going to go in anyway." Margaret lowered the eyepatch over her blackened eye.

"Of course it does," Siarl insisted. He had insisted on going with her in the first place. The woman had offered to fight him for it, letting them choose their path if Siarl bested her. Siarl had almost accepted the offer, but Sigourney had stepped in to stop him. What had happened to Justice's thugs was not a fate she wished upon Siarl. Siarl, who she loved and adored, who had begun to restore her heart.

"Her brother wants to see her. Isn't that enough for you?" Margaret opened the lock with a key she'd fished out of her pocket and held the door open.

It wasn't. They all knew that. However, it was the best explanation the woman would give. She had to dance on the edge of the unknown, finding it a pleasant place to be. To her, the mundane was a facade of true horror. Or so it seemed. Something behind the normal working eye told Sigourney that Margaret enjoyed the fact that even a saint could kill and that even the most horrendous sadist would scream if their joints were pulled apart ever so slowly. The evil eyes the Threebeanvalleyans wore on their hems were made for creatures like Margaret.

Sigourney stepped inside without saying a word. Behind her, she heard Siarl warn Margaret, "Stop messing with her."

"I would never mess with my little sister. It's just that the clock is ticking, and brothers don't wait."

"You are..." Siarl let out.

"I'm hurt. Will you call me evil? Maybe a monster. But

what will you call her when you find out what she is made of?"

The failed communication faded into the background[68] as Sigourney saw her brother behind the alchemy shop's counter. It was her brother, despite all the years showing on his face. He'd let his curls grow longer, framing his forever impish face. But instead of seeing pure evil, the one who had tormented her throughout her childhood and had made her, along with everything else, into this timid person, she saw a man who was haunted. By what, she had no clue.

"Sigourney?" Levi sounded surprised, a hint of warmth in his voice. A stack of ledgers surrounded him, some open and others closed. He had a pen in his hand, and he wore a tormented expression that melted away at the sight of her.

The door behind Sigourney creaked shut. She could hear Siarl's astonished silence. The way he always was when he saw any place for the first time. She couldn't blame him. The room was filled from top to bottom with things to marvel at. There were the cure-all bottles, which he snorted at. There were the mechanical sculptures, which he desperately desired to touch and pull apart and put back together. There were the dyes, the herbs, the alchemical drawings, the little mystery bottles, and all the pieces of equipment. Sigourney noted it all and filed it away for later use, as she could only stare at her brother.

She nodded.

"How? When?" Levi began, then he regained his senses. "Never mind that. You are here, and that's the most important part." He shut the ledgers.

The same wobbly jelly feeling from outside came back. All she wanted was to be done with all the awkwardness, which stood between them like a duck on a birthday cake, and to know what was going on.

When Sigourney said nothing, Levi stepped around the counter and continued,

"It's so good to see you." He spread his arms as if to hug her. He lowered them back down when Sigourney turned into a statue. Someone else might not be able to spot the slight difference in her posture, but he was her brother, after all. They'd spent the first half of her life together, becoming some

---

68   Siarl would never call anyone evil.

sort of human beings.

"I forgot," he said.

"You brought me here," Sigourney stated when the new bizarre turned into the new normal.

Siarl woke up from his dreaming. He came up next to her, keeping his distance, yet Sigourney knew he was ready for whatever she needed him for.

Margaret went around them to hop onto the counter. She swung her legs as she observed the moment.

"Yes, I guess I did. And now I don't know where to begin."

"How about the truth?" Sigourney suggested.

Margaret laughed. "Oh, little sister, what's the truth but a lie against uncertainty?"

Levi glanced at the woman, saying nothing when Margaret grinned back. Sigourney paid attention to the imbalance between them. The woman clearly worked for her brother, but she was as independent as a rat catcher.

"Then any explanation will do," Sigourney said carefully.

"If I must. It would have been nice to get to know you before I demanded anything from you, but I suppose it must be so..." He stopped when an otter waddled into the shop. Its whiskers quivered when it looked around the room. It soon locked its round black eyes on Sigourney, who was experiencing so many emotions at once. Some of which may have included plans to save the otter.

"*Iik,*" Otis let out.

"It seems we are going to have a full cast of characters here to witness what I'm about to say. Sigourney, you have to believe me when I say I never wanted things to go this way. I assure you, if Miss Illes treated you wrongly when bringing you here, that doesn't reflect how I feel. I needed to see you because you and you alone can shed light on how the universe works. If I find out what separates you from me, we could save lives. Who knows, we could even save the world."

"Because of the machine?" Siarl asked.

Levi looked like someone had punched him in the guts.

"They kept saying that," Margaret explained. Again, not explaining anything, just making unnecessary observations to complicate things.

"How?" Levi stuttered. The otter circled him, finally settling between Levi and Sigourney. It bared its teeth ever so slightly, wiping away Sigourney's plans to rescue the animal.

Sigourney shook her head. Siarl shouldn't have said that if they wanted to weigh their options without extra pressure. Now he had gone and ruined it all. But Siarl had already figured that out by himself. He kept fidgeting next to her.

"My abilities," Sigourney tried in the hope that it would fix the situation.

Margaret eyed her suspiciously, but then the deep lines on her forehead smoothed, and she smirked. She readily threw away convention and acted like a force that brought others face to face with the paradox of loving order over chaos despite feeling restless when faced with repeating the same mundane actions day after day in the world of abundance.

"Let me show the machine to you, and maybe then you will understand what I'm talking about." Levi was getting animated. "Sigourney, the contrast between our blood might explain why one is not like the other and what it means in the grand scheme of things. Then there won't have to be victims, not how it's made. If I can grind the mystery down to the finest speck of truth and fuel the machine with it, the quintessence, it will save lives. It will be glorious. It will be... And to think they didn't listen to me at the university, the so-called professors of physics. The pettifogging halfwits who couldn't see inventiveness, truth, or future even if it stepped on their toes... They could have helped this come to be without me having to resort to..." Levi was getting into his zone. The one so familiar from their childhood, when something excited him and nothing was his fault. Sigourney waited for the casualties. There always were. Usually, it had been her.

Otis let out an "*iik*," stopping Levi.

"I'd better show you," he said.

Seeing the past, the present, and the future in one person messes with your head, especially when the future is ever so pressing. To Levi, it was. He lived not in the moment but in the moments to come. And he couldn't take her sister's judgmental eyes, which were so like his. He could get lost in them, tearing himself apart while leaving room for self-doubt. Levi could feel the bubbling rage simmering in his gut as he observed his mute sister. There was so much he wanted to say to her about what she had done and what it had cost him. However, Levi reminded himself that Sigourney was a tool to find out how the universe ticked. He reminded himself to stay away from the personal. Through her, he could piece together what made specials special and why they fueled the machine, unlike your common person. Blood mattered. It was the key to why he and she were two completely different people. He guided them calmly to the basement and brushed off the unnecessary turmoil of human existence by returning to rationality.

Evelyn was already in the kitchen. She was pushing firewood into the oven, making the warmth of the kitchen warmer.

"Evelyn, could you open the shop for me in two hours?" he asked.

The maid glanced towards his sister and the fellow who seemed to follow inches behind her. He hadn't asked his name. Then she turned her attention back to him.

"Sure," she said, wiping her hands on her apron. "Will your guests stay to eat?" she added in a shaky voice.

"I think they will." And that was it. They had to move on, as Margaret was getting restless. So was Otis the otter. And for that matter, his sister and her paramour too. Chatting about everyday chores in the middle of a bizarre kidnapping didn't seem right.

He knew what he had to do as soon as they got into the basement. He had to detain Sigourney. He doubted she'd changed. She was slippery by nature. Always in constant motion, guest or not. Their uncle and his crew would have appreciated what she could do. He had never told a living soul what he suspected. Their mother and father would have given her to Uncle George, a brutish man. Worse than their father, who had a short temper and was embittered by the realization that he would never amount to anything more than the miserable man he already was. It was the most terrifying epiphany one can have when you lacked the elemental tools to change things. It was no wonder people found themselves at the bottom of an ale mug as their father had. The man was dead now.

Levi wondered whether Sigourney knew. Their father had drunk himself to death. He hadn't been a stupid man. Just unable to deal with the disappointments life so readily dished out, especially with a wife like their mother. Toxic to the core. But their mother had loved him, Levi, in her own twisted way. She saw in him the potential she never had, pushing him further, never letting him settle. She was the one who had gotten Levi his break, sending him to work for a clocksmith in the town. He was sure there had been coercion involved. But whatever had gotten his foot in the door, he was thankful for it.

"Our mother still lives," he said as they made their way down the stairs.

Sigourney said nothing, as he'd expected.

"She's with George, living on their small estate. She curses him to the bottomless sea every time I visit her, but—"

"That's the way she is with everyone. No one can please her," Sigourney finished the statement.

"No. No one can."

"And Dad?" she asked.

"Dead. He drank himself to death four years ago. Mother was forced to forgo the family farm."

"Sounds about right," Sigourney sighed. "Did they..." she started.

"Ask after you?" Levi guessed.

"Yes," his sister replied thinly. Her voice was barely stronger than a whisper.

"No, not really. They paid their dues to George for what you stole. But nothing beyond that. I'm sorry."

"Don't be."

This was more than he'd wanted to disclose in front of Margaret and Otis, yet he had done. Sigourney deserved to know what had happened. But he wasn't willing to go into details, because they'd arrived at his workstation, where the machine was hidden under the rag. Also, he didn't want to dwell on the past any more than necessary. Births were indeed a random lottery. The two of them were proof of that. Some might argue that life was what you made it. Levi bet they had never had to exhaust their brains and bodies to search for food, with no energy left to give a second thought to anything else. Then some smug bastard would come along and tap their shoulder and say, "Life is what you make of it." What happened next was simple justice.

Yet both of them had come from the same circumstances, and he owned a house, while from the look of it, she couldn't afford her next meal.

"Anyway, here we are." He stated the obvious, having to say something. He didn't feel like his usual, controlled self. There was something about families that blurs the line between who you were and who you are.

Sigourney kept her attention locked on him, but the boy she'd come with took in the whole room hungrily.

"I'm afraid I didn't catch your name." Levi focused on Siarl.

It took some time for Siarl to register what Levi had asked. He was too occupied with the gears and the little mechanical sculptures, whose bones lay on the table and which he was about to touch.

"Siarl, Siarl Ellis," he finally replied and stopped moving his hand towards the gears. Instead, he offered it to Levi.

Levi shook his hand. "And what are you?" he added.

"A friend of your sister." The boy nervously glanced at Sigourney when he let go of Levi's hand.

Oh, the quiet power his sister could wield, and then she pretended she didn't. Nothing was ever done right in her eyes. Other people were nothing but a constant disappointment. As kids, he'd tried to include her, get her out of her shell and be interested in something. To create something was the culmination of human life. It was ecstasy. What made everything worth it. But no. She'd rather stay away from everything and be on her own, staring at a brook or hiding in the small patch of forest behind their family farm, talking to herself as if that could ever solve her or the world's problems or make anything better. Yet if he looked more closely, there was something more underneath his sister's usual demeanor. Her shoulders weren't as hunched, she was listening intently, and there was a decisive way about her, despite Margaret breathing down her neck. There was another creature he couldn't figure out. Nor did he want to try.

"Then, friend of my sister, this machine of mine you are so keen to see will change the world as we know it. It will bring prosperity, equality, and peace." He leaned over the desk and pulled the rag off the Bufonite. He observed their reactions. They were as they should be. His sister and Siarl looked shocked, yet curious. "But I suspect you doubt me when I say this, thinking me another charlatan, a madman who promises the world to you in exchange for your last pennies. You might even consider this to be similar to those cure-all bottles upstairs. I saw you, dear friend of my sister, frown at them. This is not about your pennies. This is the real deal." He flicked the switches on, and the machine hummed.

What followed the hum was the silence of anticipation, combined with a tiny amount of doubt. Or maybe thoughts about exploding doomsday machines. But what came next was astonishment as the Bufonite spewed out a handful of perfect golden-brown seeds. As always, Levi was ready to shout from the mountain tops that he had done this, and no one else could even come close to the creation of the Bufonite. Those who'd doubted him were imbeciles and obstructed the progress of humankind with their backwater thinking.

"What you are witnessing is this machine making wheat seeds out of nothingness. When the city is full of these, we can leave the fields and forests to their own devices, feed the poor and hungry, and be content," Levi said calmly despite his heart beating fast. Somehow this was different from when he had shown the machine to the banker, Miss Pettyshare. He hadn't needed her approval, only her money. Now, he noticed, he needed Sigourney to say something.

But as always, his sister disappointed him. She said nothing, just stared at him with a frown on her face.

He continued, "As I said before, the differences between us will explain the whole mystery. Let me draw your blood..."

"No." Sigourney shook her head. "I can't."

"Why?" he asked, despite having expected her to refuse. She always said no to everything.

"Because you are leaving out all the important parts and telling me the good bits. What about the people you have locked in your basement? Do you think I can't hear them? What have you done, Levi?" She looked at him with pity. Like he was this broken wooden man.

Of course she would hear the quiet churning of existence, as she always did. Spooked by every single noise. He had forgotten.

He groaned and said, "You haven't changed at all. I truly think this is for the best. I'm sorry for what I have to do next. I didn't want it to come to this, but things are how they are, and I can't let you leave. Margaret, escort our guests to their lodgings, as I clearly didn't impress them enough to see things from my perspective or from the perspective of those who are poor and hungry. Or those who have sacrificed everything they have to make this machine work."

Sigourney clenched her fists and was ready to jump, but Siarl took hold of her before she could react, and Margaret seized them. The boy kept opening and closing his mouth, but then he spoke.

"You are saying the machine's energy system is the only thing making the wheat come into existence?" He leaned closer to the machine, letting go of Sigourney's arm.

Levi frowned. "Yes, the forces that—"

"The people, that something, the thing that lets Sigourney hide in plain sight. The quintessence that facilitates the creation of matter in the cosmos, the building blocks of life, so to speak," Siarl interrupted him.

And Levi got to experience the strange way Siarl was with everybody and everything. Those honest, inquisitive eyes were locked on his, and Levi felt naked, like the little boy who used to pick the weeds in the fields under his father's watchful gaze, dreaming of the day he didn't have to. The day when his fingers weren't numb and his back wasn't aching. The day he could concentrate all his efforts on wondering how everything came to be. Why the cosmos wasted its energy to create his flesh and blood and then let it die. What was the point of creating complexity when singularity and stillness was an option? But those questions didn't matter; reality was how it was, and keeping his head in the impossible would... would lead to the Bufonite and its like.

"Yes," he exhaled.

"And because you and Sigourney are so different from each other, you think she can shed light on the mechanics of quintessence and how it fluctuates in elements?" Siarl continued.

Levi was beginning to doubt the ever-so-innocent act. The face lit in wonder and awe by the machine. Still, all Levi managed to say was, "Yes."

No one had ever been this astute. Not even Otis, who shrugged at the marvel of the situation and simply accepted its existence, never feeling the need to explain it or tear it apart.

"What an amazing machine—although, of course, I'm not condoning your methods. I gather you fuel it through other people like Sigourney. What I'm not sure is whether their blood is enough or... Yes, I can see how and why you made it. An experiment like no other. To take it from an idea to reality... The initial calculations must have taken years of hard work. Wasn't there any other way around it than necromancy?"

"You can't possibly know that," Levi snapped.

"It's the only reasonable explanation. I highly doubt that someone like Sigourney with her ability to hide could ever power a machine to make wheat. You'd have to isolate her powers and distil her desires and wants and then combine them with something to provide energy for the production."

Levi looked at his sister. She appeared almost apologetic.

"Siarl," Sigourney said and reached for his sleeve.

Levi never meant to plead for his sister to rescue him, but he had.

"Yes, sorry. I do sometimes get carried away. What were you doing... Yes, locking us up. You can do that now. But I have to say, we will do the best we can to free ourselves and the others. What you have done here is beyond amazing, but it should have stayed as a concept until you found another way. Using living beings is not very civil."

After that, Siarl and his sister let themselves be escorted to one of the closets. Levi's head was spinning when he closed the door behind them. He fell deep into his thoughts, not even noticing Margaret and Otis' presence.

He couldn't help but think the boy was right as he returned to his work desk and the machine. He should never have gone with necromancy and with souls, but the project had been stymied for so long, and it had seemed like the reasonable thing to do.

"Don't worry, big brother. You need to break eggs to get where you are heading. The machine will be just what the city ordered." Margaret's voice startled him.

For a moment, her voice brought back memories of when he had first thought necromancy could be the key. As if she had been there with him. He shook the thought away as silliness.

"Yes, but how many eggs?" Levi asked.

"Let me stop you there, my dear brother. Never regret what you have created. It's hard to see past the immediate, both the tragedies and the glories. But you have to see all the good this will bring, as you yourself proclaimed." Margaret made a gear spin on the table.

"What are you?" Levi couldn't figure the woman out. One minute she was nothing more than a mockery of everything anyone held dear, and the next she was more rational than any other human he had come across.

"As I said to your sister, I am what I am. But if it makes you feel better, you can think of me however you like," Margaret offered.

"That really doesn't explain anything," Levi said, having expected something of the sort. No explanation, just obscurity. One day Margaret had been there, behind them at the cemetery. The early days, when he and Otis had thought that any deceased would do. She'd pretended to be a graverobber. Then she'd latched onto them like a leech, a helpful one. One that they couldn't do without.

"My darling Levi, don't worry about what I am or what I will be. For now, I'll do my duty for you and the machine. Isn't that enough? Especially when we both know that these talents of mine are reserved for the kings and queens with never-ending pennies."

"Why are you helping me then?" Levi asked, ignoring Otis, who let out a low *awk*. For once, he wished Margaret would speak the truth.

"The questions is, why wouldn't I?" Margaret went back to being her jovial self, not really made for truths of any sort. When she saw it wasn't enough, Margaret added, "To see that little machine of yours thrive—"

Otis interrupted her, having turned back into a man. "This is not right. You two speak about nonsense when the real question is how on earth he figured out how the machine functions. They know more than they are telling us."

"Dear necromancer, as always, you bore me. But I indulge you. Why wouldn't they know? Are necromancy and its ways some great secret?" Margaret toyed with Otis.

"Why do you hate me, *demon*?" Otis spat out.

"Don't worry, he will still need you, *the death merchant, the speaker of the voiceless*," Margaret countered.

Otis looked away. He couldn't help it.

"And I don't hate you. Far from it. It's marvelous what you do. Just marvelous. Before you get your panties all twisted, I was trying to point out that the boy is clever. I'd better stay here for the time being."

"But—" Levi began.

"The boy forgets that you are trying to better human lives. But you should never forget that yourself. I'm here to help. Let's leave it at that, shall we?" Margaret really didn't ask. It was more like a command. She pulled a bench from the work desk and slumped down, not planning to leave anytime soon.

"Yes," Levi whispered, looking at the Bufonite and the seeds on the table then at Margaret. "Better lives." And demons, he thought.

17

THE QUESTIONABLE DEEDS WILL
FINALLY CATCH UP

Lawyers are a curious breed. They have to be argumentative by nature. Their sole task is to find discrepancies and compare them against the laws—what can and can't be done, or more like what you can and can't get away with. And somehow, their professional personality sneaks into the personal. Hard facts are hard facts, but words are meant to bend, and if there's an issue, it should be picked at until it bleeds. Not all lawyers are like this. No. Only those who have gotten lost in the lush forest of clauses and arguments, and those who love to contest everything in the first place. Those are the ones you want to have on your side when things get sticky.

Mr. Cumberbatch was a peculiar sort of fellow. He could argue until you didn't know who you were or where you came from. Did you agree? Inevitably, you nodded your head from sheer fatigue. But when he was off the stage, during his personal hours, he lost his glasses on his nose and went on searching for them.

Rose watched as the older man with short gray hair

searched for their papers among all the documents accumulated on his mahogany desk. Percy was pacing around the room, occasionally stopping by the window looking over the back veranda. He'd failed to control his agitation. He kept telling Rose there was something wicked on its way. Luckily, he disclosed nothing in front of the lawyer.

"Here they are," Mr. Cumberbatch said and tipped over another pile. He watched as the files slithered off the desk to the dark wood floor. Briefly, the lawyer contemplated whether he should do something about the matter, but then he chose to leave the papers there. He unintentionally put his hand behind his lower back.

"Yes, I think we could draw up a contract that would leave wiggle room yet secure this project for you. That said, there's a problem when it comes to the bank branch not being established; however, I'm sure I can overturn Page Briggs' ruling and get you the license. If you let me have until next week, all this can be sorted out." The lawyer flipped the folder open and leafed through the documents. "Yes, everything is as I thought. Section B should be—"

"Then we will be back next week." Percy cut the man short, which was so unlike him. He was too polite even to interrupt Aunt Dolores'[69] minute-by-minute account of what she did on her seaside holiday. Any sane person would say, "Shoot me now."

"I'm afraid not, Percy. We need this done now. I need to secure the project." Rose refused to play along. Percy was wrong about the machine and how it was tied to the city's feverish mood. He was making connections between two facts when there was no proof that they had anything to do with each other.

Before either of the men had time to reply, there came a polite knock on the door accompanied by the words,

"Dear, people want to see you. It's about some machine."

The lawyer got up. "Excuse me."

"If I might remind you, Mr. Cumberbatch, we were here first. Our demands for any machines precede anyone else's," Rose said. She wanted to say more and in a harsher tone, but diplomacy or at least the pretense of it was better than a

---

69   Or someone along those lines. Mothers-in-law were especially good at these social games that made you wonder whether you had arrived in purgatory in advance.

declaration of war.

"Yes, of course." The lawyer gave a polite smile, making his wrinkles deeper. Then he shambled to the door.

That was as far as he got. The door was pushed violently open, and the room was filled with people wearing masks. Among them was a set of eyes that Rose would recognize anywhere. Abigail made her way in, and Justice wasn't too far behind her. They looked as bewildered as Rose did. Not as bewildered as Mistress Cumberbatch, a frail older woman who worked as her husband's secretary. She was about to faint. Rose might be inclined to follow her example if her dignity permitted.

Rose gripped the chair's arms tightly. She glanced over at Percy, who'd stopped pacing. He'd set his legs wide and put his hands behind his back. Rose wasn't sure whether he was preventing himself from attacking or trying to look as disarming as possible and failing on every count. Then she wanted nothing more than to glance back at the door, but she couldn't. Rose stared at the rows of law books behind the desk against the sickening beige wall, trying to get her nerves under control. She was sure she would collapse. Part of her insisted that if she kept staring at the books, the future would be secured and the problem would go away. But the bigger part knew that the smaller part was a moron. At some point, she had to face the music. But not right now. She stole a second to set her thoughts straight.

She was allowed that second and not much more.

"Miss Pettyshare?" Justice asked.

Rose smoothed her dress hem before standing up. When she did, she composed herself to appear calm and on top of the situation.

"Justice," Rose replied, facing the woman.

She wanted to say something snarky about not having thought Luddites needed lawyers to obtain machines. She didn't. She wasn't suicidal. Not when the Luddites clearly hadn't gathered how to use lawyers. Muskets, pipes, and brass knuckles seldom motivated lawyers. It was the money that made them perpetual motion machines.

"What an odd coincidence that we share the same lawyer," she added, not daring to see what Percy was doing.

"I don't know about lawyers, but luck and coincidence seem to play their part," Justice said.

Abigail stayed close to her master, saying nothing. What a waste of a good woman to live in servitude and have no original thoughts. Especially since Rose had found out that Abigail and her family owned the gambling house, not Justice. Rose wanted to snatch a pipe, challenge Justice, and free her teacher. But instead, she stood there unable to follow any of her impulses for fear of losing everything she wanted. The usual affliction of the living, being stuck between now and the future. Also, such romantic gestures were for other stories; here, Abigail wouldn't be impressed by her gallantry.

"Then we'd better leave you to it. Percy, we'd better—" That was as far as Rose got.

"Don't take me for a fool, Miss Pettyshare. Now, sit back down, and we will sort this out," Justice demanded.

Rose took a step backward, her heel hitting the chair.

Percy took a step forward between her and the others.

Mr. Cumberbatch had already made his way to his wife and was holding the poor woman up. The Luddites were getting restless. They had been promised action and the destruction of machines; to some of them, chatting inside a lawyer's office was their worst nightmare. It wasn't like you met lawyers in amicable circumstances.

"I'm—" Rose started.

"Sit down," Justice snapped. "It's clear we are here because of you, and you have been hiding things from me despite our understanding. We are going to find out what."

"I'm afraid that won't do." Percy positioned himself fully between the confused Rose and Justice. The Luddites took a tighter grip on their chosen weapons, but Percy didn't flinch. He stood there like some mighty defender. Any other woman would have found the situation chivalrous, but not Rose. She was getting irritated.

Before Justice had time to react, Rose got her senses back. She went to Percy, taking hold of his arm.

"It's fine."

Percy kept his rigid posture. He wasn't convinced by her words or by the fact that he was outnumbered eighteen to one. There was a slight chance a savant fighter might take them all down in the enclosed space, mostly because the Luddites were still in the hallway. But Percy was no savant as far as Rose had gathered. He might be able to lull them to sleep by reading his diary. But curse them all? She was highly doubtful.

Justice snorted. "Your kind always think they are stronger than ours. Stand down, Mr. Witch. There's no need for violence. We can handle this in a civilized manner. Miss Pettyshare owes us an explanation for all we have done for her and all we have forgiven." She looked past Percy to Rose.

Rose tried not to appear threatened by the words.

"Ahem." Mr. Cumberbatch cleared his throat. "My clients are not going to discuss anything under duress. If something is indeed owed and forgiven, then your lawyer can contact me, and we can move to arbitration." The man was still holding his wife in his arms.

Justice laughed. "Oh, how I love you humans. Always so clever. But you are right, Mr. Lawyer. This is not very just of me, and I hold justice in high regard. However, I can't let go of the matter, as Time is not on my side. He never is. If it suits you and Miss Pettyshare and her witchy companion, I'll send my men outside, except for Abigail Rivera, and then we can settle this matter."

She didn't give anyone time to answer. She added, "Go, wait outside."

The Luddites filed out, not sounding happy. They murmured as they went. Rose couldn't blame them. The promised rush of adrenaline accompanied by violence had been taken from them by the stiffs in suits. She didn't care about the Luddites or their disappointment. She was about to deal with her own.

"Now, is this better?" Justice asked.

She made her way to Mr. Cumberbatch's desk and took his seat.

Percy observed her the whole way there. He clutched his necklace.

"Let's begin, Mr. Lawyer," Justice said.

Abigail stayed at the door.

"First I have to know what is owed and what is promised," Mr. Cumberbatch said. The years seemed to shake off him. So had his wife, who had followed the Luddites out to make sure they behaved. The older woman had found a purpose, diminishing the initial shock. She was getting quite upbeat. She had always wanted to have children, but they never got around to it, and now she had a flock of misbehaving adults to boss around. A tiny part of her was fulfilled.

"Nothing was promised. All that is owed is money, and money can be repaid," Rose interrupted before some perverted course of justice got underway.

"Rose, what is this all about?" Percy asked.

There was no point in trying to lie. "Mistress Justice runs the gambling house, and I have unpaid debts to her from the games I lost." As she finished her sentence, she wanted to puke. The simple unspoken truth had held her back, getting bigger and bigger after every sleepless night.

"And we had an agreement on how you would repay the loans we gave you. Repeatedly, if I may add."

Abigail groaned at the door. She'd folded her arms, not appearing pleased at all. Rose dared a glance towards her. The woman shook her head when their eyes met, either to warn her or because of something else. Rose wasn't entirely sure.

She turned back to face Justice. "An agreement that I never promised to follow. I would protest that if any agreement was made, it was made under threat of bodily harm and loss of my position at the bank."

"If this was so—" Mr. Cumberbatch began, but was silenced by Justice raising her hand. The man staggered backward as if he saw more than the mere gesture. He slumped against the wall.

"An agreement was made. Miss Pettyshare always had the option to pay her debts and walk away. She didn't. Now I have come to collect. Where's the machine?"

"There's no machine," Rose snapped.

"Miss Banker, you don't know what you are playing at, so tell me where Lord Bufonite's machine is and your debts will be forgotten, and your position will not be jeopardized. That's my final offer, and it's quite reasonable."

"What are you?" Percy exhaled and let go of the skull necklace he'd been fiddling with.

"Welcome back, Mr. Witch. Did your curses find out what you wanted?" Justice was enjoying this.

"You are not human, that much I have gathered."

"Only a shell I have adopted, but a shell I have grown quite attached to and would like to keep. I am Justice." She stood up behind the desk and seemed to grow. Her petite frame turned menacing and larger than life. "I am your god. And I have had enough of all of this. Miss Pettyshare, tell me where the machine is, and I can do what's necessary!"

Rose couldn't. Not even in front of a god, and she believed every word Justice had said. The way the woman's voice boomed, the way it had no single shred of doubt, the way she loomed behind the desk. Every one of those things had convinced her, but Justice as a god was nothing to her, a Necropolitan, whose gods had tentacles and sank ships on a whim. Her gods had fangs and lured you to the dark side. Justice was like a girl scout when it came to supreme beings. If the woman was indeed Justice, she couldn't hurt her. It would be unlawful.[70]

"I can't. Something like the Bufonite shouldn't be destroyed. And before you say it, no, not for money. Mr. P... The man is right. If we can't stop believing the mantra that resources are tight and someone has to be the loser, then we need the machine or something like it to equalize us. Especially when the truth is that we allocate our capital to satisfy our whims[71] rather than educate, feed, house, and clothe everyone. I won't aid in the annihilation of the one chance we humans have." Rose dragged a chair closer to her and sat down, half-believing her own words. The menacing Justice and the dirty secrets didn't have any hold over her anymore. Whatever came, came.

"It will never get that far. People will tear each other apart for it. And who's to say there's going to be any equality? Or will you, your bank, and your inventor stand against the corruption the power brings? Will you give up the excess you have, which secures your and your kin's prosperity and survival, in order for others to prosper? I didn't think so. I ask you once again to give me the location of the machine. Or are you willing to die for your ideals?" Justice leaned forward, setting her hands on the desk.

If it was intended to intimidate Rose, it wasn't working. She had arrived at the point where the invisible ties had been severed and she could see how everything worked clearly.

"If I must," she said.

---

70   There she was mistaken. Gods can make their own right and wrong. The same went for anyone with enough power and capital to rule the world. They could get away with robbing a granny and feeding the grandpa to the wolves along with their granddaughter with a red hood and a generous heart.

71   Cruise ships were the bizarre culmination point of this. A lot of lost resources and failed marriages, and some people called it paradise on Earth.

Abigail sighed. But if she had any objections, she didn't let the rest of the room know them.

"The machine in question is at the Alchemist's Shop. I'm afraid I don't have the exact location; however, I'm sure this information will help you narrow your search down. The owner is Levi Perri." Percy cleared his throat.

"Percy!" Rose exhaled, her voice turning high.

"Oh, I see. The Perris," Justice began. She had a thin smile on her lips. "Anyway, thank you, Mr. Witch. You made the right call... Abigail, we are leaving. But before that, one more thing. Miss Pettyshare, don't ever come back to the gambling house. We are now square, but I don't forget easily."

Rose said nothing. She found herself staring once again at the law books. Wondering if the ultimate truth was that there were no laws, no justice, no fairness—only the figments of human imagination transformed into rules to make people cooperate. Perhaps the sole guideline one should live by when it came to others was tit for tat.

She listened to Justice and Abigail leave. Rose shut her eyes and asked, "Why did you have to do that?"

"She would have killed you. Rose, you have to believe me. I not only saw it in her eyes but in the thread of her being." Percy touched her shoulder.

She recoiled.

He let go. "I'm sorry."

"No, you are not. You wanted this." Rose opened her eyes. "But I won't let you or her take the machine from me."

"Rose, please, no. It's better this way. You have to believe me. The city is already burning. I can still feel it."

"The machine—"

"Nothing is worth it. I won't let you sacrifice yourself for it."

"We have to sacrifice ourselves for something, or we are like empty cans, swirling in the wind." She got up from the chair. "I have made up my mind. You can follow me, or..."

The Rabbit god of luck hummed. He had been doing it for the better part of an hour, to the hotel owner's misery. Mathew was tearing his hair out and wishing, from the look of it, for Justice to come back and impale the Rabbit. He continued the humming. It was fun to see at what point the man would crack and how. The Rabbit had several theories about the how. There were thoughts of stomping feet, maybe jumping up and down and screaming uncontrollably, or there could be swinging fists, coming from his misguided idea of a valuable ego living inside the man. Or there could be sobbing. If there were someone to bet with other than the subject in question, he would be having a swell time. He would go with the sobbing, but there was a slight possibility of fist swinging coming out on top, as violence was a perfectly reasonable option in the face of humiliation. Just ask any baboon after midnight in a crowded bar. Then again, the Rabbit had never understood what baboons had to do with anything. They were quite civilized compared to humans.

Nevertheless, Mathew's mood was only a minor part of the issues running rings inside the Rabbit's head. There was the fact that all of this, and he meant ALL, was beginning to repeat itself. The entrapment, Sigourney, irritated humans, humans with petty problems, and life. Life, in general, was an inconvenience. And now, Justice—he could see the allure of her reasoning, but that was a slippery slope to a maddened existence, and as a deity, there was a lot to exist. So maybe it was time to go with plan B.

There had been a time when he'd feared plan B. Seen it as a last resort when all was doomed. When humans had gone entirely mad and had started to fill their world with toxicity, their gods wouldn't be far behind. He'd walked on past that point when humans had experimented with the social, coming up with inventions, venturing beyond their tribes, then beyond their kingdoms, and lastly overseas. He had seen how humankind had spread like locusts, taking over what shouldn't be taken over. Mastering it. Shaping it. Knowing nothing of what they were tampering with.

That was what Justice was fighting against now. It was too little and too late, and for the wrong cause. You couldn't stop progress. It had a habit of sneaking around the corner and punching you in the face. Also, progress had its upsides. Life expectancy and whatnot. Things he didn't have to worry about.

But now he was worried. Worried about his overly large feet, which were clearly not feet made for this world. His velvety ears heard Sigourney and Siarl's erratic heartbeats; they were not made for this future either. Of course, he could go on as a man. There was that. He could fool almost everyone with that disguise. Yet it didn't wipe away the ears or the feet. He would always have them. His true self. He would know it. It was like losing weight. The fat person would always be there, inside, criticizing everything.

"Oh well, plan B then," he sighed and began humming again.

Sigourney wouldn't like it. She would hate him forever. And it wouldn't be like last time, when he'd released all the luck he had into her and let his body die to be reincarnated again in a year or two, when the belief in luck was strong again and Harriet Stowe was long gone. No, this time, it was forever. It was time to let go of the Rabbit.

The Rabbit wanted to feel for the last time the alluring whispers of his worshipers. But that belief was gone. The adoration was just a fantasy he'd let himself slip into for a moment. Justice was the true recipient of their worship, without a doubt. He could fool himself into thinking that they would lay down their lives for him; for her, yes, and from the sounds of it, they already had. But also from the sounds of it, Justice had gotten more than she could handle. None of them ever learned. Luck wasn't a force you could control. So many had it, and so many used it; he was the only one on good terms with it. Justice would come back enraged, looking for someone to blame. As always, the fault was in others. Again, the thing with the ego. So fragile, yet so harmful. How many wars had it caused? How many were dead because of it? How many prisons had it filled? And it was better not to even start with ideologies and ends justifying the means. Those got you into no end of trouble—to concentration camps and genocides and all the funny things where eradication became a party tune. There was no end to people doing something bad for a good reason.

The Rabbit stopped humming.

"Do me a favor," he said, snapping the hotel owner out of his trance of self-pity.

"Why would I do any favors for you after what you have put me through?" Mathew asked, proud of his small defiance.

The Rabbit scratched his ear. "I was just going to point out a way to flee."

"You said there was no escape!"

"I lied."

"Aha!"

"I never said I wouldn't. I'm not my brother Truth. He would never lie. I lie to everyone," the Rabbit said, which was a lie. He had never lied to Sigourney. Not once. Siarl's head, on the other hand, he'd made spin so often that it was a marvel it was still attached to the man. "But you don't have to believe me. You can judge the outcome for yourself. There's no harm in trying."

"With you, there has been nothing but harm. With my luck, there will be no hotel to go back to and Lucas and the rest of my family have abandoned me. Who will believe me, a ruined man who has lost his reputation and his livelihood and brought his family along with him, begging for the pity of strangers, that it was all because of you, a god? That's what you have condemned me to, and yet you ask me to comply," Mathew snorted.

"Not blindly, though. With forethought and free will to do as I suggest or stay here," the Rabbit replied.

"Then what do you suggest?" he asked. His hands shook.

The Rabbit was sure the man's hands weren't shaking from infatuation. It was the anger speaking, smothering the possibility of empathy inside him. The affliction that made humans so great. It was the cornerstone of their survival, and now they were marching towards an era where isolation and the ability to exist alone might extinguish the need for empathy. Justice was right. There was a way for man to perish along with his gadgets. Then again, they were clever buggers, like cockroaches, really. They were always coming up with new ways to correct their past mistakes with foolproof plans that might or might not backfire in a century or two.

The Rabbit stood up, or tried. The shackles forced him to crouch in an awkward position.

"Take one of those golden bowls, head to the door, and knock. There should be a guard outside. When he opens the door, hit him with the bowl, run outside, and never look back."

Mathew stared at him in disbelief.

"I promise on my mother's grave that this will work. I hear only one gentle heartbeat outside, pacing around out of boredom. He'll surely come in if you cause a ruckus. Then you will use the bowl. But it's your choice. You can hit the man with it or try to give it to him as a bribe. How you hit him is up to you, though I would suggest the good old hit on the head, as its outcome is more predictable," the Rabbit said, and sat back down in a lotus pose. When the hotel owner was finally gone, he could concentrate on meditating his ass out of here.

"It won't work," Mathew protested.

"Sure it will. You get a good swing out of using your hips. That's the key to any bodily motion. You'd be surprised," the Rabbit said, flashing a smile. A mistake on his part. The hotel owner looked like he was ready to test his theory not on the guard but on the Rabbit, and not in a funny way.

"You are trying to mess with me again, aren't you?" There was a protest, a weak one.

"No more than usual. This time around, I'm aiming to make your life more bearable."

"But what if—"

What a pitiful existence one could live. The Rabbit was annoyed that he'd misread the man's character. He'd seemed so jolly and open at the hotel. But it was unfair to hold it against the man; the Rabbit admitted he had accidentally put Mathew through more than most humans could handle. The human brain was such a delicate construction. One wrong word, one setback, one out-of-place act, a whole lot of uncertainty, and a hint of meaninglessness, and the synapses began to send distress signals. Nothing and no one would be sane after that. Then again, who was the Rabbit to judge what was rational and what wasn't? To him, sane was taking life as it came and not trying to tamper with it too much as long as enough carrots were provided. Still, to humans, sanity seemed to consist of running around in circles, following a plan, disregarding the plan, fearing the future, hating the past, taming dogs and cats, and being domesticated by those same creatures, especially of the feline persuasion, and bemoaning the repetitive days but hating change. Logical sanity was clearly not part of the original design.

The Rabbit only had sympathy towards Mathew.

"You fail? Then most likely the guard will do the hitting, and you might get a trip to la-la-land and not having to endure my ugly face."

"You think I can get out? There are no more guards

beyond the corridor?" the hotel owner asked, finally convinced by all the upsides.

"Can't hear any. Justice is a bit naive occasionally, but don't tell her I said such a thing. She would have me cut and stuffed and then mounted on a wall as a warning not to get on her bad side." The Rabbit licked his paw.

"And you will...?" the hotel owner asked.

"Stay behind."

"And you don't mind if I go?"

"Revenge is not my style. It only increases the evil in the world, assuming you go in for the concept of evil, but I can see you have an idea of it floating in your mind, which oddly enough includes unintentional events like earthquakes and bee stings. They might be distressing, but evil? I think not. Evil needs intent, and you can't really call the planet or nature evil, can you?" The Rabbit twitched his nose.

The hotel owner picked up one of the golden bowls, now empty of carrots, testing its weight.

The Rabbit wondered for a moment whether he could arrange the universe so that the man came back with a fresh stack of carrots, but then he let the idea pass. It was not worth it. Mathew bored him.

"Go on," he said and nodded towards the door. That almost ruined everything, as the man's synapses began to scream about not being hornswoggled again.

The Rabbit swallowed the rest of his encouraging words and tried to appear as harmless as he could. Others would call it a very devilish expression indeed.

The hotel owner carefully stepped down from the altar and made his way to the door. The enormous golden bowl swayed in his hands as he tried to find his balance.

The Rabbit found himself shifting his hips along with the man's, searching for that perfect fluid movement, which made all the difference in the world.

The hotel owner banged on the door while correcting the bowl repeatedly as it slipped off his hand. Mathew looked behind him to the Rabbit when there was no reply. He encouraged him to try again. The man banged on the door again, this time with more vigor, making the Rabbit wonder if it was because he realized what was lurking behind him on the altar or because he'd asked him to.

"Knock it off," the guard shouted, and the door stayed

shut.

The hotel owner stopped and once again glanced over his shoulder at the Rabbit.

"Please, sir, I think there's something wrong with him," the hotel owner said.

The Rabbit suppressed the urge to hoot aloud.

"You are lying," the guard said.

"You won't know if you don't check. I don't think your mistress would be happy if something happened to him," the hotel owner insisted.

The Rabbit was feeling proud, like a dad would be. All the good and bad rubbing off on the next generation of silly buggers, infecting them one at a time with his madness. This felt more like being a god than being a god. He wondered if this was the reason why they kept breeding, all of them. Some of them were better at it, like ants and... rabbits, and others not so much, like elephants. They were ruining their chances of survival just because they realized sex wasn't such as big deal, as it caused a screaming larva to shoot out of your butt and then what? You were stuck with it for the rest of your life, paying for its education, watching it make the same mistakes you did, and then, if you were lucky, after they were finally sane enough, you were called granny or grandpa and other names to make you feel like an outdated dinosaur. No, thank you. The elephants were clearly on the right track, getting the crit out of this planet and fast. Even more so because the funny-looking animals with their feeble bone structure had taken over, and they had stupidly gone and lost the only good thing about their construction—their tail.

The Rabbit listened as the guard's breathing changed. The hotel owner had put him in a tight spot. Damned if he did and damned if he didn't. The Rabbit liked such ultimatums. They made life ever so exciting. Boring consistency was the killer of minds.

"I need you to step away from the door," the guard said after some heavy pondering on his part about lesser evils and his future aspirations.

"Okay, I'm aside now," Mathew said, shuffling slightly to the left side of the door and lifting the golden bowl high in the air above his head.

No, no, no, the Rabbit thought. What a rookie mistake. A swing from underneath or the side was more effective than trying to drop it from above. You had to do different arithmetic with such a move. If you missed, you had an angered guard with crushed toes coming at you with their full weight—a bad combo. The Rabbit didn't have enough time to warn the hotel owner as the door creaked open and the guard poked his head in. Luckily, there was luck. The man was as big of a moron as the hotel owner, offering the most precious commodity he had on a platter. The golden bowl came down, and the guard dropped to the floor.

The Rabbit winced. He hoped there was no permanent damage to the man's intellect. Okay, it was questionable whether he had any to begin with.

The hotel owner looked like he wasn't sure what to do next, staring at the unconscious guard on the floor in disbelief.

"Go on, leave," the Rabbit said.

"But..." the hotel owner stuttered.

"He's not dead. I can hear his heartbeat. He's out of it for a while, but not for long enough if you keep lingering there," the Rabbit said.

"But..."

"Everything will be fine. I promise."

"But you...?" the hotel owner babbled.

"I'll be fine. Go, before Justice comes back and sees what you have done," the Rabbit said.

There came a saddened question of "Me?" lingering in the air like a week-old sock. No one wanted to admit the odor was coming from them.

The Rabbit could be evil and say, "Yes, you," but he didn't. The man had suffered enough, even if the utterance would technically be accurate, and the Rabbit had just been an innocent bystander with a few bright ideas.

"Go on, she'll never know," he said instead.

The hotel owner's mind had plainly caught up, and the allure of the open door was too much. He ran off without saying goodbye.

"What an odd monkey," the Rabbit said and took up a better position to start his meditation. It was time to become who he was: a rabbit.

18

LIKE A BAD PENNY

ive in the moment, they say. But what if that moment is agony? Is there permission to escape to a fantasy of your own making? How about a lie, lie like there was no tomorrow? What was so wrong with that? Why did people value mundane reality over whatever trick your neurons could pull? Sigourney had never understood reality. It seemed to contain more contradictions, misery, foolishness, hatred, fear, and evils than anything her mind could create. In her fantasies, she could save Siarl from all this. She could make sure he never saw the cruelty her brother could inflict. Cruel acts made Sigourney's head spin, or it could be the expectation-defying behavior that confused her to the core and made her want to scream. There were crimes against the person, which most would agree to be heinous, like slavery, torture, and murder. But that was the point—most would agree. Sigourney knew there were some exceptions—some governments, for one. Then there was the question of whether she and others could ever share core moral values that dictated what was good and what was not, and no consequence was worth the trouble. Or was everything forever colored by our views? Unchangeable.

She dropped her forehead against the wooden door, hearing her brother's voice behind it. He was being who he had always been, wrapped in his reality and his own desires despite the hurt he was causing. She was sure he had taken them into the basement knowing quite well that she would hear the specials. That she wouldn't agree to play along. So he wouldn't have to be the bad guy and imprison them for nothing. Or maybe he had indeed thought she would look the other way as she had done so often when they were kids. Not anymore. She wasn't the same person.

Next to her, Siarl paced around the room, his brain trying to sort out the mcoo.

The room smelled stale. Prisons always do.

Sigourney pressed her forehead harder against the wood. Was there anything to be sorted out? Could words change a person or the world? Or were she and others doomed to a static life, repeating some pattern the universe wove time and again? But that felt like sadism to those who never could get it right. Never would have an ounce of happiness in their existence. Only bruised bodies hanging from the ceiling in the make-believe prisons formed by false righteousness.

The mountain nuns had told her that the worst thing you could fear was a blessing in disguise, demanding strength from the person to see past the misery to a tomorrow with a view that didn't make your eyes water. Sigourney heard no better tomorrows as she listened to the knocking of the other prisoners, only questions about what was happening and hope for some kind of clarity. Clarity her brother would never give them.

"Sigourney, what are they saying?" Siarl asked.

"Yes," she managed to say, her voice sounding thin and lifeless. She wanted to say more, but the words got stuck in her throat as they so often did. She instead stared at the lock in front of her. It was the number seven standard issue, which was a tad harder than your common indoor lock, but an easy target for her nevertheless. A lot of good it did. She'd heard a latch slide into place and the click of a padlock.

She groaned and turned around, having wallowed for long enough in her self-pity. Siarl had made his way to the bed with a blue-and-white straw mattress. Next to the bed was a washing bowl on a wonky table.

Siarl pressed his ear against the wall and raised his hand, ready to knock.

"Please don't," Sigourney said. "You'll only confuse them."

"Then you speak to them." He lifted his ear from the wall.

"And say what? Sorry about my brother? He's the son of a bitch?" She bit her lip.

"Sigourney?!"

She had a hard time looking at Siarl's huge, innocent eyes. What a difference there could be between two creatures. One who had seen love and the other who never even had the chance to understand what it is.

"I won't apologize. It applies better than you know." She crossed her arms.

"I'm sure it does, but it serves no purpose. It's like calling someone evil, and therefore illogical and making all the wrong choices in life. A restrictive view and not helpful at all." Siarl blushed.

And she knew why. Siarl's better nature had been overruled by his idea of truth. She was sure it was his concept and not the ultimate truth. How could there ever be one? Oh yes, people swore by religions and other things that took the form of blind faith, like some scientific hypotheses, politics, and economics, as how things are and forever should be. But she had seen enough ever-elusive yetis to know that certainty was a lousy card to play in a world where time, space, and the laws of the human mind played tricks on you. Certainty and blind faith[72] got you on the fast track to ignorance and hurt, and more often than not, they were the building blocks of systems that oppressed and destroyed the impudent ones who dared to disagree.[73]

But blushing Siarl was kind of cute. You might expect him to redden with anger or go white from fear of being stuck here waiting for death or luck to intervene, but not from the embarrassment of getting caught using lousy reasoning and attempting to manipulate her.

"Evil is such a tricky concept. Some would consider me to be evil, having been in prison and all that," Sigourney offered.

"Some would, not I. Circumstances matter. They do with

72　Any kind.

73　Who know where you can stick your truth.

your brother as well. Yes, he's misguided, but he says he's doing this for the good of humanity. What if he's right and the machine is the only way to save us and the ground we walk on? Then it would be narrow-minded of us to consider him outright evil, because there's goodness in his motives. It might be better to help him make peace with his quest or find another solution for the problem. I can't deny that he's doing something amazing if he's indeed tapping into the creation of the universe." Siarl half-swallowed his last words when she looked at him from under her eyebrows.

"Of course, morality isn't black and white. Not even murky gray like some would argue. Human behavior is governed by randomness, and situations, backgrounds, and all the tiny forces in and outside have a say in what is deemed right and wrong. Not that we don't have control over it. We do. That's the problem. People say they can't change, but what they are saying is they don't want to change because it's hard, because it demands a conscious effort and so on," she replied. "But what my brother is doing is not right. You said as much yourself. I can't tell those people in the other rooms who I am." She slumped against the door and hugged her knees tightly to her chest.

Siarl stared at her, wearing his confused expression.

"I think I just don't talk," Sigourney replied, hoping he would stop looking at her like that.

"And you choose this moment to tell me that?" Siarl tried laughing, but it felt hollow.

"I have had time to think about these things. One has to when they have made as many mistakes as I have. Or are as anxious as I am. Or have sat at the bottom of a prison pit. I'm no fool, Siarl. I know what I am, but—"

"No, you are not a fool. Nor is your brother, or Margaret. But you are nothing like them either. Yes, we are all the sum of our mistakes. Still, we shouldn't forget those things we have gotten right. How we react to the randomness of life, as you put it, matters a great deal. Still the—"

"I agree that quick judgments and words like 'evil' downplay the situation. Also, I get when you ask, what if progress justifies everything? But we are not utilitarians by nature. How many of us could strangle a crying child with our bare hands to save the many? Would you help him kill me if it would save the rest of humanity? Please don't answer.

None of this matters. I'd better stop stalling and respond to those knocks. Then we can figure out how we can escape and take the machine with us." Sigourney released her hands and got up. She hopped onto the bed next to Siarl.

"Yes, let's do that. About..." Siarl began but stopped as Sigourney gave him a warning look.

"The prison thing," Siarl finished.

This was no time or place for that conversation, but he deserved an explanation. Sigourney noticed that she was clenching her hands into fists. She released them and began,

"I used to steal from people. First food, then small things they wouldn't miss to feed and clothe myself, and most importantly, to keep a roof over my head. It was so easy with my abilities. But I got too bold and stepped onto someone else's turf and got caught. Instead of putting my head on a spike, they took me in. And together, we got too bold and too daring and ended up in prison after having hurt many good people. Later I found out that one of the ex-leaders had ratted on us. They weren't happy about me getting the attention and worship of the crew. So here we are. I survived prison, bided my time, and escaped. Then I headed to Leporidae Lop, and you know the rest." She left out her visit to the nuns in between, but such details were nothing compared to the big picture.

Siarl reached for her hand, and Sigourney refrained from pulling away. She let him touch her. If she was truly honest with herself, it felt good to be touched and good to let it all out.

"And yes, you were right about luck and how it uses us. We should never have come here." Sigourney broke the silence that had followed.

"But if we hadn't, whatever this is would still be happening," Siarl said softly.

"I know. That's why we are here. To put an end to whatever my brother and Margaret are doing." She wanted to add, "*And not for me.*" But a sentence like that would sound selfish in light of recent events.[74]

---

74   Not that there was any escaping ego-centric thoughts, wishes, and wants. What mattered was how one reacted to them. Was it always about me or, you know, sometimes about the other fellow? And how about considering the entire world's well-being? Those annoying buggers who genuinely did so knew how to look good in the eyes of others, and not even in the silly "I'm better than

"Do you think the Rabbit knew?" Siarl asked.

"I don't know. But he brought us here to be free of us and finally move on, and for you to settle. I heard you two talking. Don't think I didn't."

"Sigourney, I didn't mean... I mean, I didn't know. The Rabbit said something about this being the final trip, and then we would part ways. He said everything he could ever do for us would be here. I just—"

"Thought it was a good place to settle down."

"Yes. I honestly did—"

"Why didn't you ask me?" She knew it was unfair to accuse him, but saying it aloud felt good.

"Ask you?!" He reached for her hand and turned Sigourney to face him. "You never let me ask you anything. We have been together for over three years now, and I barely know you. Don't think I haven't heard you whispering with the Rabbit, disclosing your heart, your mind, your past to him. How do you think that makes me feel?"

Sigourney's whole body shook. Siarl's hand around her arm felt tight and suffocating even though his touch was soft. Siarl would never hurt her. He just wanted... fairness and to be part of her life, and she continued denying him all those things, spitting in his face every time she froze. Tears began to pour down her cheeks uncontrollably.

"Oh, Sigourney. I'm sorry. Please forgive me. I didn't mean any of it." He drew her closer.

"Yes, you did," she whispered.

He said nothing.

Between them lingered the right thing to do. Sigourney knew how to release the pain Siarl was feeling, but part of her wanted to hold on to the anger she'd found inside her. But... that would be cruel, and she hated cruelty.

"Siarl." She struggled free of his embrace and wiped her eyes on her sleeves.

He held his breath like some broken toy waiting to be tossed aside.

Sigourney wanted to escape back to her fantasies. She didn't. She was done being the timid creature she was. Always running away from her problems and doing the wrong thing because of it.

---

you" way.

"I know you don't believe in evil, but evil is part of our everyday life. I do cruel things to you, not letting you in, while allowing you to think the fault is yours—something we all do. Then we mitigate the damage we have done with explanations, with all the buts and becauses. I know that. And I know what I have done in the past, and I have to face it, so..." She let the words drift through the disconcerting stillness of the room. The knocking had quieted. There was no longer the hollow clang of a spoon. Sigourney was sure there were ears pressed against the walls, listening in to their conversation.

"It's okay, Sigourney. I forgive you." He kissed her cheek. "About the knocking and about speaking in code... I can't decipher it for the life of me." He changed the subject.

She was glad he did. And the reason why Siarl couldn't decipher such an easy code was because he always expected things to be more complex than they were.

"Let's see." Sigourney leaned against the wall and began knocking.

"One, break, one, break. What's that?" Siarl asked.

Someone in the other room knocked on the wall twice.

"And that?" Siarl asked.

"It's usually once for yes, twice for no. But to start a conversation, you tap twice," she replied. The only thing keeping her sane in prison had been listening to other people's conversations. It didn't matter if they had been about a toothache or some other banal concern; they'd saved her life. Now, as she looked back at that miserable eight months of her life, she understood she had been lucky. She didn't want to fathom where she would be now if she hadn't gone to jail and broken free from the gang. Being part of the gang had been a glorious cage, especially since not everyone was so excited about the goose who laid golden eggs. They thought that goose was better plucked, buttered, and roasted.

The glorious cage thing Sigourney had experienced was pretty much the same for gods. Despite the gods thinking they were free and independent. There was always the head of the organized religion who imposed was always making demands and rules for the gods, or else they could make the flock walk out.

But that was beside the point. The knocking started again. This time the noise wasn't as lethargic and hollow as before.

What was presumably a spoon clanged against the wall twenty-three times.

Sigourney knocked once as a reply to confirm that she'd received the message.

Again, the spoon clanged, this time eight times.

Sigourney again knocked once.

"What's going on?" Siarl whispered. "What are you doing? What are they saying?"

"Shhh," she replied.

She knocked once after someone in the other room also knocked once. Twenty more knocks followed hers.

This went on for a while. Siarl started pacing around the room, getting more restless with every whack and thump.

When the beating ended, Sigourney frowned.

"What did they say?" Siarl asked.

"They asked me, '*What can you do?*'" Sigourney replied.

"That's all? After all that knocking?" Siarl asked.

Sigourney was about to explain that she and the other prisoner were using the alphabet. It took time. But it was better if she left all the details for later, as Siarl's mind would surely start devising a better system, designating a frequency for all the letters, like a long knock or a short knock, or even different rhythms for certain words. And he would forget that such an intricate language needed prior planning, and it was not like Sigourney had ever met whoever was behind the wall. She didn't have the time or patience for any of that, so she shrugged.

"Are you going to reply?" Siarl asked.

"Sure," she said. Sigourney thought and began to knock on the wall, telling the person on the other side that she could turn invisible.

After the prolonged knocking, the only reply was, "*Are you strong?*"

Sigourney snorted.

"What?"

"They clearly don't appreciate what I can do."

Sigourney continued knocking and after a while she dropped her hands onto her lap. Her knuckles were red and sore. Someone called Humphrey Chadwick, a clairvoyant, was imprisoned in the room beyond theirs. He had been there for over a month now. The man had lost track of time. Margaret had captured him as well. And Levi and someone named Otis had been feeding him and prepping him for something he couldn't see. Nothing made sense beyond the walls, and he was living in the past. Margaret had called him number five, which meant there was or had been four others like him. Now, there were at least two other people here. But only someone called Edith and Humphrey had been talking in code. Both of them were specials. The third one might be as well. Not in a dangerous way or a way they could use to gang up on Sigourney's brother. From the sound of it, Mr. Chadwick had given up.

She'd asked how he knew the alphabet knocking.

He'd replied that it was because of his childhood misgivings.

Also, he'd told her Levi had forced him to search for his sister. He hadn't been happy to hear that Sigourney was Levi's sister.

That was as far as they had gotten before getting too tired of the exchange.

In the meantime, Siarl had become restless and frustrated at not being able to keep up.

The last question the man had asked was if Sigourney knew how to escape. When she replied in the negative, the man had responded with a sad clang and then nothing.

Sigourney could easily get out of the room. She was good at pulling her vanishing act. Once she'd escaped through a chimney; before that, she'd dismantled the ceiling and fled through the upper floors. This simple room was no match for her. The trouble would start outside, where Margaret and her brother were, not to mention the weird otter.

"We need to find a way out," Siarl said after Sigourney had told him everything.

"Yeah, but what will we do once we are out?"

"I might have an idea. Find out what the others can do." Siarl hummed. Not actually hummed as a machine would; it was more like he radiated happiness at having fully realized his action potential.

"Okay," Sigourney said and started knocking.

Levi was alone in the basement, or as alone as he could be.

Margaret had wandered back upstairs, refusing to leave even when he'd paid her the last cash he had. She'd muttered something about destiny and Evelyn's cooking. Otis had gone back to his room, saying this was all too early for him. The necromancer wasn't happy about Sigourney being there. Using family crossed a line Otis didn't want to cross. He'd refused to hear what Levi had to say about his sister's blood. Levi pitied the man for letting personal matters get in the way of seeking knowledge. Anyone who didn't see that knowledge came first was trapped. Knowledge not only gave you power, it gave you the ability to choose.

A lunch lay next to him on the work desk. He ate his bagel and drank his coffee while he assembled everything needed to test Sigourney's blood. The Bufonite hummed next to him, producing the gold he desperately needed to build the giant machine of his dreams. Without having to take stock, he knew there were enough parts for one small Bufonite, and that was it. Maybe he should try to build it while he waited for Rose to decide? He now had the extra souls for testing. But what separated him and his sister from each other was more pressing. An opportunity he never thought he would receive. He lifted a microscope onto the desk, not getting further than that before a quiet sobbing interrupted his prepping. It was barely audible beneath all the knocking the specials did, but there it was, seeping into his consciousness.

Levi glanced over his shoulder, not seeing anyone in the room. This had been happening ever since Otis moved in. The necromancer had explained that ghosts gravitated towards him. But it wasn't only that. There were those who they'd used for the Bufonite without results and those who kept the specials in their prisons. All of this was why he hated tampering with the dead. The unwanted came with it. Science had to triumph, eviscerating the sleight of hand of the ethereal realm, one day.

He took a box of glass tubes, setting it beside the microscope, and went back to thinking about money.[75] He would have to sell more dyes and potions if Rose didn't open her purse strings soon. Levi wasn't sure if he could wait for her bank to open. Did he know anyone at the City Hall who could make sure Rose's cause got fast-tracked? Many

---

75 Money was like a bad possession—even an exorcist couldn't remove its hold on the mind.

prominent wives and daughters came to his shop, and Levi sometimes saw them outside these walls. Janet Haigs' husband was a councilor, if he remembered correctly. Of what, he wasn't sure.

The sobbing grew louder, and he couldn't continue ignoring it. It pierced his skull, making him lose his concentration. He was sure he saw a flickering image of a small girl, but it disappeared.

The dead should stay dead. That's how it was supposed to go. All this was unnatural and unnecessary. Levi's hands shook as he tried to slide a glass plate under the microscope. The plate rattled against the metal. Levi steadied his shaking hands.

"Go away. Do you think I don't know you are playing tricks on me?" Should he call Otis down to drive out the ghosts? The man would laugh, as always, seeing him as childish. But Levi hadn't grown up in Necropolis and gotten used to the creepiness factor.

But this felt different, as if someone was doing this deliberately. Levi pushed his stool farther from the desk and got up. The knocking had stopped, and there was only the sobbing, along with a faint whisper: "I'm dying."

Levi grimaced. Not ghosts, after all.

"Edith?" he tried, standing and watching the rows of doors.

No response. Maybe a slight rustle of fabric, but he could be imagining that. Levi took a step closer to the door where Edith was kept, leaning his ear against it. The only thing he heard was stillness. No dying gasps for breath. Just someone who was waiting for a mistake to happen and an opportunity to force a rush of visions on Levi to make his head spin.

"You are getting stronger," he said, moving away from the door. Edith could make tales come alive in front of your eyes, making you think they were real. Occasionally, when he had fallen asleep in the basement, he'd experienced strange dreams, but nothing this solid. Then there had been minor things like imagining tools that weren't there.

"I'm sorry," Levi muttered and made his way back to his desk.

Soon the quiet knocks resumed as the prisoners spoke to each other. Sigourney was no doubt telling stories about him, painting him to be some big bad monster and encouraging them to rebel. Not that it mattered. Why should they care about giving their lives to science?

If he were in their shoes, he wouldn't. He would do anything in his power to avenge the injustice done. That was their right. Levi wasn't monstrous enough to expect cooperation and respect. They were allowed to hate him. It was the least they could do to keep their sanity and humanity intact. Fighting felt saner than the response Mr. Wyat was giving. As soon as he'd arrived, the man had fallen into trance-like catatonia. It was disconcerting.

Levi moved closer to the shelves, pushing a wooden box out of his way. It contained all the glass tubes he used in the Bufonite's power systems. A substance other than glass would be ideal, but lead hadn't worked. He wasn't so keen on working with lead. Yes, it was a soft substance, easy to mold, and it was relatively cheap compared to other metals, but there was something that bothered him. Another project to take on when he got the Bufonite working as he intended. Behind the wooden box were the syringes. He took them and laid them on the table. Everything was ready for Sigourney. Levi only needed someone to help him keep her under control.

He'd waited for this a long time, and now, he wasn't sure whether he wanted to see the truth. Her ability had always puzzled him. Why her and not him? They were made from the same mold, yet they were nothing alike. Not then and not now. Often enough, he wondered if she was adopted, abandoned on their farm one stormy night.

Nevertheless, if that was the case, their parents never gave it away. His life would have been different if he could have been like her. Then at least he could have hidden from their father. Levi shook his head as if the slight movement could banish the squeezing feeling inside him. It didn't, but it was soon forgotten as the doors began to clatter. The hinges moaned, and the wood creaked. It sounded as if they were trying to force their way out. He was about to shout at them to stop and call Otis to aid him, but before he could, he dropped to his knees, confused. For a moment, he was sure he was in one of the rooms. But as soon as the image had come, it was gone.

The doors kept rattling. Levi took hold of the desk, dragging himself up, still feeling like his body was trapped in one of the cells.

"Cut it out," he bellowed. "I have been reasonable with you thus far. Don't force me to be unreasonable. And Sigourney, if this is your doing, and even if it isn't, I do not need your friend. Remember that."

There was hesitation, but the uproar continued.

"Sir," Evelyn said behind him, touching his shoulder.

He turned around to face her.

She looked like she had seen a ghost; her eyes were wide with terror. More because of him than the racket going on. Levi knew why. His face was twisted in anger. No wonder—his heart was racing, his chest was tight, and all the muscles in his face were tensed. It wouldn't do. He pushed his hand inside his pocket in search of the gold coin. It wasn't there, but the thought melted his anger away. Sigourney was unimportant.

"Yes, Evelyn," he said in a calmer tone.

Now she dared to glance behind him at the rattling doors. She hesitated, swallowing her words.

"It's alright." He touched her arm.

She looked at him again with a worried expression.

He smiled at her.

She smiled back.

"This is what Otis and I do. It will be fine soon."

She nodded.

"What was it you wanted?" Levi raised his voice over the noise.

"There's a lady at the shop. She's asking for you. She's not alone. And they..." Evelyn collected her courage. "They don't appear friendly." She sounded apologetic.

"Yes, I'd better deal with them then." Levi could feel the same spinning sensation from before. This time it was his doing. Why now? He snorted, thinking he'd wished this upon himself just a while ago.

"Shall I fetch Otis?" Evelyn tried to be helpful.

"Yes, do that." Levi glanced over his shoulder at the prison cells. The markings and the ghosts Otis had set there had to hold. It was a risk he had to take. But before he headed up the stairs, he took the Bufonite with him and then followed Evelyn up.

Together they pushed a showcase in front of the basement door.

"Evelyn, take this to Otis." Levi handed her the Bufonite.

"Tell him to hide it." He had a bad feeling about this. Sigourney had always brought calamity with her. She was like a bad penny.

19

THE DIVIDE COMING FROM LOCKED DOORS

he Rabbit god of luck scratched the back of his ear. You could say it was a marvel he was able to do that whilst restricted by the shackles. But all the running away from his manifold enemies had kept him nimble. Here he was, sitting with his legs raised and twisted behind his right ear while balancing with his great paws lifted, preventing him from toppling over, and scratching his ear.

He was all alone. The hotel owner had pushed the door shut behind him as he'd fled.

It was time.

His life had gone on long enough, being continuously used for others' gain. The Rabbit began to imagine living as an ordinary bunny. Yes, everything would be over in a flash. Yes, he would be at the mercy of nature. But his decisions would never again cause more harm than good. No one could curse his name as they now did in the gambling house. The games would go on, leaving most unhappy and some destitute. He just didn't want to be part of the chase any longer. But it would mean a death of some sort. His consciousness would not be his anymore. No more dreaming about cosmic scale stuff, just a desire to eat, fuck, and sleep. And not necessarily in that order. Of course, your common bunnies could be great thinkers and no one would know. They could have solutions to energy crises, could have written a constitution where everybody wins, could have understood the meaning of life. Highly unlikely given the way they behaved, but still a possibility.

The Rabbit glanced at the door again. There was a fifty-fifty chance Mathew had left it unlocked. That was only logical. But when you took humans and gods into account, reasonable odds went haywire, and there could be hundreds, even thousands of variables when it came to those whose heads were full of myths. If the Rabbit were a betting man, which he was,[76] he would put all his money on it being locked despite the futility of the thought. He, Lepus, could always kick it down, but where would he flee? He needed Justice to take off the shackles. Maybe he should have asked the hotel owner to do it before he left—but no, the Rabbit had decided. Ordinary rabbit it would be—no more Mr. Lepus.

For a moment, the Rabbit wondered if there was a danger of spontaneous combustion. He twitched his nose and ignored the warning signs. He continued meditating, pushing out all the unnecessary clatter.

The image of a soft white-gray bunny began to form in his mind. A giant for its breed, yet minuscule compared to what he was now. Should he leave one part of his consciousness behind just in case?

He concentrated on the image, making the details more accurate, more fine-tuned. He pictured those features in his place, pushing all the luck in the world out of his body. The Rabbit imagined being at the top of Mount Jadero, where evolution governed the world instead of them, the ideas.

Nah, it would be too dangerous.

"Ommmmmm." The sound resonated through his chest.

"Ommmmmmm." He continued envisioning the future.

One more "om" and he would be free. However, the last mantra was interrupted by someone, or something, struggling with the door. The Rabbit opened his eyes. Maybe a devotee,

---

76   It was just that there was no one to bet with.

but he had a hard time believing that. He tried to ignore the noise, but it sounded as if a drunk blind man was having his way with the handle.

The Rabbit twitched his nose.

The door creaked open.

The hotel owner was back. Mathew looked sheepishly at him. The Rabbit knew the look. It was the sign of a guilty conscience.

He sighed. That was godly glamour for you. He'd sprinkled it all over the man's mind without knowing it. He wondered if he should throw a cushion at Mathew to drive him away. But it would be cruel to shatter the man's sudden burst of bravery. There was only one choice to make, and that was to let the hotel owner rescue him. Oh well, he could continue his project later.

Mathew hurried to the altar.

"Let me get the shackles off." He had bolt cutters with him.

The Rabbit lifted his paws and offered the shackles, despite knowing there would be only uncomfortable electrocution for both of them in the near future. But after all this time among humans, he'd learned that they only understood things through trial and error. The man needed to be electrocuted. His whole essence begged for it.

So it happened. The hotel owner's whole body shook as the shackles activated. To Lepus' luck, he only got a mild shock. He swept the man's feet from underneath him, making him let go of the cutters, which thudded onto the altar.

The Rabbit settled back, waiting for Mathew to regain consciousness, listening to the outside world. He could hear Sigourney and Siarl and the ruckus they were making. Good for them, despite the fact that it clearly wasn't working. Lepus knew bulletproof necromancy when he saw it. Very clever to use spirits that way.

The hotel owner groaned. He sat up, clearly still out of it. He had that spacey look about him, like he was trying to figure out if there was such a concept as reality and now. The Rabbit could be helpful and say that there wasn't, but it was better for humans to think there was or there was a danger of going insane. Instead, he patted the man on his back, giving him a slight sparkle of luck that he managed to sneak past Justice's symbols.

There was another groan, but this time it was more intelligent. Or not, as the hotel owner reached for the bolt cutters.

"I wouldn't if I were you." The Rabbit stopped him.

"But—"

"But you can lead me outside and get me to the place they call Kingfisher Road, and then you will have done your duty. How about that?" The Rabbit god of luck tried to make an encouraging expression. It was more like a constipated bunny trying to look cute.

Nevertheless, the questionable expression worked. The hotel owner nodded.

"Now get me up," the Rabbit commanded.

The hotel owner did what was asked. He helped Lepus up and guided him through the gambling house. Justice had been naive to leave only the one unconscious guard to watch the Rabbit. So like the gods. They thought that if they wished for something, it would be so, reality and others be damned.

The only obstacle they found on their way out was an older woman wearing enough lucky charms to decorate a midsummer pole. The gentle *tap, tap, tap* of her cane accompanied the jingling of her charms.

The Rabbit wasn't sure if she was trying to find her way out of the building or to go back to the room where luck turned into money and money into despair. The woman wore thick eyeglasses and was clutching her purse tightly against her chest. That one devious bone in the Rabbit's body wanted to mess with her. One trick and he would be feeling more like himself. But better not. Not when the shackles restricted him and would burn his flesh.

He nodded for Mathew to move on, and the Rabbit and the hotel owner made their way around the woman. She barely saw them, but as one last good deed, the Rabbit caused the woman to spin around as he brushed past her, pointing her in the right direction—whatever that was according to her.

"Hello?" the woman asked.

They burst out into the alleyway.

The air was thickening from the smog, and for a moment, the Rabbit wondered whether he'd gone blind.

"What on earth?" he asked.

"Smog from all the coal burning. If we want to get through the city in haste, I suggest we find an omnibus to take us. They use feelers when the weather gets this bad." The hotel owner was barely visible.

"Lead the way, then."

"Will you ever tell me what happened back there?" the hotel owner asked.

"Brother-sister stuff."

"I guess I have to count my blessing for—"

The Rabbit didn't let the man go on. "Blessings come in disguise. So does calamity. But to walk alone, with no place to belong, that's no life."

The hotel owner said nothing.

The Rabbit opted out of thinking and followed the man. He had always preferred action and following his impulses over analyzing. Also, it seemed as if the hotel owner knew where he was heading. They walked on a few blocks, and the Rabbit found himself getting thirsty. If this saunter continued any longer, he might insist on stopping to get a carrot cocktail. Justice had refused to serve him alcohol. She thought it was the root of all evil, removing the ability to plan future actions and encouraging the drinker to go with their first thoughts, as any further thoughts were drowned in sweet, sweet intoxication. Maybe she wouldn't be doing all this if she had a drink or a puff once in a while? Then again, her second thoughts might have steered her away from megalomaniac world domination plans or that tiny thought that seemed to emerge in the gods every now and then—kill all humans. Or at least, the Rabbit found those thoughts in his head more than he cared to admit. The drinking helped.

Actually, he was getting insufferable thirsty. If he shut his eyes and pointed a finger in any direction, he was sure to find a pub and a persuadable mixologist. He liked the plan, as it would be disastrous to catch up with Justice when sober.

The Rabbit began to lift his paw, but that was as far as he got. The hotel owner stopped abruptly. The Rabbit almost slammed against the man. He managed to stop the motion by planting his hind legs more firmly on the ground.

"What now?" the Rabbit asked.

"I have commandeered a vehicle for us." The man beamed with pride.

In front of them was a machine, a primitive version of what they would one day call a tractor, if the future was allowed to continue. It was powered by steam and sheer human ingenuity. Electricity and gasoline would be better, and later maybe something called splitting atoms, but where was the fun in the Rabbit revealing that to the humans? The best part of inventing was the discovery, and he wasn't cruel enough to take the enjoyment away.

He clambered onto the machine and was on his way to Kingfisher Road, or if he changed his mind, to a pub.

Protests are all fun and games. Also, it's nice to stand behind your own convictions in front of so many pairs of eyes. Still, often enough, it will get you into some kind of trouble. The social type usually, ranging from social exclusion to imprisonment to off with your head, all depending on what kind of bastard you are protesting against. Sigourney wasn't sure what awaited them, but she sat inside the prison cell—or the closet made to look like one—while Siarl plotted their next move. She was on the bed, picking absentmindedly at the straw mattress. Despite being trapped, she was proud of what she and Siarl had done. Someone had to be the one to act against tyranny. And others followed. So Siarl had said, and he had been right. Edith and Humphrey had been too afraid to do anything even when they'd seen and suffered a great wrong. It had something to do with personality and internal locus of control. Plus a whole lot about circumstances and terror.

Siarl was doing all the organizing for the next attack. It seemed to make him happy, so she let him. He had quickly adopted the prison language, and as she had foreseen, he'd made some adjustments to speed up the process. Their efforts hadn't made any waves thus far, especially as the doors refused to budge. Whatever juju they had in them was strong. So, instead of exhausting her energy, Sigourney was trying to develop a more reasonable way to free them. Siarl could sometimes be too single-minded when he got an idea inside his brilliant head. Sigourney's never held anything worth keeping, so according to many, she was like a weathervane. That was a crude misconception, however. Her only crime was to be open to all the possibilities, however stupid or brilliant they sounded.

Now she was eying the door, searching for new angles.

How she'd escaped from prison didn't apply here. She'd used another sort of trickery: good behavior, trust, and then a vanishing act. Her best bet was to find the sweet spot, the one thing Levi had overlooked. There was always something. She traced the door's edges, looking for its weaknesses. Swinging the bed against it to break out had three flaws. There was not enough momentum. Also, it was not her style. Force was always the last option in her toolbox. Lastly, the juju, Humphrey had explained, neutralized any violence. But there was truly no need for it, not now, not here; her eyes caught the hinges.

Sigourney let go of the straw mattress and smiled. As brilliant as her brother was, he had no mind for this. They'd concentrated on the specials' talents, forgetting the basic things. Or at least she hoped they hadn't considered the mundane. People seldom did.

She stood up, taking the washing bowl with her, and walked past Siarl. He was knocking on the wall, talking to Edith and Humphrey. She reached for her pocket, amazed that Levi and Margaret had not searched her. She took the lockpicking set out, choosing the thick, narrow blade—the one that reminded her of a screwdriver. Sigourney knelt down to inspect the lowest hinge, and she was in luck. It was a plain hinge with a pin going through the middle without caps. Even if there had been caps, they would have been easy to remove with her tools. She pushed her pick underneath the hinge. There was no room to hit the pick with the washing bowl. She had to trust that the pin wasn't too tight or too stuck or too rusted, but even if it was, she didn't have anything better to do than shimmy and shimmy until the metal obeyed.

The pin clanged to the floor when Sigourney pushed the blade fully in.

The knocking stopped.

"Sigourney?" Siarl asked.

She said nothing, moving on to the second one. This time she used the washing bowl to aid the process, and the pin dislodged faster. The third was as easy as the previous one. Siarl had come to assist her, and he automatically took the bowl from her when she offered it to him. Sigourney lowered back down and pushed her fingers underneath the door and began to wiggle it. The hinges came apart. Siarl rushed to take the load off her, and Sigourney got up.

"Sigourney?" Siarl asked again.

She shrugged. "You seemed like you were having fun organizing the rebellion, and I didn't want to disturb you." When he looked displeased, she started to panic. Had she belittled him? "I didn't mean it that way. Just that... I needed time to think... I love you," she tried.

"It's fine. Don't worry about it; you just surprised me. I love you too." He gave her a weak smile.

Her returning smile was as anemic as his.

One of these days, they really had to have that conversation, but neither wanted to break the illusion. Pretending was so much easier. None of that mattered now as they escaped into the basement and Sigourney automatically began to open the locks, knowing well what her function was. Having a definite conviction about one's purpose in life made it manageable, giving it a simple and beautiful meaning and leaving the existential questions to others. What made the purpose more fulfilling was if it helped others, bettering their lives. Such behavior created the happiest humanoids on the planet. A bold statement would be to say in the universe, but who knew what kind of twisted creatures existed past the nearest atmosphere.

And to Justice's annoyance, she was clearly on the side of fairness here, causing every hair on her perfect body to stand up and do the lambada. But still, Sigourney was tied to her blood and her family. It mattered. It defined a person whether they liked it or not, tying them to their ancestors and society, which determined their value. On some level, she'd won the lottery with her blood, mostly because the substance pulsing through her veins hid the secret of the creation of the universe. But she knew it was a mistake. To think that a human like her held some cosmic wisdom about why everything had started was nonsense.[77]

Whatever the truth, she couldn't help but think that all this was meaningless. Of course, Siarl and the Rabbit weren't meaningless. They held significant value to her. Still, when it came to the cosmos or animals, she found them to be smarter than many humans. There was nothing special about humans —that was just the fragile human ego playing tricks on them.

---

77   Why not? According to some, we are all star children, made of the dust of
      dying suns.

Of course, she knew the specials in this basement were valuable, but to her they were mere humans.

Sigourney glanced at the staircase. It was empty. Behind her, Siarl was opening the other doors with the key he'd found. She took the set of lockpicks out of her pocket to get Edith's door open. She moved her hands with precision despite feeling like they had doubled in size. This was just too much for her.

There was a loud click.

She carefully opened the door to peer in, ready to duck if Edith Nye was planning to try her luck.

"Edith," she said, the words catching in her throat, making her sound like a mouse trying to cough. She cleared her throat and said, "Hello?!"

Unlike their room, this one was illuminated. There was the soft light of a gas lamp, reminding her of those rooms at the Royal Palace of White Cuniculus back in Leporidae Lop. The floor was covered with luscious pillows. Underneath them was a woven mat patterned with little flowers and people. Instead of a simple wooden table, there was a coffee table with golden ornamental legs and a marble counter. On it was a little porcelain tea set.

Sigourney stepped in. From the corner of her eye, she saw something coming down at her. She dived, landing flat on the rug, which wasn't there. All the clamor had disappeared. Sigourney didn't wait to see what happened next. She swirled around and was greeted again with that something that had come down at her. It was a table leg. She ducked to her left, rolling under the bed.

There was a scream from the lady who'd tried to murder her.

"It's me, Sigourney. Edith, please." Sigourney scooted deeper under the bed just in case, peering out.

No answer came. The woman who'd attacked her had bolted out through the open door.

Sigourney was glad on so many levels. She crawled out from under the bed, got up, and looked at the room, which was nothing like the one she had seen a moment ago. The marble table was now wooden, and one of its legs was missing. The rug and the pillows were nowhere to be seen.

Sigourney made her way to the door and poked her head out, wishing her hand or leg could detect the world behind the corner. She had to be satisfied with her head, which she considered to be a design flaw. Who in their right mind would put all the essential bits in the same location and think they were safe there?[78]

Despite waiting for a blow to her head, it never came. She saw Edith running up the basement stairs, Humphrey and Siarl watching behind her.

Edith shook the basement door. It didn't budge. She collapsed against it and began sobbing loudly, her raven hair hanging loosely over her face. Edith's hands clutched the hem of her gray dress.

Sigourney couldn't blame her for the reaction. If she had been in her shoes, she would lose any remaining rationality and do anything to get away, even in the wrong situation. If she'd read the knocking right, Edith had been here longer than anyone else.

Humphrey didn't look any better. He was a pitiful creature. Even someone like Sigourney could see that, and she often thought she was the lowest form of life. The man was thin, and the clothes he wore hung from his frame. A thick, disheveled beard covered his face, making his cheeks look hollower than they were. Humphrey blinked as if he was trying to relearn how to focus on someone. He clutched a spoon as he leaned against his former prison's door frame.

Sigourney had to look away. She bit her lip and thought about blood again. Not the blood coming from her mouth, but sharing the same blood as her brother. Did she carry the sins he'd committed? Was she evil by association?

"Sigourney?" the man asked, his voice sounding as thin as the one Sigourney had produced a moment ago with Edith.

"Yes?" Sigourney wasn't sure if she wanted to claim that title now. But the thought was overwritten by the fact the man was about to fall to his knees. Sigourney dashed to his aid, taking his right hand and allowing Humphrey to lean all his weight on her. Sigourney glanced at the room and saw the work desk and her brother's bench. She guided the man there. She couldn't help but notice that the doomsday machine was missing.

Humphrey collapsed on the bench and looked lost.

"Water," he gasped. "In my room." Humphrey pointed at

---

78   Octopuses got it right.

the open door.

Siarl had already moved on to the other rooms, but as always, he jumped up, ready to help.

"I can get it."

"No, I can do it." Sigourney was already running to the room, giving Siarl no time to do more than get up.

Humphrey's room smelled stale from sweat. In the corner was a full pisspot. She ignored it and went for the pitcher on the small table. She grabbed it and dashed out, more than willing never to go back.

She gave the man the pitcher.

He gulped it down, water flowing down from the corner of his mouth to his neck and inside his shirt.

"I'm sorry," he said in a clearer voice as he put the pitcher down.

"No—" Sigourney began.

"Not about this. About you getting dragged here. I should never have helped your brother." The man lowered his hands onto his knees to steady the shake.

Sigourney never knew what she should say in these situations. Everything she could come up with sounded lame, and the seconds seemed to run away with all her precious pearls, diamonds, and, most importantly, miniature porcelain squirrels.

"It's okay," she managed.

The man peered into her eyes, and all her senses screamed at her to duck.

"It's not okay. I'm glad you are here and helped us out, but okay? Never." He reached for her hand.

She stepped back. She hadn't meant to, but it happened, and there was no taking it back. She looked at the floor and said,

"I'd better go and see what's taking Siarl so long."

"Yes, I think you should." Humphrey leaned away.

Siarl stood in a doorway, immobile. He looked desperate. Sigourney spooked him when she peered into the room next to him. The room looked as empty as the others had been, but when she squinted her eyes, she noticed a man sitting still on the floor, his back facing the door. He only had light brown pants on and no shirt to speak of. His hair had been shaved off completely. Sigourney had to really pay attention to tell if he was breathing or not. His sides expanded slowly and collapsed almost as slowly.

Alive, but barely.

"Hello?" Siarl tested next to her, as he had done several times already.

No reply.

"We have come to rescue you." Siarl took a different approach.

No reply.

Sigourney had an unnerving feeling that someone was looking out from inside her.

"Will you come with us?" Sigourney decided to join in, shocked by the man's presence. She had seen people like him in prison. The pacifist protesters, the ones who'd gone away with the fairies, as they said, and the catatonic.

When they reached the man, she expected him to stink. But there was a slight smell of soap. Her brother wasn't a downright evil bastard.

Siarl was about to reach his hand out to touch the man's shoulder. Sigourney stopped him in time.

"No, not from behind. Not suddenly."

"Okay, you'd better take the lead here," Siarl said.

"Hello," she tried, circling to face him. He was in his mid-forties. There were deep lines on his face, although those same lines were now relaxed. He had his eyes open, and in this light, they were deep brown. If they detected Sigourney, there was no reaction. But again, she felt like someone was watching from behind her eyes. It was the same kind of creepy feeling as when you are alone in the room and you are sure someone is there—pressure with an awkward silence.

She wanted to flee. She would have if this wasn't her brother's doing and if Siarl wasn't here with her.

"Mister, we have come to get you out." Siarl waved his hand in front of the man's face.

No reaction.

Sigourney lowered herself onto the floor to sit in front of the man. She crossed her legs and stared at him, trying to think about what she should do.

"You don't seem to be away with the fairies," she said aloud in the hope there would be a reaction of some sort. There wasn't.

Siarl followed suit. "What are you doing?" he asked.

"He needs time. We can't shake him or touch him. For his

and our sake."

"We don't exactly have time. We should be getting out of here."

"Yes, I'm well aware of that, but while we want to dash out, he's not ready, and we aren't leaving him behind."

Siarl nodded. "Yeah. Do what you must."

Sigourney tilted her head to see if the eyes would move. "You know, I'm sorry that my brother did this to you."

No movement, no facial tic, but there was a scream from the door. "Brother?!"

Sigourney didn't want to lift her head and face the screamer. She already knew who it came from.

Edith stood at the door. Sigourney could see her shadow. Humphrey was next to her, supporting himself against Edith's shoulder.

"We came to see what's going on." Humphrey tried to soften the mood. It was a mistake. Uncontrollable rage shone from Edith's face. All pretense of niceties was a million miles away on a forgotten island with the friendly creatures who never had a chance in this reality.

As always, Sigourney found herself grasping for words to defend herself. But she really didn't have to. The other woman looked more distraught than actually angry, to the point that she might start hurting people. Fear was so easy to mistake for so many things, from snobbery to anger to hate to disgust. Usually, fear and anxiety lingered underneath every exterior.

It would be so easy to meet her with anger and hate and contempt, but Sigourney had never been good at dominating others to force their silence or cooperation.

"I'm sorry," Sigourney tried. "We should have told you."

Those magic words seemed to do the trick. Edith's whole posture sank. "I—"

"Suffered more than you should. I get it. Now please, do you have any idea how we can get him out of here?" Sigourney gave her the most sympathetic smile.[79] It wasn't a big one from ear to ear. It was small and almost non-existent, but Edith picked it up.

The effect was astonishing. Edith responded with a heartfelt smile. "What's wrong?"

---

79 Another thing that human relationships ultimately boil down to.

"He seems to be out of it." Siarl jumped into the conversation.

"Oh, I can help with that," Edith offered. As she said this, the room changed. Became brighter. But it wasn't the brightness Edith used to help them. Where the man sat, an exact copy stood up. This happened again and again until the actual man followed the example. Edith guided the ghost man and the real one out of the room to the basement door.

They all stood there for a prolonged moment of social hell, according to Sigourney. She couldn't take the closeness of the group.

"I'd better unlock the door." She knelt down and took her kit out, only for the door to clang into something heavy and big.

"Crit," she said.

20

THE LITTLE FEARS THAT KEEP US
EVOLVING

he smog swirled around Rose and Percy as they stood outside the Alchemist's Shop. This was not the first time the thick, unbreathable smoke had taken over the street, and Rose appreciated the dramatic effect. It reminded her of home. Unlike in Necropolis, here, the tangible air was a sign of cutting corners. That was the thing with money. At first, everything was done with good intentions, but soon, those good intentions turned into compromises for the profit—funny old world. Rose couldn't deny its impact on her. She had more than once advised her clients to do everything they could to make their stocks lucrative for investors. Usually, downsizing was the best option. A real way to make money, as make-believe sold better. But some poor suckers had to buy the product at some point, usually the one who was making it to begin with or someone like them. Oh well.

With Levi's machine—no, the bank's—they wouldn't have to do any of that. She only had to save it from Justice. Percy would have to keep his fears to himself. He had spoken about doom the whole coach ride here, saying things like the smog was an omen and, most importantly, she was being foolish if she thought she could outwit the gods.

Rose didn't like it when fear made decisions for her. It was too easy to let it sweep over you, especially after the realization that there was no controlling your destiny. But fear was the feeling telling you that something was novel; something was unexpected; something was beyond your comprehension. Yes, fear could cause destruction and turn evil, but in the right hands it could change the world. Rose couldn't let Percy convince her to walk away. The future lay in the novel, the unexpected, and the things beyond our comprehension. It was where she, a banker, had to be comfortable. It was where she had to take risks, especially when something was important. Without risk-takers, the human race would skulk in their caves, afraid of their own shadows.

But along with fear came uncertainty and no plans. And she couldn't quite admit that to Percy. There was only the hope that her presence would change events somehow, as caring about something was better than being an emotionally stunted calculating machine.

The hexer reached for her arm as she opened the shop door.

"We don't have a plan."

"And how do you propose we make one against the gods?" Rose asked. She knew it was a weak argument, but it was the best she could give. Maybe once they were inside, she could convince Abigail to go against her master and be on the side of humans for once.

"This is—" Percy began.

"Reckless. Believe me, I know. But I can't in good conscience let them hurt him. And he will get hurt, even if they don't mean it. He'll do anything to protect his machine," Rose interrupted him. Another argument they'd had in the coach.

"Proper authorities—" Percy began.

"There are no authorities against the gods. If there were, we wouldn't be in this mess. None of it." She headed in, pulling the door open and hearing Percy mutter to himself that there should be. The doorbell chimed as she entered.

Instead of finding Justice and her thugs in the shop, or

Mr. Perri himself, only the timid maid was behind the counter. She was helping an older man with his affairs. From the sound of it, he was a regular who'd escaped the dangerous streets to buy remedies for his soul. She could spot his kind miles away. They were the perpetual complainers and hypochondriacs. A pain in her ass when she had been a common clerk. Now, as an investor, she'd started to appreciate them. They were the ones who watched the sea and thought every surge was a tidal wave. They were the ones who pointed out the flaws and impurities of everything, and she meant everything. Rose had learned to value all the possible personalities. They kept the human race going.[80] But not only that, there was a niche market for all the wonderful things people were afraid of.

"Miss," Rose greeted the maid.

The woman nodded and then glimpsed Percy, who loomed behind Rose.

"Shall I get the master for you?" she asked past the man trying to figure out which cure was best for his rash.

"If you would be so kind... Evelyn, was it?" Rose asked. It felt like time was slowing down, while her mind was screaming, "Run, they will be here soon."

"Yes, I'll fetch Mr. Perri right away. Can you wait, Mr. Fletcher?" Evelyn nervously smiled at the customer.

The man groaned, but when he saw Rose and more so Percy, he kept his thoughts to himself. Without a doubt, he was going to take this time to list all the complaints he would unleash later.

The wait seemed like an eternity, especially when the hypochondriac started getting restless and the shop filled with other refugees. Every time the doorbell chimed, Rose's chest got tighter. The thick smog swirled in, and she was no longer convinced about its dramatic effect. It might be the reason they had gotten here before Justice,[81] but now the outside world had started to sound like a battlefield: people yelled, the horses complained, and metal clanged against metal. They didn't need anything extra to complicate things. Rose was

---

80   So there is no hope for one human prototype, despite how much some people wish it.

81   It wasn't: it was all down to the Rabbit's luck working in twisted ways. Who knew for whose benefit? The Rabbit didn't.

sure their driver had already fled, despite them asking him to wait as a possible getaway coach.

When Levi arrived, he came alone. No maid. No otter. No machine. He wore a weary expression, which he masked with a surprised smile. Before he had time to greet them, the man called Fletcher stopped the alchemist. He demanded an answer to the ingredients listed on the two bottles he held in his hands. He was adamant about it.

"I have to—" Fletcher managed to say.

"Take them both. You can have them for free. You are one of my oldest customers, and it's high time I showed some appreciation. Now, I'm afraid I have to ask you and the others to leave. The shop is closed for the rest of the day." Levi's voice was strained.

The man tried to protest. So did the two ladies who'd come in only a minute ago and were admiring Levi's mechanical sculptures.

Levi let them have one for a tenth of the price as he drove everyone away, locking the door behind them.

Rose was sure he would collapse there and then, but the alchemist managed to muster strength from somewhere.

"Miss Pettyshare, and Mr. Allread, I presume." He offered his hand first to Rose, kissing hers, and then shaking Percy's.

Rose tensed, not knowing how the hexer would react. Percy had been sniffing loudly and muttering strange words the whole time they had been there. Thankfully, Levi's entrance had put a stop to the peculiar behavior aside from his rude staring, which was better than trying to smell the alchemist, Rose had to admit.

"Pleasure to meet you, sir," Levi said while shaking hands with Percy.

Percy looked ready to open his mouth and argue. Rose interrupted him.

"I appreciate you closing the shop for us. It's imperative we talk. Can we?" She gestured at the back door.

"Yes, sure, why not." He led them out of the shop. "I gather you have had your assessment from your expert."

"Yes, Horatio Arlington found the specimens intriguing and confirmed that they are genuine. But that's—" Rose said as she followed Levi out of the shop. He was taking them into the parlor.

"He would, wouldn't he? Nevertheless, you have caught

me at a bad time. I'm in the middle of something. Would it be possible for you to come back tomorrow or later today?" Levi didn't sound sure. He halted in the hallway and turned to face them.

Altogether, he was behaving unlike the charming man she had met a couple of days ago. The mention of Mr. Arlington's name hadn't done her any favors. At this point, Rose didn't have the time to worry about Levi's past, or niceties, or for that matter reason. Pressing matters overruled everything else.[82] Justice would be here soon.

"I can't do this. I can't pretend all is well. I need you to get your machine and notes; you are coming with us. It's not safe here."

"Miss Pettyshare?" Levi frowned.

"Please, Mr. Perri, get your things. I'll explain as soon as we are in our coach." Rose looked at the door, glancing into the shop. She was sure Justice would burst in any minute now. She'd let social protocols delay the inevitable long enough.

"I can't leave just like that. I have my duties and..." He seemed unsure where to go next, or so Rose thought. But now, as Rose paid more attention, she noticed the house was more alive than before. The once quiet walls moaned. The stairs and the floorboards creaked. The air was filled with hushed voices and the smell of something greasy cooking.

Percy shifted his weight from one foot to the other behind them, sniffing the air and muttering his hexes. The man's expression had gone beyond constipation to a new level of agitation. He snarled.

"Rose, I can feel the death here. There's a necromancer hiding inside this house, and they have used their powers. I can smell it, and I mean literally. It's a sweet, rotten aroma mixed with electricity and acid. We should never have come here. Justice is right to destroy this machine of his. It's unnaturally made, I'm sure of it..."

Rose shot a glance at Percy in the hope he would stop speaking, but he didn't.

"This is an abomination. The highest offense there is..." Percy continued.

Before he could say more, she cut him short.

---

82   With ease, one might argue.

"How can you smell anything over the cooking. Nonetheless, it could be something they use. A chemical in the process. Necropolis exports a lot of necromantic remedies, and this is an alchemy shop." Both of them knew Levi wasn't a necromancer, despite dressing like one. What he was missing was the eyes that had seen the great beyond and could command it. Eyes that would make your soul shiver and want to flee out of your body.

"I'm a finder, Rose. I'm good at it, better than I am at accounting. My nose and my senses never lie. Not here, not on my previous missions. I have never made a mistake. This is necromancy." He started to prowl around the hallway.

Rose snorted. "So what? He can still make something out of nothing, and you'll bear witness to that as soon as we get out of here. No one else has been able to do that. So what if it's through the ancient ways? This is still novel, and we can't let it be destroyed."

"The Council—"

"The Council be damned."

"You don't mean that. They'll hang you or worse." Percy's eyes were wide. There were worse consequences than a hanging, especially if necromancers got involved.

Rose's stomach turned despite meaning every word she'd said, but it was a built-in feature of any Necropolitan not to go against the Council. They were the law. They were your god, your executioner, your soul, your morality, your king and queen, the bogeyman who takes you if you misbehave.

"Yes, I did," she said, sounding braver than she felt. "They are just power-hungry despots who'll destroy even a good thing if it undermines their authority, and this is a good thing. I won't let you or them stop progress."

"It's my duty," Percy insisted.

"A moment ago, you said your duty was to protect me. This is protecting me. I need the machine or..." Rose swung her hands in the air. She was ready to do more if Percy didn't stop being so stubborn.

"Destroy?" Levi asked, finally catching up.

"Yes, destroy. We don't have time for any of this. Not for the Council or to argue about Justice and what she's doing. So get your machine and your notebook, and the necromancer, if you are hiding one, and we need to get you away from here," Rose said, silencing Percy, who was about to argue back. She'd had it with him.

"Who's going into hiding?" someone asked from the opening to the kitchen. A woman leaned against the wall not far from them. She was holding a bowl in her hands and eating as she stared at them. She had an eyepatch over her left eye, and the tip of her right-hand forefinger was missing.[83]

Percy inhaled loudly, and when he exhaled, he let out, "Demon."

"That doesn't mean anything," Margaret said in a sing-song voice. "I'm more like Mr. Perri's supplier of rare goods. Don't hold my nature against me and I won't hold yours against you, witch."

Rose was starting to see how things would only escalate from here. She ignored the demon or whatever the woman proposed to be and took hold of Levi's hand, pulling him closer to her.

"You have to believe me. You and the machine are in great danger. And the only way to protect you is by leaving. The..." She wanted to say "the gods are coming," but she couldn't quite say it aloud without sounding insane.

"Miss Pettyshare, please explain. I can't do anything until you give me a reason. Not when you and your assistant are in disagreement on how to proceed. And you spoke of the Council and then about Justice. None of this makes any sense." Levi wrapped his hands around hers.

Rose could feel the seconds ticking away and hear the boots of Justice's men thudding against the ground. It was a good thing she had never told Percy the exact location of the Alchemist's Shop, or they wouldn't have gotten here on time. But she couldn't tell Levi about Justice. He wouldn't believe her, and even if he did, it would complicate things more than necessary.

"The Luddites know about your machine," she said. It wasn't a lie. It was actually the truth, which would surely make a difference. "I had to tell them, I'm sorry. But not all is lost if you come with us."

"The Luddites? You told them? I don't quite follow. What do you have to do with them?" Levi babbled.

---

83   Rose was the first to pay full attention to the woman. Others usually didn't see past the eyepatch or the blasphemous aura hanging around Margaret. What made Rose mark all the little details was that they could be the difference between empty hands and a million bucks.

"We don't have time for any of this. Please, just get your things. They'll be here any minute now." Rose let go of him.

"So she finally found you. How clever of her," Margaret interrupted them. "Not as clever as me, though. I found you a long time ago. But oh well, that's single-minded gods for you. But you'd better do what the pretty lady says and go with her."

They all stared at Margaret. She didn't flinch, just kept smiling that colossal grin of hers.

"I can't—" Levi began.

"Yes, you can. I'll stall them. It has been too long since our paths crossed. She must be missing me after having no one to dance with for so long." Margaret tap-danced on the spot, being careful not to spill her stew.

"You heard her. Get your things," Rose jumped in, thankful for her unlikely ally.

"What about Sigourney?" Levi protested.

"I'll bring her to you," Margaret said.

"How? You don't even know where we are going. Where are we going?" Levi sounded as if he was about to panic.

"Wherever you go, I'll find you. Don't you worry about that. I won't let you or the machine out of my sight. And I won't let anyone hurt you..." That was as far as Margaret got. The windows of the shop shattered.

"Here we go." She laughed.

"Please, Mr. Perri." Rose touched his arm.

"Okay, then. I'll get Otis and the machine." Levi parted from her and ran to the stairs leading to the upper floors.

Something crashed into the shop.

"That's my cue," Margaret said and headed in through the open door.

"Percy," Rose pleaded. "Please, go with Levi and get him to safety. Not to the hotel; they know about it. One of the banks you visited, maybe."

"What will you do?" Percy asked.

"I'll help her until you get away."

"This machine means so much to you that you are willing to die for it?"

"I won't die."

Percy shook his head.

"Please," Rose said, knowing how pathetic she sounded.

"The Council will crucify you if the Luddites don't."

"So be it. But for that to happen, the machine and the alchemist have to survive."

"Then you better take this." Percy opened his long black coat. Underneath it hung a short, narrow blade. Not a rapier exactly, but not a heavy sword either. Something between a dagger and a sword. He unlatched it and offered it to Rose.

"Thank you," Rose said.

"I want it back. Better see to it." With those words, he departed and followed Levi up the stairs.

Rose turned around and ran into the shop to see Margaret bash a Luddite with her soup bowl.

21

ENTANGLEMENT OF CAUSES

evi's heart beat in a way it never had before. He ran up the stairs to the upper floor as thudding feet followed after him. Rose, he thought, despite the steps sounding too heavy for the banker. But it wasn't like he had full brainpower. His thoughts were stuck in the mode of what in the name of the hairy fishmonger's wife was going on. No one had bothered to explain all the loose ends they'd obviously hoped he wouldn't notice. All those thoughts were followed by the insistence that his priority was to get the machine out of the house. But behind that, a tiny doubt whispered that he couldn't leave and let the Luddites demolish his life's work. What good would that do? The Luddites would surely be on his side if they let him explain. But he'd lived the life of the downtrodden and knew that sometimes pitchforks had to be drawn to make others listen and show how society's fabric should be woven. Unfortunately, he was in their way. Levi believed in revolutions; sometimes, everything had to be shaken so the old leeches fell off, but he preferred that to happen through progress and not at the expense of his machine or his life.

Levi ignored the tiny voice insisting he should stay. He had to leave to save those who mattered: the machine and Otis, and if possible, his sister. Levi swung Otis' door open only to see that the necromancer and Evelyn were already escaping through an open window. At least they weren't trying to take the Bufonite with them. It was abandoned on the man's bed.

"Otis?" he asked, fighting to get the words out. He felt betrayed.

Otis' long gray coat hung inside the room. As the man turned around, Levi saw that his features were sharper than they had been this morning. He looked like one of those wandering magicians with his beard and long white hair. His green eyes had stayed the same. He lingered there between the outside world and the warmth of the room, his left foot inside as he balanced on the window frame.

"So? You..." Otis didn't finish what he wanted to say.

"Leaving without saying goodbye?" Levi pretended to sound casual. He wanted to say more, but he was more like his sister than he knew. It was hard to say the words that would leave him exposed by opening his heart to the man.

"The party was getting too crowded for my liking." Otis pulled himself back in, swinging his legs in to sit properly on the frame. "Not that keen on hearing the Council's name thrown around."

"You heard that then."

"Otis?" Evelyn's eyes were wide, and she was trembling.

"In a minute."

"But..." she insisted.

"A gentleman never leaves loose ties behind." Otis stroked the maid's cheek with the back of his hand.

Evelyn shut her eyes, and Levi felt angry. She was in love, and Otis? No, he couldn't be. Not as long as he pursued adoration from every passing female to satisfy the emptiness inside him. When the initial spark with Evelyn disappeared, in would come the new, and she would be abandoned, having done nothing wrong other than fall in love with the necromancer. Otis would never learn, and Levi could never explain himself to the man.

Levi heard the thudding feet stop just outside the room. He didn't dare to glance behind him in case he spooked Otis, but he was pretty sure it hadn't been Rose who'd followed him up. It was the witch.

"So, you want us to go our separate ways?" Levi asked.

"Yeah, it seems like the best idea. You don't need me any longer, and I highly appreciate my freedom." Otis shrugged. The man couldn't look Levi in the eye.

Neither could Levi. He had hurt Otis' feelings more than he knew. The middle part was clearly a jab about Sigourney when he'd said she was the key to powering the Bufonite. None of that meant anything. Levi didn't want to lose Otis. As jovial as the man could be about everything, underneath the surface was an inquisitive mind that had helped Levi to improve the mechanical aspects of the machine. Otis had always challenged him to see outside of the box. He needed the man. In addition, there was no escaping the fact that he would likely never be able to power the Bufonite without the necromancer's help, no matter how much he wanted Sigourney's blood to solve the mystery of quintessence.

Levi couldn't quite believe that Otis wanted to abandon the project and him. The necromancer's dedication to his profession was visible in the room. There were the skulls of the deceased, who Levi was sure tapped into the continental markets through the ethereal world, analyzing the stock prices and giving Otis suggestions for where to invest his money. Or something else as absurd. Among them were the necromantic books, diagrams, and the Bufonite's tubes, which stored the quintessence. He couldn't just leave all this behind. It didn't make sense. They had worked so hard. They had become friends. They had to be able to negotiate with the witch, find a way for them to finish this and for Otis to avoid facing the Council.

"I still need you, and I won't let anyone take you. We are in this together," Levi said with more passion than he'd meant to show. "We still have a lot to do. You said you could import a syntax into the quintessence to make it more controllable. We haven't done that. We only—"

"That's all fine, but you have to see that we have come to the end of our road. While you might have a friend in the banker and while you have a great mind when it comes to the mechanics of the universe, you are no match against the Council or the hexers, witches, and monsters they'll send after me. And believe me, even if we get rid of the one standing and listening to all this in the hallway, they'll send more, especially if Mr. Allread disappears." Otis swung his legs back outside and hesitated.

The second-floor drop wasn't impossible, but there were no drainpipes or ledges close by to ensure him safe passage.

"Please stay, Otis," Levi begged him. "We can sort this out."

"I can't. I should never have stayed this long. I don't know why I did. Maybe out of sentimentality, or because I finally found someone who could match my intelligence despite you never noticing that. Mixing necromancy with machinery isn't exactly simple, even when I made it look like it was. Oh well, you'll find others. We'd better go now. Evelyn, ladies first." Otis offered the maid his arm.

"Don't!" Levi took a step forward, but his words didn't have time to take effect. Percy swept in before Otis could comprehend that there had been an actual show of care and fellowship.

"Prohibere Otis," the hexer said, making the window frame and the air around Otis ripple. Then tiny little bald, half-rotten imps with needle-sharp teeth materialized out of nothingness and began to climb all over the frame, Otis, and Evelyn. The necromancer and the maid's movements slowed as the imps pulled them back towards the room.

Evelyn screamed, but the sound soon tailed off. Her limbs collapsed, giving the imps the power to move her body without effort. But Otis didn't succumb as quickly. He fought against the imps, trying to shake himself free and get out through the window.

"What are you doing?" Levi snapped, facing the hexer, unable to watch as the imps tore into Otis' and Evelyn's flesh, commanding them like puppets.

"Get your machine, and I'll deal with these two." Percy didn't even look towards him.

"I—" Levi protested.

"I'm not in the mood to argue, Mr. Perri, and the more you distract me, the more easily the cursed imps will get loose, and I can't guarantee where they'll go." Percy kept his attention on the necromancer.

Evelyn was already inside, walking towards the hexer, but Otis hung there between the room and the outside world, holding on to the window frame. The smog whirled inside past Otis, making the imps and the necromancer look more devilish.

Levi hesitated, then he hurried to Otis' bed and snatched up the Bufonite. He hugged it tightly against his chest, feeling the notebook inside his jacket press against his flesh.

When Levi glanced up, the hexer had managed to pull Otis inside. The necromancer still fought against the imps, making every move a battle of wills. The air rippled around him. Levi recognized the sensation from when there were ghosts around. It was like this tingling of the whole body, accompanied by an uncomfortable feeling of existence.

"If I were you, Mr. Thurston, I wouldn't fight against the inevitable," Percy warned the necromancer.

Levi was sure he hadn't mentioned Otis' full name.

The hexer managed to pull Otis closer to him, but the necromancer didn't give in as quickly. He slumped onto the floor.

"Help your friend up," Percy commanded.

Levi looked at the imps and then at the hexer and then at the machine and lastly at Otis.

"He needs assistance if you want to save your precious machine and leave before the Luddites come." Percy sounded tight and unyielding.

Levi shook his head. "Can't you do that?"

"And let him hurt me with the protection he's creating against me? It has to be you."

"But the imps?" Levi knew he sounded pathetic, but anyone in his shoes would protest. The imps weren't a welcoming sight. They had the teeth and talons to latch on to your flesh, not to mention those blackened eyes of theirs. No one could call them friendly or cuddly.

"They won't hurt you as long as you don't do anything I disapprove of."

Levi didn't feel any better about touching them, actually worse. But there was no other choice. He could hear the fighting downstairs. While he thought Margaret could hold her own, she was no match for so many. Not on her own. Levi lowered the Bufonite onto the floor and carefully approached Otis. The imps moved around the man's body, sending shivers all over Levi at the mere thought of letting the creatures touch him. He hesitated when he reached for Otis' shoulders, but all the shouting and crashing made him reconsider. When his hands brushed against Otis, the imps moved out of his way. There was a slight electrified sensation around the necromancer. He helped the man up, and the imps did the rest. Otis began to walk towards the door in the same trance-like manner as Evelyn. Levi hurried after them, taking the Bufonite with him.

Percy guided them out, muttering commands with his curses.

Otis twitched as he walked. Levi was sure he heard the same necromantic commands Otis had used before when summoning spirits. Not so entranced after all. The eerie feeling he'd had before amplified tenfold. Levi really didn't like the feeling. He hadn't liked it when visiting Necropolis, and he didn't like it now. Science was controllable and real. This was a silly fantasy, and dangerous.

But he had no other choice than to follow. They didn't get farther than the stairs and the hallway. A Luddite came crashing in from the open shop door, knocking Evelyn down. The imps held tightly to the falling woman, but Percy lost his concentration, especially when a second Luddite stormed in, and the imps got loose. They began to attack everything around them, including Levi's hat rack.

When Otis was freed from their clutches, he shouted, "Spirituum." Which was the conclusion of what he had been uttering for a while. A wave of spirits surged out, causing a few of the imps to ride the air as if they had an invisible steed. Other imps had found the second Luddite immensely entertaining. They'd jumped on him and bitten into his flesh, having abandoned the hat rack. It had turned out to be too spiky and quiescent for their liking, making it a tough fighter compared to the soft, wobbly human, who screamed as they tore into him. That was more like it.

Levi didn't have time to see what was going on. He was too busy fighting off the first Luddite. The man had come straight at Levi after knocking Evelyn down. He slammed Levi repeatedly against the wall, trying to shake the Bufonite free. All Levi could do was keep a tight hold while kicking the man, aiming at the man's crotch with his knee. The only thing he managed to do was kick the air.

The Luddite knocked him down, and Levi's head slammed against the wall with enough force to make the room spin. Levi let go of the machine, which never made contact with the floor. It hovered in the air while Levi himself slumped down. He saw the Bufonite drift towards Otis. The Luddite tried to seize it, but something invisible held him back.

"Run," Levi moaned. He didn't have to say it twice. Otis took off without glancing towards Levi or Evelyn. From the corner of his eye, Levi saw the maid run as well but in the opposite direction. She was going back up the stairs. Levi was about to protest, but he threw up after seeing the imps eating the second Luddite.

Percy stepped over the second man and headed after Otis, the imps scurrying after him, leaving Levi alone in the hallway with the Luddites. Next to him, the first Luddite was going slowly insane as a spirit attacked him, forcing its way into his body and soul. The second Luddite was thankfully dead. His blood poured out of an open wound in his neck.

Levi was starting to feel queasy again. So queasy in fact that he hallucinated a giant bunny stepping in through the broken front door of the shop. Levi threw up again.

The Rabbit followed Mathew through Threebeanvalley. They'd abandoned the steam-powered lawn mower a few streets over as it had died underneath them. To his surprise, he managed to hop better than he thought while bound by the shackles. It was all about the rhythm. Occasionally, the Rabbit squinted to see where they were going, but it was pointless. The smog, which had taken over the city, was thick and tangible. Despite it, the hotel owner kept his pace, accustomed to the strangeness. Around them, people, carts, horses, and steam-powered vehicles that looked like heavy-duty reinforced mini-tanks moved out of the way, crashing into nearby lampposts and buildings. The hotel owner didn't notice or care about the Rabbit's luck bending reality to his liking, causing the little mishaps.

The Rabbit chuckled. Everything had worked out just fine. And they were already close. The Rabbit could hear Siarl and Sigourney and sense the boy's love for the small human female. The Rabbit hadn't noticed how strong it was before. Oh, he knew they were important to each other, some might even argue meant to be,[84] yet he'd filed it under the category

---

84 Not him, as eternity was a long time to be meant to be.

of things-that-seem-to-exist-without-a-good-reason. Love was such a weird concept altogether. The Rabbit liked to stay out of it. Lust, infatuation, those were more up his alley, as they didn't come with the baggage of caring, committing, and coalescing. Yet Justice and others had argued that he also loved Sigourney. Not in the way Siarl did, but his feelings could still be labeled under the big L. Nonsense, he said.

The hotel owner stopped.

"What now?" the Rabbit asked.

"I think we are here or at least nearby. Can you see anything that resembles a street sign?" The hotel owner looked around.

The Rabbit watched the smog blur Mathew's features and make him disappear from view every now and then. What a strange human invention. He wondered what use they had for the smog. It had to serve some kind of purpose, but who knew with humans.

"No," the Rabbit replied eventually. Everything was covered with darkness, and he barely knew where he was or even who he was. The latter part didn't differ much from yesterday or the day before, or any other day. Could anyone honestly know who they were? Oh yes, people gave themselves roles: mother, sister, brother, fireman, teacher, clerk, god, and so on, but was that them? Or short, tall, thin, curvy, bold, INTJ, adventurous, hairy, shy, introverted... Those were also labels created by others and comparing them to others. Was that the true essence of a person, or just a social aspect of themselves? So, who was the Rabbit, Lepus? A pure manifestation of luck? Sure. Yet it left out his emotions, the things that told him he was him, not to mention his inner voice, the thoughts that made him move his paws onward and want to see another sunset. Maybe this was no time to ponder existential questions, especially as he couldn't keep pretending that he didn't hear all the confusion inside 28 Kingfisher Road. The place that was a few strides away.

The Rabbit perked his ears, moving them from side to side to find that familiar heartbeat he seemed to love. There it was, muffled under all the arguing, shouting, and fighting. Beneath the roof beams with the others.

"I can hear them," the Rabbit sighed. "There they are, fulfilling their part in history, connected to everybody and everything. Still unable to make a connection, despite having come to be from the same atoms. Believing they are different. We are basically copies of each other, if you ask me, dear Mathew. But no one ever does. Feet and all that."

"What?" the hotel owner asked.[85]

"Never mind. Not the time to ponder these things. I'll show us the way, and then you'd better be off." The Rabbit hopped on, keeping his ears up to listen to the sounds coming from the house where Sigourney was. She was chatting with someone or someones, unaware of what was happening a room above her. Justice had already reached the shop, and she and her Luddites were repeating the same pattern that always occurred amid change. Someone always opposed it. Someone always lost, got hurt, and died. Why was change such a difficult thing? Was it because unequal resources and power distribution got distorted? Was it because altruism died when fear entered the stage? Was it because of uncertainty and loss? Whatever the reason, all this was silly, especially as he could hear the fire crackling.

To top it all, he suspected the hotel owner would follow him in. Gods or deities like him drew humans to them. They couldn't look away no matter how badly they would get hurt. Another soul to protect.

He stepped inside the Alchemist's Shop just in time. Justice was contemplating unleashing her lapdogs to break every single bone in the body of Sigourney's brother, who was slumped against the wall in the hallway. The Rabbit took in the man's essence. Just like Lord Bufonite had been: curious, single-minded, idealistic, and full of scorn. Then there were the other beings. The other sister with a strange beating heart, there but not there. She was holding a painting, testing its balance. Also, there was another woman at the back of the shop. She had a steady heartbeat. The kind that would shape the universe to her liking. All of these people would get hurt when Justice's anger reached its peak. He would have to be the hero for once rather than Mr. Lucky.

The Rabbit pushed past the Luddites towards Justice, but her men attacked him, not letting him anywhere near their god. They hit him with their pipes. He couldn't give up, for Sigourney's and the city's sake. He pressed on, trying to avoid the men and their billysticks. He could see the weird glint in

---

85 For good reason.

Justice's eyes, and he doubted that her pursuit of power would stop here. Why should it? If she could make the citizens do her bidding, she could control the world and bring justice to all. She wouldn't be a god among their brothers and sisters, but a god among the masses. They would love her unconditionally and obediently. The adoration of her Luddites was present in his aching body. Every shock they gave him made his heart find a new rhythm. But that was the thing. It was only his heart that reconsidered its actions and not his central neural system, which insisted on pressing on.

He easily shook off the first wave of humans. They were humans after all. The only trouble was that he was suffering from restrictions, making him unable to counter Justice's influence. She was adamant about making a rug out of the Rabbit and she had made it known, sending more of her people against him. He felt her godly powers make the Luddites disregard their injuries and attack him. All his luck did was build up in the shackles, waiting for Justice to collect it.

The Rabbit snorted.

This wasn't fair. But there's a thought. Maybe he should give her what she wanted. Who was he to say no to her, if it was what his sister's heart most desired? The Rabbit took a step forward. His feet were unsteady from all the dodging and kicking and because of the shackles pressed hotly against his ankles. He could hear the men getting up from the floor to protect their goddess. They panted heavily and moaned. The woman with a strange beating heart and the other had joined in the fun, but they were an afterthought now. Justice was the goal. He got closer. She bent her body away from him, which was all she managed to do as he took one last hop towards her. He swung his great paws over and around her and pulled her towards him. He hugged his sister against his chest. She tried to struggle, but the Rabbit had an unfair advantage when it came to strength.

The Rabbit released everything stored up in the shackles, shutting his eyes and seeing an endless garden with row after row of carrots. A warm feeling spread all over his body. He pictured the bright blue sky full of clouds, the white and fluffy kind. Every good dream should have sky-sheep parading around. This was going to be a good one.

"I love you, Sigourney. I always did and always will. Sorry, and clean up the mess," the Rabbit whispered before he let go completely. There was nothing anyone could do to reverse this entanglement.

296

22

I AM SURE IT WASN'T SUPPOSED TO GO THIS WAY

igourney put her lockpicking tools back in the black cloth wrapping. The desperation was present once again. She hadn't made all their wishes come true. She'd disappointed them, and they showed it with their silence. The usual shit humans do. Sigourney hated having that extra spider sense for all things social. She knew that this was the reason why she froze with people. She wished she could just ignore all the little nuances and blunder on like others seemed to do. Not her. She was meant for picking locks. It was easy. It was about mechanics and her talents rather than niceties, the right words, and politics.

She looked through the small crack in the door, peering into the kitchen. The house beyond the door sounded crowded, to put it mildly. To her, more people meant unpredictability. Sigourney took a deep breath and shut her eyes.

Behind her, Siarl peered over her shoulder and stated the obvious.

"If we push together, we can move whatever is in our

way." Siarl didn't seem to mind taking the lead. Sigourney didn't care that he did. Better him than her.

"Let me take the door off first," Sigourney sighed and took her tools out once again. She worked the pins loose, and the door came off, revealing a cupboard lodged in front of the opening.

Together, Edith, Siarl, and Humphrey pushed it out of their way. As it fell over, it let out a loud *whop*, making Sigourney want to whimper. Not only because of the loud noise, but also because it had surely alerted someone to their escape.

"Can you?" Siarl hurried to ask without having to clarify.

"Mhm," Sigourney replied. "If you give me your hands, I'll be able to hide us before anyone notices."

"I won't hide like a child," Edith stated, clearly thinking back to that hateful moment when it had become apparent that Sigourney was Levi's sister. Edith frowned but shook whatever thought she'd had off when she looked at Sigourney.

Sigourney winced. She hated Edith's pitying look, all too familiar to her.

"But..." she managed to say. Her inner child, who wasn't afraid of the world and others, wanted to add something defiant. As always, the child was silenced.

"Why should we hide? Or flee? I can drive your brother insane." Edith pushed Sigourney's offered hand away. Hatred and revenge had entered into the picture, and Sigourney had to discard her naive thoughts about escaping being enough. Of course, Edith wanted to see her tormentors suffer. A person like Edith, who had once been a respectable, headstrong, glorious puppeteer, didn't flee from uncomfortable situations or pretend nothing had ever happened. Of course she didn't. And of course Edith ignored small animals and their feelings. She and others like her ploughed on like the steam locomotives, pushing aside all the obstacles in their way. With ease, one might add. But she, Sigourney, was like the handcars, stopping even for the tiniest furry creature in her way and politely asking them to move. Even offering them food while waiting for this marvelous cooperation to occur until they both got something closely resembling a satisfactory outcome. A handcar, that was what she was.

The simple future slithered away when Edith stepped past

Sigourney to the kitchen, not listening to the protests from Humphrey and Siarl.

"We can't..." Their protests were drowned under Edith's loud exhalation. Humphrey and Siarl followed after her. The catatonic man trailed his own shadow out of the basement and past Sigourney.

Sigourney glanced behind her, back to the basement where her brother's work desk stood, abandoned. Maybe she could stay here until everything blew over, but she knew that wasn't an option. Or it was, just not a very good one. She stepped past the fallen cupboard, whose back had cracked open. She made her way carefully around the corner, considering her every movement, waiting for her brother to drop from the ceiling along with other bogeymen. Instead, Sigourney found Humphrey and Siarl in stunned silence. At first, she wasn't sure why, but then she saw that the kitchen, which had once seemed homely, looked like a nightmare escaped from Pandora's box.

The walls of the room were twisted and bloody. The light that had shone through the window was swallowed by the haunting ideas that tormented you in the wee hours of the night.[86] Everything was bathed in shades of purple and black. Edith stood in the middle of the room like a portal to another dimension, letting in all the monsters you never knew existed. Not some cuddly unicorns or fluffy Krakens. The real deals with pointy fangs, nightmarish eyes, rotten skin, distorted bodies, and a feeling of madness ready to tie you down. She'd stepped into Edith's dreams.

They were not the only ones. In the middle of the kitchen stood two men. Both beautiful, or, as it happened to be called in men, handsome.[87] One of them was pressing Levi's machine against his chest. He was covered with imps. The other one was reaching for the man's shoulder. It was like Edith had stopped time.

Behind the dreams, Edith's aggression played its tune.

---

86 Unpaid bills at first, then moving on to the worthlessness of your existence, and then to nihilistic thoughts to rub in that last bit of desperation. By that stage any ideas of sleep are gone, and soon you have to get up and face the world. You are not in any fit mental state to do that, but no one accepts your visit from the Gloom Fairy as an explanation for why you shouldn't go out and earn money.

87 Meaning easy to handle and use. Goes to show what beauty is all about.

Sigourney could feel it. She hated anger, as it rarely amounted to anything good. But she was utterly wrong. If Sigourney had paid attention to her inner emotions, she would have noticed that aggression was a built-in feature for good reason. The question was more about how to use it rather than whether to use it. It could have helped a person like her to say no when her aggression told her something wasn't right. Of course, those emotions could be wrong; that was always a possibility. But it would be an excellent spot to stop and wonder what the crit was going on. Okay, maybe not when someone was coming at you with a machete.

Sigourney glanced around at the horrors. She knew they weren't real. Still, they managed to freak her out more than they should, being imaginary and all. She could hide or flee, but Siarl wouldn't come along. He would stay, saying it was his moral duty. All this made Sigourney wonder whether there was an objective morality[88] or not. And would that morality ever let her take off or manipulate Siarl to flee with her? Maybe it was all just perception playing tricks on her. Wouldn't it then be okay to do whatever she wanted? Or would it make her a monster? And maybe she was the monster here to begin with, thinking she was in the right and understood the situation. No one ever thought they could be the evil one. It was like a protective wrapping around the package, preventing the substance from going runny and functionality draining out... Maybe the purest essence of life amounted to getting one foot in front of the other and nothing else?

None of that mattered. Next to her, Siarl struggled free from Edith's nightmares, most likely by stating what reality was composed of and what it was not.

He whispered, "We can't let this happen. We have to get the machine away from here and stop Edith. We can't afford a confrontation. Not when we don't know who those men are and what they have to do with Levi." As always, knowledge was Siarl's salvation, erasing doubt and unnecessary questions. But what about when there was no time to collect all the facts? Would any reaction be okay?

"He's right. And I have a headache to prove it,"

---

88 Or, you could say, moral truth. But truth is a funny word, with a habit of causing agreement, cooperation, and the utter destruction of other human beings simultaneously.

Humphrey said, also freed from Edith's funny ideas of what terror was composed of. You can't really frighten a man who has seen the darkness and come back. "My premonitions," he added, when neither of them reacted. As if those two words should explain everything.

One foot in front of the other, Sigourney thought.

"I can take the machine away and hide it, and..." she stuttered.

"And...?" Siarl let out, holding his breath.

"I'll come back."

Siarl ever so slightly wrinkled his nose. There it was, what he'd feared all along, that she would keep running until her legs gave out, or the edge of the world stopped her.[89]

Siarl held his breath but then said, "In the meantime, I'll clean up this mess. And if luck allows, you'll find me."

Sigourney felt her heart fall into a million little pieces. For him to put his trust in luck was like Sigourney believing her anxiety would bring her puppies and kitties. It might, but it was highly unlikely.

"Yes," she muttered.

"Go on, then." He nodded.

Sigourney disappeared. She heard Siarl sigh when she did. She bit her lip hard, trying not to cry. This was better. This was fixing what her blood had started. She crept around Edith, Humphrey, the catatonic man, and the nightmares, which had grown an extra pair of tentacles, and now, as she looked closely, there were all the faces from her past. Shivers went down her spine. Holy Bunnies, Edith was good. But truthfully, the nightmare creatures were more fascinating than fear-inducing. It was the human ones that scared her.[90] She crept past one creature who looked like her mother with six eyes. Just spooky stuff out of her imagination and not real, she reminded herself.

The nightmares were lesser around the two men, making it easier to move around. She stopped next to the man holding the machine.

---

89   Not that Siarl or Sigourney believed for a second that any edge could hold her back. She would tiptoe around it until a slight gap ensured her escape.

90   Beasts, animals, monsters, and others defined by such words were more humane, more forgiving than any man in a suit she'd met. Maybe it was the suit?

The thing was, Edith hadn't actually stopped time. Sigourney became painfully aware of it as soon as she leaned in to steal the Bufonite. The man spoke gibberish in slow motion, his green eyes trying to blink as he muttered.

Sigourney could taste blood. She was biting her lip raw. Those eyes and the words. She knew she shouldn't touch the man, but she couldn't stop now. She reached for the machine, whose golden plates captured the black and purple glow of the room. Sigourney shut her eyes and pushed her hands against the cold metal. Something seized her wrist, yanking her closer. When she snapped her eyes open, she saw the handsome man peer straight into her, keeping a tight grip on her invisible wrist. The words he had spoken came faster now. They didn't sound pleasant at all. Sigourney panicked, trying to tug her hand free.

Otis kept a tight grip.

"What are you? A fiend sent by the witch?" His words changed back into gibberish. But as nothing happened, like Sigourney turning into a frog, the man switched back to the common tongue. "Show yourself." He yanked her wrist hard.

She fought to say something. However, the man's demanding gaze, his tone, and his grip didn't make answering any easier. Sigourney didn't have to react, because Siarl, as always, did it for her.

He shouted, "Don't hurt her!" Clearly he could see where the situation was going. The only thing was, he wasn't helping. Not with his words or by rushing towards them.

"Her?" Otis turned to face Siarl.

Siarl stopped on the spot as if something was holding him back. Then he was hoisted into the air.

"Sigourney?" Otis asked.

But that was as far as anyone got. Edith's remaining charms broke apart. The man behind Otis, the hexer, began moving again. He wasn't the only one. The air stirred all around them. Fear and the feeling of someone breathing down your neck. It wasn't like the fake sensation Edith had given them. These were the genuine things. Humphrey's outcry made it more evident.

"I can't control this many at once. Please, shut up. Shut up." The man dropped to the floor, pushing his hands against his head.

Despite the spirits being invisible to Sigourney and the

others, they were there. So were the imps the hexer had used to control Otis. They were also freed from Edith's temporary alteration of time and space. The imps grasped Sigourney's invisible hands, seeing them as clearly as the stars in a cloudless night. The device shook.

Sigourney tried to let go, but the pressure from Otis' hold and the imps kept her hands in place. The coldness of the metal turned hot, burning her flesh. Sigourney yelled and tried to struggle free, but all her brain managed to do in the midst of this was insist this wasn't fair. Some detached part of her argued back, saying her mind wasn't being helpful at all. Fairness had nothing to do with the situation. So what if her brother had caused it? So what if Siarl and the Rabbit had brought her here against her wishes? None of that was useful if she wanted to survive and put things right. "Right" was a subjective word, but that was as far as the detached part got, as she, Sigourney, put a stop to its tangent. Otherwise they would be standing here for the rest of eternity combing over every single word and their possible meanings. Not to mention when the real fun started and she began to puzzle out what all the possible combinations meant.

"You didn't," Percy growled as the spirits surged against him.

Sigourney deduced that the snarl wasn't meant for her. She glanced at Siarl, who was still hanging in the air. He twitched as the spirits toyed with him.

"You left me no other choice, hexer," Otis spat out, looking over his shoulder at Percy.

The hexer didn't answer, not in the traditional way. He began to speak gibberish, making the lines around Otis vibrate, and Sigourney felt the machine get colder. It still burned her flesh, but the worst was over. Soon the necromancer staggered. The imps pulled him backwards as the man lunged towards the back door.

The hexer lifted his bird-skull necklace from around his neck, wrapping his fingers around it.

Sigourney wished she possessed some tricks that would teach them both how to behave and stop whatever this was. A disappearing act wasn't going to cut it. In the background, Siarl was fighting his way through the spirits in the hope of landing on the floor and was failing horribly. There were just too many of them.

He wasn't the only one being attacked. Otis had sent his spirits to take control of the entire room. Edith was still spinning her nightmares, making everything a whole lot more confusing, but her clothes and hair were being torn by invisible hands, accompanied with hungry whispers for her body and soul. The catatonic man was next to her, still joined to his shadow. Occasionally, Sigourney felt as if someone was looking out from inside her. The same feeling she'd had in the basement.

"What's going on?" she asked, hoping someone in the room was keeping track of what the crit this was all about.

No one paid any attention to her. Even Otis seemed gone. His eyes had rolled backward, all milky white, and he kept muttering to himself. The atmosphere got more suffocating with every sentence he let out.

The air kept shivering, sending currents all over the place, almost like a wind.

Sigourney's hair began to tickle against her face, and the fabric of her jacket fluttered. Then came the noises.

"*Sigourney, you left us to die!*"

"*We hate you.*"

"*You don't deserve to live.*"

On and on, the voices went.

Sigourney tugged at her hands, trying to free them and ignore the voices while she was at it. She was kind of used to the idea of someone hating her and her not deserving to live. They were somewhat nicer than her own voice, which constantly told her how pathetic she was and how she never did anything right. So the effect the spirits were trying to create was somewhat lacking. But if they really went the extra mile, she might show them how distraught she was. Thus far, she was her own worst enemy. But what she didn't like was the imps burrowing their knife-like claws deep into her flesh, making it hard to free the machine or her hands and get the crit out of her brother's kitchen and leave Siarl to sort out the mess. If someone could do it, it was him. She trusted him with all her heart. Although he was a bit preoccupied right now. He would find a way. But none of that could happen as long as the machine stayed in the room.

"Sigourney." Otis raised his voice over all the nasty whispers echoing in the room. His eyes had turned green again. "Leave me be and let me get this machine to safety. I promise on your brother's life, I'm doing what's right here."

Before Sigourney could say anything or snort at *"doing what's right,"* Percy interrupted his liturgy of hexes and said,

"No, the machine isn't going anywhere. Give it to me and I'll destroy it." When Sigourney didn't react, the hexer added, "Maledictus tu bubonum sequuntur demonem..."

Sigourney recognized the last word, and she guessed it was meant for her, but while she considered herself to be some sort of demon, there was no irresistible pull towards the hexer.

"Sorry, no. Neither of you gets to have it. It's Levi's and theirs." And she knew she couldn't let it be destroyed, or give it to Justice in exchange for the Rabbit, or whatever the necromancer wished to do with it. The machine and how it worked had to be acknowledged. First, she had to get it to safety, to a place only she knew to exist.

"You can't win. When the hexer finishes his chant, my spirits won't be able to keep us safe. The imps will tear us apart. They are waiting for it. Can't you sense how angry they are? Let go of the machine, and I can protect all of us," Otis insisted. His features looked haunting as the ghostly wind whipped his white hair.

The wind made the rest of the room shake. The kitchen tools, brooms, cups, curtains, flour bags, and everything inanimate was already being knocked around. Thrown, to be more precise. Siarl had fallen to the floor, but he was no longer attempting to get to Sigourney, who stood at the center of the storm. He glanced at Sigourney, as always seeing past her hiding as if their minds were connected.[91] She glanced back at him. His eyes seemed to say, *"Sorry, I have to choose."* He turned around and headed to Edith and the others to drag them to safety. Most likely behind the tipped-over kitchen table.

Sigourney bit her lip, searching for another way out that didn't involve confrontation. There was none.

"I can't let you have it. The machine has to be hidden," she said.

Otis changed his features to an otter's face. Not a happy one.

---

91   They were.

She struggled against his grip.

He didn't let her go. "I'm sorry for what I'm about to do. You left me no other choice. My life depends on this."

Otis changed his words into gibberish, making a spirit surge into her.

Sigourney took a step backward and then collapsed on the floor as Otis let go of her wrist. She became visible as she lost her senses. Another wave washed over her, and she wasn't sure who she was. Her knees didn't look like hers. They appeared twice as big. But the weirdest thing was that the usual doubt she carried with her had disappeared, replaced with the determination that she knew who she was and would always be, forever and ever—what a nauseating thought.

She fought to stop herself from shaking as the spirit invaded her, but she couldn't. She blacked out. The last thing she saw was Margaret and her brother lurching in, Margaret shadowing Levi's every move. The woman had a massive bleeding cut on her forehead, and her clothes were tattered.

"Sigourney?!" was the last thing she heard. But she wasn't sure who that was.

23

COULD YOU STOP WHISPERING ALL THOSE NASTY WORDS IN MY EAR?

ose tested the balance of the blade Percy had given her. It felt heavier than her rapier, but she didn't mind. The robust form lessened the need for the fine control she was used to with hers. There was no time for in-depth analysis. A Luddite, a tall man with a pipe, had noticed her. The man got past Margaret, who was dancing with a woman and a man. The demon was still using the spoon and the soup bowl as weapons. Somehow, she made them work for her. When the Luddites attacked her, she ducked and launched, getting the spoon under the woman's ribs and jamming it in repeatedly until the woman passed out. When she was done, she jumped at the man, who she'd tripped earlier. She bashed him several times with the bowl. It was like magic. Margaret's movements were fluid and elegant, her hands weaving in an intricate choreography of blows.

Rose could almost hear a piano being played.

Rose whirled to meet her attacker, blocking the first hit. While she blocked, Margaret had already moved on to the next Luddite. All the time, the woman laughed. Not actually laughed. It was more like she glowed, and there was this high tinkle of fairy bells—the kind that led unsuspecting travelers astray.

The Luddite attacking Rose was relentless. He lifted the pipe and was ready to swing it. Rose could use the wide opening to thrust her sword in and kill the man, but she choked. When the pipe came down, it hit hard against her neck. The blow made her right arm tingle, and her grip on the sword loosened. She kicked the man in his stomach, pushing him farther away. She switched her sword hand. The man came back, ready to deal another successful blow. He repeated the same mistake, giving Rose an opening. She thrust the blade into the man's gut, having aimed higher but miscalculating the man's height. The pipe fell as the sword sank into the soft flesh. Rose pushed it in further, hearing a pitiful sound, a gurgle with a surprised whimper.

The pipe clanged against the floor.

Rose took a step backward, drawing the blade out. She had no time to think. Another Luddite got past Margaret, who was busy toying with Justice and her men.

"Dear sister of mine made from all the wrong parts, won't you join in and show your men how it's done?"

When Justice refused to reply, the demon added, "Give me a challenge, or I'll eat them one by one. Don't you care about their souls? Or should I say about their lives? Or do you think justice should always have its victims?"

Rose ducked. This time, the second Luddite, a woman more agile than the man, thought to try her luck. Still, Rose managed to see Justice's expression. Margaret had hit a sore spot. The rest of the conversation went unheard. Rose had to keep up with the woman, who gave her no room to breathe. The Luddite managed to land several blows, but Rose had gotten used to a few bruises. She sliced at the woman's fingers and jabbed the side of her torso. The woman didn't care. She came at Rose, who struggled to keep up. Margaret came to her rescue. She wedged the spoon into the Luddite's eye.

The Luddite let out a loud yelp.

"Finish her off," Margaret sang. The woman's eyepatch was off, and her lifeless black eye was visible. It promised more than death. It promised emptiness.

Rose did. She slit the woman's carotid artery open as the woman reached for the spoon in her eye.

"Good girl. You are surprisingly good at this. But all fun has to end," Margaret said and pushed Rose into the upcoming Luddites.

A hot flash of betrayal burned in Rose's chest as she fell over. Or was it more like the loss of blind faith in the good of humanity?[92] But her emotions were a fleeting memory as instinct kicked in. She thrust her forearms forward to take the brunt of the impact. She pushed her jaw against her chest and prepared to slam against the floor or the Luddites. Justice's men pushed her off, sending her crashing to the floor. That was the worst of it. She was relatively okay, despite the bruised arms and ego. But she was sure oxygen was not getting to her head. Why else would she be seeing a giant rabbit stepping in from the broken door. Behind her, she heard Levi shout,

"Run!"

She dared to glance behind her, seeing Levi slumped in the hallway and Margaret heading towards the alchemist.

She tried to get to the hallway and flee, but she didn't get that far. Abigail stood on her hand, pinning it hard against the floor.

In the background, Justice ordered her Luddites in their red bandannas to attack the thing, the hallucination, the giant rabbit. The creature gave them their money's worth. It was fidgeting, spinning like an out-of-control merry-go-round, but instead of a ride with cute animals, there was a flea-bitten roadkill that didn't stop when the money ran out, confusing the attackers. The creature moaned as the men struck it with pipes, and there was a hint of electricity in the air. The pitiful man who'd entered the shop with the Rabbit fled back into the darkened streets.

"Find me that girl! And the machine," Justice screeched.

The men and women who'd survived the Rabbit's assault snapped to attention.

"She's somewhere in this house."

"You wouldn't dare," the Rabbit moaned.

When Justice didn't take back her words, the Rabbit snarled,

"You critting imbecilic creature with monotonous thoughts about life, get your men off me, or I'll make sure you and they will never have a stroke of good luck ever in

---

92   Or in this case, a demon.

their lives." His shackled feet crashed onto the ground.

Rose blocked the rest of the conversation out, missing the resonance of sibling rivalry. She had other things to worry about—for one, trying to get her hand out from under Abigail's foot before she crushed it into a million pieces.

She reached for her fallen sword.

"I don't think so." Abigail pushed her heel in harder.

"Help me out then. What have I done to offend you enough to do this? What do you want?" Rose lifted her eyes to meet hers.

"You have the nerve to ask me that after betraying me? I vouched for you, and you stole from us, then you killed my family." Abigail lightened the pressure. Unconsciously, Rose was sure, as the words were after blood. She was also sure she had a chance here to reason her way out of this.

"I didn't—"

"Don't!" Abigail warned her.

"I didn't mean to hurt you or anyone you loved. I wasn't thinking about anything other than myself. I should have, and I know this is the worst excuse I could give for any of this." Not far from Rose lay the woman she'd killed. Not yet, though. She lingered between life and death, bleeding slowly towards the latter with no hope of return.

"Yes, you never think. Just animal instinct. That's why you never could best me. You never knew how to turn knowledge into instinct, forgetting the mechanical and becoming part of the move. There was always a disconnect." Abigail crouched slightly, making Rose whimper from the pressure the movement put on her skin and bones.

Rose clung to the hope that there was a way out. Take that away, and everything would turn to dust. But now, she saw the burned bridges in the woman's eyes. There might be no return.

Nevertheless, Abigail crouching down was her chance. Rose surged up and towards the woman. All of which would have been easier if she wasn't wearing a skirt with yards of fabric. Still, she managed to surprise Abigail, who barely regained her balance. Rose slammed against her, keeping herself close enough to compensate for their difference in strength.

Abigail tried to push Rose away. She didn't let her. She grabbed the woman from her lower back to keep them close for two reasons—to bide time and to avoid hitting her. If she had to, she would resort to violence, but that wasn't her aim here.

"Abigail, listen to me. It doesn't have to go this way. I don't know what you're hoping for here, but destroying the machine or Levi won't help your cause. Justice is lying to you. She's doing this for her own reasons, not to save you or any one of us."

"And you're doing this from the goodness of your heart?" Abigail's voice was full of venom.

"No, Abigail. At first, this was all about money, and part of it still is, but let's not underestimate each other's intelligence and pretend the Bufonite isn't important. Whoever uses it commands everything. And whoever commands it can do good in the world. Has Justice told you what it can do?" Rose relaxed her grip on the woman's back, hoping it wasn't a mistake to show good faith.

Abigail took hold of Rose's collar and drew her close to her face.

"What is it then? Money or doing good in the world? You are mixing your intentions. And I thought we weren't going to insult each other's intelligence."

Rose opened her mouth to defend herself. She never got that far.

"Also, just so you know, Justice isn't dragging me into anything. I'm doing this for my own reasons."

"I asked you—" Again, Rose didn't get further than that.

"You are removed from this city—an outsider. You haven't seen what the march of the machines has done to the people. Children work in factories. The lucky ones get out alive with missing arms, eyes, and lungs full of cotton. Most die without seeing a good day, a day they could call their own. Tell me that is progress." Abigail was angry, but Rose was sure the anger didn't come from the hurt children. It came from something personal.

"Then change it through laws. You'll have to burn the entire city to the ground to stop the progress. There are always people like me willing to fund it. And even if you destroy everything, we'll rebuild it, and all you will have done is kill people and leave them worse off." Rose relaxed her body, wishing Abigail would too.

She didn't.

"You are naive to think they would listen to us. The laws are made for the aristocrats and the new businessmen with money made off the backs of people like me. You should know that, Miss Banker. Have you ever even talked to a common man?"

"Like you? Tell me, have you yourself seen a hard day's work once in your life? Have you worked until your hands bleed? This is about your savior complex. A game to play rather than an actual fight for your survival. That gambling house of yours is more than willing to take in the money made by the machines. I didn't see you turn away the new technocrats. You embraced them."

"I "

"You're fooling yourself here. You're a tool for Justice, and she has made your head spin so much that you can't separate what's real and what isn't. She doesn't care about you or the people. She's doing this for herself." Rose was sure she was winning this argument.

She was wrong on so many levels.

Abigail's mind had already shut down. The only thing she saw was an attack and the need to defend herself. Rose's words were empty clatter as far as Abigail was concerned. Minds didn't work the way Rose wanted them to. They didn't see a logical argument as "*Yay! Let's make some formulated attempts to test the world and the accuracy of our syntax.*" No, all they saw was an attack, and everything went downhill from there. For things to be different, they needed a conscious effort and willingness to hop on top of one's own emotions and instincts. Few could do that, and even fewer were willing to. Rose would have been better off asking open-ended questions and catering to Abigail's emotional concerns. Emotions were and always would be a stronger motivator for change than logical arguments.

"You are the one who's unable to separate what's real and what isn't." Abigail pushed Rose off her and drew the rapier. "It's such a shame that you don't have one of these."

Rose staggered backward, stumbling over the hem of her skirt. Her heels were making it worse. The other woman wore a trouser suit and could move freely. A match Rose wasn't going to win.

"Yes, a shame. If you let me take the sword, you would at least be giving me a fighting chance rather than butchering me for your amusement."

"Take it then."

Rose knelt, keeping her eyes on the woman as she picked up the sword. She put her right leg forward and held her balance steady, waiting for Abigail to make her first move.

Abigail didn't disappoint. She launched at Rose, aiming at her neck, as expected. Rose took a slight hop back to make room between her and the blade, deciding that if she survived, she would never wear high heels or skirts again.

Abigail's launch fell short.

Rose kept her feet light, shifting her weight between her front and back leg.

Abigail made another attempt.

Rose danced to the side and blocked the blade. Abigail was surprised by the force of the hit. Rose had used a lot more weight than was necessary. The rapier's point dropped down towards the floor, but the other woman was quick on her feet, and she withdrew. As she moved her blade, it screeched against the sword's blackened metal.

Abigail attacked again as soon as she had regained her balance. This time she managed to draw blood, grazing Rose's hand as she swung the sword against the rapier. It was only a scrape, but it stung. Abigail kept coming at her, excited by the small victory. Rose kicked the woman's knee, but her leg got caught on her hem, absorbing most of the force.

Abigail was winning. She landed another hit, this time cutting Rose's shoulder. She kept aiming at the throat. Soon she would succeed. The sword started to feel heavy against the lightness of Abigail's strides.

Abigail readied herself. The slight change in her posture told Rose the woman thought she'd found an opening. Part of Rose wanted to give up. She had never been able to best her teacher. The other part of her noticed that her hem was caught in a breeze, fluttering against her leg. At first, she thought someone had opened the back door, but then the whispers came. They called her name, blaming her for everything. One of them sounded like her father, telling her what a disappointment she had been, how she put her mother and him to shame. Her perfect bank clerk father saw her risk-taking as the most corrupted and evil way there was for a person to do banking, which he saw as a service—all things that Rose had heard before.

But Abigail was getting the same treatment, most likely from her dead grandmother, who'd established the gambling house. Abigail wasn't used to the Necropolis Effect. The woman's eyes were wide, and her lips were quivering. All around them, other Luddites screamed and tried to defend themselves as the spirits seeping from the back room tugged their clothes, hair, and ears and whispered unspeakable things. A few managed to escape through the broken front door. Others curled on the floor, trying to shield themselves.

The glory of necromancy, Rose thought.

Abigail had lowered the tip of her blade and was backing away. She was fully open, and Rose only had to thrust her sword in. But she couldn't. Abigail would have killed Rose if she'd had her chance. Rose knew that, yet the strength in her fighting hand was gone. Defending oneself in the glory of a battle wasn't the same thing as actual murder.

"You'd better leave," she said. "They won't leave you alone until they pick you apart with their lies."

Abigail didn't hear her. She swung her blade wildly, hoping to impale the noises tormenting her. The ones telling her that everything she'd feared all along was true. Rose pitied her for letting the outside world define who she was and what she was worth. Such a person would never be satisfied, never at peace with herself, and always sad and most likely angry. Should she guide her through it? Speak reassuring words, guide her ego into a balanced state where it could stay for now? She could do that, but why would she? While murder was out of the question, Abigail's mental preservation wasn't her duty either. But she had once felt something for her.

Rose glanced around. The necromancer had defused the Luddites' attack. Most of it, at least. Justice still stood where she had been, but the giant bunny was gone. Within the massive iron shackles lay a common rabbit, twitching its nose as it crouched there. Justice looked stunned, unable to move. Her skin crackled as the spirits surged against her, burning the vibrating air. Or Rose was sure something along those lines was happening. She could hear the sparks, see the slight smoke, and feel the electricity in the air. Rose looked at the sword in her hand and thought better of it.

The remaining Luddites rocked back and forth on the floor around their fallen comrades, the spirits raging on.

To Rose, this was just an ordinary Tuesday in Necropolis,

where necromancers hung around every corner, and you knew ghosts were always with you. There was no room to be too fussy about the creepiness factor or the dead and dying.

Justice walked past Abigail, her mind in turmoil, or so Rose thought. The god was out of it, trembling slightly, her gaze empty. And Rose thought she saw ghostly shackles around the woman's hands and legs.

Abigail clutched on to the god, who brushed her aside and knocked her onto the ground without caring.

"Leave her be," Rose said to deaf ears, trying to do the right thing. Not that anyone could tell what the right thing was in this situation.

Rose reached for Abigail, helping her up. She hugged the woman tightly against her, shielding her from the spirits. Occasionally the fencing teacher swung her hands in the air and whimpered about disappointments and not living up to some great expectations. Oh, what cruelty parents could commit by burdening their children with their dreams. Even as hopes faded and time went on, the parental expectation of perfection lay dormant. Sometimes Rose wondered if parents were the root of all evil, wreaking havoc with what they did and didn't do. But then again, the world could be a bastard too. And sometimes things just happened to turn even good people monstrous. She'd learned to ignore her father. It wasn't easy, but at least she didn't turn into a babbling wreck when the man whispered his complaints. And she didn't care much for nature versus nurture debates. What a black-and-white way to see the world. In her book, dichotomy was the surest way to get everything wrong.

Maybe this wasn't the place to get caught with such questions, especially as she could see that nothing had gone the way it should have. And she couldn't let Abigail die or lose her mind, sacrificing everything for a god who didn't care.

Rose guided them after Justice, who staggered deeper into the house through the back door.

The spirits raged on. So did Rose's father.

Colored perceptions, that was all it was.

24

YOU ARE MY LITTLE SISTER

evi leaned against the hallway wall, unable to get up. He watched as his world smashed into pieces. On the shop floor lay the broken green cure-all bottles, which crunched under the Luddites' feet. Past that lay his miniature sculptures, their metal all bent and twisted. Some of them jerked as their mechanism was triggered. He deserved it all. It was payback. But he had never actually killed anyone, and that had to count for something. It had to. Margaret and Otis had done the actual killing and... and still, he was responsible. Ada wouldn't have died if he hadn't wanted this so much. His adversary, the lady in a long, thick silk coat of the darkest red, wearing a little black dress and high heels, whose white soles shone like a beacon against the wooden floor, was right to tear his shop down.

Of course, his downfall came through eye-for-an-eye justice and not through a court of law.

Yes, he would take the beating. Still, he would argue that this perverted the course of justice. That the idea that people deserved what they got because of the actions they had taken was absurd. Such thinking was antiquated and unable to deal with modern problems. Would they chop off the fingers of the factory owners because their workers had lost theirs? Or remove the tongue of those whose words they didn't like? Or kill others just because they have killed?

Levi believed in the justice of survival. In the right to steal when hungry. In the right to defend when violated. But it wasn't perfect either. Who knew where the line between survival and self-serving motives lay?

Levi could only wait for all this to end. At least Otis had gotten away with the Bufonite. Not everything was wasted.

But he was already losing his mind. Seeing a humongous rabbit walking into his shop and starting a fight with the Luddites didn't seem right. He'd hit his head harder than he thought. He shut his eyes and took deep breaths in, mentally scanning his body. It wasn't as bad as he'd thought. He tried to get up but slumped down again, his head feeling light.

Again he took a deep breath in. He might survive if he could only get up, as the giant bunny was keeping the Luddites busy, especially the woman in charge. He tried again, and this time his feet held. Mostly because Margaret was supporting him, hoisting Levi fully up.

"Here we go, Mr. Alchemist. Our work is not yet done. We need to get you out of here before anyone thinks you should be sacrificed. And don't even think about staying to defend your shop. All this is gone, but not all is lost. I can rob banks if it's money you need to finish your machine. Where's the speaker of the dead?" Margaret was already pulling him towards the kitchen door.

Levi coughed as he tried to speak. The words grated his throat, and his mouth felt dry. Then there was the headache from being repeatedly hit against the wall. He pushed past that and said,

"He escaped through the back door."

"Good. We'd better leave too." Margaret clutched him tighter, making Levi wince. She guided him through the hallway.

"I can walk," Levi protested.

"Oh," Margaret said and let go. "I thought... Never mind."

Levi's head still felt light, but there was nothing wrong with his balance. Margaret seemed to think differently. She stayed close by, not letting him out of her reach.

They made their way to the kitchen, where Otis and

Percy's battle had reached the point where everything not nailed down was floating in the air. Including all Evelyn's baked goods, flour, kitchen appliances, and the hot stew. Otis still held on to the machine, but his whole body shook as he did. The imps Levi had seen before crawled all over the necromancer, trying to force the device from his hands. Percy wasn't doing any better. He was on the ground on his knees, fending off something invisible. Mostly likely spirits, knowing Otis and sensing the mood in the kitchen.

"Stupid necromancer," Margaret said next to him.

Levi didn't respond. There were more important things in play than Otis and his spirits. There, not far from them, his little sister convulsed on the floor, drawing flour angels with her stiff body. Her head slammed against the floorboards, and she was about to bite her tongue off. Levi glanced at Otis and the Bufonite and then at Margaret and back at his sister.

"Holy fishmonger's wife," he cursed. Sigourney was all alone. Siarl was nowhere to be seen. She was going to kill herself if she continued banging her head. He hated what he would have to do. But he had to.

"Sigourney," he shouted and rushed towards her.

Margaret yelled after him, but he didn't listen. This was never his plan. No one was supposed to get hurt, least of all his sister.

The ghostly wind tried to push him off as he moved towards Sigourney. But he fought against it. What else could he do? His sister continued spasming, her head snapping against the floor. Soon she would lose it. She couldn't die. Not now. But he was the only one wishing that. He heard whispers. They sounded a lot like their father. His voice sounded all around him, complaining that they were never meant to be born. That Sigourney and Levi had tied him down.

Levi squeezed his hands into fists and screamed, "You are the one who should never have been born. It wasn't me or Sigourney who ruined your life. It was you and your lousy choices."

Levi flinched at his own anger and waited for the blows to come. To teach him that he must never show his emotions, never question their father.

What followed was quiet sobbing.

"I'm sorry, I'm sorry... I was a bad father. I failed you

both..." the voice repeated.

Levi didn't know if the crying was any better. He'd heard it all before. In those sober moments, when their father had realized what he was and what he had done. Yet nothing ever changed. As always, Levi chose to ignore his father. He crouched down and crawled the rest of the way to Sigourney. The spirit wind was weaker at floor level.

He took hold of her head, forcing it to stay between his hands. It only made matters worse. Her head kept jerking against his hands, twisting all wrong. He let go. But he had to do something. He searched for anything to put into his sister's mouth to stop her biting her tongue. He saw the boy Sigourney had come with behind the flipped kitchen table. He and the specials were there, trying to hide from the spirit invasion and the imps. The latter had climbed up onto the table and were making rude gestures. Some of them were on Siarl and the others, trying to wrestle with them.

Levi had no time to think about what it all meant. What mattered was that there was nothing close by to stop his sister from ending her life. Levi reached for his leather notebook and forced it between Sigourney's teeth. He sat there, unable to do anything else. Feeling helpless and confused. Everything had gone crazy the moment Sigourney stepped back into his life. Maybe she was cursed, as their mother had said. Their mother thought she was the source of all their misery. The reason their father had started drinking. The reason they had to work so hard to keep the farm running. But it couldn't be. Even Levi knew that. He shook the cruel thoughts away. He looked at his sister. It would be too easy to blame her. Despite everything, all she had ever done was try to stay out of the way. That was what Sigourney amounted to—out of the way. Who could blame her?

He glanced up at the cursing Margaret. She was trying to pry the Bufonite free from Otis' clutches.

"Why, you soul snatcher, let it go!"

Her efforts were pointless. The necromancer was too far away to respond. He wore an emotionless expression, not seeing the woman or the room. His lips kept moving. Otis was summoning even more spirits. Levi was sure of it. He had been there when Otis had done that before. Margaret was only inviting calamity with her actions. If Otis lost his concentration, who knew what would break free.

"Stop it," Levi shouted. His voice was lost under the cacophony of spirits. The sobbing next to Levi got louder, and anger built up with every inhale his father took. Levi held his hands against his ears, feeling like a kid again. His, their words were toxic. It was like being back in his childhood home, hearing his mother and father fight. His father would always storm out, and for the next three days he would drink heavily.

Levi forced his hands down. The sobbing grew louder, but he had to ignore it. He had to get himself and Sigourney out of here. She was his future. Not the machine itself. All he needed was her and his notebook to solve the mystery of how to get the quintessence to work for humanity. And make sure no one had to live the life he'd lived.

Levi hooked his arms under Sigourney's shoulders and began dragging her towards the back door, pushing his heels against the floorboards. Their father's whispers, sobbing, and occasional bursts of anger followed him out. A long time ago, he'd decided that he would never end up like their father, a pitiful creature who feared life. Anxious about even the tiniest whisper the world sent towards him, always meeting them with anger. When it was his turn to die, he would leave without regrets.

Levi took them farther away from the mess. No spirits tried to stop them. It had to be Otis' doing.

It wasn't. The one inside Sigourney kept the others away. All of the dead cheered for the win, the possession. But when the body's ownership was finalized, others might try to claim the prize, as the separation of body and soul made it easy pickings for other spirits. For now, Sigourney held on tight to what was hers.

When they moved past the kitchen table, past Siarl and the others, the boy came out of hiding and reached for them. He didn't get far. He couldn't. The imps saw his sudden movement as a challenge and jumped at him. They were feeling particularly unfriendly towards the humans.[93]

---

93 Who could blame them? They had been awakened from their slumber to do grunt work. Their minds and bodies were meant to work the complex calculations of the universe. To drill holes in the fabric of reality. This was like putting nuclear scientists to work cleaning toilets. If the hexer continued being careless, or he might argue preoccupied, more would get loose. And then they would start their ultimate project, which was to make this reality like

Levi had seen what the imps could do, and he hated to leave Siarl at their mercy, but Sigourney came first. This was about survival, and you had to make choices. She would have to understand that and forgive him. Levi chose her and concentrated on getting them out of this madhouse. He almost did it. He leaned against the back door and prepared to stand up. Sigourney stopped him. She took the notebook out of her mouth and said,

"Thank you, darling, for the ride. I would kiss you, but I'm told you are my brother."

Levi stared at Sigourney, his mouth open. There was an unfamiliar tang in her speech, and the lines around her eyes were different somehow. He wasn't sure how, but the person in front of him wasn't his sister.

"Now, I might take you with me, but from the look of things, you would be more trouble than you're worth. So, here, fetch this." Sigourney threw the notebook back into the heart of the kitchen, where Otis and Percy were. A high heel with a white sole stopped its journey. Justice stood there.

Levi looked at his sister and then over at Justice, who was as dazed as Otis was. Or perhaps more like Sigourney had been, with two minds competing for control. Levi was sure the woman's hands and legs were bound with shackles, but when he looked again, they were gone. Justice turned her attention to the notebook, seeing something there, making her eyes sparkle a little. It made Levi's chest feel tight. He glanced hopelessly at his sister, or whatever the thing was. She was getting up. She moved like one of his mechanical sculptures—rigid, without flexible joints.

Sigourney smiled back. "Be a darling and move aside." The thing looked straight through him to the only sensible exit point in the building.

"Sigourney?" Levi tried.

"Not even close, sweetheart," the thing answered.

In the background, Justice laughed.[94]

---

theirs—full of secret portals to other dimensions where the laws of physics were only a suggestion. Simply put, they would unbuild reality to meet their requirement, which was to take out any certainty.

94   If the Rabbit were here, he would say his sister had lost it completely. When you started to cackle, it was only a matter of time before sentences like "take over the world," "I'm the fairest of them all," or better yet, "bow to me" were thrown around.

Levi didn't like the sound of anything he was hearing. He found himself between a rock and a hard place, with only two choices, each as lousy as the other. He could choose his notebook, despite knowing it would be a bad idea, or Sigourney, but she was as good as gone without Otis and his necromancy.

Levi grasped Sigourney's arm, but he stopped midway.

"I wouldn't if I were you," the thing inside his sister warned. "Be a good brother and go away, or else."

Levi shook his head and moved out of the thing's way. He shouldn't—he knew enough about necromancy to know that it was a bad idea to let one's creations loose—but there was no stopping it without hurting Sigourney. He was about to shout to Otis, to beg him to wake up, but the man was hoisted into the air. Margaret lifted Otis over her shoulder and was slowly making her way to him. A string of imps was holding on to Otis' leg, pulling him towards Percy. Percy had gotten up from the ground, and he looked more focused than before. Behind him, Justice's laugh was getting worse. All his formulas in the notebook would soon be gone. His whole universe existed there, and he... had to let go.

There was only one way to save what mattered the most. He abandoned the door and began pushing his way back into the heart of the kitchen.

"You imbecile," Margaret shouted at him.

25

IF WE COULD ONLY SWITCH MINDS, THEN MAYBE ALL WOULD BE WELL

igourney wondered about inner demons. She knew she should be fighting for her life and all. Still, she couldn't get rid of the nasty ideas and fears stuck inside her mind as she convulsed.

This could be her opportunity to disappear altogether, leave everyone and everything behind... and not to be, she guessed. There was reason enough to let her mind go. The person, the someone, the woman inside her felt stronger than her. She could make better use of the Sigourney mold. And everything would be a lot simpler for her. No constant heartache from uncertainty. No anxiety. No more burdens from the weird flesh she was forced to carry around. Nothing. Of course, she would lose herself, but honestly, had her self ever been that great?

But her thoughts got swept away by the present. Her body rose from the ground after it had thrown away the most precious thoughts her brother had ever produced. The notebook fell on the other side of the room, but her eyes were fixed on her brother. Her brother who'd come to her rescue.

She wanted to thank him, but her mouth spoke words Sigourney would never have chosen.

She only had to let go, and what was left of her would suffocate under the new, bolder her.

Her body opened the door, letting in the smog. She hesitated. So did the body. She needed to glance behind to see Siarl and say she was sorry. And Levi, to ask him to forgive her. She turned around, still holding on to the door, or the spirit did. It screamed inside her and fought to keep control over her movements. Her legs shook. So did her hands.

Sigourney ignored the spirit and the erratic movements, along with the door banging against the frame. The only thing she could think was that Siarl couldn't blame her for this. He really couldn't. Of course, he wouldn't. He would say nothing, and by some perverted logic he would make it alright for her to walk away. Yet she felt uncomfortable. She watched as Siarl struggled under the imps, who were constructing a Siarl-sized gap in reality, or at least trying to. Sigourney took a step forward. She would do this and then she could let the woman inside her have her.

"What are you doing?" the woman asked in her head. The noise felt like standing in an echo chamber. Or like a bee buzzing in her ear.

"I can't leave him. Not like this," Sigourney said. She could hear the apologetic tone in her voice. The whole body wanted to blush. She wanted to hide.

"We don't need him. We can get a new one. A handsome one. A rich one... for pity's sake, you can't truly mean that such things don't matter to you. Of course they do."

"Please, stop reading my mind."

"I can't do that. Can I? And no, you can't hide from me." The sarcastic tone echoed inside her. The woman tried to force the body to move, but Sigourney held on to her feet, keeping them planted.

"What's so special about him anyway?"

"Everything." Sigourney closed the door.

The woman tried to make her fingers latch back on to the brass knob.

"This would be a lot easier if you stopped resisting."

"Yes, I know."

"Then—"

Sigourney bit her lip. "I already explained to you, I can't

leave him. Not like this. And I have to set right what my brother started. Humphrey and Edith and that man deserve better." Sigourney pointed at the catatonic man. "Not to mention my brother."

"Tell me that you don't actually believe you are responsible for any of them?" the woman snorted.

"I might not be, but you are confusing responsibility with duty."

"Duty?" Decimal, the woman, snorted.

"Yes, duty. Doing something not just because you have to, but because it's the right thing to do."

"Otis never knew what to do with me. He could have given me a more useful body than yours. Why are you so afraid of everything, even your own shadow?"

"Who are you?"

"Does that really matter?"

"It might."

"Oh well, if I must." Decimal poured a flood of images, emotions, thoughts, and events from her past life as a necromancer into Sigourney's cortex. The woman was Otis' mother, who had died in an explosion. Her laboratory equipment had malfunctioned, and there was no body to be saved.

Sigourney was caught up in the history. Hating and loving all the emotions passing through her, living a new life.

The woman tugged the door wide open once again while Sigourney was distracted. The rush of not-so-fresh air made the body cough. Neither of them really planned for it, which gave Sigourney time to intercept, being more used to the quirks of the body.

"You are willing to leave your son behind?" she asked, despite knowing it was a stupid question. As she dug through the memories, she saw there was care and formality between the necromancers, but not love. Not the way Siarl had described it to her. But Siarl and his family might be the exception rather than the rule.

Decimal would disagree with the assessment. What Sigourney had missed was a tiny twinge of guilt. It was so small compared to what she felt every morning when she opened her eyes and greeted another day that she didn't consider it as proof of something major.

Decimal refused to answer. But there was something that

made Sigourney pity her. Yes, the woman was strong, and she had done marvelous things with necromancy—raised an army of the dead to fight against rat experimentation gone wrong and a whole lot more. Behind that was discontent and loneliness. But not the way Sigourney felt. This was different. Decimal couldn't participate even if she wanted to. She was forever stuck in limbo. And if there was something in life that Sigourney understood, it was loneliness.

"How about if we both stay? I mean, I'll let you stay inside me if you stop trying to push me out and control my life. Only on that condition." Sigourney pushed the door shut once again. The woman let her.

"You would actually let me stay?" She sounded astonished.

"Why wouldn't I?"

"Kraken shit, you can't be this accommodating. This is insanity..."

"You seem like a nice person, and it must be hard to be a spirit floating around there without the ability to impact the world around you," Sigourney said, leaving out the part where she hoped some of the woman's confidence would rub off on her.

"You could push me out. You must know that." The woman sighed. Or it sounded as if she did. A melancholic emotion passed through Sigourney.

"Yeah, I gathered as much a while ago. I know my body better than I like to admit."

"I once had a beautiful body, which I took for granted. You wouldn't believe how good it feels to open and close your fingers or feel your toes flex. If you are sure, then..." She let the words dangle there between the two of them, allowing Sigourney time to back down.

"I'm sure."

The woman, Decimal Thurston, groaned. "You are insane."

"That might be true. But can you help me now, please? We need to get the specials and Siarl out. Get the machine. Free the Rabbit god of luck. Do something about my brother. And preferably get far away from here," Sigourney said.

"I still think we should leave the boy behind. We could get one of those tall specimens. Otis' father was a handsome fellow. He could really make your socks turn..."

Sigourney blushed at the mucky image the woman sent

her and was about to object, but the woman sensed her mood and said,

"Oh, if you must insist. I guess he will have to do. And I have to say, it's quite beautiful what my son has done. I always knew he would go a long way. However, he should never have left Necropolis. They should have made the machine there under the Council's watchful eye. Just saying. But lead the way, dear."

People don't like it when you prioritize your passion over everything else. They think you are selfish. But gods forbid you ask them to give up anything they love human- or job-wise. They give you a list of why your request is impossible, irrational, or irritating. When you apply the same logic to your projects, they look at you like a crazy person. Yet they expect to be entertained, amazed, and pampered, forgetting all those who sacrificed everything for their enjoyment. Blind, mad compulsion and commitment, that was it.

And here they were, the forever mysterious they, fighting about who got to keep, destroy, tamper, or rule with his, Levi's, creation—the laymen, the gods, the bankers, the activists, the demons, the concerned. The only ones missing were the businessmen. But they would soon come, along with their lawyers, sniffing at the chance to steal something to make a profit.

The key to it all was in his notebook, which was full of detailed notes and drawings.

Justice flipped through the book with curious intent, looking dazed. The maniacal laugh had changed into silence, which was a lot worse.

She began to tear the pages out.

Levi's stomach squeezed into a tight ball, and he was about to cry out. He didn't. He hadn't turned around for the notebook or the machine. There was a plan, which was to rescue his sister... and part of him thought that through this he could still find the secret to creating a true Bufonite. Then there was Otis himself. Levi couldn't be mad at Otis for trying to abandon him.

He snorted. Otis and necromancy were his way out. He saw the irony of it. Levi would never get to rely solely on science. Here and now, he had to act. He leaped over Edith, who hunched behind the table as imps pulled her hair. She sobbed while the world around her kept changing its form into new, horrible iterations—none of which convinced the pests to leave her alone. Levi didn't notice. He only saw Otis and Margaret fused with their imps, and the hexer commanding them to bring the pair to him. Percy fiddled with the string of his bird-skull necklace. He had woven tiny dolls and candles into it. The latter seemed to be lit. The man turned his eyes upon Levi. They were red and present, wanting payback. No, not that. Something else. Whatever it was, it didn't matter.

It did matter.

The ghostly wind was weaker around the hexer, and Otis was out cold, while Margaret's face had turned waxy and sweaty. She tried to get the imps to release her and her precious cargo. The little demons didn't care what she did. They were like ants, who used their strength in numbers to gang up against the bigger prey.

Levi rushed to Margaret, ignoring his father's whispers. The man still hung around him, repeating the same word Margaret had said to him: "*Imbecile.*" Nothing new there.

Levi grabbed one of the imps holding on to Margaret and tore it off her.

"You fool," she snapped. Otis hung over her shoulder, which was impossible if Levi cared to stop and think about the laws of physics. But he didn't. Otis' spirits raged on around them, and the imps tore at their victims, intensifying his need to get them out of the kitchen, which had turned into a madhouse.

"I had to. He can save Sigourney... and the Bufonite. And..." Levi didn't finish the sentence. He took hold of another imp. It clawed and latched on to him. Levi shook it, but the bugger didn't come off.

"She was never part of this. You are the Bufonite. Not her. So turn around and go. I'll find you."

"I can't leave. Not without him." Levi winced. The imp's nails burrowed deep into the flesh of his neck.

"Go, mortal!" Margaret's good eye turned black, and she snarled, revealing a row of needle-sharp teeth. She snatched the imp off him.

Levi looked at her, stunned. Margaret's venomous tone

mixed with the sound of his notebook been torn. Past her and Otis, the falling pieces of the book flowed down like snow at Justice's feet. All his schematics and writing turned into disjointed windows in his mind.

"How dare you tell me what to do! None of you have a right to be here. This is my home, my machine, and my life, and I decide what goes and doesn't go here." Levi felt rage seethe inside him. This was unfair.[95]

It was Justice who answered. "Right? You dare to speak about rights in a house where there's no justice?!" she asked, sounding alive.

"And what would you call what you are doing?" Levi spat out, regretting it instantly. There was something disconcerting about how the woman held herself. She was more than a Luddite.

The god laughed. She dropped the notebook. "I'm Justice."

"You are mistaken," Levi protested. It was the only thing he could say. The rest of his thoughts fled as Justice took a step towards him. His instincts told him to run.

Justice laughed again. "Then we are making mistakes all around. You are repeating the same mistakes someone else made before you. And I made the mistake of thinking that humans could change. As always, you are so ready to eat the earth under yourself for lust, fooled by your inventions. Your machine is a conduit for sorrow, not for glory. Our Lord Bufonite bestowed the same glory on his people, who killed each other and him to own the machine. Machines can't be owned. They are the monolith that makes you the servant." Justice leaned forward, and somehow he was there next to her without being pulled in.

Levi took a step back. In the background, Margaret whimpered. She collapsed under the weight of the imps, Otis, and the machine while trying to come to Levi's rescue and being knocked over by the hexer.

Justice took a better hold of Levi's arm. "Where do you think you are going?"

"Away from you. You are insane."

---

95 Unlike Sigourney, he didn't have a voice in his head arguing that fairness had nothing to do with this. He didn't ask questions like who started this in the first place or conclude that maybe something or someone like the universe the Rabbit trusted in wholeheartedly was tallying up the score.

"That might be."

"Not might; you are. You speak of machines like they are some nasty entity trying to corrupt us. That's not how it works. The machines you so fear bring prosperity instead of the destruction you are so willing to dish up."

Justice pulled him closer. "You think you are so clever. How about this, Mister World-Changer: the concept of good isn't that simple. Neither are rights. There are so many competing views here in this room, making me wonder how you or your fellow humans ever came up with the idea of justice. Nevertheless, here I am, seeing the world from more than just one perspective. If justice is to persist, I need to persist, Mr. Perri. I choose to survive. So let me have the Bufonite, or I'll break every bone in your body and get it anyway. You can choose. I'll let you have that."

"Be my guest." Levi stepped aside as much as he could while being held by the god.

Margaret and Otis lay on the ground behind him. Percy had walked to them and snatched the machine into his arms. The demon tried to fight off the hexer, but the imps held her back. The spirits were almost all gone. Mostly because of Percy's curses. But Sigourney, or more like Decimal inside her, had done her part.

Justice's eyes burned with orange flames. Levi looked down and saw the shackles again. The god loosened her grip and took a step past Levi. Something clanged between her legs. Justice looked at her feet. So did Levi. The torn pages of the notebook caught on fire. Levi dropped onto his knees to smother the fire with his vest. They were the sole key to reconstructing the Bufonite. He was sure Sigourney was long gone, and she would have to live with whatever nastiness Otis put into her.

Justice never got to the machine. Rose positioned herself between her and Percy. She'd left Abigail sitting on a kitchen stool. The banker had her sword drawn.

"I wouldn't," she warned. Her eyes were burning as well, despite the fact that only a short piece of metal was guarding her dear life against a god. And for what? Money? No, in the end, when the question is whether my spleen bleeds when you stab it, cash loses any importance.[96] Rose wasn't risking her

---

96   At least for the moderately logically sane.

life for cash, or love, or freedom. Partly for care and friendship towards Percy, but mostly because someone had to do something. Justice couldn't win.

The god said nothing. She looked at Rose and then at the sword, yanking it out of Rose's hold as if it was a child's wooden toy. The god's hand was bleeding as she flipped the blade around. She lifted the sword to swing it down, not caring what would follow.

"You can't," Rose said, staring in disbelief at the god, having thought justice would prevail. Her protest mixed with Siarl's wail as he helped Edith with a pair of imps.

It was Percy who reacted. He dropped the Bufonite and wrapped his arms around Rose, pulling her away from the god. The machine didn't fall. For a moment, it hovered in the air, then it disappeared.

The blow never landed either, as Levi, to his surprise, jumped up from the floor and took hold of Justice's sword arm. He twisted it away from the banker. The pages he had already collected dropped back onto the ground. He hated himself for caring, but Rose's death would be one death too many. Ada all over again. And everything—if the universe indeed kept score—would be his fault.

Justice wrenched her arm free from his grip without caring if she dislocated her shoulder. She dropped the sword as she faced Levi. He seized Levi by his throat, drawing him in once again.

"You are as stubborn as Lord Bufonite was." Justice hoisted him up and dangled him there. The god grew taller, and as she did, the shackles blazed against her skin for a moment.

Levi clutched at her wrists, struggling for air. But Justice's grip was firm. There was no doubt how this would end, and everyone would see his death as justifiable. One life to spare many.

Everything slowed down. He stopped fighting for air, and his body went limp.

Somewhere, Margaret growled, abandoning the unconscious Otis on the floor. The imps had done their worst. Levi couldn't entirely focus on the demon. He saw the day unraveling in front of his eyes, making him wonder what the point was. It had started so well, and now... now Karma had come to collect.

"You dim-witted god," Margaret wheezed. "You are ruining everything." She shook the remaining imps off, and they returned to Percy. They merged into his body and faded out of existence.[97]

Margaret wasn't the only one to react. Rose tried to free herself from Percy's embrace. He didn't let her.

"You can't. I can still feel the heat. More will die," Percy insisted.

"Let me go. She'll kill him," Rose protested.

"Is that such a bad thing?"

The rest of the conversation faded away from Levi. His lips were turning blue, and Percy's question repeated on a loop inside him. He kept answering, "No, not such a bad thing. A mistake right from the beginning."

But while he could let go, Margaret couldn't. Not now. She was so close to getting all this right. She barked,

"Let Levi go, or I'll tear every tooth, every muscle, every limb from your body and show them to the other gods." She kept moving forward, pushing Percy and Rose out of her way. She knocked Abigail off her kitchen stool and took the chair with her. She bashed it against Justice's back.

The god didn't flinch. She kept squeezing the life out of Levi. There was an uncontrolled rage in Justice's eyes. There was no going back. Margaret hit the woman again and again with the stool, but Justice ignored her. Levi closed his eyes. He was sure he heard Siarl say,

"Sigourney, go and don't look back." There was a pause. If Sigourney answered, Levi didn't hear it. But Siarl replied, "I'll look after your brother. I promise I'll try to save him. But get that machine away from here."

All he could think was, *too late.*

He was wrong. Margaret crawled back towards him after Justice had sent her flying into the masonry oven. She held a spoon, and while the stool had not held terror, the cutlery did. The demon jammed the spoon into Justice's ear, and the god screamed. She released her hold on Levi, who collapsed onto the floor, holding his throat and wheezing.

In front of him, Margaret continued her attack. She had taken the fallen sword and was advancing towards Justice, who yanked the spoon from her ear. Blood streamed down

---

97   Going back to the reality where everything spooky manifested itself and broke all conventions of decency, like gravity.

the god's cheek.

"I'll kill you," she said.

"Go on, do it," Margaret snorted, meaning it. Unlike the god, the demon couldn't die and be forgotten. Not in the same sense. Humans always needed their bogeymen to take the blame for all the evil deeds.

"I thought as much," Margaret said when the god didn't strike her down there and then. But she was mistaken about why. Justice had no qualms about killing the demon. Why would she? It was in their nature to destroy each other. But unlike Rose, Margaret could hurt her. The sword was a vehicle for corruption. One cut from it and the blackness Margaret carried with her would seep in, as it had already done from the spoon lodged in Justice's ear.

Margaret advanced. She smiled like a cat who had spotted a weakened mouse. A bit confused and extremely excited.

The air around the god turned slightly electric. The shackles came back, and as they did, the oven doors snapped open, and she pulled the fire out, hurling it at Margaret. The demon cackled as her clothes ignited. Margaret dropped onto the ground, trying to put out the fire, still laughing. But Justice didn't let her smother the flames. She made her body snap back up. Hanging there.

The room filled with the smell of burning flesh, making Levi gasp for air and gag.

"Do you think this will stop me?" Margaret screeched.

"No, you'll come back. But at least you can't do anything for now." Justice threw Margaret into the corner.

The demon stopped making any noise. There was only silence and the crackle of the fire. The fire wormed its way up the wood unnaturally fast. All courtesy of Margaret's demonic body and the heat it released.

Justice turned around once again to face Levi.

Levi scrambled to his knees, trying to back away from the god.

Justice looked at the struggling alchemist.

"Is this what you thought would happen?"

Levi wished to answer. To explain why he'd invented the Bufonite. To argue how Justice was the one who had brought chaos instead of solutions. All Levi got out was a wheeze. His throat felt raw, and the burning flesh made him cough.

"Please, for the Rabbit's sake, stop. You have done

enough." Siarl interrupted them. He stood up behind the kitchen table. But his words were lost in the I-don't-care-if-you-exist-or-not land.

Justice only amplified her intensity. The shackles burned bright blue as she concentrated her full attention on Levi.

"I'll hunt your sister down. Don't think I didn't notice and don't think I won't. I'll burn everything and everyone the machine has touched to the ground. Nothing will be left."

The back door snapped shut. So did every other window and open door in the house. Upstairs, Evelyn was trapped. She had finally, after all the pacing around, found the courage to drop down from Otis' bedroom window, only for the window to snap shut and lock her indoors.

Justice was ready to use the burning corpse and make everything go up in flames. That was just it. It was what she was planning and not what was in the cards. Nor what the universe thought should happen. Sometimes it did care, contrary to what Margaret had concluded. Or maybe it was just a string of coincidences, and a bunny happened to hop into the kitchen past the fire engulfing the corner where the demon lay. The bunny had the same white and gray features as the Rabbit god of luck. It twitched its nose and made a little squeaking sound.

Justice froze on the spot.

The bunny made another sound. It seemed to say, "*This is what you decide to do when I give you the most powerful force in the world.*"

"I have done nothing wrong. Not to you, not to them. You chose to become a mortal," Justice protested.

The bunny squeaked.

"You can't say that. I'm still on the side of justice. I always have been. I'm doing this for them," Justice insisted.

The bunny twitched its nose.

"No, they don't know what they need and what's good for them. You must see how misguided they are and how they keep living wrongly. If they did as they were supposed to, there wouldn't be misery. No torment would infest their lives..."

The bunny twitched its nose again.

"...I can say that. I know what's right and wrong. And before you accuse me of not caring for the innocent, I do. I know what empathy is." Justice's voice rose high. Her shackles kept glowing, and the flames in the corner where Margaret was lying got bigger. The god stepped towards the bunny. She looked like she was ready to snap its neck and roast it.

Levi crawled back to his papers to save them. It was all he could do despite how pointless the action was. They were the only thing that made sense. Next to him, Siarl advanced in the opposite direction towards the god and the bunny, having left Edith, Humphrey, and the catatonic man taking cover behind the table.

Levi reached for the papers and Siarl for the bunny, scooping it into his lap and hugging it tightly against his chest. The bunny squeaked. Not to Siarl, but to Justice.

"I know how to listen. What do you think I have been doing all these centuries? Listening to them. The ones who don't ever get it right. The ones who do terrible things for their selfish desires. Do they care what I think? Or think of me at all? I see how they murder their children, their elderly, their innocent, and their sinners, and do they change? No. They keep doing horrendous things to each other again and again. Lying and stealing for profit. Going to war for the same reasons and turning each other into monsters to justify their actions. So don't preach to me about justice. I'm Justice. I'm what is right. And what I say should be obeyed!"

The flames billowed towards Justice, hitting Percy and Rose on their way, who both howled and dived out of the way.

The bunny pushed its head under Siarl's arm, looking away from the god.

Levi sprawled over his papers, protecting them. If he didn't survive, they would have to. They would have to right the wrongs and free humanity from whatever Justice was and the ideals she so readily believed in. Maybe he had done this wrong, but what he had done was clearly the right path.

26

THE CULMINATION OF IMAGINATION

lways on the sidelines, rarely in the spotlight even when you shape your surroundings, make other people's lives better, and leave happiness behind instead of hatred and spite. Such people were easy to ignore, especially if they were the ones who came and cleaned up the mess in the end. Oh, yes, you could blame them, say something about martyrdom, or not speaking up. But that was just a speech for those who liked to break the eggs, leave them on the floor, and run out of the room yelling, "*It wasn't me,*" or better yet, "*This is art!*" or, "*I have my rights.*" Such people might find people like Siarl disconcerting. Someone who didn't make a fuss about themselves, who was happy to help you, listen to your problems, solve them to the best of their abilities. Always nice, and most annoyingly, always adept. An egg breaker might raise their hands in the air and shout, "*look at me,*" but Siarl would never do such a thing. He would go around the egg breaker, sweep up the shattered shells, and hide them before anyone noticed.[98]

---

98   Maybe not the best strategy in life.

Sigourney was an egg breaker, despite what she might think of herself. Especially when it came to Siarl. Her brother seemed to be one too. Sigourney didn't do it intentionally or with callousness. Neither did her brother. It was just that people like Sigourney were too wrapped up in their own agonies, insecurities, worries, needs, wants, the color of their toes, the curl of someone else's mouth,[99] to notice people like Siarl smoothing it all away.

Okay, Siarl had complained a lot about luck, about the constant travel, about Lepus, about everything, but he had just reached his breaking point. That was the worst he had done, complain. State aloud that he felt uncomfortable, which made him feel like a dick, especially when it was so out of character.

Also, now that Sigourney was gone, along with the machine, Siarl was no longer certain who he was. For too long, he'd defined his existence through her and the Rabbit. Luckily, there was one more mess to sort out. There was the Levi and Justice thing. The god looked like she was ready to kill the bunny in his arms. The bunny he was sure was the Rabbit himself. Then there was the fire thing and Levi ignoring it while trying to save the remains of his work, occasionally patting the fire with his hand to keep it from spreading. As obsessed as Sigourney.

And of course, they would all burn alive if someone didn't do something soon. Siarl glanced at the back door, seeing Edith and Humphrey trying to pull it open. The god was holding it closed somehow.

"Don't you turn away from me!" Justice said to the bunny, who burrowed deeper into Siarl's armpit.

Siarl got up from the floor, holding the Rabbit tightly against his chest.

"I think he means no harm," Siarl tried.

Justice scoffed. "Boy, what do you know about harm?"

He hated that. To be called a boy just because of his size. But he never corrected anyone, and he wouldn't say anything now either.

"Look around at what you have done," he said instead.

Justice did. There was the scorched body of Margaret,

---

99 Up or down?

whose flesh was still burning.[100] Abigail lay in a ball on the floor. She was barely breathing. The spirits were gone, but they had been too much for her. Otis was lying unconscious a little further away from them, and the flames were starting to close in. Then there were Rose and Percy, who both looked like they had been in a fight—which they had been. Then there were Humphrey and Edith, who had given up on the back door and were now panicking like cornered animals. And the strange catatonic man who sat where he had been left, unaware of anything going on around him.[101]

Justice looked back at Siarl, who put his hand on her arm. There was the same electric tingle he always felt around the god of luck. He ignored the sensation and said,

"I know you did your best. I'm so sorry about what has happened to you and what is happening here. No one should witness all you have seen. It's no wonder you are doing this, thinking this is the way to solve all our problems. And maybe you're right. Losing you as our guide, as our god, will surely make the world a worse place. But at what cost? Are our deaths necessary? Let us live and show us what you mean instead of any of this. Show us how we can keep you alive in our minds and hearts. We need you. The machine is gone." He wasn't actually lying. He was willing to see the world from her perspective, and it was bleak, making him want to put everything right again. He had nothing against gods per se. He didn't care for what they did with their powers, having a say in others' destinies just because they could, but that didn't warrant hatred in his book.

Justice didn't reply. She'd succumbed to anger, and it was readily consuming her. It was the bad kind of anger, the nonconstructive kind.

Siarl had to wait for the touch and words to work their magic, if they were up to it. Words had always worked for him. People so often thought their complexity was the key, but the truth was, it wasn't. People wanted to hear their thoughts and ideas echoed back to them. That was all. If they felt fully heard, understood, then most things keeping them

---

100 The imps would say merrily. Margaret would too.

101 He was well aware. But he was damned if he was going to let others know that he was hopping from one person to another and seeing the events unravel from multiple perspectives.

back would melt away.

Then there was the gentle, loving touch of his words, which softened even the biggest doubter. People needed to be touched. It told you that you were alive and cared for. So simple yet effective.

All of that worked for Siarl, perhaps because he was genuinely empathetic towards others. He had no reason to judge anyone.

As he waited, Siarl imagined Sigourney saying sorry in her meek voice. He would reply, "*I know you are,*" then hug her tight, and all would be well. But now, she was as good as gone.

Only a passing thought. Justice was coming around, despite the fact that justice and luck were fighting inside the god, making everything more confusing. At first, Justice's anger was too great, but then the confusion of the words and the touch set in, and what followed was numbness and then sobbing—the so-called byproduct of Siarl being Siarl. Justice's shackles faded away. She staggered forward, and Siarl caught her. Her shoulders hunched down, and she collapsed into a position impossible for anyone with a working spine. The god, the sister of the Rabbit, felt feeble in his embrace.

The back door snapped open, and Edith and Humphrey fled, causing the fire to blaze.

Siarl hunched over, holding on to the mumbling Justice, whose words made no sense. She said, "This went all wrong... like oil and water."

A beam crashed down next to them as Justice's concentration and luck stopped holding everything together. Siarl couldn't stay there to decipher what the god meant. He took a firmer hold of Justice and guided them through the kitchen. Farther away, the hexer had dragged Rose towards the door. She was fighting him, saying things like, "I can't leave him." But she had to give up. Not because she was wrong or Percy's dragging had made her change her mind, but mostly because Percy's arm caught on fire and she instead took charge and pushed the man out.

Siarl was too focused on his own struggles to pay much attention to what the banker and the hexer did. He tried to keep the pace fast and maintain his hold on the god and the bunny. Both were heavy and fidgety. Especially the bunny, who tried to squirm its way to freedom. Siarl did his best to get them to safety, but it wasn't enough. Not when his companions were as entitled and stubborn as gods and about as cooperative.

The bunny wiggled out of his hold and hopped under a blazing stool, refusing to come out. The Rabbit forced Siarl to lower Justice onto the floor, where she continued to mutter about oil and water, luck and justice.

Siarl knelt down, reaching for the Rabbit's hind leg to drag him out. But with every reach, the god huddled farther away from him. All he got was lungs full of smoke, making him cough forcefully. He was sure he would pass out soon from the heat. But he didn't pass out. A hand took hold of the bunny and picked it up. Siarl looked up and saw Rose. She offered her hand to him to help him up. He took it happily. The banker was a welcome sight. She had torn off a piece of her skirt and tied it around her mouth and nose. She pulled him up from the floor, handing the bunny to him.

"Go," she said.

Siarl glanced at Justice.

"Don't worry, I'll bring her out. We will be right behind you."

He didn't wait for her to tell him twice. He dived out of the kitchen with the bunny into the night air. The smog from earlier was still thick and tangible, but it was fresh and clean compared to the smoke inside. He saw Edith and Humphrey on the lawn, frozen in place. Percy was doubled over on the ground. His long jacket lay next to him. The hexer muttered curses to heal the burns on his arm. He was wheezing, having to gasp after every word he said.

Rose came out behind him, helping Justice out, who appeared to weigh thousands of pounds. Rose turned around as soon as she had dropped the god on the lawn.

"Rose," Percy protested weakly.

The banker spared him a glance but headed in anyway.

"Hey, wait up," Siarl said before the woman dived back indoors.

Siarl gave the bunny to Justice and went after Rose, not noticing the slight tingle transported from the god to him. Before he got in, Siarl stopped to lift his shirt's collar against his face. Crit, he thought and tore a piece from the hem of his good shirt and tied it around his face, following Rose's example.

The mask didn't do as much good as he'd thought it would. Not to him, at least. Rose seemed unfazed by the fire and smoke. She crawled on the floor towards Abigail, who was closest to the door. Levi was still gathering the pages. Then there was the catatonic man and the necromancer.

Siarl hesitated. His lungs were in flames, making him want to puke after every sip of air he took. But this wasn't the time to back down. He did what Rose had done and dropped to all fours. Levi was the farthest, and... if he was honest, he would help him over the others anyway... because of her.

Siarl crept forward, trying to stay out of the fire's way. He saw an imp huddled under a bucket. The imp jumped at the opportunity and got on Siarl's back. The others of its kind were nowhere to be seen. Siarl continued crawling towards Levi.

Rose had gotten her fingers around Abigail's shoulders, and she was hauling her out in a crouched position.

Siarl got to Levi, who was stuffing the pages inside his black shirt.

"We need to go," Siarl said.

Levi didn't reply. He reached for another stack of papers. Siarl touched his hand.

"Leave them. We really need to go." The imp pushed its claws deep into Siarl's flesh, as if to remind him that time was running out. He was more aware than the imp thought.

Sigourney's brother looked up and shook his head.

"I can't let them destroy everything. This is our hope. This is all that is left, and you must see that the Bufonite could have—"

Siarl cut him short. "They mean nothing if you die."

"And I mean nothing if they are gone."

There were no words to argue back, to make Levi reconsider what he was doing. Siarl understood the man's logic. Everything Levi was, was in those papers. Siarl knew he would either have to force the man to come with him or leave him there. He could try one more thing, but...

"Sigourney still has the machine, and she won't destroy it. She'll hide it, and..." He left the hope there to jolt the man back into reality.

Levi looked up from the papers and then to those already scorched.

"It won't do any good. It should never have been built the

way it was."

A cupboard crashed farther away from them. Siarl wanted to scream, "we really don't have time for this," but he said,

"Then you have a chance to do it right if we get out of here alive."

"It won't matter, but I'll come with you."

Levi crawled behind him towards the door. The alchemist panted as he moved. So did Siarl, despite the mask.

"You know, I would never have thought she could connect with anyone," Levi said.

"It wasn't easy. It took a war between gods for her to accept me," Siarl replied.

Levi snorted.

Siarl let the man believe it had been a joke. It was easier that way. All his emotions about her leaving and most likely never coming back had to be smothered for now. If there was a later, he would let them out. Now, he crawled onward, trying to ignore the blackened fingernails pressed hard into his back.

As soon as the door was closed, the imp jumped from his back and ran outside, disappearing out of sight. Any other person would have shouted after the creature that thanks would have been nice. Not Siarl. Instead, he crawled the rest of the way out and took his mask off, and took long sips of air in. Levi followed his example.

"The necromancer," he heard Percy moan to Rose, who was lowering Abigail onto the ground.

Rose nodded but added, "Someone needs to go to the other side and get the remaining Luddites out." She looked around the yard and found Humphrey and Edith. "You." She pointed at the clairvoyant and then at Edith. "Get them out."

Rose didn't wait for a response. Everything important had been said, and she had other things to worry about. She ran back into the house.

Siarl looked at the two prisoners. "One of you needs to call for help as well, or the fire won't stop here. The whole neighborhood will go up in flames."

Humphrey got up and said, "I'll go and help with the Luddites. Edith can run for help."

"Thank you," Siarl said.

But as much as he wanted to, he couldn't stay lying on the lawn. He would have to go in as well. The catatonic man was still there. He crawled back inside. The smoke had gotten worse. He could barely see Rose's outline, but there she was, helping Otis up from the floor. She would have to deal with him. Siarl searched for the catatonic man. He was still there behind the kitchen table, his trousers on fire. Siarl ignored all his own warnings and got up, dashed through the flames to the man, and knocked him down, rolling him around in an attempt to smother the fire. He managed to quench it, somehow managing not to burn himself. Siarl grabbed the man and wormed his way to the entrance. The fire stubbornly licked at them, determined to engulf them, but the flames seemed to bend around Siarl and the man. Siarl knew what it meant. It was the effect of pure, concentrated luck and maybe a hint of justice keeping him safe. Siarl sighed and relaxed a little.

There was no need to fear the inevitable or the facts of life. He stopped wiggling across the floor with the man and got up instead. He dragged the man out with the last of his strength and, once outside, dropped onto his back. He drew the mask off and gasped.

"I, Justice, live inside all men, guarding them against the beastliness of human nature. I'm where society begins and where it will end," Justice muttered to herself, her voice lifting high at first, and then falling to the level of a whisper. "These won't keep me." She rattled the shackles. Then she hugged the bunny tight against her chest.

The bunny snuffled.

Siarl exhaled, unable to get up and ask Justice to shut up, which he would never in a million years do anyway. But at least he could free the Rabbit from his sister's clutches. Not now though; his ears were ringing, and his heart was hammering against his chest. He had to lie there. He just had to.

Siarl heard the muffled sound of Rose asking, "Is there anyone else in the house? Where's the maid?"

If there was any strength in his body, he would react. He didn't have to. Levi did.

"Evelyn?" the alchemist let out. He got up inhumanly quickly, clearly not thinking as he stormed into the blazing kitchen.

Rose ran after Levi, shouting, "You fool, the fire is too strong! Come back!"

Levi ignored the banker. Siarl didn't. He got up and reached for the woman before she headed in. He brushed his hand against her back and let her go. Rose had no knowledge of his small act of kindness, but it was the least he could do to aid her safe return.

Siarl shut his eyes and walked in as well, letting the luck guide him into the shop to help with the Luddites.

Soon after, the windows on the upper floors exploded.

No one saw or cared about the invisible girl, human-wise at least. The only ones who could intervene were the gods. But Justice was too preoccupied, the Rabbit was no more, and the named ones, the ones who people worshiped somewhere on this rock, were too interested in their own affairs to be aware of the flight of a single human being, even when they held the possible futures in their hands.[102] Yes, there were the demons like Margaret, who sensed her. Every part of their being told them to chase after her and hunt her down like a dog. However, inside her, Decimal had made a spirit wrap around them, hiding them to the best of her ability.

So Sigourney ran. She ran past the red gates of Blue Songbird Park. She took refuge inside the carts of vendors, guiding her out of Threebeanvalley. She let them take her away, as hiding the machine inside the city would be too risky. She couldn't trust any human to protect it, including herself. No building would keep people or gods away. She was proof of that. So nature had to do it, and she knew a place that was only hers.

This was what she was good at. She could run and hide until there was no tomorrow. With her speed and determination, there might not be. Decimal tried to slow down their travel. To reason with Sigourney that there was no need for speed. But every shadow, everything reminded Sigourney that they were being pursued. They weren't. That was beside the point.

To Decimal, being alive seemed to be the point. There was no end to her taste for *everything*. She was even willing to stay with the mountain nuns for weeks, wishing to learn their

---

102 Paws. Always paws, if you asked Sigourney.

secrets. Their dual nature was too much for the nuns. They were forced to leave. Or it might have been the relentless, inquisitive questions Decimal asked.

So they, she, kept going across the continent, and it felt good to be alone. Finally, Sigourney could hear her inner voice without distractions. Finally, she could put the pieces back together. And finally, she saw her history from a different perspective, not only from hers or Decimal's. Levi's words rang inside her. He'd suffered as severely as she, and instead of helping him, she'd hated and abandoned him. She hadn't seen past her ego and the agony of existing to comprehend someone else's pain. She'd thought she was unique, one of a kind, the only one battling with the fiendish, obsessive loops going through her head, and now she realized there was nothing special about her, not even taking into account her ability to hide.

And why had she kept everyone at arm's length? Out of fear? All she should have done was show kindness and compassion, listening to them. Oh, people did and said the silliest things. However, that was okay. Their spectacles were as tarnished as hers.

"You know, life would be a lot easier if you thought less and acted more," Decimal said as they hiked through a thick forest. They were almost where they should be—Sigourney's secret place, where happiness and meaning lay.

"It doesn't work that way," Sigourney protested. She dropped to sit on the trunk of a fallen tree.

"You overcomplicate things. Everything is straightforward if you strip the extra layer of balderdash off. This brain of ours makes things unnecessarily problematic. Look at my son and your brother. Instead of bringing gods down upon them, they could have occupied their time with less invasive pursuits and they would have flourished."

"But there has to be—"

"Meaning?" Decimal cut her off. It was an annoying habit of hers. She read Sigourney's mind before she fully formed her thoughts. They'd discussed it several times before, but it was hard to get Decimal to change her mind.[103]

"Yes," Sigourney said, looking from under her eyebrows at nothing in particular. The only one experiencing the effect

---

103 Mind, what a troubling thing to carry around.

was a random bird on a branch, who had no clue what human expressions meant. So it chirped away happily.

"You can't deny that what they made could have made a huge difference. Isn't that worth pursuing?" Sigourney got up and continued moving.

"Everything is worth pursuing if you explain it correctly to yourself and, if necessary, to others. That includes any form of abuse."

"You are..." Sigourney changed her words into a hum to drown out what she thought.

"I have been called a lot worse."

The rest of the way to the lake, Sigourney sulked. Decimal wasn't what she had pictured when she thought an inner voice to guide her through life would be a good idea. The woman had often encouraged Sigourney to do unspeakable things. Also, Decimal had a weird fascination with death. Sigourney didn't really care to know what parts of her body animals found incredibly delicious or easy to eat. Cheeks and nose were good starting points. Not that humans were excellent protein sources; there was better and easier prey on the market. Not to mention the sky-scraping death towers she had been planning to build on Necropolis' soil or the corpse-eating relatives or water burials. Anything rotting got the necromancer animated.

Sigourney climbed up a tall hill. At the end of it would be the lake. The target of all this and the end of their flight. It should be deep enough to hide the machine but shallow enough for someone really determined to retrieve it. When she reached the highest point, she opened her backpack and took out the device. She looked at the silvery forest lake and then at the Bufonite. They were both so beautiful under the soft morning light.

"It's such a shame to throw it away. Your brother and my son were poets when they built that thing," Decimal sighed.

Poets indeed, although others might think of them as madmen. The golden plates, the carvings, the soul inside the mechanics was their language. Whatever Levi had done, however much she'd feared him then and even now, she had always loved him with all her heart. She had once looked up to him. His cleverness, his charm, his perseverance, his brilliant mind, and for the fact that it was never dull around him. The adventures they'd had as kids were what fueled

Sigourney's restlessness. She had to see the entire world before she was satisfied. To visit the tallest mountain, which she had, to dive to the deep caves on the shore of Jadero, which she would do, to hear the wind chimes ring as she gazed down at valleys full of life. Levi had shown her the power of needing to know more. And now she had taken away the culmination of his imagination.

"You'd better chuck it before you change your mind. The Necromantic Council can't convict Otis without it," Decimal said, as she'd said before.

While Sigourney disagreed with the woman that her son shouldn't be put on trial for what he had done, she knew the machine couldn't get into the wrong hands. Maybe one day it could surface. Siarl would know who to give it to and when. But there was no forgetting that so many had died already because of the machine.

How could something so beautiful be so dangerous? Was the apparatus the reason for the deaths or the people who couldn't handle it? An inanimate object couldn't be a mover of evil. Or could it? Could an artifact make the entire human population spin around it to serve its survival and renewal? Like termites building and feeding the hive without ever understanding why. Thinking about their motivations, needs, and wants, blinded by the strings that kept pulling them back and forth.[104]

Could motivations take away the evil of a deed? Make it all better? But it wasn't anger that she'd witnessed back at the alchemy shop. It had been fear. Were fear and evil always tied together?

"Who cares... But if you don't throw it in already, we'll freeze to death here, and I'm already starving."

That was another thing the woman did, always craving food. Making Sigourney taste everything they came across.

"Can't you think about anything else except food?" Sigourney asked.

"What do you want me to say? That the cost of the imbalance the machine causes would be too much? That we humans who are always on the brink of conflict would only repeat our father's and mother's mistakes? Or how about if I argue for it? Saying things like the bruises of violence are

---

104 Okay, that was giving meagre credit to the inner life of termites.

justifiable in exchange for unlimited resources? How can any of us see the future and predict it correctly?"

Decimal was right. Sigourney had seen enough gods, empires, and humans to know that it was impossible to control the tidal wave of all the possibilities. The great always thought they could take control and shape the wave to conform to an idea. Some of them could, for a while. Then the chaos came with multiple factors and forces, and the great needed more and more arms to keep all the balls in the air, having to move faster than light to play catchup with the desires of others.[105]

Among all this, reason was never the strong suit of man. Even the brightest person with novel thoughts could be blinded by their own visions, not understanding the pitfalls, like the idea of free information. Freedom came with a price, one that the next generations had to pay. Sigourney knew that the stories we told ourselves mattered. You become what you think you are. She had done just that, become her own worst fears.

"Go on, tell your story as you see it," Decimal replied. This time Sigourney had no stamina to argue back and say she was being impolite by listening in. What was the point, as the thought had been as much for her as for Decimal and the universe. But unlike the universe, Decimal had said something.

Sigourney released the machine from her hands. It splashed against the lake's still surface, causing ripples and then bigger and bigger rings that distorted the pale blue and yellow of the sky reflected in the water. Soon they died out, and the wholeness of the reflection returned to the serene, perfect moment of a quiet, lonely morning. Somewhere in the distance, a bird sang its song. Sigourney sat on a stone, listening to the surrounding forest come alive. She wondered whether they had made the right call.

Most probably, they would never know.

By unleashing the doomsday machine, as Justice would see it, there was no telling what catastrophes would be created in the profit-making system, but neither was there room for hope for all the good that might have come to be. All denied

---

105 And nature. No matter how much humans wanted to be the masters of their environment, to remove it once and for all from the equation of life, it wasn't possible. Not with their constrained views and hearts.

because of uncertainty, never allowing the opportunity to shape a better tomorrow or take responsibility for their own actions.

Or all this was silly, and the sun would rise and set without having to take humans into consideration.

"Sleep well. Maybe someday you will surface again," Sigourney said aloud and got up.

She began to hike back to so-called civilization. Monster or no, she had forgiven herself for her past and how she handled it. She could pretend she was some alien creature, or a bird, who had been raised in the wrong nest. And ever since then, her destiny hadn't been hers. Now she understood that she couldn't control her past, her surroundings, or what chance threw at her, but she could command her reactions. She could follow her usual instinct and keep running, or she could go back.

"Or we could take the world by storm." Decimal smiled.

Sigourney was sure she did.

27

THROUGH ALL HOPES AND DREAMS TO THE SEA OF ENDLESS POSSIBILITIES

ercy gazed at the horizon, watching the sea churn. He could breathe again, knowing he was on his way to the shores of his motherland. He never thought he would miss Necropolis as much as he had. Even the familiar sea birds swooping against the cloudy sky made him feel at ease. Creatures of poets, making people dream impossible dreams. All they did to him was remind him that he was tied to the land. No great poetry came to his lips.

"Can't we go inside already?" Otis groaned next to him. The scars on the necromancer's forehead had faded. Still, the man would be marked for life. He could always shift form to hide them. But they both knew they would be there—the imps' and the fire's parting gift.

Of course, Otis couldn't change shape now, not as long as he was with Percy. Percy had put a curse on the man, stopping him from using his necromancy or matter transmutation.

He was taking Otis to the Necromantic Council. There he

would be judged for all he had done. Aiding in the creation of the machine and unleashing spirits in Threebeanvalley. Some were never found and sent back to the realm of the dead. Even leaving Necropolis' soil without the Council's permission was an offense. Not to mention all the other sordid things he'd carried out. It would be a miracle if the man saw the light of day after this. An execution was possible. Even soul destruction wouldn't be off the table. The last thought made Percy shiver.

Percy kept his attention on the sea when he answered Otis.

"Not yet. The guide for traveling by sea says that you have to spend—"

"You and your rules," Otis groaned, cutting Percy short.

"They are—"

"Spare me. I'm here, ain't I?"

"Sure." Percy corrected his posture and moved his hand behind his back. He winced from the pain in his right hand. The burned skin was still raw and one size too small. No curse or medicine had gotten it back to normal. And unlike Otis, he couldn't disguise it out of existence. He tensed his jaw and tried to bite the pain away without having to reposition himself.

In addition to the pain, he felt uneasy around the necromancer. All that had happened in the kitchen couldn't be forgotten. He had almost been unable to protect the city against the spirits. One wrong move on his part and they would have been set loose. Then there were the imps and what they had done. He hated to admit that a few had broken out of his control and done their worst. Luckily, no one had noticed a couple of holes in the fabric of reality. They would be there forever, causing spooky action in the distance.

Nor was he keen on leaving after the messy situation. Half of the block around the alchemy shop had burned down, and the explosion had taken lives. However, his duty lay elsewhere, with the Council. The world would turn into a hellish place if there was no one to hunt down the renegade necromancers and force them to face the consequences of their actions. Otis might have caused a spree of Kraken only knew what horrors if the hungry poltergeists had gotten their hands on fresh bodies. But hypotheticals were not his concern; nor were the deaths Otis had caused. Death and dying were perfectly permissible in the eyes of the Council. It was the actual rule-breaking that concerned him. To be exact, clause number 250, especially addendum b-78. All of which might have led to a massive conflict between nations and to necromantic wars. A few lives against the many were small fry. His duty was to ensure the rules were followed to the letter. Otis had caused at least fifteen offenses. All of which Percy had noted down carefully.

"Can't you just let me go? Have some leniency towards me. I did save you when the windows exploded. You let me go, and I can turn myself into an octopus, and no one has to know..." When Percy didn't react right away, Otis added, "I can pay you. While we grappled over the mastery of the spirits, I had a chat with your grandfather and, oh boy, is he a loony, but a rich one. He told me—" Otis began.

Percy corrected his posture again and slowly turned his gaze from the sea to the necromancer.

"I can't be bribed.[106] Also, if I remember correctly, you only *saved* me after I knocked you over for trying to flee..."

Yet, despite the motives, Otis had shielded Percy from the worst of the explosion while they wrestled after the necromancer had woken from his trance.

"And you will not turn into the image of our god," Percy added.

"Don't tell me you believe that octopus nonsense?" Otis leaned against the railing.

Percy would laugh at the pitiful attempt to get under his skin if he were the type of person who laughed. He wasn't. And if Otis thought he was so easily shaken, they would have an interesting sea voyage ahead. Of course, he could explain to the man about the consciousness of octopi. The color-changing ability, the complex nervous system, and the tentacles, which seemed to have a life of their own. The copper blood. That there was no central brain the way humans had. That they were one of the most alien creatures on this planet. Not to mention the god they both knew existed, Kraken, ruled the sea and Necropolis. But Percy's fascination with the animal wasn't because of the father of the sea. It had started one late summer day when he was only a boy. At an aquarium, his eyes and the now-dead octopus'

---

106 Others might add "with my own money." Not Percy. He wasn't one for money. Although the salaries the Council paid would make any grown man cry.

eyes had met, and he had lost his soul to the creature. Ever since, he'd needed to understand it fully. A creature so marvelous, so creative, who could teach a thing or two to humankind. And to think they only lived a few years...

Percy harrumphed and thought up a perfect act of revenge.

"Octopi, also commonly referred to as octopuses, are soft-bodied mollusks who belong to the order of Octopoda. There are around three hundred recognized species, but I'm sure that we'll find more in the near future. They are masters of hiding in plain sight. One interesting fact about them is their blue blood, due to copper..."

Otis sighed. "Can't you just kill me now?"

"Where would be the fun in that?" Percy smiled.

"Is that a smile I detect? You know, underneath the rules and facts beats a cruel heart," Otis said, looking out to sea.

"Only for rule-breakers." Percy began his monologue once again.

"For Kraken's sake, shut up!"

A year had passed. It had gone relatively quickly. Emphasis on relativity. Time is a tricky force, never the same to everyone, and never equal. To the young, it ticked on slowly, almost eternally. To the old, someone kept stealing pieces of it away every night. To Levi, the year had gone in the blink of an eye. He was hunched over his desk, humming happily. Using necromancy had been a mistake, he was sure of that now. It had been a shortcut he had been willing to take in his moment of weakness. But now, he understood better how the machine and the universe ticked. A universe he'd started to consider as an egg after reading Kepler's ideas and the data Wilkinson had gathered about the cosmos. He'd run with the notion, abandoning the original design and going with a mechanical egg in constant motion. Now he was back to the question of what to use to fuel the creation. He had lost the secret Sigourney held. Maybe it was better that way. He had been obsessed with the notion, tying his thinking down.

He'd come up with new thoughts about plants and the enigma they hold in their leaves—one possibility to reveal the building blocks of quintessence. A good one, as plants had a more complex structure of memory and creation than humans or animals, despite no one wanting to admit that. But for now, plants had been a dead-end when it came to creating something out of nothingness. So he'd turned his gaze back to the skies, especially the dark bits between the stars. There was something there. Maybe similar to what human souls held inside, made of the same atoms.

Levi was sure Otis had tapped into it without knowing it. And those with specialized skills have a soul more in tune with the creation and the manipulation of time, space, and matter. This was why they had been easier to use, but every soul had the same potential. This much he was sure of. Or he hoped to be. Otherwise, inequality was written into the cosmos, making the universe a dolorous place to exist.

He called all this the theory of souls. Not in the traditional way, nor with a religious connotation. It was about matter and energy and powering creation. Every living, breathing creature could create, shaping one form into another.

Levi wrote down several book titles on a piece of paper and folded it on the table. He opened it again and added two more books. Then he took another piece of paper and wrote down what he would need to grow plants. Just in case.

He was so immersed in his planning, he didn't hear the door opening or the footsteps getting closer to him.

"Mr. Perri?" Rose asked.

She startled him. The letter "s" in the word "soil" gained an extra loop, looking more like a snake than a letter.

"Levi is fine," he replied, not turning to face the banker.

"Oh, yes, I forgot. So how is everything? Have you made any progress?" The banker exhaled. Half of her face was burned, but it didn't seem to stop her. She wore it like a badge of honor, having saved Evelyn and helped Levi escape into the night so everyone would consider him as good as dead. She'd shielded them with her own body as his alchemy supplies had exploded, turning the fire into an inferno. It had been a miracle she had gotten off so lightly. None of them should be alive, not according to his calculations. A miracle indeed, but he didn't believe in miracles. There was always a reason behind them, something people had missed; like the disappearance of wealthy Evelyn to the sunny lands where she could say nothing of what she had seen or about the fact that

Levi was alive. Some might think of it as a gift from the universe, her rising from her low position to a countess, but in reality it was only the wonders that money and a determined banker could do. And a determined banker could make the world spin around, or so Levi had come to witness. Rose was a force to be reckoned with.

"What day is it?" Levi struck out the word "soil" and wrote it again.

"Tuesday, as always," Rose said carefully, leaning over the table to see what he was writing.

Levi pushed the folded note towards her.

"I need you to get me these. It would be easier if I came with you to see what they have in the—"

"You know that's not possible. For now, this has to go as we arranged." Rose took the note and put it inside her jacket pocket. As always, the woman was impeccable. Her green coat looked almost black. It was made of the finest, thickest satin you could find. Underneath the jacket, Rose wore a pantsuit, which Levi had read caused quite the stir in Threebeanvalley's social circles. He snorted at the thought.

A nasty thought occurred to Levi. Maybe she dressed fancy to draw attention away from her burned face. He groaned.

"Then you need to bring me lists of the library and bookshop inventories. Plus newspapers and gossip about the latest scientific breakthroughs."

"Yes, I'll try to get what you need. I brought what you asked for last time I visited. It's all waiting for you next to the door." Rose glanced towards where she'd come from at the pile of books and a stack of newspapers.

"Oh, yes, good. Here's something else I need." He gave her the other list.

"Seeds and soil? What are you going to do? I thought the egg was enough?" She looked at him intensely, making her red, scarred skin tighten, causing her to wince.

"Yes, but we need something to fuel it into creation. Now it's a mechanical mystery box and a marvel on its own, but not the miracle we are looking for." Levi leaned against the back of his chair, casting his gaze out of the window. The city's rooftops were endless, and if he moved a little bit, he might be able to see out to the sea.

"If you say so. It has been a year, and hiding your expenses has been..." She stopped, as both of them knew it was pointless for her to continue. She was too invested in getting the machine working again. Even so, she'd suggested acquiring him another necromancer. He'd refused, infuriating her.

They'd argued about the use of souls. She'd said it was the same as the skulls they used back at home in the banks. His qualms about using the dead were for nothing. But he refused. She had been helpless against him. She'd tried to impress upon him the good that would follow. To appeal to his past and to his only weakness. He still believed in the machine. Nothing had changed that. But he wouldn't let her desire to rush ruin his redemption.

"No more lost souls," he'd said.

Rose put the other note in her pocket and took one of the finished eggs from the table. This one was made of gold and blue sapphires.

"At least they will be worth something as they are," Rose sighed and put the egg back on the table.

"Have a little faith." Levi restored the egg to its rightful place among the others with emerald and ruby stones.

"I have, but you have to admit, I took a great risk hiding you here. If the Council finds out, I'm as good as dead. Or the Worthwrites... And if Siarl finds out, he won't—" Rose said.

It was always Siarl this and Siarl that. How he had picked up banking instantly. How he had a curious mind and high morals... The annoying little bugger. At least his sister was free of such a man.

"How's our young friend?" He cut her short.

When Rose was about to reply, he said, "Yes, yes." He leaned back on the table, flipping his notebook open, and scribbled down his thoughts.

Rose sighed and left him alone.

He watched after her and turned back to his notes. Yes, plants or the atoms had to be the key, combined with the egg shape, which was perfect in its design. Eggs weren't the source of so many creation myths for nothing. The oval was the shape of the universe.

He listened to Rose shut the door behind her. So many times he'd wanted to say to her that making money was easy; building value was harder.

28

THE MACHINE LIVES ON

iarl walked behind the doctor, carrying a basket with him. The doctor kept glancing behind him uncomfortably, but Siarl couldn't help it. The Rabbit came with him. He'd tried to leave him behind in the boarding house they lived in, but he kept chewing everything. Even the cage Siarl had built for him couldn't hold the bunny. Some of his powers had stayed behind; Siarl had often caught glimpses of the Rabbit teleporting around the room, especially at the sight of carrots. Followed by a horrible sound as the Rabbit devoured them. It was a mix of snorting, chewing, and moaning. The neighbors had complained. Siarl didn't blame them. He could imagine what the landlord would say if she knew what was going on in the room. Siarl might have to buy the place just to get away with all the damage the god of luck had caused.

"You said you were here to see your aunt?" the man said. Most likely to mask the noise of slow chewing and sniffling coming from the basket.

"Yes, Aunt Meredith," Siarl replied. It had been Rose's idea to call Justice Meredith to hide her from the Luddites,

Abigail, or whoever came looking. But a new name didn't wipe away the fact that they'd committed a god to a mental health institution. What else could they have done? Send her to jail? That hadn't seemed right.

The god had kept hugging the Rabbit on the lawn, watching the city burn around her. She'd rocked back and forth, unbalanced and out of this world. Nothing Siarl had said, or anyone had said, had brought her back.

"As far as I can tell, she's calling herself Justice. Your aunt, I mean." The doctor turned at the end of the corridor.

In the distance, hearty singing echoed through the building.

"Has she started to remember?" Siarl asked.

"No, not as far as I know. She keeps up the fantasy of having burning shackles around her hands and legs, and she wakes up screaming in agony. Sometimes she professes to be a god. We would like to up her dosage. Or we could use the new model of treating hysterics and delusions like Meredith's by drilling a hole in the side of her skull. It will relieve pressure and help her get herself back." The doctor stopped, snapping his heels together.

They were standing behind Justice's door. This wasn't the first time Siarl had visited the god. It had seemed wrong to abandon her here and forget all about it. Yes, she'd attacked the alchemy shop and done only the gods knew what to the Rabbit. Also, based on the newspapers Siarl had found, she'd caused havoc among the city's entrepreneurs with her men. But even with all that and the fire and the death of Margaret, Levi, and the others, condemning someone to oblivion was still cruelty.

"Isn't that kind of archaic?" Siarl asked carefully.

"Yes, in the way it was initially used. It's pure nonsense that drilling a hole into the skull would release invading spirits. But through my studies, we have found that these systems actually have some scientific merit—"

"I'm sure they have, but I'm afraid it won't help my aunt," Siarl cut the man short.

"I do have—"

"I would like to see Meredith now." Siarl again blocked the subject from going further.

The doctor pushed the key into the lock and opened the mint green door for him. The man glanced into the room, finding Justice sitting on her bed, looking outside through the bars. When he was satisfied, he left Siarl alone with Justice, muttering as he went that he should have sent a nurse to guide Siarl here if he was going to be so close-minded about what modern medicine could offer. Then he went on muttering about the little incidences around Justice. How the world seemed to arrange itself so she always got what she wanted, no matter how crazy and hurtful it was to the others. She should be thrown out onto the streets.

But they couldn't do it. The Worthwrite Bank of Necropolis paid the bills. Or more like the shell company Rose had set up to hide everything that should be hidden. Siarl was sure she hid more than she told him, but he should be thankful rather than suspicious. Rose had given him a job at the bank. It was all due to the rescue work he had done when the fire had started to spread. He and Rose had worked relentlessly until the city's fire brigade had taken over, and even after that, they had done their best to help. Blocking the fire from spreading, rescuing people from the burning buildings, and finally organizing a water line. Edith and Humphrey had been there to help. And most importantly, he had been there to wrap Rose's head in a cloth soaked in cold water, preventing the worst. He had been there for her first.

Siarl shrugged and made his way to the bed and sat next to Justice. She smelled of soap, or the room did. She didn't react to him.

"Hello... Justice," Siarl said. "I brought Lepus to see you." He took the bunny out of the basket and tried to give it to her.

She hissed and drew away from him. "Get that rodent away from me!"

Oh good, she remembered something. Siarl put the Rabbit back into his basket and sat silently, looking out through the window with Justice after she'd calmed down from seeing Lepus.

Siarl wasn't sure what he could say or do, but he'd read that company and closeness were necessary for the mind to be whole. So he came here every Tuesday to sit with Justice and look out of the window. Sometimes she said things like, "*See what he did. My mind is not mine,*" or "*They ask too much from luck.*" But mostly, she stayed silent. She didn't like to be close to the Rabbit, and whenever she was, she hissed insults and accusations.

A bluebird flew back and forth between the widow and the nearby tree. He followed it from branch to branch, letting the time go by. At least Justice had a pleasant view over the hospital's garden. Rose and Siarl had made sure of that. It was one of the reasons the hospital staff was somewhat hostile. But smiling helped. So did money.

Rose graciously let Siarl come here during business hours even though the bank was ever so busy a year after opening. She felt like it was her duty after Levi had died and no one had known what to do with Justice. In a way, the mental health institution served as a prison. Justice was under lock and key and was subject to constant supervision and chatter from the professionals and the so-called nutters.[107] But at least here, Justice had a comfortable bed, warm meals twice a day, and garden therapy. A luxury many on the outside couldn't afford.

Siarl liked working for the bank. There was never a dull day, and he was continually learning new things. Science and technology moved forward in leaps here in Threebeanvalley, and he was at the heart of it. Also, he'd started to take night classes from the university and planned to get a degree. In what, he wasn't entirely sure yet. The possibilities were so endless. He glanced at Justice, but she refused to engage.

Siarl let the minutes pass. He used these moments as meditation, a practice the Rabbit had taught him.

When an hour had passed, he stood up.

"I'll come back next Tuesday. See you then."

"Please don't," Justice said, not taking her eyes off the window.

She always said that. But Siarl was sure she was better after every visit, or so the nurses told him.

He closed the door behind him and headed with the Rabbit back to the bank to perform his clerical duties.

Justice whispering as he walked away,

"The blind lead the blind onto the path of destruction. More shackled than me in the never-ending circle where meaning always has to be pursued with something new. Desire dwells in the hearts of men. Never stopping to see the present. Never seeing that they have stripped down their

---

107 Sometimes, it was hard to tell who was who.

humanity for the sake of profit. The machine lives on."

Rose sat behind her desk. The room was an exact copy of the one Mr. Worthwrite had back in Necropolis. Made of dark mahogany with a colossal desk, bookshelves, and dark leather couches. All very grand. All shipped here from home. All very not like Rose. Everything was too pompous for her taste. She rested her leg over her knee as she tried to concentrate on the task at hand. She was going over the bank's new acquisitions, and then she would have to read the letters sent here from Necropolis. Being the head of an offshore bank wasn't as glamorous as one might think. Of course, there were the social engagements, with lavish dinners and balls, but they'd lost their glamour. There was no excitement, as she was the biggest whale that everyone wanted to hunt. She would rather be the huntress. Then there was the fact that the sight of her made people squeamish. Her burned face made them want to run, but since she was the whale, they instead spewed out honeyed words, mostly about her heroism. How she'd saved the city from ruin with her swift actions. How on earth had she been there when the fire had started? One day, someone who hated her enough would search for the reason and use it as ammunition against her. She kind of looked forward to that day. She made bets with herself on who it might be. The stakes were high. A significant chunk of her yearly salary would be donated to the charities of her choosing.

Her leg began to shake against her knee, and she found herself thinking about the gambling house and Abigail. She scratched her open left palm and tried not to let her thoughts go there. Thus far, she had been able to stay away from both. Setting up the bank had taken all her mental capacity. Now it was all coming back. It had started innocently at the high society affairs, a way to get through the dull evenings. She loved the look on men's faces when she took them for all they were worth. Then it had become painfully evident that she was doing more harm to the bank than good. Oh, they praised her for her brilliant way with the coins, but behind her back, it was another story. She'd stopped going beyond the basic socially acceptable level. People frowned upon full humiliation. All of which would have been different if she had been a male banker.

Her brutal method would have given her a reputation like no other. To top it all off, the burned face would have made her a legend. But ruthless women were seen as freaks of nature —evil, one could say. But a man, he would only be doing what was expected from the head of the biggest bank in the world. To her, the burned face had become a mask behind which to hide. She was no longer anything but a figurehead.

And Abigail? Her former fencing teacher refused to see her. Something had shattered in the woman's mind. Most likely caused by her grandmother. What nasty creatures they could be. The guardians of the way things should be done. Or to some, a source of warmth and comfort. Rose's grandmother had been a wild one. Always daring to do the impossible. Mostly with her penny-farthing. Her grandmother had wanted to bicycle around the world. She never did. But nor would Rose accomplish her dream. She was no longer sure what her dream was, if she had ever had one. Thus far, she'd lived for the rush she got from her work and her extracurriculars. Now she'd started to think that basing one's life on feeling high wasn't exactly a life to begin with. But what else could she do?

She opened the remaining letters and glanced through them, looking for anything that required action. Nothing to get herself worked up about. Nothing about what she was doing off the books or anything indicating they were sending someone to monitor her. She was doing too well for them to care or to notice she had cooked the books in order to fund Levi. But she had been able to pay back everything, and now what Levi needed came from her own pocket. More like the pocket of the shell company she'd made. Not the one Siarl knew about to cover the expenses of their fallen god.

Rose got up from behind the desk. Everything that needed her immediate attention had been dealt with and would be left for her secretary to pick up. Rose headed to the door and opened it. She was instantly welcomed by a thick cloud of tobacco. The smell was overpowering, and she wanted to cough her lungs out. She didn't. She couldn't give her secretary the satisfaction in their small war.

Page Briggs leaned against an open window behind her desk. The short-haired woman was rolling a fresh cigarette as Rose approached her.

"I have left papers on the desk for you to pick up. See they get delivered."

The woman scowled, saying nothing.

Page Briggs being her secretary was proof of what money and influence could accomplish. Rose left her alone with the only rebellion the woman could come up with. This was cruel of her. She knew it. But sometimes, the satisfaction of payback was worth not being the bigger person.

Outside, Rose hailed a coach. When she stepped in, she thought about the bank and the financial world and how she could spice it up. Maybe they could bet on the future weather and water supplies, or how about the smog. It could be a short-term way to make money with market fluctuations. Hmm. She would have to revisit that idea later. Now she knew what she was doing, and she was willing to take the risk of her own downfall. Rose headed to the gambling house. She already anticipated the electrified atmosphere. The sound of cards being shuffled. The chips clicking. And the sighs and cheers of the other players as they experienced the full force of Bluff the Prime Mover.

Maybe Abigail would come around and accept everything that had happened with them, her, and with Justice.

29

A UNIVERSE TO BE HAD

igourney stood at the ruins of the alchemy shop. Some of the other houses were being rebuilt around it, but not her brother's place. Its orange stone walls were scorched black, and the windows were shattered. The roof had collapsed, and the beautiful drawings her brother had done were obscured by the smoke. Sigourney stepped in through the door, seeing the shop floor had been fully demolished, revealing blackened stones.

The distant chatter of the workers echoed inside the empty room. Everything that had survived the fire had been stolen, including all the burned and bent items thought to hold the secret to transmuting gold. The symbol of alchemy, at least here in Threebeanvalley's soil. Somewhere else, alchemy had been about eternal life. There, the gleam of metal held no glory against immortality. But those who'd stolen the precious items would find them as empty of substance as a jar of cookies after a relative's visit. Or at least those who knew nothing of the mathematical symbols Levi had drawn. To the educated eye, there was a universe to be had.

"I don't like it here," Decimal said. "I..." she started but didn't finish what she was saying.

But Sigourney knew what the woman had meant. "I can hear the whispers too." Some of the dead had stayed behind. She could see their edges. Decimal's necromantic abilities had started to rub off on her. Sigourney had come to notice that necromancy was mostly about being open to all possibilities, being able to speak with anyone, and knowing more than the next fellow. The last thing made Decimal a bookworm. She'd forced Sigourney to read every book they'd come across, slowing their travel back here.

"There's more..."

Sigourney heard what she meant. Behind the desperate voices was one almost gleeful sound, repeating, *"Little sister, you came back. For me?"* On and on it went.

"We shouldn't have come back. He's not worth the trouble," Decimal said, referring to Siarl, or Levi, or all of them. This was not the first time she'd complained about coming to Threebeanvalley.

"Don't you want to know what happened to Otis?" she asked.

"I already know what happened to him." The necromancer refused to say more.

"*Little sister,*" Margaret whispered.

"Why are you still here?" Sigourney answered the call.

No coherent answer came, just an echo of the word "sister."

Maybe even demons needed to belong somewhere. The same basic yearning that people had as a built-in feature. Sigourney guessed it was only to be expected from the creations of the human mind. Demons were just that. A product of human imagination that had taken bodily form. And they would forever remain. Sigourney was sure, especially after tapping into what Decimal knew about spirits, the dead, and corruption. Margaret could never change who she was. Not according to Decimal. But Sigourney couldn't quite believe that. Such a default setting installed in a living thing seemed cruel. To remain the same and be trapped by one's nature. Who would want such mercilessness to exist? Decimal disagreed. To her, deterministic nature was absolution.

Sigourney felt a twinge of pain, thinking the demon's soul

would be trapped here in the ruins for eternity, or until she could find a poor sucker to latch on to, feeding on their fear and hatred. Then there would be no person left. It was stupid to feel guilty about Margaret or any of what her brother had done. She hadn't done anything wrong to merit the feeling, but it was her default to feel guilty about things she had no control over. Stop making shadows to your being, she'd said to herself, like Decimal had taught her.

"*Here for me?*" Margaret repeated, sounding as if she stood behind Sigourney.

Sigourney's skin formed goosebumps.

"Not for you," she said. Her chest suddenly felt tight. Who would ever come for a monster?

"No," Decimal protested. "Stop even considering it."

"But..."

"She's not worth it."

"What if I had thought the same about you? A nasty spirit and a necromancer. Or what if someone had thought the same about me, a monster, a thief, a spy, not deserving a second chance?"

"That's not the same," Decimal snorted.

"*The same,*" Margaret repeated. Sigourney was sure she echoed it to annoy Decimal. The demon wasn't making this any easier.

"And for that matter, she'll find a target eventually." Decimal crossed their arms.

Margaret would. Sigourney knew that. But could she condemn the demon to these ruins for the unknowable future? Or the innocent passer-by to their fate? And if nature was a starting point and actions mattered, then wasn't it her duty to do something? It was all fine to think noble thoughts and say noble words, but when push came to shove, if she didn't act, wasn't it all empty? Here in the ruins under the early morning sky, Sigourney could show kindness.

"Sigourney, no! Please... she'll consume us both..." Decimal pleaded.

If she thought she would be selfish about this and focus only on her own survival, then the necromancer had another think coming.

Decimal intercepted, reading Sigourney's thoughts.

"She will be."

"She'll be what?" Sigourney asked to annoy the necromancer.

"Be selfish. It's not always about who you are and what you do. The other person can be a jerk as well. And Margaret is a major jerk. If you let her come with us, she'll destroy everything she touches, including Siarl. Care for him if you don't care for us."

"What do you want me to do? Leave her here?"

"That would be what a normal person would do. But no, ask her the questions you want answered and be done with it."

That she could do.

"Margaret," she began. The spooky feeling of the demon pressing against her back grew stronger. Every fiber of Sigourney's being wanted to run. She didn't. "What happened to the others?" she tried.

"*Others, others,*" Margaret repeated.

"Cut it out," Decimal said with Sigourney's mouth.

"You really should kick the woman out," Margaret said, appearing more solidly behind them.

Sigourney spun around, and instead of seeing the woman with the eyepatch, there was a thinner, ghostly woman with bony joints and no eyes. Where the eyes should have been were holes that sucked the light out of the place. Her mouth had pointy fish teeth. She wore her usual grin. It was like she mocked the whole of existence with it.

"Why should I answer if you are going to leave me here?" the demon asked, tilting her head when Sigourney stood there in stunned silence.

"Because it's the right thing to do. And we can always force you, demon," Decimal answered on Sigourney's behalf.

"Would you do that too, little sister?" Margaret asked.

"No. But please, I need to know if they are all dead. Levi, Siarl... Otis. The specials." Sigourney finally found her own voice. The pale demon with the grotesque appearance looked pathetic rather than at the top of her game.

"What makes you think I know?"

"Don't play games with the girl," Decimal intercepted before Sigourney could make another pitiful plea.

"I like you, little sister. I do this for you and you alone, but never tell a living soul I helped you."

Sigourney nodded.

"None of them are dead. The banker woman faked your brother's death and took him away from here. Find her, and you find him."

"And Siarl?" Her heart was beating fast.

"Find her, and you find him. That's the answer to everything, and it's all you'll get. Now, if you don't mind, leave me alone. You are cramping my style. I have been eying one of the builders, or maybe a housewife would do. I'm not sure if I want a man. They are such boring creatures."

"You can—" Sigourney began to say, but Decimal cut her short, snapping their mouth shut.

"Leave her," the woman said inside her head.

"But... I can't let her take an innocent life," Sigourney thought.

"Who's to say it will be that. And she has as much right to survive as any of us."

"But before—"

"Before this was about us. We have as much right to survive as she does. So does the builder, but he better learn quickly to defend himself against a demon."

"You know he can't... And taking a life is evil."

"I thought you hated that word. Besides, all of this is a matter of opinion."

Sigourney was about to protest, but Decimal flashed back to her previous failed argument, and she blushed.

"Are you done?" Margaret asked.

Sigourney nodded.

"Then be gone, fiend," Margaret said and disappeared from sight. Her laughter lingered in the ruins, sounding like the distant ringing of bells—the big ones.

Sigourney fled back outside, finally able to breathe fully. Margaret's words repeated in her head. *Find her, and you find him.* Finding the banker would be easy. They tended to gravitate to certain things. Like big buildings, grandeur, and money. Some to horses and others to powerful engines. The city had a lot of the latter. She would find the banker and hopefully Siarl and her brother, then she would search for the specials. For now, she would head to the place where the banks usually stood and find out if she was among them.

Sigourney left the street where the alchemy shop had once

stood, leaving behind the horrid house and what had happened there. She didn't get much farther, as the universe delivered an answer to a question she hadn't asked on a platter. Or more like it smelled and felt like luck. The Rabbit was still alive. Sigourney's eyes welled with tears, and relief washed over her whole body.

She watched as a man plastered posters on a wall. It was the catatonic man. He hummed loudly as he did his work. On the posters read: *Great Clairvoyant Humphrey is back!!! Book your tickets to the show of a century, tonight.* The smaller letters read: *Featuring the illusionist Edith Nye.*

Again, there was a tight feeling in Sigourney's chest. Part of her wanted to go up to the man and greet him. The bigger part choked and hid herself.

"Go on," Decimal encouraged.

"I can't." Sigourney resorted to her go-to answer. Before Decimal insisted, she said, "Tonight, I'll see them tonight. When I have gathered my thoughts."

"If you must."

Sigourney passed the catatonic man, Barnabas Wyat, and headed to the banking district. It was going to be a beautiful day. Sunny, warm, with the right kind of breeze. A good day for a reunion. A good day to see the Rabbit again and hug the god tightly and never let go.

Decimal chatted as they walked. "It's a shame they never got their justice."

Sigourney said nothing.

"Maybe you should offer the specials a chance for revenge. There has to be a payment for what they went through."

"My brother and your son's life?" This was what the stories taught them. Revenge had to be taken. No courts, just taking justice into your own hands and beating someone to a pulp. That the evil should always pay their dues at the hands of the hero. And it was the hero who got to decide who was evil and who wasn't. Did that mean societies' noble ideas would always be thrown out when the eye of the judge evaded or people cried wolf? If she fancied, she could take the spot and be the hero, and condemn them. Levi and Otis deserved to be hanged in the darkness when no one was looking.

"Yes, there's that." Decimal fell silent and said nothing else.

They found the banking district easily. And without having to ask around, they found Rose Pettyshare and Siarl. They were taking an early lunch on the café terrace opposite the Worthwrite Bank of Necropolis Ltd. Siarl looked happy. So did the banker woman. She kept smiling at Siarl and occasionally touching him, squeezing his hand.

Sigourney swallowed. This wasn't what she'd expected. Not that she knew what she'd expected, but still, this wasn't it. She had no right to expect Siarl not to have moved on. It had been over a year since they last saw each other. And he had no inkling whether she would ever come back, despite her promise to do so. She didn't exactly have a perfect track record of keeping her word, especially when the inner part of her screamed, "I feel uncomfortable."

She could take endless pity on herself, but Rose had it worse. Her beautiful face was scarred. It wasn't only that she'd lost her conventional beauty—more than one passer-by glanced at her with a horrified expression. Then there was the fact the banker winced every now and then when the lines around the burned flesh grew tight.

"He doesn't love her, you know," Decimal whispered.

Sigourney couldn't answer. The words got stuck in her throat, unwilling to be spoken.

"I have seen the way the boy looks at you. I feel it in you. He doesn't look at her the same way."

"I guess." That was all Sigourney could say.

"Now let's use that talent of yours and poke around in the bank and find out more. Maybe there's more to the story."

There was a creak of the floorboards. Levi lifted his head up to see if Rose had come back. The attic was empty. The mid-afternoon sun shone through the small, round windows, casting shadows on the floor, but that was it. He watched as the dust fell and lifted like snowflakes on an icy morning. Light as a feather. There was a disturbance to the pattern—a very slight one.

"So you came back," Levi said, turning to face the room.

There was hesitation, and he understood why. He didn't press her for another reaction. If she wanted, she would show herself.

Eventually, Sigourney did. She had a bunny on her lap.

"Hello," Levi said.

Sigourney was tongue-tied. She said nothing.

"Where did you find that?" he added. She had always been good with animals.

"Under Siarl's desk." She carefully mouthed the words as if he would use them against her. There were several ways he could. It was so easy with her, but why would he?

"That's nice," he said, staying in neutral territory.

"The machine was not destroyed," Sigourney blurted out. Levi was sure he heard her sigh with disappointment at her own words.

"Good to know. I truly appreciate that, for Ada's sake." Levi twirled the tweezers he had been using on one of the eggs between his fingers. He watched his sister curiously.

"Oh," Sigourney replied, sounding somewhat disappointed. Or he could be misreading her.

"I shouldn't have done what I did. I... never mind. Explanations don't matter here. Using people was a mistake to begin with, and I take responsibility for it."

"You do? Do you truly mean that?"

He'd walked into that trap. His sister was more devious than he thought. But there was no taking back what he'd said. Not that he even wanted to.

"Yes." He lowered the tweezers back onto his work desk next to a golden-red egg. "So, what do you want?"

"I don't want anything. It's just the others. And..."

"Then what do you need me to do?"

"You could tell me what happened to Otis." Sigourney lowered the bunny onto the floor and sat down to watch it hop around. It didn't. It stayed close by, reluctant to depart.

"Percy Allread, the hexer, took him home. Or so I was told."

Sigourney snarled, not looking like herself at all.

"To Necropolis?" she spat out, sounding different from the soft-spoken, almost apologetic person she had been a moment ago.

"Y-yes," Levi stammered, unsure what to say or do. He hated that feeling, but he guessed he was at the mercy of his sister from now on and should get used to uncertainty.

Sigourney muttered under her breath. Her eyes kept flickering as if she was looking inward.

"They'll kill him." Then she went on muttering, "I thought... Don't finish that thought. He's my son still." What she said next was so low that Levi could barely hear. Two people clearly lived inside his sister's head. She had finally gone mad. But then he remembered the voice in the kitchen and how different it had sounded. Levi shuddered from the thought of what Otis had done. To his mother, it seemed. And to his sister. The reckless... He never got to finish the sentence. Sigourney interrupted him.

"I'm sorry that I left you there like that. Back then, you know, and then you came for me," she said, sounding louder and more like herself. Sigourney let her gaze focus back on him.

Levi hadn't expected that. He'd thought there would be more incoherent babble.

"I... You did what I would have done if I were you," he said, and for the first time, he meant it. "You should have left earlier. We both should have. Our parents..." He shook his head, not wanting to go back there.

Sigourney scooped the bunny into her lap and just sat there mute, as if all that was necessary had been said. Most probably it had.

"So, what now?" Levi asked, unable to take the silence his sister so readily lived in.

"I forgive you too," she finally said and stood up. "But that's not why I'm here. Or I don't think I am. I should have forgiven you a long time ago and let the past go. The same goes for our parents. They were far from perfect, but they did their best with what they got from life. Granted, their best wasn't much, but it would be silly of me to carry it around as this shield, so I don't even have to try. I lost the only people who mattered to me because of it—"

"I'm sorry to hear that, Sigourney. They were cruel, and I wasn't much better." He stood up as well, having an inkling where this would lead.

"We were what we were. But I need you to come with me and face what Edith and Humphrey have to say. I can forgive you, but I'm not sure if they can."

"Alright, if that's what you want. I'll come with you, and

they can deliver whatever punishment they see fit. But I beg of you, let me give you something first."

Levi chose the green egg from all of those on his desk. There were fourteen others, all with a different color and pattern. All made out of gold and gemstones. The one he was holding now had tiny emeralds embedded among the diamonds. Levi had made it with Sigourney in mind. Ever since she was little, she'd loved green.

"One more thing," he said and closed the notebook on the desk and took it with him.

"Take this to that boy of yours and tell him to look after them." Levi walked to his sister and handed her the notebook. "He'll know what to do with it. But tell him to never give the notebook to Rose Pettyshare. Rose can sell the rest of the trinkets on my desk for more money than she ever put into them or me.

"And this is for you." Levi offered the egg to Sigourney.

Sigourney handed the bunny to him, and they made a switch.

"Can I?" she asked.

He nodded.

The egg spun on her hands on its own. He'd designed it to do so. The other eggs, too, had a mechanical side to them, but none of them was anything close to as intricate as the one in Sigourney's hand. He had been right about the egg shape and quintessence. He had been right about so many things. Levi just wished he had gotten there without all the mistakes and the heavy price he was about to pay. At least now he was ready to go. He had given everything there was to give of him.

Sigourney opened the egg, and she gasped.

Inside the egg was a sparkling night sky. An entire universe.

"I made it with you in mind," Levi said.

AUTHOR'S NOTE

Writing Mechanics of the Past took longer than I expected. The story kept evolving and changing. When I started to write the book, it was about blood—the blood of specials and Sigourney's past. I knew Sigourney would have to face the life she left behind and meet her brother. The mechanical aspect came later as her brother's personality and Threebeanvalley evolved. The turning point of the story was when a friend asked when I would write about Sampo, the mythical Finnish machine that was a way for riches and good fortune. So the Bufonite came to be. I wondered what it would mean for such a thing to exist and how people and, in this case, gods would behave. I'm not sure if it is cynical of me to expect sorrow and heartache, but that followed here.

Machines and new inventions are astonishing, but they bring a changed world that affects the balance of human affairs. When the balance is altered, there has always been turmoil. Luddites acted the protect their lives and livelihoods in the era of the industrial revolution. They did what they saw was correct. If the age of AIs and algorithms will see something similar, it is yet to be seen.

But mostly, this was a story about Sigourney, family, and the past, and who we were and are. Her transformation, growth, and courage fueled my writing. I needed to see if she would stop running or not. I'm not sure if she came back to Threebeanvalley to get Siarl to go with her or not. Maybe we will find that out in another book.

Past and family relationships are tricky. Several lives with their own needs and wants are twisted together, not to mention the hopes, wishes, demands, and actions of the past generations. If any, there is a volatile cocktail or source of great strength.

Thank you for reading Mechanics of the Past.

Sincerely,
K.A. Ashcomb

ABOUT THE AUTHOR

K.A. Ashcomb lives in a small town in Finland. She is a satirist, and she grew up reading books by Terry Pratchett and other comical fantasy authors. After acquiring her MA in Comparative Religion, spiced with Social Psychology and Sociology, she found herself working part-time behind a shop's counter. With tons of free time on her hands, she began to create stories about gods, unfortunate heroes, and other jerks to amuse herself. The stories grew bigger and bigger, and she had to put them on paper, and so her first book Worth Of Luck was born, then Penny for Your Soul came along, and now Mechanics of the Past came to be.

When she isn't writing books or crafting short stories for her blog, you can find her in the local forest reservation taking macro-photographs. Trying to roam back to her keyboard, beloved two mischievous cats, and husband.

COMING NEXT FROM K.A. ASHCOMB

Petula Upwood, the Mayor of Necropolis, has an Otis-sized problem. She has to figure out what to do with him and the Bufonite incident. The Necromantic Council has imprisoned Otis and will do anything to get their hands on the machine. Petula can't let that happen. There would be no end to the Council's rein. It is just that no one goes against the Council and survives. Not even the Mayor.

www.ingramcontent.com/pod-product-compliance
Lightning Source LLC
Chambersburg PA
CBHW031244160726
47993CB00001B/17